STARGATE SG·1

MURDER AT THE SGC

AMY GRISWOLD

FANDEMONIUM BOOKS

An original publication of Fandemonium Ltd, produced under license from MGM Consumer Products.

Fandemonium Books
United Kingdom
Visit our website: www.stargatenovels.com

S T A R G Å T E
SG·1

METRO-GOLDWYN-MAYER Presents
STARGATE SG-1™
BEN BROWDER AMANDA TAPPING
CHRISTOPHER JUDGE CLAUDIA BLACK
with BEAU BRIDGES and MICHAEL SHANKS as Daniel Jackson
Executive Producers ROBERT C. COOPER & BRAD WRIGHT
Developed for Television by BRAD WRIGHT & JONATHAN GLASSNER

WWW.MGM.COM

Print ISBN: 978-1-905586-69-1   Ebook ISBN: 978-1-80070-033-8

Historical note:
This book is set during season ten of STARGATE SG-1
between the episodes *Insiders* and *Uninvited*.

CHAPTER ONE

COLONEL Cameron Mitchell climbed up the last few meters of the precarious trail leading to the cave they were exploring, rain running down the back of his neck, and levered himself through the cave opening. Inside, the team's lamps lit an uneven, branching cavern, its floor rising into jagged pillars and dropping off into pits like the world's most dangerous playground. It was damp enough inside that his dripping on the cave floor didn't seem to be making it any wetter. "Are we finding anything yet?"

"Yes," Sam Carter said, at the same time that Daniel Jackson said, "No."

Cam turned up his hands, inviting them to make up their minds. They'd been trying ever since they got back from Atlantis to find any sign of the Sangraal. Now that they had the gate addresses of Castiana and Sahal, Cam had hoped that finding the Sangraal had become a simple exercise. Try one, try the other, and figure at worst they'd hit the jackpot on world number two.

Instead, the team currently exploring Sahal hadn't found anything of interest, and Castiana was slowing them down by possessing a toxic atmosphere that made even Daniel reluctant to just charge in and start digging. Instead, he'd come up with another gate address on his own from his research in the library on Camelot. After a week of twiddling his thumbs at the SGC, Cam had been willing to try anything that meant getting out in the field.

P2H-144 was making him change his mind. They'd spent three days in a damp cave, they'd hit a lot of dead ends, and he'd listened to a lot of speculation about what Welsh poetry might have meant. Without knocking Daniel's ability to put together clues, Cam did wish that they had something a little more solid to go on than speculation about where Merlin might have hidden the prize on a cosmic scavenger hunt.

"I believe the question is what we are finding," Teal'c said. He was holding one of the lights for Sam, who was adjusting the dials on her ground-penetrating radar setup. At least, the piece of equipment she'd brought had started out as a ground-penetrating radar setup, although Cam would be the first to admit that he didn't understand half its readouts at this point. If she'd told him that it could measure their distance from the nearest coffee shop, he would have been tempted to believe her.

"I'm getting some really interesting energy readings," Sam said. "Nothing that I can explain as a natural geological feature. I'm increasingly sure there's a power source down here somewhere."

"The question is whether we can get to it from this direction," Daniel said. "If there's an Ancient installation somewhere down there, this isn't the original entrance."

"I should hope not," Vala said. She was perched uncomfortably on a rock outcropping, her face smudged with dirt and her interest in the caves clearly flagging. "This doesn't look like an entrance to me unless whoever built this place really disliked visitors."

"I think they really disliked visitors," Daniel said. "But that's not the problem. The problem is that the part of this system of caverns collapsed a long time ago, and I think the original entrance went with it. It's possible that we could make our way down through these caverns and find an alternate route into the installation, but it's also possible that all these tunnels could turn out to be dead ends."

"Or that the power source you're reading could be buried under about a hundred tons of rock," Cam said.

"We're trying to think positively."

"If we can't find the door, we could always make a door," Sam suggested. While they'd only been working together for a few months on SG-1, Cam knew Sam well enough from their previous friendship to be wary of her enthusiasm for explosions.

"Are we sure that's a good idea?" he asked.

There was a momentary pause as Sam and Daniel seemed to be trying to align their definitions of "good idea." "Let's try exploring our other options first," Daniel said.

Sam shrugged, undaunted. "Fair enough. We'd have to do a lot of work down here anyway putting in supports in order to make it safe to blast through the rock. I'm just saying it's an option."

"An option we'll try after we've tried all the other options first," Daniel said.

"After that, yes."

They seemed to have resolved the question without needing Cam to issue orders, or even provide an opinion. He'd been noticing that a lot on SG-1. It wasn't that he minded having a team that ran like a well-oiled machine; most days he was honored just being on the same team with the rest of them. But there were times when he wasn't sure how he fit into that machine, let alone whether he was actually driving it.

"How important is it that we keep searching this particular planet?" he asked, feeling the need to at least remind the two scientists that they needed a reason for their investigations other than sheer curiosity.

"Pretty important," Daniel said without turning around. He was scraping mud away from a crack in the rock, peering through it as if trying to figure out whether it led anywhere interesting or just led to more rock and more mud. "If there's any possibility that this might be the final resting place of the Sangraal…"

Cam gave him a moment to finish the sentence, and then prompted, "Is there any possibility that this might be the final resting place of the Sangraal?" Merlin's clues had pointed them to three planets Arthur and his knights had definitely visited during their adventures. They hadn't provided the gate addresses of those planets, because that would have been much too easy. Now that they'd found them it was starting to seem increasingly unlikely that the Sangraal was on any of them. Cam was starting to feel that Merlin had a lot to answer for.

Daniel sat back on his heels with a frown. "Probably not. It was always a long shot — this isn't one of the three planets we were focusing on. All I can tell you is that this planet's gate address is a partial match for what may or may not be gate symbols in a single illustration in a single manuscript that I found in the library on Camelot."

"So you're practically sure we're in the right place, then?" Vala said, in the tone of someone who'd been spending a lot of time in a damp cave and really wanted something to show for it soon.

Given what he'd seen of Vala, Cam was guessing she was hoping for something shiny as much as she was hoping for hidden Ancient knowledge. On the other hand, given what she'd just been through at the hands of the Ori — having a daughter, watching her grow to spooky maturity as the Orici, and then losing her in a matter of days — maybe a weapon against the Ori was high on her list of priorities too. Cam was aware that he still didn't have Vala figured out, but there wasn't exactly time to stop and do getting-to-know-you team building at the moment.

"I'm still marginally hopeful," Daniel said.

"What we can be more certain of is that there's something down there with an Ancient energy signature," Sam said. "That in itself makes this site worth checking out. Even if it's not one of the planets named in Merlin's message, any planet with functioning Ancient technology on it that could possibly have been visited by Merlin is worth checking out at this point."

It was an explanation of what she and Daniel were doing here, not a request for permission to keep on doing it. Cam couldn't really argue with her, although he did wonder just how much of a wild goose chase this was going to turn out to be. It might have been more useful for Daniel to be searching more of the books on Camelot, but Daniel had made it very clear that he needed to be out here in the field searching this planet instead. Cam was just finding it hard to shake the suspicion that after a certain amount of time spent poring over old books, archaeologists developed the incurable desire to get out into the field and dig something up.

Cam's radio crackled. "Okay, carry on," he said to Daniel and Sam, and retraced his steps with care back through the cave to reach the entrance where he could get decent radio reception. Below him, a trail wound down the face of a steep cliff, reaching the bottom only after a series of hair-raising switchbacks and roughly-carved stairways. The steady rain made the gray river below blend with the equally gray sky. He could just see the Stargate in the distance, a smooth man-made arch rising above the trees that filled the river valley. "This is Colonel Mitchell."

"General Landry here," the man's voice said. "Round up your team and get back here with them. I have a job for you."

"Yes, sir," Cam said, but didn't switch the radio off. He was having an intense premonition of the immediate future in which he ordered Sam and Daniel to report back to base that moment. He decided to save himself the steps of going in and listening to their arguments and then coming back out again to relay them to Landry. "I think Dr. Jackson and Colonel Carter would appreciate more time to track down the source of the weird energy readings they've been picking up."

"You think they're onto something?" Landry asked.

Cam considered his answer for a moment, and then decided that he did trust his team. "Yes, sir. There's still a non-zero chance the Sangraal might be here."

"All right. Leave them to it and get yourself back here as soon as you can, then. We have a situation on our hands that I cannot wait to turn over to you."

Cam tried to find some way to interpret that statement that wasn't *I have something unpleasant to dump on you as soon as you get back*, and couldn't find one. "Yes, sir," he said.

"I'm also available right now," Vala said brightly, appearing in the cave mouth. Cam raised an eyebrow at her, and she mouthed 'please' and looked up at him through her lashes in entreaty.

"Perfect," Landry said, and cut the radio connection before Cam could decide whether that was irony or not.

"I thought you'd want to stay and see if they dig up any shiny things," Cam said.

"Shiny things that would belong to your Stargate program and will not produce any profits for anyone on the team," Vala said. "As has been extensively explained to me. Besides, this doesn't strike me as a very shiny kind of place."

It was on the tip of Cam's tongue to point out that Vala had never had much problem in the past acquiring things that technically belonged to the Stargate program, and that it also wasn't like her to pass up any chance of a treasure trove, even if it came in the package of a muddy, cold cave that would probably take the next several days to explore.

He opened his mouth, and then closed it again, realizing that Vala looked tired. He had seen her in a number of moods so far — mostly various shades of bravado, flirtatiousness, and stubborn determination — but at the moment she actually looked faded, and older than he usually guessed. He wondered how old she really was, and knew better than to ask and expect he'd get an answer. It had been a long few weeks for her, he thought.

"All right," he said. "Go see if Teal'c wants to stay and play archaeologist, or if he'd rather come deal with whatever Landry's cooked up for us."

Vala ducked back into the cave, and emerged promptly with Teal'c following her.

"Not going to stay and help them dig?"

"I am sure Daniel Jackson and Colonel Carter will locate the source of the anomalous power readings without additional assistance," Teal'c said. "I will return to Stargate Command to assist you." He didn't add *with your permission*, but Cam chose to believe it was implied. He was still very aware that he'd twisted Teal'c's arm to return to the team, and that Teal'c had done so in large part as a favor to his friends. While he knew Teal'c respected the chain of command in theory, in practice he wasn't sure Teal'c would stick around if Cam ever needed to give him orders he really didn't like.

That was, at least, better than the position he was in with Daniel, who didn't even respect the chain of command in theory, and who Cam suspected would never have considered staying on SG-1 if he'd managed to get to Atlantis without being waylaid by Vala Mal Doran. And then there was Sam, who Cam knew respected the chain of command with every bone in her body, and who had never said a word to remind Cam that she shared his rank, could have been in charge of SG-1 herself if she hadn't preferred to go to Area 51, and was so critically valuable to the Stargate program that if she asked for an office with a window, Stargate Command would give serious thought to drilling a hole in Cheyenne Mountain.

"All right," Cam said, putting all of that aside as unproductive thinking. "Time to go home."

It was a long hike down the mountain, and an even longer one back to the Stargate, with the rain swelling the river and reducing the trail to one flat, muddy part of a slightly less flat, slightly muddier field. The sun set while they were walking, and slowed their pace further as they tried to avoid stepping into deep puddles or veering too far toward the river. In the trees that climbed the slope, he could hear the hooting of some kind of nocturnal monkeys, and occasionally see a flash of white as they swung from tree to tree. As far as Cam was concerned, if he were a monkey, he'd be somewhere dry taking the night off.

When they finally reached the Stargate, Cam gazed up at it in appreciation, shading his eyes against the spitting rain.

"Finally," he said. "Let's dial the gate."

"Gladly," Teal'c said.

"You know, you might be missing the moment they find the Sangraal."

"I believe Daniel Jackson has established that this is unlikely to be the location of the Sangraal. While their finds on this planet may provide clues to its location, I am willing to sacrifice the opportunity to watch."

"On the up side, now we know one more place that the Sangraal isn't," Vala put in. Her bright tone sounded a little forced, but Cam was grateful for any attempt at raising morale.

"There are an infinite number of places that the Sangraal is not," Teal'c pointed out as the gate began grinding its way through the dialing sequence, spattering them with spraying raindrops as it turned.

"So, it's just like that famous Earth author says, once you've eliminated the impossible, whatever is left is your answer."

"Holmes is the detective," Cam felt he had to clarify. "The fictional detective. And that's not what he meant, anyway. He meant that once you've ruled out all the ways something couldn't happen, whatever's left is what must have happened, even if it's unlikely, because it's what you've got."

"Or maybe there's something else that's possible and even less unlikely that you just haven't thought of yet," Vala said.

Cam flicked on his radio to avoid having to come up with an answer for that. "This is Mitchell," he said. "Transmitting iris code now."

There was a longer than usual pause before General Landry's voice came back over the radio. "What took you so long?"

"Next time I'll call a cab," Cam said, and stepped through the Stargate.

Nearly a year in this job, and he still wasn't used to the tugging sensation of passing through the wormhole in a shower of lights, like tumbling through a kid's kaleidoscope. It was cold and disorienting and still exciting, and as always he was a little disappointed when it ended. He stepped out on the solid ramp in the gate room, only to be met by the flashing red lights of an alert. Vala and Teal'c closed formation behind him, and Cam raised his own weapon, scanning the room.

"Stand down, SG-1," Landry said from the control room. "We've put the base on lockdown after an incident while you were gone, but we're not under attack."

"If the base is on lockdown, why were we recalled?" Cam asked.

"Because I have a job for you. Get cleaned up and meet me in the briefing room in ten."

"Ten of what? Because it's going to take a lot more than ten of your Earth minutes to get cleaned up," Vala said.

"I have faith in you," Landry said, and cut off the speaker.

"Ten minutes," Cam said, as Vala opened her mouth to speak. "He means it."

"Right," she said after only a momentary pause. "I'll be there!"

"That's the way we like it," Cam said, and headed for the showers.

Vala had been at the SGC for several weeks before she had learned that the design of the Cheyenne Mountain base was not deliberately intended to be depressing and grim. She had been assuming some kind of psychological warfare against their opponents, but Daniel had assured her that it was just that the military wasn't very good at decorating.

The locker room was, in her opinion, a perfect example. For a place intended for tired people to reassemble themselves after missions, it lacked every amenity Vala could imagine except for hot water. On the other hand, it was possible that her ideas about bathing chambers were a little skewed by having experienced Goa'uld luxury, if not from a position where she could thoroughly appreciate it. She had to grant that rose petals and scented oils were probably luxuries not in the military budget, but she thought they could at least have managed soap that didn't have a chemical sting.

She toweled herself off in the echoing emptiness of the women's locker room, wishing that Tau'ri notions of propriety didn't mean she had it entirely to herself. She wasn't in any mood at the moment to enjoy her own company. For a moment, her fingers traced the faint stretch marks that marred the curve of her belly, one of the few reminders that her experiences in the Ori's home galaxy were more than just a bad dream.

Adria had healed her hours after the birth, and she felt no lingering pain or weakness. She moved with none of the caution that she imagined she might have felt after a normal childbirth. Or not. Maybe she would have been filled with energy, bustling around the kitchen with a baby tucked in the crook of her arm. Not that she had ever wanted such a thing. But there was no baby now, only a self-possessed young woman off conquering planets with a fanatical gleam in her eye.

Vala shook back her hair, banishing all unproductive introspection, and tugged on the clothes she had been issued on her return, a drab olive jumpsuit that she couldn't imagine flattering anyone. Her reflection in the mirror raised an assessing eyebrow. She looked — if not precisely like herself — very unlike an innocent villager's wife.

"Good enough," she told her reflection, and squared her shoulders as she strode out.

Carolyn Lam was already waiting in Landry's office. She nodded to Vala but didn't smile as she sat down, or maybe it was just that she was carefully avoiding smiling at General Landry as he sat down. Apparently it was unusual for the Tau'ri to work with their grown children, and even after they had done so for the better part of a year, it was clear that a certain awkwardness still lingered. Carolyn bit her lip, looking uncommonly unhappy, and Vala decided there was more to it than that.

Mitchell and Teal'c took seats on the other side of the table, Mitchell glancing at General Landry as if wondering whether they were in trouble, and if so, what for, and Teal'c practicing his usual measured calm. Vala expected that all the Jaffa learned as children how not to let their feelings show on their faces unless they wanted them to. It was a skill she'd never quite mastered, instead having to fall back on displaying some other feeling loudly enough that no one noticed the one she didn't mean for them to see.

Landry waited longer than usual before he spoke, clearing his throat and shuffling the folders in front of him, and Vala fought the urge to squirm. Surely if anyone was in trouble it wasn't her. She hadn't done anything to be in trouble for, certainly not in the last couple of weeks. And surely he already knew the general outline of her prior misdeeds, so even if they'd found out about anything in particular, it shouldn't come as any kind of a real surprise.

She was preparing an impassioned defense along those lines when Landry finally spoke. "One of the civilian archaeologists was found dead in his office this morning," he said. "Dr. Vincent Oliver. He'd been working on the artifacts that SG-11 brought back from P5B-078."

Vala recognized the gate address from the peek she'd taken at SG-11's briefing folder when one of them had left temptingly unattended on a lunch table. It obviously wasn't that classified if they were that careless with it, she had reasoned. The briefest glance had made it clear that they were after odds and ends of interest only to scholars, not anything valuable either for its decorative qualities or its technological uses. Pothunters did sometimes stumble on something interesting among their old dishes and buttons, but it wasn't a particularly rewarding approach to treasure-hunting in her opinion. There were better ways.

"What did he die of?" Mitchell asked. "Some kind of killer virus? Or some kind of booby-trapped artifact — hang on, whatever killed him isn't loose in the base, is it?" His voice rose with a note of manfully repressed alarm.

"Surely not," Vala said, and then reflected that it probably wasn't certain after all. She had thumbed through a number of the reports from the team's prior missions, and far too many of them for comfort had ended with things being brought back to the SGC that should have stayed far away from it. It was one thing that had made an attempt at psychological warfare make sense to her. The gray walls and clashing colors of the base might well scare any creature with an aesthetic sense into fleeing back through the Stargate. She would have to ask Daniel about it again, she decided. Perhaps he had been joking. She still wasn't sure she understood his sense of humor.

"Nothing's loose in the base," Landry said. "Believe me, that was one of our first thoughts. We've searched it, and scanned it, and all but turned the place upside down. I feel confident in saying that there's nobody here but us."

"Dr. Oliver was poisoned," Carolyn said flatly.

Landry nodded. "Not entirely coincidentally, he'd been studying some kind of primitive weapon that was found coated with... what are we calling this stuff?"

"Targonine," Carolyn said. "It's a highly toxic substance that's extracted from the seed pods of a species of tree that's particularly common on P5B-078. Oliver's theory is that the weapon he found was used for warfare rather than hunting, because the poison was potent enough that you wouldn't want to eat anything you killed with it."

"You could ask the people who live there," Vala said.

"And we would," Carolyn said, "except that as far as we can tell the human population of P5B-078 was collateral damage in a war between rival Goa'uld a couple of centuries ago. We're not actually sure who won, but what we are sure of is that neither side considered the place valuable enough to resettle it with humans or Jaffa after that. The humans who lived there were mostly farmers and hunters. Oliver theorized that the planet's value was strategic, and that when the war was over and the territorial lines were re-drawn, it was no longer near enough to a territorial boundary to make it worth anyone's attention. But really all we have are guesses."

"What we know for certain at this point is that Dr. Oliver died of targonine poisoning," Landry said, and Carolyn nodded assent. "The poison on the weapons he was working with killed him."

"So we're talking workplace accident here," Mitchell said.

"I really wish we were," Carolyn said after a pause that hung in the air just a little too long. "Certainly that's what I thought when I first examined him. I just couldn't find any signs of a scratch or a cut. Targonine isn't absorbed through the skin — it would have to either get into his bloodstream through an open wound or be ingested. Which was my next theory, but I still couldn't figure out how he'd gotten the poison into his mouth. Not until we got back the lab results on the coffee he was drinking. We sent it in just as a routine thing, just so we didn't leave any stone unturned. As it turns out, that was a very good thing."

"There was poison in his coffee?" Vala prompted, when it seemed as though someone was going to have to.

"Enough poison that it couldn't possibly have gotten there accidentally," Carolyn said. "Based on our analysis of what was left in his cup, I think someone must have scraped off the sticky residue from part of the weapon and stirred it into the coffee."

"Wouldn't he have tasted it?" Mitchell asked.

Carolyn looked at him askance. "You've drunk the coffee here, right? My best guess, having done everything short of put the stuff in my mouth, is that the poison had a mildly bitter taste. I don't think you'd taste it in strong coffee, at least not distinctly enough to make you suspicious until you started feeling ill. It's a fast-acting paralyzing toxin, so by the time Oliver realized something was wrong, he probably wasn't able to call for help."

Mitchell frowned. "The poison couldn't have just… I don't know, dripped into his cup?"

Carolyn shook her head. "Not in a dose large enough for

drinking half a cup to kill him."

"Not unless he was in the habit of using irreplaceable alien artifacts to stir his coffee," Landry said. "And I like to think our people have more sense than that."

"Yes, sir," Mitchell said.

"Vincent Oliver was murdered," Landry went on. "And I want you to find out who killed him."

"I have to ask, why me, sir?" Mitchell asked. Vala admired his tone, very nearly an innocent inquiry, with only the barest hint of *it's not fair to make me do something that's clearly going to be unpleasant.* "My last attempt at playing detective didn't go that well."

"You weren't my first choice," Landry said. Mitchell looked as if he didn't actually prefer hearing that. "No offense, but I'd normally like to have somebody who's used to running investigations running this investigation. The first thing I did was call General O'Neill at Homeworld Security. He wants us to handle this without involving the NID if at all possible."

"I think we'd all like to avoid involving the NID," Mitchell said.

"I thought they were good guys now," Vala said. "As opposed to the IOA, who we're all still not sure about." She was doing her best to keep up with all the different factions of the Tau'ri, but there were times when she felt she should have been issued a handy crib sheet.

"The IOA are our oversight committee," Landry said. "We are officially required to believe that they're the good guys."

"Not literally," Mitchell said, noticing the set of Vala's mouth. She was relieved at that, having had just about as much of mandatory faith in the last few months as she could stand. If they were just required to lie, that she could do easily enough.

"But the NID are actually on our side now," she persisted. "We think."

"We took down the rogue agents in the NID," Mitchell said. "As far as I know, everyone who was dirty is either in prison or on their way to join the Trust, where at least they'll have to figure out some other way of taking over Earth for the Goa'uld other than spying on us from inside one of our national security organizations."

"Which I hope they will find exceedingly challenging," Teal'c said.

"And there are some good guys over at the NID," Mitchell went on. "I know they've been working hard to clean house. I'm just not sure how comfortable anyone feels giving them free rein to investigate inside Cheyenne Mountain, especially after what happened last time when they sent Barrett over and he let Ba'al get away. I know he was brainwashed, so maybe it wasn't really his fault, but it's not good for anybody's comfort level."

"I can tell you how comfortable General O'Neill feels about having the NID in here, and the answer is that we're not doing it unless we don't have any other choice," Landry said. "On the other hand, there's only so long that he can keep Oliver's death quiet without it looking like a cover-up. He's given us 72 hours to sort this out before he has to let the NID take over the investigation. The alternative to that is getting the IOA in here directly, and I can tell you right now that General O'Neill doesn't want Richard Woolsey in here either."

"Understood, sir," Mitchell said. "I'm still a little less than clear on why SG-1 is going to be taking the lead on this one."

"On the most basic level, because all of you have been off-world for the last three days," Landry said. "Which means you couldn't possibly have been involved in Oliver's death. Three days ago, he was walking around in perfect health, as far as any of us know."

Landry looked at Carolyn, who flipped through the file in front of her as if it were suddenly very interesting. Vala watched with interest, wondering who wasn't saying what, and whether they would come out with it in the meeting or whether she was going to have to try to pry the interesting parts out of them afterwards.

"I like to think that you wouldn't assume we had anything to do with killing one of the archaeologists even if we'd been on base," Mitchell said.

"I try not to assume anything," Landry said. "But for what it's worth, no, I wouldn't leap to the conclusion that you're secretly a murderer. Of course, since I've approved every single posting to this base, it looks like I was wrong about someone. I expect you can imagine how happy I am about that right now."

"I think I can, sir," Mitchell said. Vala gave Landry a sympathetic look, which he ignored.

"You and SG-1 were off-world, so there's no way that anyone can argue that you were involved in the death yourselves and are trying to carry off some kind of cover-up. This has to be airtight enough that we don't have to get the NID into the loop to chase loose ends. Normally, I'd take the lead myself, and figure that O'Neill trusts that I'm not going to murder my own staff in a way that makes me look incompetent. But in this case there's a potential conflict of interest that makes that a bad idea."

"I'm not sure it really rises to the level of a conflict of interest," Carolyn said. She closed the folder reluctantly, and took a deep breath before she spoke. "Dr. Oliver and I were… at one point earlier this year… romantically involved."

"I did not know that," Mitchell said after a moment. Vala hadn't known it either, which bothered her a little, as she tried to keep track of important personal undercurrents. It was still hard for her to interpret the Tau'ri's signals about romance, though, especially when they failed to follow the easy rules laid out in so many magazines and television shows.

"We were trying to keep it out of the office. And 'romantically involved' makes it sound more serious than it was. We dated briefly. We ate some dinners together, we went to the movies a couple of times, and… the usual sort of thing." She wasn't looking at Landry, and Vala thought if she'd ever been required to explain just what she did on romantic evenings to her own father, she might have had the same expression. Although her own father was more likely to have told her more than she ever wanted to know about his own romances instead.

"So what happened?" Vala prompted when Carolyn trailed off and seemed reluctant to continue.

"I think we both knew it hadn't really been… clicking. We broke things off. I'll admit that made things awkward, but that's no reason to believe that I killed him."

"I don't believe you killed Oliver," Landry said.

"Thank you," she said dryly.

"But you're the first person I've found who has any motive whatsoever for killing him. It's bad enough that you did the initial tests on the body, all of which you will have someone else repeat. You can't afford for there to be any question of whether you were cleared in a murder investigation because your old man was the lead investigator. That's the kind of thing that ends careers. Not with a bang, but with a whole lot of whispers."

"He's right," Mitchell said. "You can't afford to have this hanging over you." He turned to Landry. "SG-1 will take the lead on the investigation."

"That's what I wanted to hear," Landry said.

CHAPTER TWO

"TELL me what you know about Oliver," Cam said over the radio. He hadn't meant to take up quite so much space in the control room in order to call Daniel, but the rest of the team had trailed along with him, Teal'c looming over his shoulder and Vala roaming around looking like her fingers itched to poke buttons. He wished he knew whether to put their desire to accompany him down to enthusiasm or to a lingering feeling that he couldn't necessarily be trusted to get it right otherwise.

There was a crackle of static from the other end that resolved itself into Daniel's voice as his face appeared on the video screen above Cam's head. Behind him, the cave was illuminated by the team's lamps and the dim glow of the radar set, which Sam was bent over, fiddling with its controls.

"BA from Cornell, PhD in Classical Archaeology from Berkeley," Daniel said. Cam refrained from pointing out that Oliver probably wasn't killed because of where he went to school. He was learning to let Daniel follow his meandering trains of logic along their track, and hoping that they eventually reached a station. "We brought him on three years ago because we needed someone else to work on cataloguing Ancient objects, although of course that's not all he worked on once he was here. Most recently he was working with the items from P5B-078, including a weapon coated in an unknown toxic substance."

"Apparently it's targonine," Cam said. "At least according to Dr. Lam's analysis. We've got Dr. Patel re-doing that analysis now so that there's no question about anyone having cooked the results."

Daniel frowned. "Oh, come on, you can't really believe Carolyn faked the lab analysis."

"I don't," Cam said. "But Landry's right that it's not a matter of what we think, it's a matter of what people will say. If we end up having to have the NID in here…"

"Or the IOA," Teal'c said darkly.

"Knock on wood when you say that," Daniel said.

"What does that do?" Vala asked from over Cam's shoulder.

"A Tau'ri superstition to avert ill omen," Teal'c said.

"Actually it was a joke," Daniel said.

Cam tapped his knuckles on the control room table. "I think we'd all like to keep the IOA, the NID, and any other strings of initials out of this investigation."

"I think the table is metal," Vala said.

"Let's focus, people," Cam went on doggedly. "Dr. Oliver was working on the poisoned — well, poisoned what? What was this thing exactly?"

"When we find toxins on weapons, it's usually for hunting," Daniel said, which was the kind of non-answer that Cam was getting used to. "This was interesting because the weapon was pretty clearly intended for warfare. It's a kind of a spiked club — I guess you'd call it a morning star. If getting hit by the thing didn't kill you, the poison definitely would."

"Nice," Cam said. "Oliver was studying this thing?"

"Probably just taking a cursory look at it. It's not something that fits with anyone's primary research interests or with our current priorities, just a curiosity. If I had to guess, I'd imagine he was just interested in the thing because it was unusual, and he wanted to go ahead and get it photographed and catalogued before something else more important came up and shifted our priorities and it got shoved in a box."

Vala shook her head. "It seems that it might have been a better idea to shove it into a box."

"I can't argue with that," Daniel said over the video feed. "I'm trying to think of anything else I know about Oliver." There was a pause, the static crackling. "He did some interesting work before we hired him on what turned to be Ancient sites on Earth, not that he understood what he was looking at. Published a few papers, nothing too on the nose, but heading down some of the right paths. Very cautious, though. Unwilling to speculate too much about the meaning of what he'd found."

Cam drummed his fingers on Oliver's personnel folder. "We've got his personnel history on file," he said. "Tell me what's not in the file. Who was this guy, and why would one of our people want to kill him?"

"I didn't know him that well as a person," Daniel said. "He wasn't an easy man to get to know. He really didn't open up except about work. A couple of times he talked about going hiking. Outdoor photography. I think he went skiing sometimes in the winter. Nothing out of the ordinary."

"As far as we know," Vala said. "No one admits to *all* their hobbies." She threw an amused glance at the rest of SG-1 when no one answered. "Do they?"

"Some people do," Cam said after a moment. "And I expect some people don't. So we'll keep an open mind there. What else do we know about Oliver?"

"He was very careful in his work," Daniel said. "Methodical. He kept his workspace neat. He did unimpeachable work and reported it clearly."

"That doesn't sound like the world's most enthusiastic endorsement," Cam said.

"Honestly? Oliver didn't have a tremendous amount of imagination. He was a good excavator and cataloguer, not really given to big theoretical leaps of faith — he had all the clues in front of him to figure out Ancient interference in human history, and he couldn't quite make that last step."

Cam rolled his eyes. "You mean like all the other archaeologists on the planet, except you?"

"I was in the right place at the right time," Daniel said. "Oliver was in a right place at a right time, and he kept looking for conventional explanations. I'm not criticizing the man. He was a good archaeologist. He did important work. I wished he'd carried it a little farther, gone out on a few more limbs." He let out a frustrated breath that made the radio crackle. "But it hardly matters now, does it?"

"We will find his killer," Teal'c said.

"We'd better," Cam said. "You're saying he was careful. That makes accident seem even less likely. But I'm still not hearing a motive for murder."

"Have we ruled out suicide?" Daniel asked. "It's a weird way to do it, but Oliver certainly had access to the artifact and knew it was poisoned."

"I don't think we've ruled anything out yet," Cam said. "You tell me. Does it seem plausible to you that it was suicide?"

"I don't know of any reason why he would have done that," Daniel said. "But his personal life was a closed book to me. I didn't even know that he and Dr. Lam were dating. If you're asking me if he was deeply unhappy or troubled in some way… I truly don't know. But suicides usually leave notes. Normal suicides."

"As opposed to?"

"Working with the kind of artifacts we work with, there's always the possibility of some kind of alien influence or weird side effect. Nothing about the weapons SG-11 found suggested that they were anything other than inert. But it's still remotely possible that they exerted some kind of mind-controlling influence, something that either resulted in Oliver committing suicide or resulted in someone else killing him. We've dealt with addictive light, artifacts that caused bizarre hallucinations, all kinds of brainwashing—"

Cam broke in before Daniel could finish listing past causes of uncharacteristic behavior in SGC personnel. "Okay, anything's possible, and we'll do a thorough workup on Oliver's colleagues and anyone else who looks like they had the opportunity to do this. And I'd also like to think that whoever killed Oliver wasn't in their right mind when it happened. But if someone's running around here having homicidal delusions, that's even more reason to find them before they hurt anyone else."

"Yeah, I know. All right, let's think. If he was poisoned using scrapings from the artifact, we're looking for someone who had access to it. It should have been locked up in the archaeology lab overnight."

Vala raised one eyebrow. "Does 'should have been' mean it really was?"

"We need to find out," Cam said, leaning back in the control room chair. "Let's assume for the moment that it was. Who does that give us as possibilities?"

"Oliver shared a lab with three other archaeologists, Dr. Chen, Dr. Jefferson, and Dr. Carr," Daniel said. "Dr. Niles was also in the same lab, but she left to take a university job a couple of months ago. It was still a little cramped, because they were all on day shift, but there wasn't any reason to ask any of them to work nights. Cataloguing artifacts isn't usually a specialty that has midnight emergencies."

"And if it is, they get you," Cam said.

"Pretty much. That said, all of them have the access code for the lab, and all of them sometimes work late or come in at odd hours to catch up on work when it's quiet. Any of them could have been in there at pretty much any time of the day or night without it being suspicious."

"The security footage should reveal whether anyone was in the archaeology lab overnight," Teal'c said. "And the base logs will reveal their times of exit and entry."

"Check them," Cam said.

"I don't know how much that will tell us. The scraping could have been taken from the artifact at any point," Daniel said. "And if Oliver put the poison in his coffee himself, he had a million opportunities to collect the poison while he was working on the artifact."

"It's still a starting point. It would be nice if someone were on camera sneaking into the lab at three in the morning with a guilty expression."

"I doubt any intelligent murderer would provide us with such convenient evidence," Teal'c said.

"I doubt it too, but it's worth a look," Cam said. "Even if we can't figure out when someone took the scrapings, maybe we can find out who could actually have been in a position to put them in Oliver's coffee. Other than Oliver himself."

"Do you want me to come back and talk to the archaeologists?" Daniel asked. "It is my department, and I feel responsible in a way for whatever's happened."

"I'd better talk to them first, for the same reason we're keeping Dr. Lam out of this," Cam said. "You weren't here, and you can't have killed him, but it's your department, and I don't want there to be any question of a kind of cover-up. That said, wrap up what you're doing and get back here as soon as you can. I want a second opinion on those artifacts, and somebody who understands what all this archaeology stuff is about."

"What, didn't you take a combat archaeology course at the Academy?" Sam asked, appearing in the video behind Daniel.

"In the Air Force, that course is awfully short," Cam said. "'See that historic site down there? Try not to bomb it.' The days when we manage that are the good days."

"We'll wrap it up," Daniel said.

Sam frowned. "The latest imagery I'm getting from the radar set suggests there's a way through that passage we found," she said. "We could be very close to getting in there and finding the source of those energy readings."

"It'll still be here in a couple of days," Daniel said.

"Yeah, but will we? You know something more important is going to come up."

"Unfortunately, I think something more important has come up."

"I know, you're right," Sam said.

"Great, I'm glad you're on board with your orders," Cam said, trying not to sound too short about it. He hadn't, in fact, been offering a suggestion for debate. "Get back to base and let's figure this one out so that I can go home."

"We're on our way," Sam said soberly, and Cam cut the connection.

He turned to the half of SG-1 that was at least present. "Teal'c, you get the fun job of going through a couple of days of security footage of a door. Vala, you're with me."

It occurred to Cam the moment after he said it that taking a notorious art thief into the same room as a collection of irreplaceable artifacts might be a bad idea. He opened his mouth to second-guess himself and then shut it again. If she was part of SG-1, they had to trust her. And he did trust her. Mostly. On a good day. That was going to have to be good enough.

"Ouch," Sam said as the video feed blinked out. "I probably shouldn't have pushed back that much."

Daniel shrugged. "It's not like we never argued with Jack." He still missed those arguments. There had been a perverse comfort in knowing that he could push just as hard as he could, and that Jack wouldn't let him go too far, or stay too long, or stray too far down some intellectual path that in the heat of the moment felt like the most important thing in the world. He had never had to rein himself in, and he wasn't sure he enjoyed doing it now.

"Colonel O'Neill wasn't in Colonel Mitchell's position. It's awkward for him having me back on the team."

"He practically begged you to come back."

"He did beg me to come back," Sam said, humor lighting her eyes. There was a time when she might have shrugged off the implied compliment awkwardly, Daniel thought, or found it necessary to list the reasons why she was vital to the team. Over the years she'd settled into an easy confidence in her own skills, secure in her importance to the Stargate program without ever needing to boast about it the way some of the civilian scientists did. He wondered if he'd changed as much in ten years, and whether it was for the better.

"So I don't think you need to worry that he doesn't want you here."

"I didn't say he didn't want me here," Sam said. "Just that

it's awkward. We're both at a rank that usually comes with a command. The last thing Cam needs is me second-guessing his orders. Even if this is just a temporary situation until we get our current problems with the Ori straightened out."

"You say that with such confidence," Daniel said, with a glance at the radio to make sure it was switched off.

"Daniel. You're not worried that we're going to lose?"

He shook his head. "Aren't you? We found the three planets Arthur and his knights visited, and we're not any closer to finding the Sangraal. The Ori are moving fast, and I don't think they're going to give us much more time to look. And even if we do find it, we're putting our trust in Merlin, who doesn't seem to have been the most stable and reliable of the Ancients, and that's saying something. The Sangraal might not even do what we hope it will."

"I won't say I'm not worried," Sam said. "But we've got Morgan le Fay's word on the Sangraal now, too."

"I'm not sure that reassures me."

"More than that, I have to believe that we're going to figure out a way out of this, whether that's the Sangraal or something else. We have before, and we've been in some pretty bad situations. It's not as bad as the time it was just the four of us and Bra'tac up against Anubis's entire fleet." She smiled in memory. "I'm never going to forget Bra'tac's face when we told him *our* entire fleet was the space shuttle."

"So now we've got, what, two battle cruisers?"

"And a whole lot more experience," Sam said calmly. "And some of the best people on any planet. We're going to get through this."

"Shouldn't Mitchell be doing the big pep talk?" Daniel asked, embarrassed by his own moment of doubt. They were going to find the Sangraal, and they were going to kick the Ori out of the Milky Way galaxy, because anything else was unthinkable. That had nothing to do with faith in the Ancients, a commodity he felt he no longer possessed; it had everything to do with having faith in themselves."

"Colonel O'Neill never really pep-talked."

"Jack never really had to," Daniel said.

Sam began packing up her equipment. "You shouldn't blame Cam for not being Jack, you know," she said. "That's not any fairer than when he spent most of a year blaming Jonas for not being you. And not any more fun for the rest of us, either."

"I don't," Daniel said.

"Mm-hmm."

"I just don't know Mitchell as well."

"It's been almost a year," she said. "Cam is a good guy, I have every confidence in his ability, and I think you'd like him if you tried to get to know him better. I know that for him this whole thing with SG-1 has been like being the new kid at the lunch table."

"Is this a pep talk or a lecture?"

"Which do you need?"

"A lecture, probably. I've been told I need keeping in line."

"I'm not touching that one," Sam said. "Let's get our gear packed out before it rains any more. I don't want to leave any equipment down here."

"You don't really think we're going to get a chance to come back," Daniel said.

"Let's just say I'm being realistic," she said, and started packing.

Vala hurried her steps to catch up with Mitchell as he strode down the hall toward the archaeology lab. "So, do you want to be the good cop or the bad cop?"

Mitchell gave her an odd sideways look, and she turned to walk backwards so he wouldn't have to crane his neck. "How do you even know about that?"

"Teal'c said it was traditional for interrogations on Earth. Besides, it's not like you people invented the idea. Believe me, the Goa'uld know how to use the potato and the stick." His expression became even odder. "Carrot and the stick?" she hazarded. "I'm sure that root vegetables were somehow involved."

"We're not doing an interrogation," Mitchell said. "We're just going to ask these people some questions."

"So you're the good cop."

"We're both the good cop. Nobody's under arrest. Yet. We're still trying to figure out what happened here."

Vala considered this as they made their way through the corridors. "These artifacts your archaeologists are looking at, are they valuable?"

Mitchell gave her another sideways look. "Why would you be asking?"

"Someone was killed. Take it from me, valuable artifacts can make even the nicest people act... not so nicely."

"I am not ready to believe that someone in the SGC murdered one of their colleagues over money," Mitchell said flatly.

"Surely it depends on how much money?"

"Not for everyone."

Vala felt that was an awfully innocent view of human nature, but she held her tongue as Mitchell pushed open the door to the archaeology laboratory.

She found herself immediately disappointed. "Archaeology laboratory" had suggested shelves full of beautiful shiny things, or at least something more impressive than a small room with barely room for four work tables and the metal shelves that crowded each wall. The shelves were stacked with cardboard boxes, trays containing uninteresting fragments of pottery, and a few loose artifacts that were clearly not the sort that would raise interesting sums at auction. In the corner, coffee was stewing down to a brown, caramel-scented sludge.

The three scientists in the room, two men and a woman, huddled glumly around one of the tables, nursing cups of the sludge in question. Clearly they hadn't been put off the drink by their colleague's untimely demise.

"General Landry's asked me to take charge of the investigation," Mitchell said.

"Are we under arrest?" the woman asked. She raised a stubborn chin, tossing back her shoulder-length black hair. "I need to feed my cats."

"We'll get someone to take care of that for you," Mitchell said. "I think you can assume you're restricted to base until we get to the bottom of this."

"Great."

"You're Dr. Alice Chen?" When she nodded, Mitchell turned expectantly to the other two.

"Dr. Gideon Carr," one of them said. He was the oldest of the three, heavy-set and pale in a way that suggested that he didn't go out in the sunlight much even on his days off. He was dressed in what Daniel called a sports coat, although Vala had yet to decide what sport it might possibly be practical attire for. One of his hands was also bandaged, which she would have concluded was clearly the result of a fight to the death with Oliver if it weren't for the fact that Oliver had been poisoned rather than stabbed.

"And I'm Dr. Barry Jefferson," the other man said. He was dark-skinned and younger than Carr, and wore a button-up shirt and a tie with brightly colored line drawings of humans in improbable clothing. He was fidgeting with his coffee cup as he spoke, turning it around in his hands until it made Vala nervous just to watch.

"We've been stuck in here all day," Chen said. "General Landry said to wait, so we're waiting. Still waiting."

"So why don't you come with me, and I'll get your statement first," Mitchell said. "Vala, why don't you take a look around the lab. Get Chen and Carr to show you what Oliver was working on."

She wasn't sure if that meant he intended to be the good cop or the bad cop, but all she could do was make meaningful eyebrow motions at him while he led Chen out, which he either failed to notice or ignored.

Fine, then. She could take a look around the lab. She turned to the two men and gave them her most brilliant smile. "I'm terribly interested in what you do here. What exactly is it that you do here?"

"We work on —" Carr began, while Jefferson said, "Basically, we —" The two men exchanged glances, and Jefferson waved Carr on. Deferring to seniority? Resolving that the less he said, the less likely he'd be to be caught out as the murderer?

She wished she had the powers of detection that appeared to be standard for Tau'ri detectives. If so, all she'd need to do was examine the pattern of the coffee rings left on the work tables to conclude that one of the scientists had been raised by a single mother with a pathological hatred for men whose surnames began with "O." As it was, all she could do was listen with attentive interest, a technique that had reaped many rewards for her in the past.

"We mainly work on cataloguing objects that the SG teams bring back," Carr said. "For example, we've got this box of pottery from M8D-874. It's interesting because we're seeing definite relationships between the style of pottery-making there and on P4G-230, which suggests there's either been trade between the two worlds, or that the human populations were both taken from the same area of Earth."

"You could ask them," Vala suggested.

"Unfortunately, on both worlds evidence suggests that the human populations were entirely wiped out by — well, on M8D-874, by a series of natural disasters, and on P4G-230, by an unsuccessful attempt to revolt against the Goa'uld. P4G-230 was later mined by Jaffa until the naquadah mines there became played out, but their artifacts are very different. In this dig we're concentrating on trying to learn more about the initial human population."

"Why?" Vala asked, after a pause into which Carr failed to volunteer any reason why the Tau'ri were busily digging up shards of pottery made by dead people who hadn't accomplished anything notable other than being enslaved by the Goa'uld and then dying.

"Dr. Jackson is interested in how humans spread throughout the galaxy," Carr said. "He thinks it might shed light on current human civilizations in other parts of the Milky Way. I'm really more interested in their ceramics technology. I've actually published a book on ceramics techniques — although not those used on other planets, obviously." He smiled as if that were intended to be humor.

"We know you wrote a book," Jefferson said.

"It was called *Ceramics Techniques of the Pre-dynastic Period: An Overview*. I have a copy around here somewhere, if you'd like —"

"You must find some that are actually in one piece," Vala said, looking down into a divided box that held shards of pottery, each neatly labeled. It seemed like the best way of warding off that invitation to come up and see Carr's etchings. From the variation in the handwriting she saw, all of them had done their share of labeling. She felt that wasn't exactly a revelation worthy of Conan Doyle.

"We find a few. That's much rarer. People don't tend to dispose of ceramics that are still intact, and they don't tend to stay intact if they're exposed to the elements for very long. Now, we have found a few, well, I suppose if you want to be sensational about it you could call them treasure hoards —"

"That seems like a perfectly reasonable description to me," Vala said. "Do sit down right here and tell me all about the treasure hoards."

"They're actually not as scientifically interesting," Jefferson said. He cleared his throat, as if used to needing permission to speak. Vala wondered how long he had been out of a classroom. She'd seen students sitting in rows in their classes on television, and tried to picture the man folded into one of their little desks. "The system lords — well, really the minor Goa'uld too — tend to collect artifacts that they perceive as exceptionally valuable — jewelry made out of gold or naquadah or other precious materials, monumental sculpture, that kind of thing. But it's not like they keep records of where they got it. There's no provenance for most of the objects, so unless we can sort out where they came from, they don't tell us much."

He reached up to take down a box from an upper shelf. "This, for instance. It's very pretty, but the most we can say about it is that it's a gold mask, made in a style that's derivative of Ancient Egyptian work. It could have come from any of a hundred planets. It's probably a portrait mask, and if it were from Earth, it would have been made for someone's tomb. If it had wound up there, it might have told us something about the man it was made for. As it is —" Jefferson shrugged. "All it tells us is that the Goa'uld collect gold artwork like magpies."

"How very shallow of them," Vala said. The mask was lovely, heavy gold enameled in black around the eyes with a square, stylized beard and angular wig or headcloth worked in gold and black stripes. Her fingers itched to hold it. "Do you think I could…"

"Don't take it out of the box," Jefferson said. "Not unless you want me to get you a pair of gloves."

She weighed the box in her hand thoughtfully, tilting it to examine it at various angles in the light. "That won't be necessary. It is certainly a beautiful piece." She added a little frown of disappointment when Jefferson closed the box again and set it back in place. "But I'm sure its scientific value is far beyond any value it has as pure gold."

"It's pretty valuable as pure gold," Jefferson said. "But you're right, of course."

She did take note of its location. It was only what Conan Doyle would have done, she told herself. A good detective took note of all the important details.

Cam unapologetically borrowed Daniel's office to use as an interview room. His own was several floors away, and besides he preferred to see the archaeologists on their own turf. Daniel's office was cluttered with what looked like the weirdest objects from every antique store Cam's grandmother had ever dragged him through as a child, although most of the stuff was probably either alien or genuinely ancient in origin.

Chen sat, her mouth pressed together firmly. Cam settled into Daniel's chair and resisted the urge to stack the books that covered the desk in some kind of facsimile of military order. That probably wasn't the way to get Daniel to warm up to him, if such a thing was actually possible. He respected Daniel Jackson for his accomplishments, and trusted that Daniel respected him for his record. That wasn't the same thing as actual friendship, and he was finding that a lot harder to achieve.

"Tell me what happened in the lab yesterday," he said.

"I was working on a set of gold finger rings that were found on P7X-245," Chen said. "Barry had cleaned them and taken measurements the day before, and I was photographing them and packing them up to put in storage."

"You weren't working on the weapons SG-11 found?"

"Not yesterday," Chen said. His ears pricked up at that, and Chen shifted a little in her seat. "I took some photographs of them day before yesterday. I do most of our photography. But I never actually handled the artifacts. Dr. Oliver set them up for each shot exactly the way he wanted them."

She was awfully quick to protest any suggestion that she'd touched the artifacts, Cam noted, but he let that go for the moment. "Was that typical of Dr. Oliver?"

"I'd say it was. He liked things his way."

"You disagreed with him?"

"I didn't think it was important to obsess over whether each of twenty arrowheads was lined up at exactly the right angle," Chen said. "For example. He had a fit about that the last time I did any photography for him. This time I let him fiddle around as long as he wanted getting each one lined up. It took about twice as long as it should have to get the shots."

"It was frustrating," Cam suggested.

"It was pretty frustrating, all right. He drove us crazy about that kind of thing. If you moved anything in his sorting trays, or put an artifact back in the wrong place in a box, he'd read you the riot act. Barry borrowed his office keys once and didn't put them back on exactly the same hook on the wall, and you would have thought he'd murdered —" She broke off abruptly.

"Dr. Jefferson borrowed Dr. Oliver's office keys? When was that?"

"I don't remember. We all did at one point or another. Oliver had books we all needed to refer to. He kept his office keys on a hook in the lab, so we usually just grabbed them if we needed something and Oliver wasn't in the lab."

"And he was okay with that?"

"As long as we didn't move any of his stuff."

"Let's talk about last night. How was everyone acting when you left? Anything out of the ordinary?"

"Not really. Everyone was in kind of a bad mood."

"What about?"

"Nothing in particular. Just one of those days when everyone's cranky. It's a small lab — I think we've all pointed out that it's too small for four people, but Dr. Jackson said that there's no more room available. We get on each other's nerves sometimes."

"So there weren't any arguments you remember about any particular subject?"

"I remember Dr. Oliver complained at one point that Barry hadn't labeled some pottery fragments he was working on, and Barry said that he would when he was finished and that he knew where all of them came from. Which you can imagine didn't go over well with Mr. 'What if you were hit by a truck tomorrow?'" She broke off again, shaking her head. "I guess you don't notice until someone dies how much we talk about death like it's no big thing."

"Any other arguments?"

She shook her head. "I kept out of it. Gideon was in a bad

mood, too — I asked him to pass me a book at one point and he shoved it at me without even looking at me. I think we were all glad when the end of the day came."

"It didn't strike any of you as unusual that you were all getting along badly?"

"It wasn't unusual," Chen said. "I mean, I don't want you to think that we all hate each other, but, like I said, it's a small lab, and we're up in each other's faces all the time. Gideon gets on everybody's nerves by being pompous about every publication he's ever had — you'd think that book of his was a New York Times bestseller. Barry drops things and knocks things over and gets in everyone's way. And there's no sunlight down here, and you can't even go take a walk outside. It gets a little grim."

It would have been nice for Cam to be able to say that her description of the afternoon pointed to an alien influence. Well, maybe nice wasn't the word, but at least he wouldn't have had to suspect a more ordinary motive for murder. However, he had to admit that even SG-1, which was one of the closest-knit teams on the base, had occasional days when he suspected they'd all rather be working alone.

"Was anyone still in the lab when you left?"

"Barry and I left at the same time. Gideon and Oliver came out a few minutes later. It couldn't have been more than five or ten minutes, because we were still waiting for the shuttle back out to the parking lot when they came up. We all caught the same shuttle bus."

"And in the morning?"

"I came in a little early. I'd left my laptop in the lab, and there were some notes I wanted to look at over breakfast. I let myself in, got my laptop, and took it down to the mess hall. No one else was in the lab at that point."

"Did you notice if Oliver's spiked club had been interfered with since the night before?"

"I didn't even look at it," Chen said. "My mind was on breakfast. I came back up to the lab at a few minutes after eight. I remember being relieved that Dr. Oliver wasn't in the lab, because he would have jumped down my throat for being a few minutes late."

"He was usually in the lab in the mornings?"

"Sometimes. When he had reports he wanted to write up, he usually did that in his office. It's quieter in there, and he's got all the books if he needs them. I figured that was what he was doing."

"I understand you were the one who found him," Cam said, using his most sympathetic tones despite the fact that she didn't seem exactly broken up by Oliver's death. Sometimes grief took a while to creep up on people.

"I did," she said, sounding at least more subdued. "I was going to tell him that I'd gone through a tray of tile fragments that he said needed to be re-catalogued. He'd been pretty insistent about it, and I figured if I told him before he nagged me about it again, it might put him in a better mood. I opened the door, and he was slumped over his desk, like he'd fallen asleep. Only he would never have slept on the job." She shook her head. "As soon as I saw him like that, I knew he must be dead."

"Dr. Chen, can you think of any reason why someone would have wanted Dr. Oliver dead?"

"Certainly not. I mean, you don't kill someone just because he argues with you about your work, right? Who does that?"

"Hopefully no one," Cam said. "But we're going to have to find out."

Daniel stowed the last of his equipment in his pack and turned to see that Sam was fastening up her own. "I'm sorry we're having to leave just when it seemed like we were getting somewhere."

"That's pretty much par for the course, right?" Sam said. "Besides, as much as I'd like to stay, it's probably just as well that we're getting out of here. All that rain is going to make the hillside out there unstable —"

Her words were cut off by a rumbling crash that shook the cave floor. Daniel crouched low, arms over his head, wondering if the ceiling of the cave was about to come down on them. He could feel Sam's shoulder pressing against his, but he didn't dare look up at her. It would be awfully ironic to survive the Goa'uld, the Ori, and everything else the galaxy could throw at them only to be crushed by falling rocks.

Damp, crumbling fragments of rocks showered down on them, but the cave ceiling held. After what felt like an eternity, the rumble stopped, replaced by a quiet in which Daniel could hear his own heart pounding in his ears. Daniel and Sam exchanged looks and straightened up, moved as one toward the cave entrance.

It was just possible to piece their way through tumbled rock to reach the mouth of the cave, although both of them held their breath as they did so, uncertain whether part of the ceiling might come down on their heads at any minute. Once they were able to look down, Sam winced and shook her head, and Daniel felt his spirits sink.

The trail that had led up to the cave mouth was gone, obliterated by the tide of rock and mud that had slid down the face of the mountainside, smashing everything in its path. It had left them with no obvious way to get back down to the valley floor other than painstaking rope work down a cascade of fallen boulders resting on treacherously unstable mud.

Sam looked at the jumble of rocks and mud without any more enthusiasm for negotiating it than Daniel felt. "I think 'as soon as possible' is going to be a little later than we thought," she said.

CHAPTER THREE

CAM walked Chen back to the lab, where she dropped sullenly into a chair. Vala was prowling the lab, peering into boxes and examining the artifacts laid out on worktables. He hoped she was getting a better idea than he had of what the archaeologists actually did on a daily basis. And that she wasn't planning to walk off with anything particularly pretty.

"Jefferson, you're up," Cam said, and led the man back to Daniel's office.

Jefferson picked up a pen from Daniel's desk as he sat down, turning it round nervously in his fingers, and then seemed to realize what he was doing and dropped it. It clattered to the desk, and then rolled off onto the floor, Jefferson's elbows flailing as he tried to catch it.

"At ease," Cam said. "I just want your version of what happened yesterday and today."

"I was working with some pottery fragments," Jefferson said. "Yesterday and today."

"I understand you and Oliver had a disagreement about your work."

"He thought I ought to stop and label everything before I did any sorting and cleaning. As if I was going to forget where the whole box of pottery shards came from. That was just Oliver, though. He was always breathing down your neck, waiting for you to make some mistake, or do things differently than he would have done them."

"I take it you weren't friends," Cam said.

Jefferson breathed a humorless laugh. "You could say that again. He wasn't the easiest man to work for."

"Because he criticized your work?"

"He criticized everybody's work. He obsessed about having little details perfect. Frankly, he was a pain in the ass. I'm sorry he's dead, of course," Jefferson added, as if abruptly remembering the reason for their conversation. "It was a shock to all of us."

Not to all of you, Cam thought. *Because one of you probably killed him.*

"When you came in this morning, was Oliver already here?"

"No, he came in a few minutes late. I got here early — I was kind of trying to smooth things over after yesterday. Gideon was already here, too, working on inscriptions. Alice wasn't in the lab, but she must have stopped by the lab already, because her laptop was gone."

"You noticed that."

"Archaeologists notice things."

Cam leaned back in Daniel's chair, wondering how long it was going to be before he got to go home to his waiting bed. "Did you happen to notice whether Oliver's mug was still where he left it?"

"It was. I'm almost sure it was. No, it was, because I saw him take it down from the shelf and pour himself some coffee."

"He didn't rinse out the mug before he poured the coffee?"

"He always rinsed it out the night before. He just took it down and poured his coffee into it." Jefferson frowned at him. "The rest of us all drank coffee too — at least, Gideon and I did. I don't know about Alice. But the poison must have been in the cup."

"Were you alone in the lab at any point this morning?"

"No," Jefferson said. "Well… Gideon went out for a minute at one point. To the men's room, I presume. That was right before Oliver got here."

"So what I'm hearing is that everybody in the lab was alone with Oliver's cup at some point." Cam rubbed his forehead. "And everybody had access to the poisoned weapon."

"It was in a locked case," Jefferson said. "But Oliver kept the keys to all the locked cases in his office drawers. We all knew where they were, and he labeled the keys by which case they opened. It was mainly just a way for us to make sure that visitors couldn't stick their fingers anywhere dangerous."

"Do you usually have a lot of dangerous things in the archaeology lab?"

Jefferson shrugged expressively. "If this were a normal job, I'd say the artifacts were in a lot more danger from the visitors than the other way around. But working here, we've had our share of ordinary-looking objects that turned out to fire disintegration beams or take over people's brains or actually be alive. A plain old poisoned weapon isn't even that exciting."

"Can you think of any reason why someone would have wanted Dr. Oliver dead?"

"Not an actual reason," Jefferson said. Cam didn't need to be a great detective to notice that wasn't the same thing as just plain saying no.

"I'm listening."

Jefferson let out a long, slow breath. "Well. He and Gideon had been arguing—more than usual, I mean. And I don't think it was about work. A couple of days ago I left my jacket in the lab and came back for it. I heard raised voices, but I just thought they were off on how the shelves should be arranged again. They were arguing about that the other day, about some boxes that had been moved from where Oliver wanted them, and Gideon said he didn't do it, but try telling Oliver things like that."

"But?" Cam prompted.

"This was different. When I came in, they were squared off with each other like they were about to start mixing it up. I mean, I seriously thought one of them was going to throw a punch. I said, 'Hey, what's up,' and Gideon said 'It's fine,' but he didn't sound like he meant it. I grabbed my coat, and Oliver said something like 'I meant what I said,' and Gideon said Oliver didn't have to worry about it, and I got out of there."

"That's all you heard?"

"That's all. I wasn't thinking about anything like this happening, I just didn't want to be there because whatever was going down seemed…"

"Awkward," Cam finished for him.

"That. But maybe it didn't have anything to do with what happened."

"Maybe not," Cam said, but he didn't really believe it.

By the time he brought Jefferson back and nodded to Carr to follow him, Chen was arguing with Vala about whether she really had to stay there.

"I'm certain that your cat will survive without you for a few hours," Vala said, shooting him a glance over Chen's shoulder as if to verify that Tau'ri cats didn't expire if not constantly attended.

"We'll get someone out to feed your cat," Cam said, nodding reassurance to Vala in case she was visualizing some kind of ferocious animal the size of a pony. Although didn't the Egyptians have cats, in which case didn't the Goa'uld probably have cats? He could ask Vala sometime, although getting a straight answer out of her was never easy.

"That's what you said hours ago," Chen said.

Cam's patience was beginning to wear thin. "You have to understand the position you're in," he said. "All three of you had access to the poison that was used to kill Dr. Oliver. None of you seems to have liked him very much. You see why it doesn't look good."

"If you come clean, I'm sure General Landry will go easy on you," Vala said. That wasn't, frankly, true — Cam was pretty sure a confession to cold-blooded murder wasn't going to make anyone's day easier — but Vala did sound persuasive saying it.

There was a resounding silence, very much like the sound of three people failing to confess.

"Dr. Carr, it's your turn," Cam said.

Carr was calmer than either Chen or Jefferson as he took his seat in Daniel's office. He shook his head regretfully. "A terrible business," he said. "I can't believe he's gone."

"You and Dr. Oliver were friends?"

"I wouldn't say that," Carr said. "Not friends as such. We

had our disagreements, our little arguments—he felt some of my translations were inaccurate. He expressed himself quite strongly on that point only last night."

"So I've heard," Cam said.

Carr turned up his hands. "An awkward scene. Especially under the circumstances."

"Dr. Jefferson got the impression that your disagreement with Oliver was for more personal reasons."

"No, no, it was an archaeological dispute. You may imagine that it's a peaceful and cooperative profession, but coop four of us up in a space the size of a walk-in closet, and you'll quickly see our true colors. It didn't bring out the best in any of us."

Cam put his head to one side, considering Carr. If he were one of the detectives on the shows that came on TV late at night, he'd be able to sense that Carr was lying. Actually he had no idea, but it seemed worth trying, and since Vala wasn't there to play bad cop, or good cop, or whatever she'd been proposing, he figured it was up to him.

"You don't expect me to believe that, do you? You weren't arguing about archaeology last night. Jefferson made that very clear. If you're innocent, I need you to tell me the truth, even if it's something you wouldn't ordinarily want anyone to know."

"When you put it that way," Carr said. "There is something that I wouldn't ordinarily have mentioned. A personally awkward situation. But it had nothing to do with the murder, nothing." Cam waited, hoping he hadn't just put the idea of confessing to some embarrassingly trivial argument into Carr's head. "Dr. Oliver and I both thought a great deal of Patricia. Dr. Niles," Carr added when Cam looked blank. "We worked with her for a number of months. Her methodology was suburb."

"Okay," Cam said, unsure where that was going.

"After several months I asked her… I invited her to have coffee with me outside of work. I told her that I wanted to get to know her better." Carr's cheeks flushed. "And she said that she was happy to have coffee with me as a friend, but that she was already going out with Dr. Oliver. She hadn't told anyone because she didn't want to make things awkward. She hoped things between us wouldn't be awkward."

"And were they?"

"Of course they were. I had been… effusive in my compliments. It was a personally embarrassing situation. But we were both professional adults, and we didn't speak of it in the office. For what it's worth, she and Oliver always behaved professionally whenever any of the rest of us were around, although sometimes I came into the lab early in the morning and saw them… well, talking very closely together."

"So what was the subject of your disagreement?"

"Patricia left the SGC very suddenly two months ago to take a job in the private sector, in Denver. It seems she hadn't told anyone she was applying, even Oliver. My impression is that she broke off their relationship when she left. I expect he was angry with her, and that's perfectly understandable. What made the situation so awful was that he seemed to think that I had persuaded her to leave. I made a couple of trips to Denver — for unrelated reasons — and made the mistake of mentioning it. Oliver accused me of carrying on an affair with Patricia, of having stolen her from him. He was completely overwrought."

"Overwrought."

"What would you call it when a middle-aged man behaves like a lovesick teenager? He told me to stay away from Patricia. I assured him that I would, that we hadn't even spoken since she left the SGC. I barely have time for a social life at all. I certainly don't have time for one that requires driving to Denver."

"What was the upshot of your argument?"

"Barry came in as Oliver was still lecturing me. Neither of us wanted to air our dirty laundry in front of him; I think he asked if something was wrong and I told him everything was fine. Oliver said something like 'I meant what I said,' and I said I knew. I was planning on talking to Dr. Jackson about it when he got back from off-world — it was becoming unbearable to work with someone who was so paranoid about his personal life. But of course that's a moot point now."

"You were the first one into the lab this morning," Cam said, striking off at a tangent. "Is it possible that someone had already tampered with Oliver's coffee cup?"

"I frankly wouldn't have noticed. I poured my own coffee, but I don't pay attention to how other people keep their things. Unlike Oliver, I don't consider it any of my business. Oliver did make a habit of looking into other people's business."

"How so?"

"Strictly professionally. He was our supervisor, in a sense, but he took that very much to heart. We were all trained professionals, and it rankled sometimes to feel that he didn't have much trust in us. Toward the end it seemed to me that he was getting paranoid about our work, as well, always expecting someone to betray his trust one way or another."

"Looks like that was for good reason," Cam couldn't help saying.

"It's hard to believe this could have happened."

"You weren't working with anything that could have exerted some kind of, I don't know, mind-controlling influence…"

"I wish I could say we were. Alice was working on photographing a number of objects that were going into storage, but none of them had any unusual properties — they were merely nice examples of material culture from various sites visited by SG teams. Jefferson was working on a set of pottery fragments, and I was doing translations. Oliver himself was writing up a report about the poisoned weapons."

"Then I'll ask you the same question I've been asking everybody. Why do you think somebody killed him?"

Carr let out a slow breath. "Colonel Mitchell, I don't think anyone did kill him. I think it must have been suicide. The way he'd been acting about Patricia — it wasn't reasonable, even if their relationship was more serious than I had assumed. He was practically unhinged. I can only assume that the combination of losing her and the stress of working in such a dangerous environment…"

"Try being out in the field sometime," Cam said, but he knew even as he said it that he wasn't being fair. Most archaeologists didn't work in conditions where they might go in to work in the morning and find their office overrun by runaway plant life, occupied by homicidal aliens who were threatening to turn all the humans into their personal slaves, or counting down to nuclear self-destruction. "If you think of any reason, any reason at all, why someone else might have killed him, I'd appreciate it if you wouldn't keep it to yourself."

"Believe me, we'd all like to get to the bottom of this," Carr said.

"By the way, Dr. Carr, what happened to your hand?"

Carr looked down at it as if he'd forgotten about the injury. "A tool I was using to clean some pottery slipped, a few days ago. I had it stitched up in the infirmary, and got a tetanus booster. Nothing important."

"You should be more careful," Cam said. "We don't want any more people around here getting hurt."

He returned Carr to the lab, and called security to escort the scientists to comfortable quarters for the night. He left the security guards to explain to them that they weren't going to be going home that night, and headed up to the gate room. Apparently Sam and Daniel needed reminding that "wrap it up" meant "sometime today" in Cam's book.

Sam was clearing rubble away from one of the more promising campsites in the cave, in that it was dry and reasonably flat, when the radio crackled to life.

"I'll bet you that's Mitchell calling to find out why we're late," Daniel said.

"No bet."

"Carter and Jackson, come in," Cam said over the radio.

"We're here," Sam said. "And I'm guessing your question is

why we're still here."

"Got it in one."

"A rockslide just took out our way down from here. I'm guessing that all this rain destabilized part of the hillside. We're just lucky it didn't seal up the cave mouth entirely."

"A rockslide," Cam said, sounding like it was all he needed at that moment.

"We're sorry," Sam said. "I think we can still get back down to the Stargate, but the sun's already down, and I don't want to try it in the dark unless there's no other choice."

"And I hope we don't wind up with no other choice," Daniel added.

Sam nodded agreement. "For now, the chamber we're in seems stable, and there's still the possibility that we can find the Ancient installation. We've got lights and supplies, and in the morning we can take a better look at that rock fall. If it doesn't look like we can make it down on our own, you can send backup when you check in with us."

"Sounds like a plan," Cam said.

"If that works for you."

"It's fine. Keep me posted."

"What have you found out?" Daniel asked.

"We're still trying to piece it together. Nobody says they saw anyone stirring poison into Oliver's coffee, if you were still hoping it might be that easy. Teal'c is pulling the security footage, and I sincerely hope it answers more questions than your archaeologists did."

"You think they're stonewalling you?"

"I think somebody's lying, but I don't know who," Cam said. "And I could sure use your opinion, so just get back here as soon as you can."

"Will do," Sam said, and Cam cut the connection.

Daniel cast a thoughtful glance toward the dark shadows at the back of the cavern, where a number of more or less navigable passageways led back into the unknown. "You know, going on looking for the Ancient installation while we're stuck here tonight isn't a bad idea," Daniel said. "If you've found a way down there—"

"I think I've found a way through the cave passages that might lead to the vicinity of the energy readings," Sam said. "The question is, do we want to explore it in the dark, when we're both tired, knowing that if we get hurt, we'll still have to climb down over all those boulders to get out of here..."

"I didn't say it was a great idea."

"Let's just get some sleep and hope that they've already caught the killer by the time we wake up in the morning."

"Do you really think that's likely?" Daniel asked.

She shrugged, looking more optimistic than Daniel felt. "You never know."

"So, have we found the killer yet?" Vala asked as she came into Daniel's office, where Teal'c was seated in front of Daniel's computer. Vala had made at least one discovery in the archaeology lab, but she wasn't yet certain how it bore on their problem.

"I was intending to ask you the same question," Teal'c said.

"That would be a big 'no,'" Mitchell said as he followed Vala into the room. "Except that Oliver and Carr were involved in some kind of love triangle with Dr. Niles, which is more soap opera than usually goes on around here. I've just tried calling her in Denver, but she's not answering her phone. I'll try again after a while—if we can track her down, at least we can get her opinion on whether Oliver was upset enough about their break-up to poison himself, and find out whether Carr was telling the truth about not having seen her since she left town."

"Any luck with the security cameras?"

"I have reviewed the security footage from the previous two days," Teal'c said. "It shows the entrance to the lab, but not whatever may have transpired within the lab itself."

"Even so, it might help tell us whether one of them is lying."

"At 12:30 yesterday," Teal'c said, bringing up the security footage on Daniel's computer, "Dr. Oliver returned from lunch and entered the archaeology lab." Vala watched him walk down the hall and enter the room, a white-coated figure with thinning hair and wire-rimmed glasses with no idea that he was going to be dead within twenty-four hours.

She found the idea unutterably depressing. As opposed to everything else that had happened lately, which was all so pleasant and cheering. She told herself firmly to stop thinking about it, and focused her attention on the video.

"Chen and Jefferson entered the laboratory shortly thereafter, followed by Carr," Teal'c continued.

"So everyone's in there together," Mitchell said. "But the poison probably isn't in his cup yet, because both Chen and Jefferson said they saw him drinking coffee after lunch."

The cameras kept rolling in an empty hallway. Teal'c sped up the video feed, and hours slid by.

"At 18:02, Chen and Jefferson left the laboratory, followed by Carr, followed by Oliver." Teal'c froze the frame.

"That confirms that none of them hung back and put the poison in Oliver's cup," Mitchell said. "If he was poisoned last night, it was in front of the rest of the scientists in the lab."

"Would they have noticed?" Vala asked. "We all know how self-absorbed archaeologists can be. Sometimes Daniel doesn't even seem to notice me."

"Maybe not," Mitchell said after a moment. "People get wrapped up in their work. But it couldn't have happened while Oliver was still drinking coffee, or he'd have collapsed last night rather than this morning. And it wouldn't have been before he rinsed out his mug, or there wouldn't be any point. So it would have had to be at the very end of the day, after Oliver had already rinsed out his coffee mug and hung it up to dry."

"While others were also putting away their own mugs."

"I don't think so," Mitchell said. "Chen has a travel mug. You can see her leaving with it. And Jefferson and Carr both say they usually left their coffee mugs at their desks and then rinsed them out in the morning. Apparently Oliver used to get on their cases about it."

Teal'c's eyes went to Daniel's clutter of coffee mugs left absently in various places around the office, but he refrained from saying whatever was on his mind. Jaffa were usually tidy, in Vala's experience. She felt it came from living aboard ships and dealing with unbalanced gods who might have you executed if you annoyed them.

"No one entered the laboratory overnight," Teal'c said. The night passed without anything more interesting to see than a few people walking down the hall past either the office or the lab; none of them opened either door. "At 07:35 Chen entered the laboratory, and then exited again carrying her laptop computer. At 07:42, Carr entered, followed by Jefferson at 07:47. Carr left again at 07:53. His destination did not appear sinister." He brought up the next camera, which showed Carr entering the men's room at the end of the hall. "Oliver arrived one minute before 08:00 hours, and left the room a few minutes later carrying his coffee."

"Now with added poison," Vala said.

"It appears so." He split the screen between two camera feeds; on one, Carr was entering the archaeology lab, while on the other, now-doomed Oliver was opening his own office door.

"Oliver was planning to write up his notes on the artifact," Mitchell said. "The rest of the team all had work to do. Presumably they're working, until… there."

At 09:27, Chen left the lab, walking down the hall and appearing on the second security camera as she approached Oliver's door. She opened it, froze in apparent shock, and then disappeared inside. At 09:29, Dr. Lam and one of the medical technician entered the frame, running down the hall and hurrying inside Oliver's office. Teal'c froze the picture there.

"Dr. Lam was the first one on the scene," Mitchell said. "That doesn't make this any better for her."

"It was only natural for her to respond to an emergency

inside the base," Teal'c said.

"I know. Still, I wish she'd been at lunch or tied up treating someone's sprained ankle. Run that back a minute." Mitchell ran the footage back to watch Chen enter the office again, and paused it on the moment when her expression changed as she saw what was inside. "She sure looks surprised."

"She also knows the cameras are there," Vala said. "She must have known her life depended on appearing to be surprised. If she's guilty, that is. If she's innocent, it was probably just a very disturbing morning at work."

Mitchell shook his head. "I don't think any of this tells us much, except that everybody was alone with Oliver's coffee cup at some point." He looked around the group. "Any thoughts on where we go from here? This detective thing isn't really my strong suit. I'm not even really a big fan of detective shows on TV."

"I admit to a personal weakness for the genre I believe to be known as noir," Teal'c said. "Dashing private detectives in hats and beautiful women with ulterior motives."

"That's so unrealistic," Vala said.

Mitchell shook his head. "Do those movies even make sense if you're from another planet?"

"Surprisingly much so. I have found some other detective stories that Daniel Jackson recommended to be mystifying. Very often they turn on subtle points of Tau'ri culture that are lost on me, or that do not seem to be true to the present day. I have not noticed most people sealing their correspondence with colored wax or changing all of their clothes for dinner."

"When everyone dresses like this, how could you tell?" Vala put in, waving a hand to indicate the unrelieved olive drab of her jumpsuit.

"Also, the assumption in many of the 'cozy' mysteries is clearly that violent death comes as an unexpected shock, despite the number of murders that seem to occur in peaceful villages inhabited by elderly women."

"I can see where that would be a little hard for you to identify with," Mitchell said.

"Indeed. The works of the 'hard-boiled' school are more familiar stories. They deal with criminals who steal or kill from greed, or from a desire for jealousy or revenge. I believe those things to be universal. And the heroes in those stories are no strangers to death."

It was hard to trump that as a dramatic line, but Vala felt she had to try. "I did find out one thing," she said.

"Tell me it's something that's going to tell us who killed Oliver," Mitchell said.

"I don't know about who, but it might answer more than a few questions about why," Vala said. "Those lovely gold artifacts that are scheduled to be put in storage? They're forgeries."

Mitchell rubbed his forehead. "Forgeries," he said. "And you know this because…"

"Well, I've had to become something of an expert on Goa'uld art," Vala said. "For, well, professional reasons. There are collectors out there who will pay good prices for genuine Goa'uld pieces without too many questions asked about where they came from or if there's a system lord who might want them back."

"That is a dangerous practice," Teal'c said.

"Less dangerous than it used to be, now that there are a lot fewer system lords around. A power vacuum means a lot of pretty pieces have become more… accessible. If you were interested in that kind of thing. Which of course I'm not anymore, because I am strictly interested in helping people as part of SG-1 rather than making any kind of personal profit."

"Right," Mitchell said after a moment. "Let me rephrase. What is it about these artifacts that tells you that they're not Goa'uld?"

"It's obvious," Vala said. "They look completely wrong. It's not any one thing. It's the whole feel of them, the way they make you feel when you look at them." She put her head to one side as if he ought to understand what she was talking about. "You know? I mean, take the mask Jefferson showed me. There's something about the nose that certainly isn't right."

"Excuse me if this sounds like it might be just a little bit of a wild goose chase," Mitchell said.

"It's not a wild goose chase," Vala persisted. "I am telling you that a number of the artifacts you have in that laboratory never came out of a Goa'uld treasure hoard. They weren't made by the Jaffa or by any humans who cared what the Goa'uld thought about them. And I'm not even certain that they're solid gold."

"That, at least, can be tested," Teal'c said.

"Then let's test them," Mitchell said. "I'll ask Landry to get our archaeologist buddies settled down in guest quarters for the night."

"That's a euphemism for 'in a cell,' right?" Vala asked.

"Well, in our actual guest quarters, which you're familiar with, because we use them for actual guests," Mitchell said. "Which do happen to have locks on the door that don't necessarily open from the inside."

"In a comfortable cell," Vala said.

"We are both still residing in guest quarters ourselves," Teal'c pointed out.

"I think it's the lock that makes the difference."

"Meanwhile, I'm going to call Daniel back," Mitchell said. "He can tell us if there's anything to the idea that they don't 'feel right.'"

"They don't," Vala said. "He'll say the same thing."

CHAPTER FOUR

"THAT'S impossible," Daniel said. "They can't be forgeries."

"Vala says she's sure there's something wrong with them," Mitchell's voice said over the radio. "In particular that gold mask thing that was about to go into storage."

Daniel sat back on his heels wearily, trying to remember the piece. He had seen it when it was found, its gold lines so appealing that he felt a stab of guilt at having brought it home, like a treasure-hunter only digging up tombs for the valuables he could find there. It had helped to remind himself that this particular treasure came from a Goa'uld stronghold that had been assaulted to free the human slaves kept there and deprive the system lord of a valuable tactical resource, and that leaving the pieces where they were found would only have meant leaving them for looters like… well, like Vala Mal Doran.

"That mask was definitely genuine," Daniel said.

"So there's nothing to this 'I have a feeling' talk of Vala's."

"I'm not saying that," Daniel said. "There's a kind of intuition about pieces that you get when you're an expert on art from a certain period. I've talked to museum curators who've taken one look at a sculpture and been certain it was a reproduction or a forgery. It's not one big thing, usually, it's a lot of little things. The way the sculptor worked the metal, or the way the piece was cast. The shape of the features. The decoration. Whether it's too close a copy of something famous — ancient art wasn't made with a cookie cutter — or too far away from anything we've found before. I don't know what she's seeing. But I can't imagine why she'd lie about it."

"I have noticed a certain tendency to place herself at the center of attention," Mitchell said, sounding as if he was choosing his words carefully.

"Yes. Yes, there's that. I'm not saying Vala wouldn't lie, but

I'm not sure she'd lie about this. This is her profession, in a twisted kind of way. Not even that twisted by Earth standards. There are a lot of art dealers and private collectors who deal in pieces that have a questionable history. If she were trying to sell the thing to a gullible buyer, maybe, but not when it's a matter of actually putting her professional judgment on the line."

"Then what's going on?"

"Were all the pieces that Vala says are forgeries scheduled to go into storage?"

"I don't know," Mitchell said after a pause. "I can find out."

"Because if so, the obvious conclusion is that someone was replacing the genuine artifacts with copies, and figuring that no one was going to find out about the switch because the forgeries would be in storage. I mean, eventually they might, if we ever take the pieces out of storage, but that's not likely to happen anytime soon."

"Then why do we have this stuff?"

"Because there's useful research we could do if we had time to study artifacts that don't blow things up or lead us to Ancient sites out of Arthurian legend," Daniel said. "But we don't have that time, certainly not right now with the Ori breathing down our necks, and it's not like we can put any of this on display. We're just filing it away in hopes that someone's going to come along later and have more options about what to do with it."

"So you think somebody… what, stole the originals?"

"The idea does spring to mind. Something like that mask… we're putting it away in storage because it's not actually any use to us. It's just a really nice piece of art typical of Egyptian-influenced Goa'uld work. Or, really, Jaffa work — I doubt a Goa'uld actually made the mask, they're not typically very creative that way. A Goa'uld probably commissioned it. Anyway, my point is that we don't think it's very interesting, but a private collector would probably be a lot more interested in the fact that it's made out of solid gold."

"A private collector here, or off-world?" Sam asked, coming

up behind Daniel, her hair tousled from sleep. Daniel hadn't managed to nod off himself before Mitchell called with his latest piece of bad news.

"That's a good question. Jackson, do you have a good answer?"

"It could be either one," Daniel said slowly. "Disposing of it on Earth would probably be easier. They'd have to get the pieces out of the SGC, which would be running a risk, because there are random bag checks. They're not supposed to be removing any objects brought back from off-world from the base."

Sam put her head to one side. "Are you telling me you've never taken anything from off-world out of the base?"

"I'm not actually saying that," Daniel said. "Which is why I'm saying they'd be taking a risk, not that they couldn't do it."

"I assume you're not selling pieces on the black market," Mitchell said.

"No, it's just that sometimes I want to work on the weekends without being underground in a base where the coffee…" He trailed off, realizing that all jokes about coffee were probably insensitive at the moment. He was trying hard to focus on the problem at hand, rather than thinking about the fact that three days ago he'd been talking to Oliver about his work, and now the man was lying cold in the SGC's morgue, waiting for the investigation to end so that his family could put him in the ground.

"But it could happen."

"It happens all the time in archaeological circles on Earth," Daniel said. "It's always been a problem. Or, at least, it's been a problem since we decided that it wasn't actually ethical to dig up whatever you can find as haphazardly as you want and sell it all off to the highest bidder. I do see one obstacle, which to my mind is more serious than the problem of how you'd get the artifacts out of the base."

"And that would be?" Mitchell prompted.

"They're not really Egyptian," Daniel said. "And you'd have to sell them as Egyptian, because you can't very well explain that they were made by aliens on another planet. Anyone who'd believe that, you could sell the Brooklyn Bridge. And anybody who'd believe that decorative objects made by the Jaffa actually came from a dig in Egypt…" He ran a hand through his hair, realizing too late that he was only streaking it with mud. "It is complicated by the fact that some of what we've found in Egypt actually did come from off-world, or was made under the influence of the Goa'uld. But, still, whatever you're claiming the provenance of these pieces is, you're going to be lying. And I would think that anyone who would swallow your story would just as easily swallow the forgeries, at a considerably reduced risk."

"Except that the forgeries probably aren't real gold," Sam pointed out.

"Probably not," Daniel said. "A collector who only cared that they were solid gold…" He frowned in distaste at the idea. "Well, you wouldn't get the kind of price you would from someone who thought they were paying for priceless Egyptian antiquities. You'd make some money. Just not that kind of money."

"And off-world?"

"I don't know what the market is like," Daniel said. "I think Vala is evidence that there is a market, and that there are collectors out there who will pay more for artifacts than just the price of the gold that went into them. But she's the one to ask about that. If anybody's an expert on the interplanetary trade in stolen goods, it's Vala Mal Doran."

"Okay. We'll do that."

"You should still check out the possibility that they've come up on the antiquities black market on Earth," Daniel said. "No museum would touch them, but it's just possible that there's a private buyer out there who's rich enough to pay serious money for these things and ignorant enough to believe they're really Egyptian."

"That would be a great idea," Mitchell said patiently, "except that I have no way of doing that, and by the time you get back here, this whole thing may be out of our hands."

"Only now it'll include an investigation into incredibly classified materials being smuggled off the base and sold," Daniel said. "Just what we all wanted. No, it can't wait until we can get out of here. You need someone who can ask the right people the right questions on Earth."

"You're going to say Vala again, aren't you?"

"She doesn't have the contacts on Earth," Daniel said. "At least I hope not. She works fast, but we've kept her pretty busy, and besides she's not doing that kind of thing anymore. No, I was thinking of Sarah Gardner."

"Osiris's host."

That was probably all Mitchell knew about her, from the SGC's files. Daniel had once known her much more closely. He hadn't seen her since just after the Tok'ra had freed her from Osiris's control.

"Temporary host," Daniel said firmly. "But she's a good archaeologist, she's done some work on trying to stamp out the black market trade in antiquities, and she already knows about the Stargate program. There's no time to get anyone else cleared to tell them the truth about what we're looking for, and it's going to be a lot easier for her to ask the right questions if she knows."

"Why am I sensing some kind of catch?"

"The catch is that I'm not sure she'll even pick up the phone," he admitted. "The last time we talked she said she didn't want anything to do with the Stargate program, and that she never wanted to hear another word about it."

"And this is your best suggestion?"

"It's the best suggestion I've got. All of our people are either possible suspects in the theft, if there has been a theft — in which case you'd be giving them the perfect opportunity to cover their tracks — or they're in the Pegasus Galaxy. If Catherine were still alive, I'd suggest you ask her; she always kept her finger on the pulse of everything going on in

Egyptology. But this is what I've got."

"Understood," Mitchell said. "It's worth a try."

Cam checked on Teal'c and Vala on his way to his office, and found them investigating the composition of the gold mask in Daniel's office.

"Have we got our suspects squared away in guest quarters?"

"All safely tucked away," Vala said. "If not happily."

"Believe me, the faster we solve this thing, the happier I'll be, too."

He left them to it and went up several floors to his own tiny office, kept perfectly neat and largely unused. Having an office at all made him a little uneasy; it seemed one step away from having a desk job, which he was trying hard to avoid for at least the near to medium-term future. But there were the inevitable reports to be filed, explaining where they'd gone and what they'd meant to do and, usually, what had happened instead.

Cam called Walter to get Sarah Gardner's number. He was learning to assume that Walter knew everything, and once again he wasn't wrong. He dialed the number Walter gave him and listened to the phone ring, wondering if Dr. Gardner was going to pick up.

"Hello?" a woman's voice answered finally.

"Dr. Gardner, this is Colonel Mitchell at the Cheyenne Mountain facility."

"Cheyenne Mountain?" Her voice grew very clipped. "Has something happened to Dr. Jackson?"

"He's fine," Cam reassured her. "We're just having a little bit of an archaeology problem right now, and he thought you might be able to help us until he can get back from his latest trip."

"His latest trip," Dr. Gardner said, and now he could hear the irony in her voice. "I take it this isn't a little out of town junket."

"That would be classified," Cam said.

"Right, of course. I will never understand why he's still willing to…"

"Very classified," Cam warned.

"I'm alone in my house," Dr. Gardner said. "Or should I worry that my phone might be tapped? I should like to know who might be doing that, if it isn't you."

"I don't know anything about any surveillance you might be under," Cam said, although he suspected that if he checked, he'd find that she was at least on the NID's list for long-term monitoring. "But you can't be too careful."

"I think working for you people is a good way to be killed or endure unspeakable horrors," said Dr. Gardner. "Is that clear enough without requiring any censoring?"

"Loud and clear," Cam said. "We're not asking you to do anything dangerous. We just need information. There are some artifacts, some… particular artifacts that might have come up on the market as Egyptian antiquities."

"I take it they are not Egyptian."

"You got it. Dr. Jackson thought you might be able to find out whether anything like that has been offered for sale recently, especially anywhere near Colorado Springs."

"No," Dr. Gardner said.

"Come on, we really need your help —"

"No, nothing like that has been offered for sale recently. Not in any of the circles of private buyers who might possibly be interested. For reasons that you might be able to imagine, I have a particular interest in Egyptian artifacts being offered for sale, especially those whose provenance is unknown or implausible. The last thing I want is for anyone else to go through what I did."

"I hope that's not possible," Cam said. The idea that more Goa'uld symbiotes might be lurking in undiscovered stasis jars was one he tried not to entertain.

"I hope so, too. Are you certain it's impossible?"

"I'm afraid we can't be certain."

"Lately I've been assisting the Egyptian Supreme Council of Antiquities in their inquiries into who might be in the market for artifacts smuggled out of their country. I'll do some asking around, but I can already tell you that everything I have heard of for sale lately is genuinely Egyptian, which is unfortunate from the point of view of protecting their cultural heritage, but a relief from my point of view."

"And ours," Cam said. "Suppose someone really wanted to sell some supposedly Egyptian artifacts without attracting that kind of attention. How would they go about doing it?"

"They might have a particular buyer in mind," Dr. Gardner said. "A personal friend or acquaintance, so that they never had to pass the word that there was anything for sale. If it were someone who intended to hoard the pieces in a private collection rather than exhibiting them anywhere ... yes, it's possible. You might check the bank records of your suspects. Unexplained large cash deposits are a good sign that something interesting may be going on."

"We'll start with that," Cam said. "Thanks. You've been helpful."

"Tell me, if it's not too very classified," Dr. Gardner said. "These pieces that are missing... how worried should their buyers be?"

"Only a little," Cam said. "I hope."

"I'll certainly sleep better at night knowing you're so certain," Dr. Gardner said. "Goodbye, Colonel Mitchell."

"It seems a shame that we have to cut into it," Vala Mal Doran said, turning the mask back and forth in her hand. Teal'c held out his hand for the artifact, and she handed it to him with visible reluctance.

"You have said yourself you believe it to be a forgery," Teal'c pointed out.

"Yes, but it's not a bad forgery. It fooled trained archaeologists."

"You believe that some of them were fooled?"

Vala raised an eyebrow. "You think they were all in on it? I saw a movie like that on television, where everyone on the train stabbed the man because it turned out they all had grudges against him for… admittedly somewhat contrived reasons."

"No one has been stabbed," Teal'c said. "And it is possible that only one of the archaeologists was criminal, and that the rest were merely careless and negligent."

He selected a knife from among Daniel Jackson's tools, and carved a fine line down the face of the mask. A darker metal was clearly visible underneath.

"Gold plate over nickel," Vala Mal Doran said. "Someone has an electroplating setup and a criminal mind." She shrugged in response to his expression. "And I don't have an electroplating setup."

"Nor would you have pointed out the forgery if you were responsible."

"Well, of course not. Credit me with some common sense, if nothing else."

"Indeed I do."

"What have we got?" Colonel Mitchell said as he came into the room.

Vala Mal Doran handed him the mask wordlessly.

"The mask is not solid gold," Teal'c said.

"I take it there's no way it was made like this by the Jaffa."

"A Jaffa artisan would only make such a thing for the Goa'uld if he had a death wish," Teal'c said. "Nor would a human slave of the Goa'uld be likely to take such a risk."

"It wasn't made by either one," Vala Mal Doran insisted. She turned to Teal'c in appeal. "You can't believe this is a genuine piece made for the Goa'uld."

"I am no expert on art."

"Well, I am," Vala Mal Doran said flatly. "And I was right that it wasn't real gold. Could we all entertain the possibility that I'm right about this too?"

"I'm entertaining it," Colonel Mitchell said. "If you're right, it puts a different light on Dr. Niles's decision to leave town in a hurry."

"I do not think Dr. Niles could be solely responsible for the forgeries," Teal'c said. "The original of this mask—assuming there was an original—was only brought back to the SGC after her departure. She could not have replaced it with a forged copy."

"Great. I was hoping for at least one thing to make sense. All right, let's assume Vala's right, this is a forgery, and someone who's still at the SGC cooked it up, probably one of the archaeologists we've got locked up right now. How do we figure out which one?"

"Whoever made this needed raw materials and an electroplating setup," Vala Mal Doran said. "Where can you buy those around here?"

"A jewelry-making store, maybe?" Colonel Mitchell did not sound certain. "It's getting too late to call around, but we can do that in the morning."

"The electroplating set must be somewhere," Vala said. "It might be somewhere on base, although that's taking a risk. I'm getting the picture that there's not much privacy here."

"There's some," Colonel Mitchell said. "We can search the archaeologists' workspace and check the security cameras to see if there's anywhere they might have stashed an electroplating kit."

"As I was saying," Vala Mal Doran went on. "It might be less of a risk to keep it at home."

"It's going to be a little harder to get permission to search their houses," Colonel Mitchell said. "But I'll see what I can do."

Vala Mal Doran nodded reluctant assent. "I expect you have laws and things."

"We do, actually."

She put her head thoughtfully to one side. "I don't suppose it would help if I volunteered to feed Dr. Chen's poor hungry cat?"

Colonel Mitchell took a breath as if to speak, and then let it out again as if reconsidering his first words. "That would be very neighborly of you," he said.

"I would be pleased to transport you," Teal'c said. While

he had given up his apartment off base as a source of more problems than it solved, he still found that the freedom a car afforded was well worth the effort of maintaining it.

"Great. I don't want to know any more about it," Colonel Mitchell said. "Unless you find an electroplating kit completely accidentally, without actually searching the apartment, which would be very wrong. Understood?"

"Perfectly," Teal'c said before Vala Mal Doran could speak.

"Oh, I see," Vala said, with a conspiratorial wink.

"Not another word," Colonel Mitchell said, and went out.

"Let's ask Dr. Chen for her keys," Vala Mal Doran said. "For the sake of that poor cat."

"I would in fact recommend that we not request Dr. Chen's permission," Teal'c said. "It might be better to go to her apartment intending to acquire a key from a neighbor or property manager."

"You think if we ask she'll say no."

"It seems entirely possible that if we request permission, and Dr. Chen is the guilty party, it will occur to her that her illicit activities might be exposed. Given my experience with Tau'ri bureaucracy, it will be far more difficult to get permission to enter Dr. Chen's apartment once she expressly refuses it."

"We wouldn't want to bother her," Vala Mal Doran said experimentally. "After all, she might have gone to sleep already. And we know this is a difficult time for her."

"Indeed," Teal'c said, withdrawing his car keys from his pocket.

"I don't actually need to get a key from a neighbor," Vala Mal Doran said.

"I did not believe that you did," Teal'c said, and she smiled.

After weeks underground, it was a relief merely to breathe the air on the surface of Earth, even if it reeked of vehicle fuel. Vala followed Teal'c onto a multi-person vehicle that transported them to a wide parking area for smaller vehicles. He kept a stern eye on her, as if expecting her to announce at any moment that she was a visitor from another planet. Vala mimed zipping her lips to reassure him, and his own lips quirked in something that looked very nearly like a smile.

His own vehicle was black and boxy and made an alarming noise when he started it. It seemed tactless to ask if it was supposed to sound like that, and besides, it was no louder than the cars and trucks in the movies she had seen. On the other hand, in the movies, they crashed into each other and exploded into fireballs with an alarming frequency.

"Your seatbelt," Teal'c said, and Vala strapped herself into the safety harness without hesitation.

It was hard to see much from the vehicle except the contrast between light and dark as they sped past pools of light from the street lamps and brightly lit signs that mostly seemed to advertise food and motor fuel, although she had to admit that many of the names were lost on her. Starbucks she recognized from Daniel's coffee cups, and several of the food shops from the bags that often littered the scientists' work areas.

She craned her neck trying to see out the window. A single slivery moon rode high in the sky among stars that shone only dimly in a sky dull with light pollution.

"You can see the stars clearly if you leave the populated area of town," Teal'c said.

She leaned back in her seat, looking up at the tiny sliver of sky visible between signs and the car roof. "Do you look for Chulak?"

"Chulak's suns are not visible from Earth," Teal'c said, but she saw him glance up for a moment before returning his gaze firmly to the road.

"So you do."

Teal'c didn't answer that, pulling off the busy road onto a slower side street instead. Vala folded herself into her seat in order to put her feet up on the front instrument panel. There was no point in looking for her own home world in the night sky, nothing there she wanted to see. All the same, when they pulled into another parking area and she climbed out of the car, she had to force herself not to gaze up at the sky.

"Well, sentimental pining gets you nowhere," she said briskly. "We need to keep our minds on the job."

"You are correct that we must keep our minds on the case," Teal'c said, and straightened his collar. "Search out the clues and uncover the wrongdoers."

"Find out who done it?" she offered.

"Indeed."

He led her to a charmless, squat apartment building that made her reassess her ideas about the SGC's architecture. If this was an example of a place civilians paid money to live, it was possible that the Tau'ri genuinely found little boxes attractive. The doors were numbered, and Teal'c stopped in front of the one that matched the address he had written down.

"We could in fact ask neighbors if they have a key," he said.

"Is there a security system that will fire weapons at us if we don't use the key?"

"Such systems are not in common use," Teal'c said. "I am not certain that they exist on this world at all."

"Then we're fine," she said, extracting a lockpick from her jumpsuit. She felt this might need some explanation, and struggled to come up with one. "I forgot that this was in my pocket," she said finally. "Until this evening, when obviously I remembered." Teal'c shook his head, but made no comment.

The lock popped open absurdly easily, and she reached out cautiously, not quite trusting that the doorknob wouldn't be electrified or primed to set off an alarm when she touched it. She opened the door, froze momentarily at the rusty yowl from within, and then relaxed as she identified it as an angry cat, which twined around her ankles while continuing to protest.

"She does indeed have a cat," Teal'c said.

"Having a cat doesn't make her not a thief," Vala said. "The

Goa'uld like cats, but does that make them good people? I think not."

"I meant only that she was truthful in that detail."

"All the best con artists are truthful in the details that don't matter," Vala said. "That's why people believe them when they lie." She looked around. "What do the Tau'ri feed cats?"

Teal'c held up a can from the counter. It bore a picture of a cat, which suggested it was either meant for feeding cats or contained cat. She decided to take his word for it that the former was more likely. He opened the can and emptied its not-particularly-appetizing contents into a dish on the counter, and Vala turned away to examine the other contents of the room.

Nothing that met the eye resembled electroplating equipment. She prowled the room, peering into its corners, and quickly concluded that if the equipment was there, it wasn't in the main room. There was a door into a second room, though, and she reached for the knob. "I think the cat might want to get into the other room," she said. "Probably that's where it sleeps."

"Clearly you are only thinking of the creature's comfort," Teal'c said.

"Clearly." She opened the door. "Of course, there's only a one in three chance that it's here, one in four counting the possibility that Oliver himself was the one who was stealing the artifacts." Vala circled the bedroom, examining the unmade bed, the cluttered dresser, and the open closet with nothing more sinister than mismatched shoes at the bottom of it. She opened the bathroom door. "But we could get lucky."

Teal'c came to look over her shoulder. The electroplating kit was set up on the bathroom counter, with several pieces of costume jewelry lying next to it, coated thinly in gold.

"We've got her," Vala said.

"None of these are off-world artifacts," Teal'c said.

"She was probably practicing. And left these here in case she had to explain what she was using this for."

"Do they not, in fact, provide a plausible explanation?"

Vala let out a frustrated breath. "Due process and all that. Like on that show with all the lawyers."

"Indeed. It is sufficient to persuade me, but it may not be enough to convict her of the thefts in the absence of more evidence."

"The thefts and the murder," Vala said. "She must have killed Oliver to cover up the fact that she was stealing."

"I do not think we can jump to that conclusion yet."

"It's obvious. Just as obvious as the fact that if she was making fake artifacts, she must have been making them out of something." Vala was opening the drawers beneath the counter as she spoke, and hit gold on the lowest one. Or, more to the point, some metal duller and darker than gold, but nearly as heavy. She extracted one of the bars stacked in the drawer and set it down triumphantly on the counter.

Teal'c failed to return her smile of triumph. In fact, he was scowling, his brow furrowed.

"Isn't this what we're looking for?"

He picked up one of the bars, turning it over to reveal a familiar seal, the serpentine sign of Apophis. "This was mined by the Jaffa of Apophis."

"Several years back, I should think," Vala said. "But then it's metal, so it could have just been sitting in a stockpile somewhere." She turned it around in her fingers. "I think this is definitely a clue."

"Indeed," Teal'c said, but he didn't sound happy about it.

Sam woke up, and then wasn't sure she had. It was completely dark, far darker than it had been when she went to sleep, when light had been filtering in through the mouth of the cave. She held up her hand in front of her face, and felt her palm touch her nose without being able to see even the faintest outline. She felt at her eyelids to make sure her eyes weren't covered, and blinked until she was sure blinking wouldn't help.

Her heart was hammering in her chest, and she drew a

deep breath, trying to judge whether there was enough air to breathe. It was difficult to believe that a cave-in hadn't woken her, unless she'd been knocked unconscious. She felt her head, finding no painful signs that a rock had struck her. Her breath came without an effort, and she felt none of the signs of hypoxia, although she knew all too well how treacherously a lack of oxygen could sneak up on a person.

"Daniel," she said, and reached blindly until she found his shoulder. "Wake up."

"Hmm?" he mumbled, and then, much more sharply, "Sam, I can't see."

"It's pitch black in here. There must have been another landslide."

"It took out the cave mouth and the radar equipment but it didn't even wake us up?" Daniel was right, she realized — the radar equipment had lights that should have been shining brightly in the darkness. "I just turned my flashlight on," he said.

"It's not working?" The darkness was undiminished.

"I can feel the flashlight getting warm the way it usually does," he said. "I just can't see the beam."

"Okay," Sam said slowly. "This is strange."

"Tell me about it. I think — did you hear that?"

She started to say no, and then she did hear something, the sound of something large breathing in the darkness, a snuffling noise and then the sound of a heavy body dragging or slithering against stone.

"I think we need to get out of here," Sam said under her breath.

"I think you may be right." She heard Daniel scrambling to his feet, and took hold of his sleeve as she stood up. She reached for her pack, shrugging into it, and found her own flashlight by feel, picking it up and switching it on. It didn't make the darkness any less total, and she switched it off again, not sure if whatever she could hear in the darkness could see it. She didn't like the idea of becoming easy prey.

She took firmer hold of Daniel's arm and began steering him

toward the cave mouth, or at least where she thought the cave mouth should be. She didn't disorient easily, but it was unnerving trying to piece her way across the uneven cave floor while something unseen moved and breathed in the darkness.

Sam found the edge of the cave mouth with her foot, and edged sideways until she felt one side of the cave opening. When she crouched down and felt around, there was an alarming drop below the lip of the cave mouth. She would have to lower herself down trusting there was something to stand on beneath her, something that wouldn't immediately give way under her feet, and then make her way down without being able to see where she was going.

When she put it that way, taking her chances with whatever was in the cave sounded better. Sam felt her way around the inside wall of the cave instead, with Daniel following her, his hand resting reassuringly on her shoulder. She could still hear something else moving in the cave, but it didn't seem to be coming closer.

Instead, there was a new series of sounds, the unmistakable sound of teeth crunching through bones and flesh, and then a gulping noise that might have been something large being swallowed. Daniel's hand tightened on her shoulder, and she spread her hand against his arm as a silent "I know." She sped her steps as fast as she dared, hoping that at least retreating into the farthest corner of the cave might provide some shelter while whatever was eating finished its meal and left.

Light glimmered in the darkness, and she brought herself up short to be sure that she hadn't imagined it. No — it was the beam of Daniel's flashlight striking stone. When she looked in that direction, she could definitely see the curves of the cave wall and floor, dim but growing more strongly lit as she moved. She led the way, lowering herself carefully down as the bottom of the cave sloped and curved its way into a tight squeeze between walls of rock.

When she could see the flashlight in her hand, she turned, putting her back to solid rock. She edged over to let Daniel squeeze in next to her, half-crouching in the mouth of the narrow tunnel behind them. It felt better to be facing whatever was back there rather than to have her back to it, anyway.

She shone the flashlight back toward the cave entrance. The flashlight beam shone for a few feet and then vanished into darkness, as if a dense cloud hung in the air, so black that it absorbed all light that shone on it. And yet she'd felt and smelled nothing as she moved through a cloud that now looked as though it should have choked her. She could still hear sounds that suggested noisy eating, and the shuffling of something moving over stone.

"Tell me you have some idea what's going on," Daniel said in a whisper.

Sam shook her head. "Maybe some kind of natural defense used by whatever's out there?"

"Defense or hunting strategy."

"I was afraid you'd say that."

"Stay here, or try to get further back?"

"At least we can see where we're going." She shone her flashlight through the narrow opening. It was one of the paths through the system of caverns that had looked promising on radar, and she closed her eyes for a moment trying to visualize its shape. "I think this passageway goes pretty far back, and it should open out into a cavern about twenty meters back."

"Sounds good to me right now."

"I've got rope in my pack. If we get lost back there, though…"

"It'll be worse than meeting whatever's out there?"

She drew her sidearm to feel its comforting weight in her hand. It offered a solution to their problem, but there would be no hope of an accurate shot without getting close enough to be in range of claws, teeth, or tentacles. And firing blindly in a cave that was already unstable was probably a good way to bring the ceiling down on their heads.

Reluctantly she put it away and worked a metal cam into a crack in the rocks as an anchor, tying a rope to it, and headed back through the passageway.

CHAPTER FIVE

THE PASSAGEWAY narrowed and curved, and then began climbing steeply, and she was just beginning to wonder if she was going to need to tie on another length of rope when it opened out into unexpected brightness. The blue light of very early morning filtered down through a broad crack in the roof of the wide cavern, and she didn't entertain the speculation that the crack was a result of the mudslide for more than a moment; the cavern floor was thickly carpeted by grass and even small trees straining up toward the roof, nourished by water that trickled down from one wall and flowed like a wandering stream into a sinkhole in the middle of the cavern.

"Pretty," Daniel said.

"Do we think our predator lives in here?"

"Maybe hunts in here. There might be rodents, bats, maybe salamanders or fish in that stream. What am I saying? Given that we're on another planet, there might be just about anything in that stream."

"Large prey, though?"

Daniel turned a circle thoughtfully, and picked up a branch. "Tooth marks," he said. "And claw marks. And look at these prints." He crouched to shine his flashlight's beam on something that she had to admit looked to her like a barely-visible depression in the silt of the cavern floor. "Hand-like. We saw monkeys in the forest outside. This would be a protected place for them to shelter at night." He peered up at the crack in the cavern ceiling. "Think they could climb down the cave wall?"

"If they can, does that mean can we climb up?"

"We're a lot bigger than they are," Daniel said. He shone his flashlight beam up along the cavern wall, although its light diffused too much toward the top of the cavern to see clearly. "I don't much like the idea. Do you?"

"Not really, no," she admitted. "We'd still have to get down that rockslide, only starting from farther up. Besides…"

"You want to know what's farther back in the caves."

"Don't you?"

"You know I do."

They cautiously explored the edges of the cavern, listening for any sound of movement. Once Sam froze at a rustling in the grass, but it turned out to be a rodent the size of a rat, large-eared and large-eyed. It stared at her and dashed away, apparently horrified by her invasion of its territory. Daniel found another set of tracks, these oddly deep and hoof-like, or maybe the marks of a creature with two large claws on each foot.

"There can't be actual deer in here, can there?" Sam asked.

Daniel frowned skeptically. "I suppose if there are more of these areas where sunlight penetrates from above, it might support a very small herd of something like mountain goats. But I've never heard of grazing animals living in caves."

"There's a first time for everything?"

"Certainly there is on SG-1."

On the other side of the cavern, they found a narrow crack that seemed to be going in the right direction to connect with a passageway on the other side.

"It's going to be tight," she said skeptically.

"I think we can do it," Daniel said, peering in. "Besides, I'd still like to put some distance between us and…" He nodded back toward the way they'd came.

"Worth a try." Sam opened her pack, pulling out rope and working another cam into the nearest crevice that she thought would hold it. Daniel looped the rope around himself and began painstakingly squeezing himself through the crack. He stopped, came back out and shrugged his tac vest off, and tried again, obviously needing that few inches' clearance to get through. He moved forward, tugged Sam's pack into the crack behind him, and then moved forward again.

"Don't get stuck," she said.

"Trying not to."

"I mean, stop before you get stuck."

"That's always the trick, isn't it?" He sounded like he couldn't draw a deep breath. "Like taking eggs out of the pan just before they're done."

"Why would you do that?"

"The residual heat finishes cooking them, otherwise you get —" He winced as the rocks scraped his chest.

"I really mean it, we can't afford for you to get stuck."

"I know," Daniel said impatiently, and wrenched himself through the crack with a visible effort. There seemed to be more room beyond it, because he kept going while Sam shrugged off her own vest and struggled through the same passage. All the rocks seemed jagged and determined to puncture her in a dozen places, and at one point she wasn't sure she could get through at all. She felt for a widening of the rock, found it an arm's length further on, and deliberately exhaled, moving as quickly as she could through the tightest spot until she struggled free on the other side.

"How does it look past here?" she asked once she had breath to speak, while wrestling with her pack to extricate it from the rock. "Daniel?" she prompted when he didn't reply.

"I think we're going the right way," he said. "There's writing on this wall."

"The Jaffa," Cam said, taking a swig of his coffee in hopes that it would bring the world into sharper focus. He'd grabbed a nap in one of the guest rooms, and it was now either wearily late or painfully early, depending on how you looked at it. "We think the bars of nickel you found in Chen's apartment used to belong to the Jaffa who served Apophis?"

"It is unlikely that it was legitimately in the SGC's stores," Teal'c said. "As far as I am aware, the Stargate program has never traded for base metals with the Jaffa."

"We wouldn't need to," Cam said. "Nickel is cheap, that's

why we make nickels out of it." Vala looked bewildered, but Teal'c inclined his head in a nod. "And other stuff. It's not like we have a shortage. Do we?" Cam asked the question without really expecting an answer, and wished Sam was there to provide one. She hadn't yet checked in, but it probably wasn't nice to radio her and wake her up to ask her if Earth was having a nickel shortage.

"It is possible that an off-world contact was providing these raw materials to Dr. Chen in order to assist her in producing the forgeries."

"That's possible," Cam said. "It would mean she wouldn't have to charge bar nickel on her credit card. Useful if we found out about the forgeries and didn't immediately trace it back to her. The problem is, what off-world contact? Dr. Chen wasn't assigned to an SG team. I checked her records. She's never been through the Stargate."

"Perhaps she had a confederate," Teal'c said.

"It's always useful to have a good accomplice," Vala said. "If you want to do something criminal, which of course I would never…"

"Let's just take that as read," Cam said. "The two of you, ask around and see if anybody knows who Chen's friends on base are." He shook his head. "I mean, ask around in the morning."

"Technically it is morning," Teal'c said.

"There are always guards around," Vala said. "I've had some interesting conversations with them in the middle of the night. When I wasn't sleeping. Which, usually, I have been. Perfectly soundly."

"You do that," Cam said. "I'm going to go wake up Chen and have a little chat."

"Are you sure you don't want me to play the good cop?" Vala asked.

"I'm pretty sure you'd be the bad cop," Cam said. "And, no. I want to give her the chance to come clean. It would save us all a lot of time."

"If Dr. Chen was forging artifacts, is it not a strong possibility that Dr. Oliver was killed because he discovered her crime?" Teal'c said.

"I know," Cam said. "I'm still hoping there's another explanation, but, believe me, I'm keeping that one on the table."

He went up to the control room first. "Dial P2H-144 for me," he told the sergeant on duty. "I want to check in with the rest of SG-1." To hell with it, he decided; if he wasn't getting any sleep, he wasn't going to let them sleep either. Daniel had worked with the other archaeologists, and he ought to have some idea whether Chen had any friends who were assigned to gate teams.

"SG-1, this is Mitchell," he said. "Come in, SG-1." There was a resounding silence on the other end of the radio. "Hey, Sam, wake up Jackson for me. I have a question for him." The silence continued, and the video feed didn't cut on. "Carter? Jackson? Anybody?" He turned to the sergeant. "Are they having some problem transmitting?"

"I'm not picking up any interference with the connection," the sergeant said. "Their equipment is transmitting a signal, they're just not answering you."

"Can you activate the video feed remotely?"

"Let me see." The sergeant's fingers moved over the keyboard in front of him, and abruptly the video feed turned on. It showed a portion of cave wall, and what looked like more fallen rocks than Cam remembered seeing, which made sense if there'd been a cave-in. On the other hand, clearly the radio set wasn't buried under rock or smashed to pieces, which weighed against the idea that the entire cave had now collapsed.

"Carter, Jackson, come in." There was still no answer. The video transmission continued showing completely uninformative cave wall. Cam looked at the blue rippling surface of the wormhole in the gate room below, which didn't provide any more hints about what might be happening on the other side. "All right. Let's get a backup team out there. Who's on base?"

"SG-15 is available," the sergeant said.

"Okay. Get Parker and his people up here, I'll brief them."

The young lieutenant in charge of SG-15 appeared in the briefing room within minutes, although he had a bleary look that suggested that standing by in case of emergencies had involved napping. "The rest of my team is on their way up, sir," he said.

"This should be pretty straightforward," Cam said. "Go to P2H-144, take some climbing gear, and find Colonel Carter and Dr. Jackson. They were exploring a cave, a rockslide took out their way down, and now they're not answering their radio. Knowing them, they probably stumbled into the fabulous lost treasure trove of the Ancients and are having too much fun to call home, but… just go find them."

"Yes, sir," Parker said.

"And, lieutenant?"

"Sir?"

"I know the base coffee is terrible, but you and your team might try it anyway."

"Yes, sir," Parker said, flushing, and went out hurriedly.

Cam tried not to worry as he headed down to confront Chen. Probably Sam was fine. Sam had spent years on SG-1, and she had a lot of practice in being fine. And Daniel was luckier than any man had a right to be. Chances were that a cave-in hadn't taken them both out, and running off with the rest of SG-1 to look for them wouldn't help if one had.

"Damn it, Sam," he muttered under his breath. "You and Jackson had better be okay, or when Landry gets in he can take over playing detective whether or not he likes it." And that sounded like the fine, traditional spirit of insubordination that he was discovering characterized so many of SG-1's decisions. It probably wasn't going to help discipline on his team if the person blatantly ignoring orders was him.

He buzzed the door signal on Chen's door, and waited until she opened it, scowling. "It's a little early," she said.

"I hadn't noticed. We need to talk."

She let him in. The guest room looked more like a hotel room than a prison cell, but as Vala had pointed out, it did have the essential feature of a lock on the door that couldn't be opened from the inside. "I've already told you everything I know," Chen said.

"About Oliver's death, or about forged artifacts?"

Her expression froze. "I don't know anything about any forged artifacts."

"I find that hard to believe," he said. "You were the one photographing the artifacts before they went into storage. Am I supposed to believe you didn't notice they were fakes?"

"Were they?"

"You tell me."

"I was just photographing them," Chen said. "Goa'uld art isn't my specialty. Are you implying that somebody, what, replaced the real artifacts with fakes?"

"That would work," Cam said. "If that somebody had a market for the artifacts they were replacing. Why don't you tell us where they were going?"

"I told you, I don't know anything about it."

The door buzzed again, and Cam opened it. It was Vala, looking triumphant. "Why don't you ask her about Sergeant Green?"

"Tommy Green is a friend of mine," Chen said. "I don't see what that has to do with it."

"A friend who's been assigned on the team acting as a liason to the Jaffa on Dakara," Vala said. "Which made him a perfect fence for your little scheme, didn't it?"

"Hang on there, Vala," Cam said. Apparently it was going to be good cop, bad cop after all. "I'm sure Dr. Chen had a good reason for what she did."

"I didn't do anything," Chen insisted. "I didn't take the artifacts. I didn't replace them with copies. And I certainly didn't give them to Tommy to fence for me on Dakara."

"A likely story," Vala said, narrowing her eyes.

"Then where did they go?"

"If the artifacts in storage are fakes, I don't know where the real ones went. And neither does Tommy. Ask him and he'll tell you the same thing."

"I intend to," Cam said.

"We'll be back," Vala said menacingly. "We know where you live."

"I'd rather not be living here," Chen said. "If I'm not under arrest, can I go home now? Or at least get back into the lab and do some work?"

"Maybe later," Cam said. "Vala here already fed your cat. Just so you won't worry."

He could see Chen stiffen at that, and any questions he had about her guilt were immediately answered. The only question now was how to prove it. "I didn't give her a key."

Vala shrugged innocently. "They were very helpful at the…"

"The property manager's office," Cam said.

Chen frowned. "In the middle of the night?"

"That's not what I'd worry about right now," Cam said. "I'd worry about the penalties for theft."

"I took home a few bars of nickel to test out my electroplating kit. Tommy brought them back to the base as souvenirs. They weren't worth anything. I mean, all right, technically I shouldn't have taken them out of the base —"

"You shouldn't have taken the artifacts you replaced with gold-plated replicas," Vala said.

"I didn't take any artifacts, and I didn't use that electroplating kit to do anything but make some earrings to give people as Christmas presents," Chen said.

"And I suppose you didn't murder Dr. Oliver, either?"

"You've got to be kidding," Chen said, as if it were the first time it had occurred to her that the two might be connected. "Even if I had taken the artifacts — and I didn't — I certainly didn't kill anyone."

"I think Oliver found out what you were up to," Vala said.

"He was blackmailing you, wasn't he? Threatening to reveal your secrets, while all the time you were just lurking in the shadows, waiting for the perfect time to strike."

"Or something like that," Cam added.

"That's not true," Chen said, and crossed her arms. "And I'm not saying another word."

Out in the corridor, Vala put her head to one side. "I honestly don't know what comes next among the Tau'ri," she said. "Torture? Interrogation drugs? Or is this the part where we tell her that she has the right to remain silent?"

"No on the first and second, and… probably no on the third," Cam said. "I doubt we can bring her to trial, so it doesn't really matter that she has a right to remain silent, because we're not going to be able to use whatever she says against her in a court of law. We can't try a civilian in a military court when we're not in a war zone —"

"Aren't we in a war zone?"

"Not officially in a war zone. It's complicated. We might be able to make a case for it if she had been on another planet when she committed a crime, but she wasn't. And we can't let her take the stand in a civilian court and talk about aliens and the Stargate and traveling to other planets. I expect we'll fire her, and revoke her security clearance for cause, but that's about all we can do."

"That hardly seems like much."

"Well, it'll make it a lot harder for her to get another job," Cam said. "I bet people don't like to hire archaeologists who've been fired for theft. So there's that. We're going to have to handle Green more carefully, though, because we could court-martial him, and I bet Landry won't like it if we screw that up."

Green was asleep in quarters on base, and came to the door blinking and rubbing at his untidy hair.

"We want to ask you a few questions about your involvement with Alice Chen," Cam said.

Green snapped to military attention. "I don't have to tell

you anything," he said.

"That's true enough," Cam said. "Anything you might like to tell us?"

"It'll go easier for you if you do," Vala said. "We won't have to get out the…" Cam shook his head at her firmly. "All right, we wouldn't do that, but we also won't have to use the…" He stepped on her foot. "It'll all be much nicer for everyone," she finished, with an exasperated look at Cam.

"I want to see my lawyers," Green said, and repeated it like a broken record after that until Cam gave up and called security to collect him and escort him down to an actual holding cell. He remained stubbornly silent through the process, his mouth a firmly set line.

"He's a hard nut to crack," Vala said.

Cam looked at her sideways. "Where are you getting this stuff?"

She shrugged. "Television."

"You're maybe watching a little much television."

"I don't have a lot else to do with my time off, do I? Sometimes I read magazines. Or talk to the security guards. It's very quiet here in the middle of the night."

Before he could come up with a response to that, he saw Teal'c striding toward him down the hallway. "General Landry has arrived at the base," Teal'c said. "He is eager to hear how our investigation is progressing."

"I bet he is," Cam said. "All right. Let's go report."

Landry heard out Mitchell's summary of their progress so far with an expression that suggested he was less than enthusiastic. Vala helped add detail to his explanation, which she felt lacked color. "And Green swears he'll never talk," she finished.

"That is, he wants a lawyer," Mitchell said.

"Well, he can't have one right now," Landry said. "But that means we can't question him right now, either. Haven't you got anything better than a jewelry-making kit in Chen's bathroom?"

"And the nickel stamped with Apophis's seal," Mitchell pointed out.

"Any archaeologist might have brought that back. I've seen them bring back rocks. You can't tell me that metal bricks stamped with the seal of Apophis's Jaffa are less interesting than rocks."

"I have checked the artifact catalog records," Teal'c said. "There is no record of such nickel bars being brought into the base."

"Which is suspicious right there," Mitchell said.

"Maybe she hadn't gotten around to recording it."

"So she was just taking her work home with her?" Mitchell looked skeptical, and Landry shrugged as if granting that his skepticism might be warranted but unwilling to commit himself on the point.

"She was using the nickel as the base material for the forgeries she was making," Vala said. "We're practically certain that she's the thief." Landry looked a question at Mitchell, and he nodded agreement. Vala felt it would have been nice if Landry had taken her word for it, but she did appreciate the vote of confidence from Mitchell.

"Yes," Landry said, "but is she also our murderer?"

"Absolutely," Vala said, at the same time that Mitchell said, "We don't know."

"It is the best lead we have so far," Teal'c said calmly into the ensuing slightly awkward silence. "If Chen is guilty of the theft, it gives her a potential motive for the murder, which all the other suspects lack."

"As far as we know," Landry said.

"Anyone could have had a motive," Vala granted. "But we know Chen actually did."

"You think Green was selling this stuff for Chen on Dakara."

"That is what we believe," Teal'c said. "With your permission, I will visit Dakara myself and investigate Green's movements there. It would be difficult for him to have formed a criminal partnership with one of the Jaffa without anyone being aware of their meetings. There are few enough Tau'ri stationed on Dakara that they are conspicuous and attract considerable notice."

"Sounds like a plan," Mitchell said, although once again he felt that constituted rubber-stamping someone else's plan which had been already fully formed without consulting him. "Do that."

"And let's hope Green was wandering around saying 'Does anyone want to buy these stolen artifacts I have for sale,'" Landry said. "Meanwhile, SG-15 just reported that they can't find Colonel Carter and Dr. Jackson."

Mitchell sat up straighter in his seat like a watchdog pricking up its ears in alarm. "Couldn't they get back up to the cave we were exploring? I thought they were supposed to be taking climbing gear with them."

"They found it, all right, although even with proper gear they didn't have much fun getting up the cliff. Apparently that rockslide took out the path completely. When they got somebody up to the top, they saw that Colonel Carter and Dr. Jackson weren't there, although their radar setup still was. Apparently there's no sign of a cave-in, or anything unfortunate but explicable. They did find the carcass of some kind of dead animal — not human, probably some kind of monkey — but Carter and Jackson were nowhere in sight. SG-15 guesses that they might have ventured farther into the caves, but they've got about six different possible routes to explore, and it's going to take them time to check all of them."

"Permission to go and look for them," Mitchell said at once.

"I was afraid you were going to say that."

"Sir, there's not much I can do here while Teal'c is asking around on Dakara and Dr. Gardner is checking for potential buyers here on Earth. This is the only lead we've got, and I want to follow it. But while we're waiting for more information, I think Vala and I should go look for Sam and Dr. Jackson."

"Go," Landry said. "But don't fall down a hole in a cave, or whatever's happened to them. I need you back here. Promptly. Understood?"

"We won't fall down a hole," Vala assured General Landry earnestly.

"Try hard," Landry said.

Teal'c stepped through the Stargate and out onto the surface of Dakara. A hot wind scoured the courtyard, and the reddish sky was darkening as the sun sank toward the horizon. He started toward the complex of old buildings that had been taken up as the council chambers, on the theory that someone there could tell him which Jaffa had been the contacts for the liason team from Earth.

"What are you doing here?" a familiar voice asked. He looked up in pleasure to see Bra'tac striding toward him, his eyes sharp under his hooded cloak. "I thought you were still too busy with the Tau'ri to have much time for our affairs."

"My business with the Tau'ri is in the service of our people," Teal'c said. "Or would it serve better for me to debate politics here on Dakara while the Ori invade more of our worlds?"

"Perhaps, and perhaps not," Bra'tac said. "There are many places where you are needed, and I do not expect you to find a way to be in more than one of them."

"I am most needed on Chulak, and that is the one place I cannot go at all," Teal'c said heavily. "Have you heard any news of our friends there?" It had been nearly ten years since he had lived on Chulak, and many of their people had scattered to other worlds in the chaos of the Jaffa Rebellion, but he could not help imagining old neighbors and friends suffering under the yoke of the Ori. Just the thought of the Ori and their servants walking past the house where he had lived for years, and where his son had been born, turned his stomach.

"I have heard nothing from Chulak," Bra'tac said. "The Priors guard the chappa'ai and allow no one to pass through unless they serve the Ori. But do not lose heart. Whatever lies they are telling our people, our people will not believe."

"It might go better for them if they did. The Ori are not kind to those who will not worship them."

"We have had long practice in pacifying false gods," Bra'tac said. "Do not worry for the people of Chulak. There is nothing you can do for them until the Ori are driven forth. So what are you doing about that?"

"We are searching for a weapon," Teal'c said, looking around to ensure that they were alone. There were other people on the road from the Stargate to the old temple complex and the newer buildings taking shape on the plain, but none of them were in earshot. "Daniel Jackson believes it can defeat the Ori."

"I will believe it when I see it," Bra'tac said, but he sounded reassured all the same. "You have been missed here."

"What has been happening on Dakara that has made me so missed?"

"The council has chosen Se'tak as our new leader," Bra'tac said.

"Se'tak," Teal'c said, troubled. "He was one of Ba'al's Jaffa. I do not remember him having ever had a reputation as a wise leader of men."

"But he is a great warrior," Bra'tac said. "At least, that is his reputation. Myself, I think some people are confusing reckless aggression and courageous tactics. He tells our people that our first priority is finding a weapon against the Ori, and that is a thing they like to hear."

"I hope to find a weapon against the Ori as well."

"But you are not here to say so."

"As you say, I cannot be in more than one place at once."

"And yet you are here now. What message was so important that it could not be brought by the Tau'ri's liason team?"

"No message," Teal'c said. "I am here on another errand. Tell me, who have the liason team had dealings with, particularly Sgt. Green? Who are their contacts among our people?"

Bra'tac's expression sharpened. "You suspect a traitor among us."

"Nothing so dangerous," Teal'c said. "A receiver of stolen property, artifacts the Tau'ri have brought back from their explorations on uninhabited worlds, and from the Goa'uld strongholds they have taken."

Bra'tac frowned. "They have spoken to most of the members of the High Council who have been on Dakara," he said. "But it is difficult for me to believe any of the High Council would abuse their positions for profit."

"I cannot believe it either," Teal'c said. "We have had our disagreements, but they are all honorable men and women." He shook his head. "Have you known Sgt. Green to speak often to anyone else?"

"There are a number of our people who the Tau'ri have dealt with in the course of obtaining lodgings and meals. Perhaps one of them might have done such a thing."

"You have no suspicions?"

Bra'tac considered the matter as they walked, and then stopped while they were still well short of the temple complex. "There is one who I think is Sgt. Green's friend," he said slowly. "But I cannot believe he would stoop to theft. His name is Da'shak, and he was an assistant to Maz'rai." A shadow of grief passed across Bra'tac's face at the mention of his old friend, dead in a valiant attempt to cleanse himself of Ba'al's brainwashing. "I am certain he was not brainwashed. He is an honorable man who has served our people well since we threw off the false gods. And yet..."

"And yet?" Teal'c prompted when Bra'tac faltered.

"He was building a new house on Imrak," Bra'tac said. "He settled there when our people first rebelled against Apophis, but he brought little with him. I visited him there, and saw the meager quarters in which he lived. And now I hear that he has hired men to build a spacious home, and purchased furnishings for it from many craftsmen."

"His fortunes have risen as he has grown more prominent," Teal'c suggested.

"I have not noticed you growing rich from your seat on the council."

"Nor have I," he admitted.

"It is not proof. But it makes me wonder about him. I would prefer not to wonder."

"You see, you may regret that I came," Teal'c said.

"Never that," Bra'tac said, and clapped him on the shoulder. "Will you not stay and meet with the council? I am concerned that many of Se'tak's ideas are unwise."

"You know that if I begin debating with the council, I will be here a week from now, and no nearer to leaving," Teal'c said.

"I know it," Bra'tac acknowledged. "If you are looking for Da'shak, you will not find him here. He has returned to Imrak to see to more improvements to his house."

"Then I am bound for Imrak as well," Teal'c said, and turned to retrace his steps back toward the Stargate as the sun touched the horizon.

CHAPTER SIX

CAM hustled his way from the Stargate toward the base of the cliff, with Vala right behind him. The rain had finally stopped, but the drying mud didn't make the hike any easier. The swollen river was running brown, and casting up drifts of broken branches on the shores.

"I'm sure they're all right," Vala said. "Don't you think?"

"Probably," Cam said. It didn't sound like they'd been in a cave-in, at any rate.

"Because it would be really ridiculous for them to have survived our latest encounter with the Ori, just to get eaten by some kind of oversized..."

"Centipede," Cam offered.

"I was thinking bats."

"Bats don't really eat people. They eat insects and things."

"It depends on how big the bats are."

"They're probably fine," Cam said. "Jackson's probably up to his knees in some kind of archaeological discovery right now."

"I'm sure," Vala said, and strode along behind him in silence for a minute. "Why is it that the more we say reassuring things to each other, the less reassured I feel?"

"The perversity of human nature," Cam said.

"But they're probably fine, don't you think?"

"Let's just get up there and find out."

They found SG-15 fixing a more-or-less stable route over and around the boulders that were tumbled across what had been a nice, easy path to the cave mouth the day before. "It's not an easy climb," Lt. Parker said, shading his eyes to look up to the top. "We got up there to take a look right away, but I didn't want to leave any of our people up there until we were sure the way down wasn't going to collapse."

"How sure are we?" Cam said, gazing skeptically at the fallen rocks. Bouldering had never been his sport even before the 302 crash that had ended his career as a combat pilot. He hated to think of himself as flinching from anything in its aftermath, but he couldn't help picturing in vivid sensory detail how it would feel if one of the rocks slid and smashed all the bones that had been so painstakingly pieced back together.

"I can do it, piece of cake," Vala said. "Why do they call it a piece of cake?"

"Because eating cake is easy?" Cam offered.

"So I'll go find them, and then we'll have cake." She was already slipping into the climbing harness one of the members of SG-15 had left unattended, toying with the carabineer until she figured out how to clip it onto the fixed rope. "Or are we going to stand here all day while a centipede bat creature eats them?"

"You're getting into the spirit," Cam said.

She turned, all humor gone from her face for a moment. "I'm here to help," she said. "I know that may be hard to believe, given my past… well, my past everything. But I really do want to do my part on SG-1. I want to help stop the Ori. I really want to help stop the Ori. And right now I want to do the right thing and help keep my teammates from winding up eaten."

"I believe you," Cam said.

"It doesn't seem like a lot of people here do. You apparently live on a very virtuous planet."

"No, it's just that the Stargate program is very picky. That's why everyone's so upset about what happened to Dr. Oliver. We're supposed to make better choices than this. There's not supposed to be anyone in the Stargate program who would kill somebody for reasons that don't involve alien possession, or who would steal artifacts and sell them for a profit."

"And you know this because of your extremely reliable psychological testing?" Her skepticism was palpable.

"That's sort of the theory," Cam said. "In practice I think there's more of an element of personal judgment involved."

"I'm ready to go up," Vala said, her chin set.

"All right. Take it slow and easy. When you get to the top, radio down and let me know what you can see."

He tried radioing Sam and Daniel again, but got no answer. He wouldn't have expected one if they were deep in the cave; they'd been getting bad reception anywhere but near the cave mouth. On the other hand, there was no reason for them to have gone deeper into the cave, unless they were pursuing a lead. Or being pursued. He paced at the bottom of the cliff, watching Vala ascend, and decided he couldn't stand it just as she pulled herself up onto solid rock at the cave mouth.

"I'm up," she said over the radio. "I see their radar set, and something… unpleasantly eaten. I agree that it looks more monkey-like than centipedal."

"Any idea what ate it?"

"Something with teeth that could snap bones like twigs. I'm afraid zoology isn't really my specialty. Daniel's pack is here, but Sam's is gone." There was the sound of rustling fabric. "Daniel's flashlight is also gone. I'm trying to see any signs of where they went, but it's all very muddy and confusing. We were all walking around up here for hours."

"Stay there," he said. "I'm coming up."

Parker had been right; it wasn't an easy climb, even clipped onto the rope to ensure he wouldn't go crashing to the valley floor if he fell, just probably be crushed between tumbling boulders. It helped that he had no fear of heights — pretty much required for the Air Force — but even so he was sweating as he worked for handholds and footholds, straining to lever himself upwards without kicking rocks out from beneath his feet.

He hauled himself over the lip of the cave with profound relief, and unclipped himself from the ropes, giving a thumbs-up sign to SG-15 beneath.

"What took you so long?" Vala asked, her head to one side.

"I stopped for coffee," Cam said. "There was a Starbucks halfway up."

She shone her flashlight into the back of the cave, down a precipitous slope toward a narrow crack in the rock. "I think they went this way."

He squinted at the floor. "You see tracks?"

In answer, she shone her flashlight at the bolt anchored in the rock, with a rope still clipped onto it.

"Okay, that's a better sign than tracks. SG-15 must have been blind to miss that."

"It may be a bit of a tight squeeze."

"Piece of cake," Cam said without much enthusiasm at all.

Imrak was a colder world than Dakara, and Teal'c stepped out of desert heat into the chill of an early morning in a thick grove of pines that filled the air with their sharp scent. The path from the Stargate was deserted at first, but as he walked, he began to pass farms and houses, young children out herding goats and older people starting out into the fields or walking into town toward shops and factories.

He asked each person he passed if they could direct him to the home of Da'shak, and before long a boy who reminded him sharply of a younger Ry'ac nodded emphatically.

"I can show you," he said. He looked up at the seal on Teal'c's forehead that marked him as Apophis's First Prime. It had been a mark of honor, once, and then a reminder of his people's slavery, and finally a reminder of both parts of his past, which had shaped him beyond any erasure. "You are Teal'c the warrior."

"I am Teal'c," he said, inclining his head in acknowledgement.

"I wanted to be a great warrior," the boy said. "But the war with the Goa'uld was won before I was old enough." He sounded disappointed by that.

"There are enemies enough still," Teal'c said. The boy bore the mark of Apophis on his forehead, but he would never bear a Goa'uld symbiote; his prim'ta would be a ritual celebrating freedom, not slavery. And this boy's younger brothers or sisters would bear no tattoo on their foreheads, unless it was a symbol chosen to mark their kinship to their people, rather than their servitude to a false god.

"The Ori," the boy said, kicking at the dirt as he walked. "Is it true they've taken Chulak?"

"It is true," he granted.

"Is everyone there dead?" The boy asked the question casually, either too young to truly understand the weight of so many deaths or so used to death and disaster that it was an unremarkable part of his world.

"I do not believe so," Teal'c said. "The Ori want worshippers — slaves — and dead men cannot serve them."

"My mother's people were from Chulak," the boy said. "Like Da'shak. I was born there, but I don't really remember it."

"Perhaps you will be able to visit Chulak soon."

"You think we'll beat the Ori?"

"I do. You must have faith in our people's strength, and in the strength of our allies the Tau'ri. If the Goa'uld did not destroy us, the Ori will not."

"Yes, but the Ori have superweapons that blast things into tiny bits. And they're led by a demon woman."

Teal'c raised an eyebrow. "Are there truly demons in the world?"

"I don't know," the boy said, but he scuffled his feet in the dirt again as if he knew the answer Teal'c wanted.

"There are not," Teal'c said. "The Ori have great power, but they are beings like ourselves and the Tau'ri and the Goa'uld. They are not gods, and they are not demons. And their leader Adria is the daughter of a very brave woman who is also not a demon."

"You know an Ori?"

Teal'c shook her head. "The Orici's mother is human. She was made to bear a child for the Ori."

The boy nodded, and Teal'c knew that was entirely within his experience of life under the Goa'uld. He hoped that a time would come when the idea would be as shocking to his people as the Tau'ri seemed to find it. "Are you fighting the Ori?"

"Indeed," Teal'c said, and the boy seemed content with that.

"Here's Da'shak's house," the boy said. The house was palatial in its spaciousness, and a new wing was being added, the stones going up in courses and the roof being tiled from a stack of painted roof tiles set under the eaves of the finished part of the house to shelter them from the rain. "I think he's here, he was in town yesterday buying lamps."

"Thank you," Teal'c said. He rested a hand on the boy's shoulder for a moment. "Tell your friends that our people will defeat the Ori as we have defeated the Goa'uld."

"I'll tell them," the boy said, his eyes alight with hero worship. Teal'c smiled at him as he dashed off, no doubt to embroider the tale of their meeting until he was helping Teal'c fight off bandits on the road and defeating ten of them at a time with mighty blows from a tree branch used as a staff.

He turned his attention to the house in front of him, and strode to the door. He knocked, and waited for an answer. Da'shak came to the door brushing dust from his hands. "Forgive me," he said. "I was clearing space for the workmen. Please, come in."

Teal'c nodded and stepped inside. The entryway was lit by lamps of figured brass, and tiled beautifully underfoot. It reminded him of the palace on Chulak, albeit at a smaller scale. "I have come to speak with you," he said.

Da'shak nodded. "You are always welcome," he said. "Come, sit, and I will bring you food and drink."

"There is no need," Teal'c said, and Da'shak frowned at his failure to observe the pleasantries of social visits. "We have a serious matter to discuss."

"If you are trying to persuade me that Se'tak is in the wrong, you may as well save your breath," Da'shak said. "So he argues that we should attack the Ori. Is that not our only hope of winning back Chulak, and freeing the others of our people who have become slaves of the Ori just as they had won their freedom from the Goa'uld? We will have to find weapons that will work against them, and strategies, that is true. But we cannot simply sit by and do nothing."

"I have not come here to argue politics," Teal'c said. "Although if I had, I would say to you that sometimes the hardest task a warrior must face is to sit by and do nothing, when any action would lead to greater disaster."

"That is not what you did," Da'shak said. "Or we would not now be free."

"That is what I did more times than you can imagine," Teal'c said, his temper kindling at the younger man. Da'shak was too young to understand what those long decades of serving Apophis had been like, or to imagine the weight of Teal'c's vivid memories of all the times he had stood by despite the misgivings in his heart, all the times he had done nothing. "Myself and every other Jaffa my age who still lives. But I am not here to instruct you in our people's history."

"Then why are you here? Not that you are an unwelcome guest, but as you can see, I have work still to do here before the laborers arrive."

"I see that you do," Teal'c said. "How have you afforded such luxury?"

"Is it any of your concern?"

"I am afraid that it is. You have befriended Sgt. Green of the Tau'ri."

Da'shak's eyes slid away from Teal'c's, and he was certain that his suspicions were correct. "And what if I have? It is to all our advantage to be on good terms with the liaisons from the Tau'ri. As you have said yourself, their aid has been valuable to our people."

"Sgt. Green stole valuable artifacts from Stargate Command," Teal'c said. "I believe he disposed of them among the Jaffa. But I do not believe that they remained here. There is no one on Imrak who has the wealth to buy such things simply to display them. What did you do with them, Da'shak? Did you sell treasures made by the hands of the Jaffa to off-world strangers, or did you melt them down for the gold in them?"

"I would not have sold treasures of our people," Da'shak said, his pride clearly stung. "These were human-made. My father guarded human slaves who made such things on Chulak. He examined all the pieces that were brought and guaranteed that they were the work of the wretched humans who served the Goa'uld."

"What did you do with them?"

"I sold them off-world," Da'shak said. "There are collectors who will pay well for such things, so that they can say that they are living in the same luxury as the System Lords. Green had no idea what price they would fetch. I gave him gold chains, which he said jewelers on his world would buy without asking questions about where they came from. It was the least fraction of the profits I made when I sold the artifacts."

"I do not understand how you can say such things without shame."

Da'shak rounded on him. "Am I the one who should be ashamed? Those artifacts never belonged to the Tau'ri. They should be ours, now that we have overthrown the Jaffa. Enough Jaffa suffered and died for them."

"And the human slaves who made them."

"Not Tau'ri slaves. The Tau'ri dig in the graves of their betters and pick through the ruins of their conquests like crows. Their SG teams care for nothing but treasure."

"If that is what you think, you do not understand them at all."

"Do you think they would have carried off masks and bracelets and lamps if they had been made of clay rather than gold?"

"I do," Teal'c said. "They have brought back many such things, and their men of learning study them, to understand those who made them."

"That does not give them the right to rob us."

"You cannot escape your own guilt so easily," Teal'c said. "If you believe our people should own the treasures Green showed you, why did you not speak to the council? The Tau'ri would have returned them if they believed our claim was just."

"A likely story."

"Likely, but not certain," Teal'c granted. "That is true. But it is equally true that you knew full well that Green had no right to the things he offered you. He was given them by one of the Tau'ri who betrayed her superiors' trust. You willingly received his stolen property, and in return you cheated him by paying him a fraction of what they were worth."

"I paid him what he asked," Da'shak said.

"Be silent. I have not finished. You then took these treasures, which you claim belong to our people by right, and sold them to off-worlders who were not Jaffa. And when you had done all that, and turned a considerable profit from your righteous acts, did you use your profits to aid the poor and desperate among us? Have you bought food for the hungry or helped to expand the council chambers of our people on Dakara?"

Da'shak opened his mouth to reply, and then closed it again, unable to reply.

"I see that you did not," Teal'c said inexorably. "You enriched yourself and bought luxuries by selling treasures made by slaves." He stepped back, sweeping his gaze over the richly furnished room. "This is a fine house," he said. "Worthy of one of the Goa'uld."

"I cannot get the pieces back," Da'shak muttered.

"I expect that you cannot."

"What will you do to me?"

"I will do nothing to you. You have committed no crime under our laws. I will remember what I have learned of your character. That is all."

"What about Green? I told him that it would be all right to sell the artifacts to me. That he was doing the right thing."

"It was not your place to relieve him of his guilty conscience," Teal'c said. "Nor to reassure him that his crimes would not be found out. I will return to tell his superiors what I have found out. He will face trial among the Tau'ri for selling stolen property." Da'shak's expression twisted in misery, and Teal'c relented enough to relieve him of his obvious assumption that such a trial would end in torture and death. "They will imprison him for a time, and he will lose his rank and his place among their warriors. Assuming that he has done no more than sell these things, and is not guilty of killing a man to cover up the theft."

"I knew nothing about any killing," Da'shak said, looking even more troubled.

"I am certain you did not." He waited a moment to see if Da'shak meant to make more excuses for himself, or to take responsibility for his actions and repent of them. He did neither, only rubbing his dusty hands on his trousers as if he could clean them of any guilt for the death of a man he had never met. "How long has this been going on?"

"Green sold me the first of the pieces not long after he first came to Dakara," Da'shak said. "Perhaps a hundred days ago."

"Describe them."

"Two bracelets, gold set with sapphires. A gold lamp in the shape of an ox. A gold wall plate with inscriptions, some kind of poetry." Teal'c frowned, knowing that Daniel Jackson would regret the loss of such a thing more than any amount of gold. But at least the inscriptions would have been photographed before Chen replaced the genuine plaque with a cheap forgery. "A gold necklace with a wide breastplate. A gold statue in the shape of a cat. And several masks, gold with black enamelwork. He said he had another mask he would bring me next time he came."

"I am afraid you will have to disappoint your buyers."

"You said yourself I did nothing wrong by our laws," Da'shak said, and Teal'c shook his head. He had hoped that at least Da'shak would offer no more excuses.

"I am finished here," he said, and turned to leave, not wasting any words of farewell on the man who stood silent behind him. The heavy door closed between them, and Teal'c left him to consider what price he had paid for his comforts.

"So what have we got?" Sam asked, wrenching her pack free of the crack in the rock and shrugging it back onto her shoulders.

Daniel was rubbing moss away from the stone with his sleeve, and stepped back to examine his handiwork. "Definitely Ancient," he said. They were in a low rock passageway, just big enough for both of them to stand, which ran on into darkness past the inscriptions Daniel's flashlight illuminated. "'And then Arthur triumphed over them, and in every heart, and in every, umm, in every world' — I've seen this before, this is from the Welsh Triads, although it's usually 'in every nation of the world.'"

"What are we looking at?" Sam asked patiently. She knew Daniel well enough to know that he'd get to the point sooner or later, but she preferred it to be sooner rather than later.

"It's a quote from a set of Welsh medieval manuscripts," Daniel said. "Or, probably the manuscripts are actually quoting whoever wrote this."

"You think it was Merlin?"

"I think it might have been." His eyes were alight, his expression intense. "We have to find whatever's creating that energy signature."

"Any clue to what that might be?"

"Well, obviously I'd like it to be the Sangraal, but… I'm trying to remember. I don't think the part of the Triads that mentions King Arthur is talking about the Grail. It's a long list of threes, listing Arthur's knights, and some of their deeds, and… I need Merlin's library. Or any library."

"Unless you suspect there's one down here, we're going to have to make do," Sam said. "Do we keep going down this passageway, or is there a door of some kind?"

Daniel ran his fingers up and down the cave wall next to the carvings. "There's no sign of any kind of opening."

"Actually, I think there is," Sam said, shining her flashlight on the cave floor. Muddy, reptilian footprints led away from the cave wall, cut off in mid-curve to make it very apparent that whatever had made the tracks had come through a hidden door.

"Not monkeys," Daniel said.

"I'm no biologist, but I got that far," Sam said.

Both of them turned to look back the way they had come. Sam couldn't hear anything that sounded like slithering coils coming closer, but as she and Daniel looked at each other, she thought they both felt a renewed sense of urgency at getting the door in the wall open.

"On the other hand, whatever came out of that door was able to open that door," Daniel said, apparently following her thought.

"Yeah, but wouldn't you still feel better if the door were between us and it? And maybe there's a way to lock it from the other side."

"Unless there are five or six of that thing's friends on the other side," Daniel said.

Sam looked at him sideways. "You want to walk away and leave whatever mysterious Ancient artifacts may be on the other side of this door to the lizards? If they're lizards."

"I didn't say that."

"Good," Sam said. "I'd start worrying that you'd been possessed."

"Don't even say it." Daniel worried at the stone with his fingers, trying various combinations of letters in the inscription. "It could require a password of some kind."

"That's possible."

"If this were anyone else, I'd say it could be anything, but Merlin liked tests. He would have made it something that you could figure out from this inscription if you knew... if you knew the rest of the Triads, probably. Which I can almost remember. Damn it."

"You'll remember."

Daniel nodded without taking his eyes off the inscription. "It's just a little frustrating knowing that at one point when I was Ascended I knew everything, and now I can't remember something I read this year. I've just been reading so many medieval manuscripts about Arthurian legend that they're all running together. Okay. Arthur triumphed. How did he triumph?"

"The Sangraal?" Sam offered.

"No. It wasn't the Sangraal. And that's not the right kind of answer, anyway. Or at least it's not the whole answer. Merlin built weapons for Arthur because he thought that Arthur and his knights were worthy of using them. Arthur triumphed…" He closed his eyes as if seeing a page in front of him. "Through the strength of his spirit, and the sharpness of his sacred weapons, and the virtue of his warriors."

Stone ground against stone as a door in the cave wall slid open in answer to the passphrase. A sudden blaze of light dazzled Sam, and she blinked, realizing as her eyes adjusted that it wasn't sunlight, but a glow no brighter than lamplight. She drew her sidearm and stepped cautiously inside, sweeping her light back and forth in search of any glimpse of movement.

The stone chamber revealed had once been a round room with pillars forming a walkway around its central expanse, but one side of the chamber had clearly collapsed long ago, tumbled stones and pillars lying in a pool of murky water. The muddy lizard tracks filled the room, crossing and recrossing one another, but there was no sign of anything moving. Still, she kept her back to the wall, circling the perimeter of the room cautiously.

In the center of the chamber, three low, narrow platforms looked as if they had been carved out of the stone of the cave floor. None was big enough for a person to lie on them; the largest looked more the size to hold a rifle or perhaps a staff weapon, but its surface was bare. Each platform was set with gleaming crystals from which the soft glow emanated. Daniel moved toward them like a moth drawn to a flame, his weapon in his hand but his eyes on the inscriptions carved into the surface of each platform.

He stopped in front of the longest of the three platforms, and crouched to read the lettering. "Rhongomyniad," he said. He looked up. "Arthur's legendary spear." He moved to the second platform, the shortest of the three. "Carnwennen," he said. "Arthur's dagger. This is another one of the triads. The last one should be…" He nodded as he saw the inscription on the third of the platforms, running his fingers across the lettering reverently. "Caliburnis," he said. "Which is just another name for Excalibur."

Sam ventured over, her own curiosity pricking. "We've already established that Excalibur isn't the legendary sword in the stone," she said. "If it's actually some kind of weapon created by Merlin, it would be awfully nice to have right now."

"Tell me about it."

"Do you think there's some way to open these platforms?"

"Maybe," Daniel said. He tried pressing the letters of the names, and then tried various sequences of letters, to no avail. "If this is another riddle, I'm not even sure what the question is. Except the names of the weapons, which I've already given.

"Maybe you need them all in Ancient? Or Latin?"

"Maybe so, which is a problem, because I don't know the names for the spear and the dagger in anything but Welsh. This is an obscure part of the legend, and as far as I know it's not referenced anywhere but the Welsh triads. Unless there's something in Merlin's library about it, which there might be. There's so much there, and so little time for research."

Sam traced the contours of the nearest platform. She thought she could feel almost imperceptible seams in the rock, as if there might be a part of the platform that was intended to separate from the rest and sink or rise or open, but pressing did nothing, and neither did manipulating the lighted crystals. Finally Daniel shook his head. "I'm not sure there are any controls to find."

"Are we sure there's not some kind of test we have to pass first?"

"That would be nice. Then we might have a chance of passing it. No, I'm beginning to think this was where these weapons were stored when they weren't in use, and that they weren't ever returned here after the last time they were used. There are a lot of mythological accounts of the fate of Excalibur, and most of them are very clear that it was returned to the Lady of the Lake after one of Arthur's knights obeyed his instructions to cast it away."

"You think she was an Ancient?"

"I don't know. But I don't think Excalibur is sitting here for us to find. Or Arthur's spear, for that matter. I'm not so sure about Carnwennen. There's a legend about how Arthur used Carnwennen to kill one of his enemies when they were hiding in the darkness of a cave, but there's also a version where Arthur was the one who was hidden in the darkness."

"You think the dagger is what's creating the darkness out there."

"That's my theory," Daniel said. "We should see —" He broke off abruptly, listening. "Do you hear something out there?"

Cam followed the rope, which ended near the opening to a high, vaulted chamber, big enough that there were actually plants growing in it.

"Carter? Jackson? You back here?"

"This certainly would have been a more pleasant place to camp than out in that damp, drafty cave," Vala said.

"Yes, but if they moved their camp, they moved it in a hurry. Or they wouldn't have left the radio and Jackson's pack behind, let alone Carter's pet radar setup."

"Maybe the cave-in alarmed them."

"So they ran further back in the cave?"

Vala shrugged. "They might? This sort of underground exploration isn't really my strong point."

"We don't do a lot of it in the Air Force, either," Cam said.

"On the other hand, there are definitely animal tracks in here. And the tracks of those terribly unattractive boots you people wear."

"They're comfortable."

"The tracks go this way." They led up to a narrow passage in the rock. It looked like a tight squeeze, but possible.

"If you can get through there, I certainly can," Vala said. He was halfway through the narrow passage when the lights went out. "What happened to the light?"

"What do you mean?"

"Is your flashlight turned on?"

"There's plenty of light," Vala said. "I'm turning it on anyway, but… oddly enough the beam does seem dimmer than it was a minute ago."

"I can't see a thing."

"It isn't that dark. Or maybe it is," Vala said, surprise in her voice.

"Something strange is going on here," Cam said. He pushed forward, wedging himself between two rocks until he wasn't sure he could move. He felt Vala's hand reaching out for his, and grasped it firmly.

"Mitchell? Vala? Is that you?" Daniel's voice came as a welcome surprise, but the sudden change in his tone came as an unwelcome one. "Uh-oh."

"What, Jackson?"

"There's something down here that's creating an area of total darkness," Sam said from somewhere nearby. "We ran into it upstairs, and came down here to start with because we were trying to get away from —"

She broke off at the sound of hissing from out of the darkness. Something scraped across the rock, a dry, slithering sound that sent chills down the back of Cam's neck. Whatever was out there hissed again, louder and apparently angrier.

"Okay," Cam said as calmly as he could manage. "I don't have a lot of room to move, here."

"The good side is that unless that thing is a lot smaller than I'm thinking, it's going to be a tight squeeze for it to get to you," Daniel said. From the sound of his voice, he was somewhere on the other side of the narrow passageway, but Cam couldn't tell any more than that. Out of the way of the angry creature, he hoped.

The hissing came again, and now he could hear heavy breathing in the darkness as well. The papery slither was coming closer, along with a scraping that might have been claws on rock.

"That doesn't help me much if it can get to me. Especially not if it's poisonous. Do we think it's poisonous?"

"At least I've got you between me and it," Vala said from behind Cam.

"Forgive me if that's not very much comfort to me."

"I think the field of darkness centers around the creature," Daniel said. "There's an inscription on the wall from the Welsh Triads that references Carnwennan, the dagger of the legendary King Arthur—"

"If there's a short version, give me the short version," Cam said, wrenching his shoulder back so that he could draw his sidearm. The sound of something massive breathing was coming closer, and then he heard a rumbling growl that he could feel in the soles of his feet and all the way up his spine. "Think Cliff's Notes."

"It could shroud its bearer in darkness."

"We think a lizard is carrying a knife?"

"It may not literally be a knife. I think something that lives in this cave complex carried off or maybe even swallowed Carnwennan, maybe because it was shiny, or maybe because it carried the scent of human beings and the creature thought it might be edible."

"Right now I'm guessing it thinks we're edible."

"If it gets too close to you, shoot it."

"I'm way ahead of you," Cam growled.

"But maybe you can scare it off."

"Go away, lizard!" Vala called. "Shoo!"

"I have a better idea," Cam said. "Everybody get clear." He fired at the ground in front of him, the shots resounding like thunderclaps in the confined space. There was a furious hiss, and then the scraping of scales on stone and a thudding noise as if heavy flesh was buffeting against the cave walls.

"Whoa!" Sam called, and then, "I'm okay. I think that thing caught me with its tail."

"It's probably making for the water," Daniel said. "I'm going to try to stop it." He fired, more thunderclaps, and Cam froze where he was. There was a splash, a grating of stones, and the sound of something thrashing in the water. "If it's got Carnwennan, we need to stop it."

"And just how do you propose to do that?"

Suddenly Cam could see the beam of Vala's flashlight flickering unevenly on cave wall. The darkness lifted as swiftly as it had come, and Cam wrenched himself through the narrow passageway in the rock to see Sam picking herself up off the cave floor, and Daniel scowling at the murky pool of water at one end of the room, still rippling as if something large had disappeared into its depths.

CHAPTER SEVEN

"WHAT we need is tranquilizer darts," Daniel said. "If we could immobilize that thing, we might be able to get the dagger back."

"If it is a dagger," Sam said. "It would certainly be nice to get a look at whatever's causing this effect. If we could duplicate it, I can see plenty of uses in the field."

"So can I," Cam said, shining his flashlight at the water, still rippling from the creature's passage. "But none of us are crawling into a hole filled with water to wrestle a python that's swallowed one of Merlin's weapons. That's just not happening."

"We're going to have to take the wall apart," Daniel said. "And move the stone that's blocking the outlet."

"Correction," Cam said. "Somebody is going to have to do those things. Probably Parker and poor unlucky SG-15, since they're already standing around outside. Talk about drawing the short straw as far as missions go."

"We were fine," Sam said. "More or less fine."

"I'm glad to hear it. But I need both of you back on base right now. Landry wants results from this murder investigation, it's turned into an investigation of stolen artifacts at the same time, and I don't know how much I can rely on Dr. Gardner, since she obviously hates the Stargate program's guts."

"I'm not sure it's the Stargate program she hates," Daniel said. "More like everything we represent. The threat of alien invasion, the knowledge that most of accepted archaeological explanations for Egyptian history are wrong and that she can't tell anyone in the field the truth about it, the personally traumatic things that happened to her... it's understandable that she's not our biggest fan."

"My point is that I need you two back at the SGC to help me figure out what's going on. You can hunt for Arthur's dagger later."

"Later," Daniel said, skepticism heavy in his voice. He was probably right, Cam knew; the chances that he'd get to putter around looking for a device that might be down here, that might create a field of darkness, and that might turn out to be useful were minimal. "Come on, Mitchell. We need a few more hours here, we're getting so close—"

"It's not the Sangraal," Cam said. "We need the Sangraal. And we need to solve this case. And we are leaving now, and that's an order."

Daniel took a deep breath and let it out. For a moment, Cam was afraid his next words would be *I don't care*. "You're right," Daniel said instead. "I know, you're right. And as much as I hoped that this might be at least a stepping stone toward finding the Sangraal, it doesn't look like it. All the same, I want SG-15 to go over this place with a fine-tooth comb. I don't want there to be any chance that we had the answer right in front of us and let it slip through our hands."

"They'll check it out," Cam said. "But for now, we're going home."

"I want to talk to Chen myself," Daniel said, toweling the last of the mud from his hair. It still rankled to be pulled out of the field, but at least it meant he could finally get clean and dry, and that there was some possibility of sleeping in his own non-lizard-infested bed.

Mitchell frowned as he pulled on a clean shirt. "I still think that's a bad idea."

"Come on," Daniel said. "You know I didn't kill Oliver. I was off-world, and even if I hadn't been, you can't really believe that I murdered him because, I don't know, because his over caution as an archaeologist got on my nerves—"

"I know you didn't kill him, Jackson," Mitchell said, cutting Daniel off just as he was working up a good head of indignation. "But it's getting pretty messy. These disappearing artifacts are your department."

"I know," Daniel said, feeling a stab of guilt. There had been little time lately to spare for actually managing his department, and he'd left the other civilian archaeologists to catalog and write up what the SG teams brought back without anything that he could really call supervision. He'd never had any himself, and he hadn't needed any, but he knew that wasn't an excuse. "But that's exactly why I want to get to the bottom of this. You don't believe I had anything to do with the artifact theft, do you?"

"I think if you decided to steal something, you'd do a better job of it than this."

"Thanks. I think."

Mitchell reached for his uniform jacket. "If you forged something, it wouldn't look obviously like a forgery. If you wanted to sell something off-world, you wouldn't need Green to help you do it. And if you wanted to murder someone, you wouldn't use a poison that points to one of a tiny handful of people."

"Do I really need to tell you that I didn't do any of those things?"

"No. I think your record speaks to that. If what you wanted was to get rich, there are approximately a million things you could have done that would be easier ways to make money than trying to sell the academic world on crackpot theories and then coming to work for the US government."

"At the point where I did, they were offering me more money than anybody else," Daniel said. "Which is to say, more than none. But I take your point."

"This whole thing bothers me," Mitchell said, shaking his head. "I mean, these are supposed to be our best people. If the levels of scrutiny we put people through here can't even screen out thieves and murderers, what does that say about us?"

"That most of our people are very good, and a few of them aren't," Daniel said. "That's always been a problem. I don't know if you ever read the reports about Jonas Hanson, the one who set himself up as a god on one of the first planets we ever visited." It hadn't been an auspicious start to their exploration of the galaxy, and Daniel was glad that Sam wasn't around for this conversation, because it was an episode he tried not to mention when she was around.

"That was unfortunate."

"He was a real bad apple, and Hammond chose him personally for the Stargate program. Sam even vouched for him. We screen out people who have suspicious associations, or who've gotten caught committing crimes, but as hard as we try, I'm not sure we can reliably screen out people who haven't ever gotten caught."

"And then there's Vala," Mitchell said.

"Give her a chance."

"I am," Mitchell said, doing up the buttons on his uniform jacket. "She's helped us a lot. I even think her heart is in the right place. But if even the people with perfect records turn out to be criminals sometimes, it's hard to make a really good case for handing Vala the keys to the candy shop."

"Look at it this way," Daniel said. "We need to know if we can trust her, right?"

"True enough."

"So we give her access to the archaeology lab. There aren't any amazingly powerful weapons in there, or pieces of irreplaceable technology. There are just some interesting pieces of art and material culture that should be catalogued and put into storage, where hopefully someone will look at them someday. Some of them are made out of gold. Well, gold is nice. But there's not a single thing in that lab that's worth more than what we stand to gain by trusting Vala."

"Her help fighting the Ori?"

"And an asset to the SGC. If we can trust her, and it's worth finding out now whether we can trust her with valuable objects."

"I hate to think that we're somehow entrapping her."

"We're not. I'm not. It's just… trusting her has to start somewhere. Let's start here."

"All right, we'll play it your way," Mitchell said. "Let's go talk to Dr. Chen. I can't wait to hear her side of all this."

Teal'c's information had been enough for Landry to move Chen to a holding cell rather than the more comfortable prison of guest quarters, and to have Sgt. Green escorted to a cell as well. Chen was sitting with her head in her hands when Daniel and Mitchell walked in, although she sat up and straightened her back defiantly when she saw them.

"It's all over," Daniel said. "We know you've been replacing artifacts that you were photographing with gold-plated replicas. We know you gave the originals to Sgt. Green, and that he sold them to Da'shak. I assume he gave you a cut of the profits, or maybe you gave him a cut of the profits, since you took most of the risks — smuggling the artifacts in and out of the base, particularly. It might be a little hard to explain why you needed to take several pounds of solid gold home with you."

"They never asked," Chen said. "They searched my bag once, when I had the lamp in it, but I just said it was one of the artifacts I was cataloguing and showed them the catalog record from our database. They seemed to think that covered it, as if it were just like checking out a library book. It was easy."

Daniel tried not to wince. He probably bore some of the responsibility for that, too. He'd taken objects home, over the years, carried them back and forth along with books and notes, and the guards had gotten used to it. It honestly hadn't occurred to him that it created a risk if other people in his position were less honest. He could just hear Jack telling him that he had an overly optimistic view of human nature. Which wasn't true — it was just that he had a hard time remembering that other people's temptations were different from his own.

"Why did you do it?" Mitchell asked softly.

"I needed the money," Chen said. "I had bills, debts — you don't know what it's like, you've never had student loans or tried to scrape together a living on an adjunct professor's salary."

"I have," Daniel said flatly. "I've been unemployed, evicted, too broke to buy a cup of coffee, you name it. Believe me, I've been there. But I never stole from people who trusted me. I never even considered doing that."

"Then maybe you're better than me," Chen said miserably. "I thought — the things were going into storage, we'd already photographed them, they weren't doing anyone any good in boxes. I knew how to use the electroplating kit, I'd made jewelry before as a hobby. The first time, I wasn't even thinking about forging anything, I just thought — the bracelets were so pretty, I wanted to see if I could copy them, make a replica. It came out really well, and I thought, if I switched them, no one would know."

"Was that when you got Green involved?"

She nodded. "We were talking, just kind of trying out the idea, and I said it couldn't work because I'd get in so much trouble if I tried to sell them anywhere in the world. And then I just thought, maybe somewhere that's not in the world."

Daniel waited, and then when she didn't continue, asked, "Is that why you killed Oliver?"

Her head snapped up. "I didn't kill Dr. Oliver. I don't know who did, but it didn't have anything to do with the artifacts I gave to Green."

"The ones you stole," Mitchell said, and she nodded reluctantly.

Daniel shook his head skeptically. "He didn't find out what you were doing?" She hesitated, clearly unsure what to say, and he pressed on. "If you didn't do it, you need to tell me the whole truth. I can't keep you out of trouble for what you did, but I'll do my best to keep you out of trouble for what you didn't do. If you're telling the truth."

"He suspected," Chen said. She leaned back against the cell wall, turning her face up to the unforgivingly harsh lights. "He called me into his office the day before yesterday. He asked a lot of uncomfortable questions about the artifacts I was photographing, and I guess he must have known it was making me nervous. Then he said that he wasn't happy with the photographs of certain pieces, and that he was going to get them back out of storage and have me redo them. I tried to bluff it out — saying the photographs were fine, telling him that you'd say the same thing and that he could ask you if he wanted to — and finally he came right out with it, saying he'd looked at the pieces in storage, and he knew they weren't the same ones the SG teams brought back. I told him I had no idea what had happened, but I could see he didn't believe me."

"And that's when you decided to kill him," Mitchell said.

"No! But I knew I had to do something. And I thought… I knew he'd been making a lot of phone calls to Patricia Niles after she left for Denver. But he was so secretive about it — he'd hang up if anyone else walked into his office, and he looked so guilty. A couple of times I heard enough to be sure he was talking to her, but then when I asked him, he said he'd been on the phone with a repairman. Pointless lies. And then one weekend I actually saw him in Denver, but when I asked him what he'd been up to, he said he'd spent all weekend at home."

"Sure," Mitchell said. "They were dating and they didn't want anyone to find out about it."

"Because she's married," Chen said.

Daniel frowned. "Are you sure about that?"

"Why else would he have been sneaking around that much?"

"Dr. Carr claims he was getting generally paranoid," Daniel said. "That it would have been entirely in character for him to hide his relationship with Dr. Niles because he was afraid that having people know about it would somehow endanger it."

"Maybe he was, but he sure didn't want anyone to find out about her," Chen said. "It was kind of a shot in the dark — I was desperate for a way to keep him from turning me in. I told him I knew about the phone calls he'd made to Patricia, and that I didn't expect he wanted everyone at the SGC to hear about his relationship with her. I really thought he'd just laugh at me, but he asked me what I wanted, and I said I wanted time to tell you myself. That I thought things would go easier for me if I confessed rather than having him accuse me."

"It might have," Mitchell said. "Why didn't you do it?"

"You were never going to confess, were you?" Daniel asked, already knowing the answer. "What did you want the time for, if it wasn't to kill Oliver?"

"I was going to try to get the artifacts back. I thought if I could replace them, it would be my word against Oliver's. But when I talked to Green, he told me there was no way. Da'shak wasn't keeping the pieces, he was selling them himself. We couldn't buy them back from him because he didn't have them. I was afraid Oliver would say something about it again yesterday, but he never brought it up, like something else more important was distracting him. And then before Green and I could figure out what to do…"

"Someone got rid of your problem," Mitchell said. "You figure it was Green?"

"I don't want to think so," Chen said. "And I think I've got nothing more to say."

Cam assembled the team around a conference room table, everyone falling on the coffee as if enough caffeine would make the problem solve itself. It was mid-day, but he hadn't done more than catnap the night before, and he didn't think Sam and Daniel had gotten much sleep between the cave-in and their reptilian friend. "So, do we figure it was Green?"

"Two problems with that," Daniel said. "First, Sgt. Green doesn't have access to the archaeology lab."

"She could have given him the poison."

"But he couldn't have gotten it into Oliver's cup. And, second—"

"He is not on the security tapes," Teal'c finished.

"And if his story matches hers, we've got nothing to pin the murder on him," Cam said. He shook his head. "This business with Dr. Niles is sounding more and more fishy."

"Tell me about it," Sam said. "Carr says she broke up with Oliver for him. Chen says she was married, but it's possible that she's just guessing. Oliver's strange behavior about her might have been guilt, or paranoia, or an attempt not to create more drama with Carr when they'd wound up in some kind of weird love triangle."

"It's a mystery, and I really dislike mysteries," Cam said. "Let's try one more time to get the mysterious Dr. Niles on the phone." He picked up the conference room phone and dialed, not really expecting an answer, but she picked up on the third ring.

"Hello?"

Cam put the phone on speaker and gestured for silence to the rest of the team, who all addressed themselves to their coffee thirstily, with the exception of Vala, who was sipping hers as if she still couldn't decide whether she liked the stuff or not. "This is Colonel Cameron Mitchell at Cheyenne Mountain," he said.

"Colonel Mitchell," Niles said, without enthusiasm. "If you're calling about a consulting position, I already told Dr. Oliver I wasn't interested."

"Dr. Oliver is dead," Cam said bluntly. "And I have some questions I need to ask you about your relationship with him before you left your previous job."

There was a momentary pause. "I don't want to talk about Gideon," she said. "I'm sorry he's dead, Colonel Mitchell, but I'm not going to be able to answer any questions for you. I'm going to ask you not to call me at this number again."

"Hang on, I just need—" The line went dead, and redialing produced only a long series of unanswered rings. "Okay, that was short."

"And very suspicious," Vala said.

"Tell me about it."

"Do we have a forwarding address for her?" Sam asked.

"Yep. 42 Rosewood Drive, apartment 3A, Denver, CO."

Sam looked sideways at Daniel. "We could go see if she's

more cooperative in person."

"I doubt she's going to be really glad to see me," Daniel said. "I tried to talk to her when she left, but she shut me down pretty hard. I thought it was just that she felt guilty about not having stayed in the job very long. Whether it was or not, I'm not sure that I'm the best person to get her to open up. We never really clicked while she was here."

"Just as well, or we'd be looking at a love… what would you call it? Square? Quadrangle?" Vala asked. "Are we sure you're not just protesting too much?"

"Vala Mal Doran might be a good choice to accompany Colonel Carter," Teal'c said. Vala looked sideways at Teal'c as if not sure whether she was pleased or suspicious or both, although at least she did stop speculating about his nonexistent affair with Patricia Niles. "It would also be instructive for her to see more of Tau'ri culture firsthand, rather than on television."

"You mean television isn't entirely representative of our culture?" Sam asked. "I'm shocked."

"Not even Wormhole X-Treme," Daniel said. "Sure, I think it's a good idea, if Sam's okay with it."

"I think it's a good idea, too," Cam said. "So we're doing it. Do I have to give the 'this is not a democracy, and you all don't get votes' speech?"

"General O'Neill preferred the 'Does it say Colonel on my uniform?' speech," Sam said. "I mean, when he was a colonel and it did say colonel on his uniform. Now it says general, and people usually know that already. I'll be fine with Vala."

"We'll be perfectly fine," Vala said. "What could go wrong?"

"Just please never say that," Cam said, and waved them on their way.

Once they got out to the highway, Sam watched Vala out of the corner of her eye as she drove. Vala rode with her feet up on the dashboard, her neck craned to see out the window and her nose pressed against the glass. The mountains rose stark and dramatic against the wide blue sky, their white caps shining in the sun, a view Sam always appreciated after long days spent underground. Vala seemed more interested in advertising billboards and signs promising shopping, dining, and gas.

"We've got about an hour's drive," Sam said. "I keep hoping we'll get something civilian-appropriate out of the transport rings we've been taking apart at Area 51, but we haven't been able to come up with a reliable transport system based on them that doesn't eat more power than it's worth." She gunned the engine to pass a car that was crawling along in the right lane. "I guess this is all really different from what you're used to."

"I'm used to a lot of things," Vala said. "Your world is a bit slower-paced than a lot of the real hotbeds of interplanetary theft, admittedly. But you certainly have more technology than a lot of backwater worlds like the one where I grew up."

Sam waited, wondering if Vala intended to say more, and not wanting to push her if she wasn't. "I grew up all over the place myself," she said. "That's what comes of being an Air Force brat. We moved around to different military bases, and then I joined the Air Force myself, so I've never really settled down anywhere."

"I could never settle down," Vala said, but there was a wistfulness in her tone that made Sam not entirely believe her.

"It's not like I don't see the appeal myself," Sam said. "The idea of actually having a house somewhere, and maybe even living in it with someone… but life makes that complicated."

"It certainly does that," Vala said, and Sam winced, wondering how tactless she had been. She wasn't sure how Vala felt about Tomin, whether he'd been strictly a means to the end of protecting herself when she discovered she was pregnant, or whether she'd developed genuine feelings for him. For that matter, she wasn't sure Vala knew how she felt about him, and she couldn't even imagine how Vala felt about Adria.

"We should try to get you out of the mountain more often," she said instead. "At least that's easier for you than it was for

Teal'c. The whole idea of having aliens on Earth was a lot newer when he first started living here, and it was a long time before anybody even managed to take him to the mall. Shopping," she added, not sure if "mall" was a concept that translated cross-culturally. "Clothes that aren't standard-issue fatigues, scented candles, maybe a plant? That kind of thing. And food that you'll probably think is weird, but that at least you can pick out for yourself."

"All of that sounds nice," Vala said, but distantly. Then she seemed to catch Sam watching her, and brightened with a visible effort. "Any expensive pretty things lying around without owners?"

"Are there really ever expensive pretty things lying around without owners?"

"It's more of a euphemistic way of putting it."

"You're not really planning to knock over a shopping mall, though. Because then you'd get kicked off of Earth, to start with."

"No, I'm not, but it is what people expect to hear, isn't it?" Vala was looking deliberately out the window, not meeting Sam's eyes.

"You could cut everyone some slack," Sam said. She was beginning to feel like she needed to record this particular pep talk so that she could cue it up at intervals, which felt a little weird, because she'd never thought of herself as a pep talk kind of person. But with Jack battling bureaucrats in Washington, all of them were having to pitch in to keep the team on an even keel, even if she would have preferred a literal naval engineering problem. "It was just as hard for Teal'c when he joined the team. Harder, because he was the first person from another planet anyone had ever dealt with."

"He had a more virtuous record, though."

Sam shrugged. "He'd been Apophis's First Prime. Even after he switched sides and saved our lives, that made some people nervous. Colonel O'Neill and General Hammond had to really go to bat for him to persuade their superiors to let him stay."

"Still, I'm getting the impression that ever having done anything unfortunate for personal gain is… well, perhaps not quite right up there with murder, but definitely equally shocking. And yet if one can believe your television programs, your world is filled with criminals. You should surely be used to the idea that money matters to people."

"It's not that money doesn't matter to us," Sam said. "Believe me, I like getting paid. Speaking of which, has anyone set up a bank account for you?"

"They have. Teal'c has even promised to show me how to shop on the Internet."

"Well, don't go crazy. And it's usually a bad idea to buy anything people are trying to sell on television. There are a lot of scams out there."

"I have a certain amount of experience with people who make a living selling other people worthless goods," Vala said. "I think I can manage."

Sam stopped the car in front of another apartment building, this one steel and glass, a shimmery box rather than a dull concrete box. Vala unfolded herself from the car and stretched, wondering if Daniel could explain the ritual significance of boxes to the Tau'ri people, or if it was only that boxes were cheap to build and Tau'ri architects unimaginative.

"She probably isn't home this time of day," Sam said, and Vala followed her up the front steps of the building. "But it's worth a shot."

Inside, the air was chill; what the Tau'ri saved on architectural frills they made up for in their investment in climate control. Sam pressed the button to summon the elevator, and Vala examined the signs posted on a board nearby. Offers to sell things were clear enough, but she was still trying to puzzle out whether "baby sitting" and "dog walking" involved babies, dogs, or exercise positions, or were euphemisms she hadn't yet deciphered, when the elevator doors opened.

Upstairs, the door to Dr. Niles' apartment was closed, as all the doors were — the Tau'ri were clearly not a trusting people in that respect — and there was no answer when Sam knocked, and then called "Dr. Niles?" After a minute the door down the hall opened, and a harried looking woman wearing soft and shapeless clothes with a blanket thrown over her shoulder emerged. "She's not here," the woman said. "She has her afternoon class. Now could you…" She put her finger to her lips for quiet. "I just got the baby down."

"What do you have to get babies down from?" Vala couldn't help asking once the door was closed, although she did it in a stage whisper.

"Down for a nap," Sam whispered back as they made for the elevators.

"Right, they take those," Vala said. She'd spent precious little time with babies, and Adria had skipped the napping stage, going straight from inexplicable baby to spooky child to agent of intergalactic domination. She tried to visualize herself putting a child in a bed to nap, and could only imagine it as a con game, the child borrowed, or actually a bundle of handheld weapons wrapped in a blanket. The thought still ached, a dull, nonspecific hurt that she resented for existing. The last thing she could afford was any weaknesses to slow her down.

"I could let us into her apartment," Vala offered once they were in the elevator.

"If we'd had a key, we wouldn't have knocked," Sam said. "And that next door neighbor is likely to pop out of her apartment the moment we try breaking in. Besides, it's not very fair to break into the apartment of someone who for all we know doesn't have anything to do with either crime."

"Well, if fair is what we're going for."

"We try," Sam said dryly. "Dr. Niles left to take a teaching job at the University of Denver, and her neighbor said she has an afternoon class." She pulled out her cell phone and dialed.

"Hey, Daniel — no, not yet. Listen, can you look at the University of Denver's class schedule online and figure out what Dr. Niles would be teaching right now? We're going to try to catch her as she's coming out of class."

They stepped out of the elevator, and Sam fished a pen out of her purse and grabbed one of the flyers off the board to write on. "Okay. All right… no, but I can find it. Oh, you did? Great, let me get that too, just in case." She scribbled fast, and then said, "Thanks. Tell Landry we're on our way."

"We know where we're going?"

"More or less. And Daniel got her license plate number from when she applied for a parking permit at Cheyenne Mountain. If we can find her car, we can catch her on her way back from class."

Vala was curious about the university, as Daniel seemed to feel that universities were the repository of all human knowledge. Unfortunately, what she could see from the street was more buildings shaped like boxes, as well as small crowds of Tau'ri carrying packs on their backs and books in their arms. Many of them also had the ubiquitous coffee cups in their hands. Teal'c had warned her that the drink was mildly addictive but central to many rituals of Tau'ri culture, which she was finding to be true. Certainly no one ever had a meeting without it.

"That's her car," Sam said abruptly, and pulled into a parking lot. It was plastered with stern warnings about permits being required, but Sam merely pulled her car in behind Niles's car, blocking her avenue of escape.

"Keep an eye out for anyone who looks like they want to tow us," she said. "That is… just let me know if anyone looks very unhappy that we're parked here."

Vala regarded the young people who passed by with a steely glare designed to discourage them from commenting on their choice of parking places. Some of them looked back curiously, but none of them volunteered to tow the vehicle, which Vala assumed to be a local custom.

"How do you sit like a baby?" she asked.

"What?" Sam put her head to one side. "Do you mean sit cross-legged?"

"Babies can't sit like that. I'm sure they can't. I'm not even sure babies can sit up."

"It depends on how old the baby is," Sam said.

"How do you walk like a dog?"

"I think I'm missing a punchline," Sam said. "Is that her?" She shaded her eyes, and then climbed rapidly out of the car. Vala followed a moment behind her. "Dr. Niles?"

The woman approaching them was tall and shapely, with a halo of red curls framing her face, although if Vala was interpreting them correctly, her woven-wool jacket and pressed trousers suggested practicality more than a desire to impress. "What happened to my car?" she said, frowning at theirs, and then her frown deepened as she recognized Sam. "Colonel Carter. I already told Colonel Mitchell that I don't want to talk about the reasons I left."

"We really do need to talk to you for a minute," Sam said.

"This isn't the place," Niles said tightly. "I'm trying to put my previous job behind me professionally. Being stalked by Air Force officers isn't going to help matters."

"We could sit in your car," Sam offered, with a pleasant smile that made the absence of an offer to move her own car exceedingly clear.

"Fine, let's get this over with," Niles said, and climbed into the driver's seat.

Sam sat in the other front seat, and Vala climbed into the back.

"Is this about Gideon's work?" Niles asked. "Because I don't know anything about his projects. I've been trying not to even think about my work at the SGC. That's what I'm supposed to do, anyway, isn't it? It's all classified. I can't give any kind of reasonable explanation of what I've been doing for the last year, let alone have any publications to show for it. Just an unpleasant gap on my CV to explain when tenure time rolls around."

Sam didn't look particularly sympathetic. "With all due respect, Dr. Niles, you knew that was what you were signing up for when you took the job at Cheyenne Mountain."

"When I took the job, I expected to be able to stay in it."

"So why didn't you?" Vala asked.

Dr. Niles craned her neck to see Vala where she perched in the back seat. "Should I even be talking to you? I thought you were some kind of alien hijacker who kidnapped Dr. Jackson."

"Kidnapped is such a harsh word."

"This is Vala Mal Doran, the newest member of SG-1," Sam said firmly. "And I would also like to know exactly why you left your job at the SGC."

"What's happened to Vincent Oliver?"

"It looks very much like he was murdered," Sam said.

Vala watched Niles closely as she reacted to the news. She seemed to be shocked, her eyes widening and her breath catching. On the other hand, it was very much how Vala would dramatize shock herself in a situation that called for it to be persuasively performed. "I can't believe it," Niles said.

"I understand the two of you were close," Sam said.

Dr. Niles laughed, a humorless sound. "Close. Is that what people are saying?"

"That's what Dr. Carr says. That you began dating Dr. Oliver after you turned down Dr. Carr, and that the two of you were seeing each other until you had some kind of falling out a few weeks ago." Sam leaned back, looking perfectly comfortable in the front seat of Dr. Niles's car. "Is he right?"

"Gideon Carr is one of two reasons why I left the SGC," Dr. Niles said. "The other one was Vincent Oliver."

"I take it things had gotten awkward."

"That's one way of putting it. I had been working at the SGC for less than a week when Gideon started sticking to me like glue. At first he was very flattering about my work—wanted to hear all about what I'd been doing in the academic sector, suggested that we might write a book together if our work was ever declassified. I went out to coffee with him. Once. And he made it clear that my mind wasn't what he was interested in. I told him no. I expected that to be the end of it. It wasn't."

"You could have reported it," Sam said. "Landry wouldn't have put up with harassment on base."

"I thought about it," Dr. Niles said. "But I didn't want that to be my introduction to everyone at the SGC. And it never crossed the line into anything that couldn't pass as friendly interest to anyone watching. It was just… persistent. I was relieved when I started working more directly with Oliver. It meant I could move my work space next to his, and have lunch with him to talk about our project rather than being trapped at a lunch table with Gideon."

"And then?" Vala prompted when she fell silent.

"And then Vincent made it clear that his interest in me wasn't entirely professional either. He asked me out. I turned him down. And after that, working with him became a nightmare. I wish there were one thing I could point to, something I could say for certain was retribution. Instead, it was every little thing. He had always been a perfectionist, but he became obsessively critical. Nothing I did was right. After a few weeks of being berated about every piece of work I finished, I knew I had to get out. I was lucky to get back into an adjunct professorship here. I'll be even luckier if I get a tenure track position out of it."

"You should have gone to Landry," Sam said. "He would have gone to bat for you."

"Are you sure? You've been working under him for, what, a couple of months?"

"Hank Landry has a good reputation. And Dr. Jackson would have been on your side, no questions asked. The last thing he wants is for people in his department to be treated unfairly."

"I didn't want to run to Dr. Jackson. Especially when I didn't have any hard evidence for him."

"You could have come to me," Sam said. "Do you think I don't know how hard it can be for a woman in a field full of men? This kind of thing happens. I've seen it a lot. It's not your fault."

Dr. Niles twisted her hands on the steering wheel. "I didn't think about that. And you were at Area 51 while a lot of this was going on. Anyway, it's done now. I'm not going back."

"Not even now that Dr. Oliver is gone?" Sam asked. There was something in her tone that made Dr. Niles raise her head abruptly.

"You can't imagine that I…"

"I know you didn't poison him," Sam said. "You left the SGC before the poison that killed him was even brought back to Earth. But I wonder if you have any idea who might have wanted to kill him."

"Besides you," Vala said.

"I have no idea. I was trying to keep my mind on work. With limited success, but the last thing that I wanted was to find out more about the personal life of anyone I worked with. I just wanted to do my job, Colonel Carter. I wish that had been possible."

"So do I," Sam said. "If you think of anything else, anything that might be relevant to Dr. Oliver's death, I hope you'll let us know."

"I will if I think of anything," Dr. Niles said. "You'll excuse me for hoping that I don't."

CHAPTER EIGHT

ONCE they were back in their own car, Sam pulled out to free Niles, who wasted no time driving away. Vala was looking at her a little curiously from the other seat, her head tilted to one side.

"You seemed sympathetic."

"I am sympathetic," Sam said. "That kind of harassment — I don't like to think that it was going on at the SGC under our noses. Daniel's not going to like thinking that he missed it, although he's been a little busy lately. We all have. But the fact that the Ori want to take over the galaxy doesn't mean that we can stop doing the rest of our jobs."

"It's the way of the world," Vala said.

"Only when people don't do anything to stop it. There are a lot of things we don't have to accept about the world."

"And some things we do."

"No argument there. The trick is telling the difference, right?"

"We're back to a dead end, though," Vala said after a momentary pause during which Sam would have given a lot to know what she was thinking. "She couldn't have killed Oliver."

"No, I don't think she could have. But I think it's worth taking another look at Carr. I realize that being a jerk doesn't make you a murderer — if that were true, we'd have a lot fewer astrophysicists — but he did lie to us about what was going on between Niles and Oliver."

Vala shrugged. "Unless he really believed they were romantically involved, because Dr. Oliver acted so paranoid whenever Carr showed any interest in her. It's all very dramatic."

"The paranoia is what seems weird to me," Sam said, and then reconsidered that. "Actually, it's not that it's weird for someone who works at the SGC to be paranoid. We're all a little jumpy, understandably. But I'd expect it to focus on the chances of getting killed in some interesting way at work, not on his personal life, unless —" She broke off abruptly, frowning into the rear view mirror. "I think that black car is following us."

Vala twisted around to see. "Are you sure?"

"We're about to find out." Sam spun the wheel and changed lanes efficiently, other vehicles honking furiously as she settled into the traffic two lanes over. Behind her, the black car was also changing lanes. Sam took the next exit off the highway, and the black car followed as well.

"They're definitely following us," Vala said.

"Right," Sam said grimly. "Let's see if we can lose them."

Sam swerved wildly through traffic again, winning more angry honks from motorists behind her. Vala seemed unruffled, although it was possible that if she'd been marathoning TV and movies in an attempt to understand Earth culture, she'd concluded that every drive necessarily ended in a car chase.

Sam put the pedal to the metal, hoping that she wasn't about to earn a speeding ticket and involve the Highway Patrol in something far out of their depth.

"We might have lost them," Vala said after a minute. There was a longer pause, and then Vala added, "It's possible you might want to slow this vehicle down at some point in the future, considering that."

"Possible," Sam said, slowing to the upper bounds of reasonable safety. "But I don't like this one bit. We talk to Niles, and then someone follows us home? We've all been assuming that Oliver's murder was for personal reasons, but if there are enough people involved in it for them to be tailing us, we may have miscalculated."

They were heading into a long stretch of highway that cut through open countryside, with only a few jutting mesas and scrub trees to break the featureless grassland. Most of it was parkland, with only a few houses and farms visible in the distance among the foothills of the mountains. It was, Sam couldn't help thinking, a perfect place for an ambush.

"Are they still behind us?"

"I can't tell," Vala said, and then with an explosive bang, one of their tires blew out. The car swerved out of control, shuddering. "I'd say that was a yes!"

Sam couldn't risk more than a glance at the mirror, which showed someone leaning out of the window of a black car well behind them, aiming a weapon in their direction. She wrestled with the wheel, and with another bang, they lost another tire, the car jolting along on the rims and then fishtailing across the road despite her attempts to steer.

For a moment, all she could do was pray that they didn't smash into another driver as the car spun. Then they were off the road and jolting down the uneven shoulder. For a moment, Sam thought she could bring the car to a stop on the slope, and then she felt it pitch sickeningly as they rolled, crashing down the slope into a ditch between two scrubby trees.

She shook her head to clear glass from her face, and felt the world swim. Hands were tugging at her, and she realized Vala was trying ineffectively to free her from her seat belt. She reached down automatically and snapped herself free. "We should get out of here," she said, but she was moving too slowly, still dazed from the crash.

Vala reached inside Sam's jacket to draw her pistol and leaned over Sam's shoulder to fire through the window. Sam jerked her head around to see a man in black stumble and go down, sliding down the bank. She couldn't see any blood, and suspected he was in body armor. Wonderful. All the cards stacked against them.

"I think this is the part where we run away," Vala said.

"I'm on it," Sam said, and managed to heave herself out of the car. She dropped to one knee, grabbed the gun back from Vala, and fired in the direction of their attackers. Zat fire spit towards her as she yanked the back door of the car open as some minimal cover. Sparks flew, and she could smell the stench of scorched upholstery fabric.

"I thought your people didn't have energy weapons!" Vala

called from the other side of the car. Sam dived in front of the car and rolled as she scrambled behind it, putting her shoulder to Vala's. Below them, the slope descended into a windbreak that was scarcely more than a ditch between scrubby trees, and beyond that, open field ran toward what might have been a creek.

"They don't," Sam said grimly. "Either these guys aren't from around here, or they've got friends who aren't. Like the Trust." She raised her voice. "Let's talk about this! We can work this out!"

There was no reply, only an ominous sewing-machine rattle that sent her diving for the ground. That wasn't a zat, but the all-too-Earthly sound of an Uzi firing. Bullets rang off the body of the car and splintered glass. Sam crouched, trying to present as small a target as possible, and fired off a couple of shots under the car to discourage anyone from doing the same.

Vala looked sideways at Sam and raised her eyebrows in a "what now?" expression. They were clearly outgunned, and the very slowness of their pursuers in moving in gave her a bad feeling. It suggested they might be waiting for reinforcements, and as if in answer to the thought, she could hear another car slowing down and stopping on the road above. The highway patrol would eventually show up, but it didn't look like they could wait around, and besides she suspected the highway patrol would be outgunned too.

"Let's go," she said, and gave Vala a shove toward the minimal shelter of the trees. Vala rolled as Sam lay down covering fire, and then threw herself into the ditch, disappearing into brush. Sam did the same, hoping that she wasn't just presenting a tempting target. She hauled herself up behind a tree and fired twice. The man she'd hit was up again, and she swore and wished she had a zat. There wasn't any Earth-made body armor that was a good defense against zat fire, although she wouldn't put it past these guys to be wearing armor not made on Earth.

Her mind was working even as she watched two men edge

around the wreck of her car, wondering who was after them. The Trust? Or interplanetary spies, or rogue NID agents… they had a lot of enemies. At the moment, Sam was more interested in just getting out of range.

She squinted at the open field between them and the stream. On the other side was more open field running all the way to the distant mountains. She could see the shapes of buildings in the distance, farms or houses, but they might as well have been on another planet for all the good they did at the moment.

"I think we've got to try to take them out," she said.

"I just love a good firefight," Vala said, squaring her shoulders and nestling down further in the shelter of a tree. There were footsteps crunching down the underbrush, and Sam readied herself to fight.

Her first shot took down one of the men who rushed them, though a second went wild as a second man ducked behind a tree. Vala swept a third's legs out from under him, dropping him neatly to the ground where she kicked him in the head and turned to drive her elbow into the throat of the man who'd evaded Sam's shot.

It all seemed to be going well until Sam felt the familiar numbing buzz of zat fire catch her in the chest.

"Damn," she said, and fell to the ground unconscious.

Cam found Carolyn brooding over her lunch, pushing around stalks of broccoli with her fork without showing any inclination to eat them.

"What's your diagnosis?" he asked, putting down his own lunch tray. "Is it broccoli as we know it?"

"The broccoli's fine," Carolyn said. "I'm just not really in the mood."

"How are you holding up?"

"Seriously? I'm not happy that I'm apparently a suspect here."

"I don't think anyone thinks you did it," Cam said. "It's just that the circumstances look bad."

"For my father," she said in frustration. "He's bending over backwards to make sure that he suspects me so that it doesn't look like favoritism. Which is exactly why I didn't want to stay in this job in the first place once I realized it involved working for him. He swore it wouldn't be a problem, and it hasn't been a problem, until now."

"Don't tell me you'd want to have missed all the fun we have around here."

"How could I want to miss worrying about whether the Ori are going to take over the galaxy and we're all going to join their cult?" Carolyn shook her head. "I like the work. I just don't know how to get out from under this accusation. If we don't figure out who did it, and I have this hanging over me from now on..."

"We're going to figure out who did it," Cam said. "We make great detectives."

"I hope so. Because I'm pretty sure that Landry isn't going to go to bat for me otherwise."

"He'd never do anything to hurt your career."

"Or anything to get me out of this mess."

"It probably wouldn't help if he tried, under the circumstances."

"Which is exactly my point. If I were working for General Hammond or General O'Neill, their good opinion of me would mean something."

"You've got our good opinion of you," Cam said. "That has to mean something."

He'd been skeptical of doctors by the time he got to the SGC, having seen all too many of them in the days after the crash, most of them either pessimists who thought he'd never go back on active duty or relentlessly cheerful believers in just one more lap around the physical therapy room when he was ready to fall exhausted back into his hospital bed. Carolyn had checked him over after his first mission with SG-1, which had involved unexpected sword fighting, and he'd answered her questions with cautious versions of "I'm just fine, thanks for asking," until she finally put his folder down on the table and closed it firmly.

"You think I'm the enemy, don't you?"

"I don't know what you mean," he said.

"Sure you don't. You think I'm looking for a reason to bench you."

"Why would you do a thing like that?"

"Oh, I don't know, maybe because you've sustained major injuries in the last year that nearly took you off active duty for good."

"I'm fine," Cam said firmly. "Never been better."

"You don't actually have to lie to me," Carolyn said. "I know, I know, you're fine, and for what it's worth, I think you are fine right now; apparently you'd have made a good medieval knight. But medieval knights were old men at forty-five. When you're forty-five, I hope you have a plan for what you want to be doing that doesn't involve SG-1."

"I've thought about a battleship command," Cam said. "Who hasn't? Or a desk job wouldn't be too bad if it were someplace like the SGC." And that was a lie, he knew; a desk job would be terrible. He wanted to be out in the field, and if it couldn't be in a fighter anymore, and it couldn't be on SG-1 forever, he wanted one of the battleships. But he also knew the kind of thing that would make him sound like a well-adjusted realist. "I'm keeping my options open."

"Good," Carolyn said. "This job chews people up and spits them out. I'm not saying people shouldn't do it. It needs to be done. But no one's done ten years on an SG team without a break, and I think ten years is optimistic in your case. You only get to walk away from so many major injuries. You've walked away from one. You have fewer left."

"I get the point."

"I hope so. My point is, I'm not here to bench you. I'm here to keep you in the field as long as I can, and hopefully get you out of the field still fit for a ship command rather than so badly injured that you have to retire. I'm on your side."

"I appreciate that," Cam had said, and he'd started to believe it.

Now she smiled at him wanly from across the table. "It does mean something to have your good opinion, and SG-1's. I know how close the original team was to Janet Frasier, especially Sam. I'm glad that they've accepted my stepping into her shoes."

"Believe me, I know all about stepping into someone else's shoes."

"That can't be easy, either. But General O'Neill hasn't been on the team for a couple of years."

"And Colonel Carter was in charge of the team for a year. It makes things a little awkward."

"Awkward is apparently the order of the day. But you've done a good job with the team. I don't think anyone can argue that we'd be doing better if someone else were in charge."

"I expect Jackson could argue it," Cam said. "Jackson can argue anything."

"Does he say so, though?"

"Not that I know of," Cam admitted.

"Well. From what I know about Daniel Jackson, if he thought you were doing a bad job as the team's leader, he wouldn't hesitate to tell you. I gather that he told General O'Neill what he was doing wrong on a regular basis."

"And, see, now I feel bad that he's not telling me how I'm getting it all wrong," Cam said. "Maybe if he were, it would make me feel more like the team had really come together."

"I'm not sure you can have it both ways," Carolyn said, and then broke off abruptly. "And there's Daniel now."

Cam scooted his lunch tray over to make room, but Daniel wasn't carrying one of his own. "We've got a problem," Daniel said bluntly. "SG-15 just reported back in. They ran into our reptilian friend, and it didn't go well. They have injuries and a man missing."

"Did Landry clear us to go?"

Daniel nodded. "Reluctantly."

Again, Cam felt that pushing Landry should really have been his role, but since he would have pushed him to do the same thing, he didn't really feel that he could argue.

"Did Landry clear me to go?" Carolyn asked.

"I didn't ask."

"He'd better," she said, pushing her uneaten lunch away. "I'm coming with you."

Landry regarded them with a fish eye when they assembled in the gate room. "Dr. Lam, you are not going with them."

"SG-15 has injured team members."

"And we have other medical personnel."

"It's not like she's going to be out of our sight," Cam said. "Even if she were under arrest — and she's not under arrest, right? — it's not like she could escape or conspire with other desperate criminals while she's on an uninhabited planet with SG-1 watching her."

"Theoretically uninhabited," Teal'c said. "I believe SG-15 may have encountered inhabitants."

"If reptiles count as inhabitants."

"Don't make me regret this," Landry said.

"You won't regret it," Cam said, and stood back as the gate dialed.

They set a brisk pace from the gate, jogging down the long path toward the cliff face.

"When I went to medical school, I never thought it would involve this much sprinting," Carolyn said, although she didn't sound out of breath. "Emergency medicine, sure, but in general practice usually the patients come to you."

"You're telling me," Daniel said. "Archaeology doesn't usually involve sprinting either. Generally when something's been there for a few thousand years, it's going to stay put for the next few minutes. Although depending on where you're digging, you may still get some practice in running away from men with guns."

"Sounds like good preparation for this job," Mitchell said.

"It was. I just had to get used to more running and more guns. And to situations where it was more acceptable to shoot back."

"Personally, I joined the Air Force so that I wouldn't have to run," Mitchell said. "That's what we have airplanes for."

"It's probably overkill to use an airplane to go from the gate to the dig site," Carolyn said. "Even if we could fit one through the gate."

"That's why we're running. Remind me that this counts as my exercise for today. Possibly for tomorrow, too."

Daniel could see SG-15 now, clustered around someone sitting at the top of the rubble field. Sitting was better than lying down, and from Carolyn's expression she took some comfort from that as well. She quickened her pace, though, and made her way up the rocks with deliberate speed, although she kept her mouth pressed firmly together all the way up.

Daniel scaled the uneven slope behind her, and found Carolyn kneeling to investigate an airman's wounded leg.

"The thing bit him," Parker said.

"What was it?"

"We couldn't see," one of the other airmen said, a woman with a dark ponytail and a smudge of dirt across one cheek. "All of a sudden we couldn't see a thing, like all the lights went out. Then something jumped out of the darkness and bit a chunk out of Henderson."

Mitchell hauled himself up over the lip of the cliff. "How are you holding up, Henderson?"

"Fine, sir," the man said, and gave him a thumbs-up, although he winced when Carolyn started unwrapping bandages.

Parker shook his head. "When we got back to where we could see, we realized that Collins was gone. We yelled for him and didn't hear anything, and I didn't want to send anyone in after him without backup."

"Okay, we need to get Henderson back to the gate," Carolyn said, re-wrapping bandages around his injured leg. "The quicker we get that leg cleaned up and stitched up, the less chance of permanent damage."

"We can rig a harness to get him down," Parker said. "But somebody has to go after Collins."

Daniel shone his flashlight into the back of the cave. "It looks normal to me," he said. "I mean, it's dark, but I can see the cave wall."

"The darkness started right after that tight squeeze between the rocks," Parker said. "We had a hell of a time getting Henderson through there, let me tell you."

"I bet that was fun," Carolyn said.

The airman gave her a thumbs-up again. "I'm lovin' it."

"You two take Henderson back to the gate," Mitchell said. "We'll find Collins."

Parker frowned. "With all due respect, sir, I don't like to leave one of my people behind."

"We'll find him," Mitchell said. "I want Dr. Lam here if he's injured, and the rest of your team guarding the gate to make sure we have a safe way home."

Parker nodded reluctantly. Carolyn patted Henderson on the shoulder and came to peer around Daniel's shoulder. "So where's this weird darkness we're dealing with?"

Daniel scrambled down the rocks to the point where they narrowed into the corridor leading back to the sunlit cavern. His flashlight beam illuminated it nearly to the opening at the other end, but the opening itself was cloaked in impenetrable darkness.

"I think it's come back to the cavern where it hunts," he said. "That room may also be warmer than the rest of the cave complex, which may be part of what's attracting it. When SG-15 started exploring, they must have run straight into it. Or more likely it ran into them, because they would have stopped as soon as they saw the strange darkness."

Carolyn followed, looking over his shoulder again. "I'm still not seeing the darkness you're talking about."

"Right there," Daniel said, shining his flashlight beam. "In an uncertain radius around something with sharp teeth and a bad temper, so I wouldn't get much closer until we've figured out a plan, here."

"Where?" Carolyn said. She pulled out her own flashlight and joined its beam to Daniel's, the light disappearing into a dark fog before reaching the end of the rock chimney.

Daniel stared at her. "Tell me what you're seeing."

"The passageway we're in climbs up sharply and then opens out into some kind of wider space. There's light filtering down from the opening, so I'm guessing that's your sunlit cavern." She moved her flashlight up and down, with no apparent effect as far as Daniel could see. "I can see right around the opening to the cavern, but the angle's wrong to get much idea what's through there. I don't see anything moving."

"No flashlight beam disappearing into a cloud of utter darkness?"

"No," Carolyn said. She looked at him as if he were the one who wasn't making sense.

"Mitchell," Daniel said. He handed his flashlight to Mitchell and sidled out of the way to make room for him.

"I can't see the opening at the other end," Mitchell said. "Because there's a big dark cloud in the way."

Carolyn shook her head. "I am still not seeing your big dark cloud."

"The ATA gene," Daniel said, pieces fitting together in his head. "This device, Merlin's dagger, it's meant to shroud whoever carries it in darkness, but there's also a part of the legend about being able to penetrate darkness."

Mitchell looked at him sideways. "He built a weapon that doesn't work on Ancients?"

"Or on people who have the ATA gene, which I'm going to assume Ambrosius — King Arthur — did. Which unfortunately means this probably isn't going to help us directly against the Ori. For that, we need the opposite, something that works on people with Ancient genes but not on us."

"Let's stick with the positive," Mitchell said. "We've got somebody who can see what we're up against. So let's find out what that is."

Carolyn edged around Daniel and cautiously began ascending the corridor. "It probably won't come out here, right?"

"Umm," Daniel said. "Actually it was hunting in the mouth of the cave last night."

"I did not want to know that."

"What can you see? Because right now all I can see is the back of Jackson's head," Mitchell said in obvious frustration.

Carolyn froze abruptly and held up her hand for silence. She slowly edged forward, disappearing into darkness as she did. It was on the tip of Daniel's tongue to protest, but he could still see her holding up her hand for quiet as her palm, then her fingers, faded into black.

There was a pause that seemed to go on for an eternity, as Daniel strained to hear the sound of her footsteps and her jacket scraping against stone. Then she reappeared, and he let out the breath he'd been holding.

"Okay," she said. "That's the weirdest thing I've seen in a long time. I would say it's a snake — the head and neck look like a snake — but it's got legs, too. Sort of a snake-lizard? I bet the biologists would have a field day."

"Is the body spotted?" Daniel asked.

Mitchell looked at him oddly. "Have we seen one of these before?"

"It's in the mythology. Maybe. Spotted, or not?"

"It's spotted."

"And the feet, do they look like hooves?"

"Kind of. They're definitely clawed, but they're small, weirdly proportioned."

"That's the Questing Beast," Daniel said.

"It's a beast on a quest?" Mitchell asked.

"It's a beast people quested after," Daniel said patiently. "Sir Pellinore and later Sir Palamedes hunted it as part of a charge laid on Sir Pellinore's family. It's supposed to have hounds barking from its belly, but I think we can put that down to a little bit of exaggeration — presumably a creature that people hunt incessantly gets associated with the sound of hounds. It's kind of ironic, though —"

Mitchell broke in. "Tell me that the next words out of your mouth are going to be relevant to our current situation."

"Ah… I was going to say that most Arthurian scholars have speculated that the legends were actually attempts to describe a giraffe."

"That was not a giraffe," Carolyn said. "I have seen giraffes before, and that was not a giraffe. I can't really imagine how you could get 'giraffe' out of that."

"Well, obviously the scholars were wrong, but you can't really blame them for not getting all the way to 'something that King Arthur and his knights saw on another planet.'"

"I wish they'd done something about it while they were here," Carolyn said.

Mitchell nodded. "Weren't they supposed to kill dragons, not leave them around for us?"

"Actually, they may have tried," Carolyn said. "I didn't want to get very close, but it looks like this thing has a dagger — at least, it might be a dagger — stuck between its scales. Like maybe someone attacked it with the dagger —"

"And let go of it, and this thing got away," Daniel finished.

"That would make it thousands of years old," Mitchell said.

"Fifteen hundred years old, give or take a bit," Daniel said. "The Questing Beast was supposed to be long-lived."

Carolyn craned her neck as if trying to get another look at the creature. "It's also supposed to be mythical."

"There's a lot of that going around lately," Mitchell said.

"Myths are ways of explaining things people don't understand," Daniel said. "Sometimes they're memories of things that existed on Earth but don't anymore, or that never existed on Earth but existed somewhere that was visited by people from Earth—like the knights of the Round Table. Merlin turned Ambrosius Aurelianus and his knights loose on the Stargate system, they went out and had adventures on planets like this, and eventually they returned home and told stories about what they'd seen."

"Not having signed a non-disclosure agreement," Carolyn said. "I bet not many people believed them about the Questing Beast, though."

Daniel shrugged. "They might have. Remember, most people in the Middle Ages never travelled very far from their homes. It probably seemed plausible that there might be a beast that looked like that in other parts of the world, even without bringing other planets into it. And it probably wouldn't have seemed much more credible if you had tried to describe a giraffe."

"Later," Mitchell said. "What do we do about this thing?"

Daniel looked at him sideways. "Want to try slaying it?"

"Somebody stabbed it, and that didn't work."

"Those scales look like pretty good armor," Carolyn said. "I'm guessing the point didn't actually penetrate very far. It looks like most of the blade is stuck between the scales."

"So how well do we think bullets are going to work?"

"Zat?" Daniel suggested.

"It would be great if this were that easy," Carolyn said. "I'm willing to try it."

Daniel handed her a zat, and she aimed, her body tensing, and fired. For a moment, nothing seemed to have happened, although Carolyn's eyes went wide. Then the black cloud was shot through with crackling sparks, the energy of the zat crawling across its surface.

"Watch—" Carolyn managed, and then collapsed. Daniel tried to leap backwards, collided with Mitchell, and elbowed him to get him moving faster.

"I'm on your side, Jackson!"

"Just move," Daniel said, but at that moment one of the crawling sparks struck him, and the world went dark.

CHAPTER NINE

SAM woke up somewhere dark, cramped, and vibrating uncomfortably. It took her a moment to realize she was in the trunk of a car, being buffeted from side to side as the car swung through a series of turns. Not still on the highway, then. Her hands were bound behind her, but twisting allowed her to see that there was a trunk release. She was jammed against something soft and moving, which she realized after a moment was another person.

"Vala," she said.

"Still here, yes," Vala said from somewhere in the vicinity of her elbow. "I take it this is not a quaint local custom of your people?"

"I think we've been kidnapped," Sam said. "At least they wanted us alive."

"People who want to take you alive don't usually want to bring you back to their house so that they can have a pleasant tea party," Vala said.

"Don't I know it. There's a lever that should open the trunk, but I don't want to try to jump out of a moving car with my hands tied behind my back."

"I can do something about that," Vala said. "Let me get to your hands."

"They're zip tied."

"That shouldn't be a problem."

Sam twisted to get her arms within Vala's reach. After a few moments she felt the pressure of the zip tie release, and stretched cramped fingers gratefully.

"I'm going to need a knife to get yours off." Something cold was pressed into Sam's hand, which indeed turned out to be a short knife. "What else have you got up your sleeve?"

"A detective never reveals all her secrets."

"I think that's a magician," Sam said. "Okay, got it." The car swayed into another turn, and then slowed. "You ready?"

"As ready as I'll ever be."

She took a deep breath and pulled the trunk release.

The car was slowing to a crawl, and Sam jumped out and rolled as she hit the ground, scrambling up to her feet as soon as she could. They were parked next to a two-story building, maybe a warehouse or an abandoned factory. Two dumpsters stood near the loading dock, and she dove for one of them as cover as the car doors opened.

Vala joined her, and Sam looked around, trying to gauge just how much trouble they were in. She wasn't sure where they were, and couldn't see the main road from the parking lot. A second car was now pulling up beside the one they'd just left, and any moment now they'd be back in a firefight again, only now with the added entertainment of wondering whether it had been long enough since they'd been zatted for them to survive getting zatted again.

Vala pointed up toward the roof of the building, and Sam shrugged assent. Vala hoisted herself up to the top of the dumpster and sprang from there to catch the edge of the roof, pulling herself up with ease and flopping down flat on the roof so she could watch without being seen. Sam could see that there were handholds in the brick that would let her climb the building herself, but not with Vala's speed.

The car doors were opening, and Sam edged around the dumpster, putting her back to it. That would only buy her a few seconds, though. The car trunk was standing open, and it couldn't be that much of a mystery where its occupants had gone. She reached for her sidearm, and was sorry if not surprised to find it gone. If she couldn't think of a way to run, she was going to have to talk her way out of this one.

There was a creaking noise from above her, and then a thunderous crash as something metal and heavy came smashing down into the parking lot. Sam knew her cue, and moved at the same time, leaping for the wall and using the handholds in the brick to scramble up toward the roof. She tried to resist the urge to look over her shoulder too often, afraid of both slowing down and wrenching herself off the wall.

She heaved herself over the edge of the roof to the accompaniment of more rattling gunfire. "What did you drop on those guys?"

"I have no idea," Vala said. "Probably it wasn't an essential life-support system for the people in this building, I hope?"

"Probably part of an exhaust duct system," Sam said. "They'll live." There was the metallic clank of feet on the dumpster below. "And we're about to have company." She looked around, hoping for a good way off the roof. There was a trap door with a heavy padlock that she hoped led down into the warehouse below. "Can you get that lock off?"

"Piece of cake," Vala said. She fished a metal hook out of her pocket and began working.

"I mean really fast."

"I'm sorry, I thought you meant next week. I was trying to work you into my busy schedule." The lock popped open, and Vala snatched it off the door, turned with her arm already drawn back, and threw the padlock over Sam's shoulder, hard. There was a yell and a sound that might have been someone falling off the edge of the roof and hitting the dumpster on the way down.

Sam hauled on the trapdoor and managed to get it open. "Nice aim."

"Thank you."

Sam glanced through the trap door just long enough to see that the floor was a reasonable distance below and then lowered herself through.

"I can't close it behind us," Vala said.

"Come on," Sam said. They'd cross that bridge when they came to it. Vala dropped down through the trap door, and Sam looked around. They were in a cramped storeroom, its walls lined with metal shelves full of dusty boxes and a bare wooden stairway leading down toward a heavy metal door.

Footsteps sounded on the roof, heavy and approaching fast.

"Door," Sam said, jerking her head to motion Vala towards it. Her own lockpicking skills were better than she would ever have liked to explain to her father, who would probably have felt that her Air Force career shouldn't have included quite so much breaking and entering. But she figured Vala was faster, and indeed Vala selected another tool also apparently concealed about her person and twisted it in the door's lock, popping it open immediately.

Sam threw herself through the door as soon as Vala opened it, pulled Vala through after her, and dragged the door closed. "Lock it again from this side."

"Don't they teach locksmithing in Air Force school?"

"More like the school of hard knocks," Sam said. "And I've been to that one, too. I just figure I shouldn't try to teach an expert."

They'd only bought themselves time. They were up against professionals, who'd have no more trouble with the lock than Sam and Vala had. She considered trying to bar the door, but decided that running was the better option.

The main floor of the warehouse was cavernous, shelves extending up to the ceiling and the length of a football field toward distant doors. Pallets lined the shelves, heavy with boxes that appeared to contain kitchen appliances on their way from some distant manufacturer to some even more distant consumer. Vala examined one with every sign of speculative interest until she seemed to decipher its contents and abruptly lose interest.

"Front door?" Sam asked under her breath.

"I'd stake out the front door," Vala said. "If I were them."

"Okay, think like the bad guys," Sam said. "Which exit aren't you covering?"

"I'd cover all of them."

"Assume there aren't that many of you."

"I wouldn't keep someone on the roof where we came in."

"My thoughts exactly," Sam said. They doubled back cautiously. The door they'd locked was now standing open. She slipped through, trying to put each foot down too lightly for it to make a sound. Vala followed her, silent as a ghost, and waited while Sam found a ladder that would get them back up to the roof.

It rankled to leave these guys here rather than taking them down, but they were outnumbered and outgunned, and just getting out of there was probably the better part of valor. Sam climbed the ladder to the roof, and waited while Vala crept to the edge and looked down. She nodded Sam forward, and Sam joined her. There was only one man below, staking out the loading dock next to the parked cars.

He wasn't looking up. Sam glanced at Vala and shrugged, willing to try jumping him herself, but also willing to let Vala take the lead. Vala shrugged in return. Sam held out her hands for "rock, paper, scissors," and then realized that Vala probably had no idea what she was doing.

Vala pointed down, and then pointed to herself. Sam nodded acceptance, and Vala moved swiftly and silently toward the edge of the roof. She swung down and over the edge of the roof, hanging by her hands, and then swung herself out from the roof and let go.

Vala landed squarely on the man guarding the loading dock, and they went down in a tangle of arms. Either she'd knocked the breath out of him or he was too surprised to yell, because he only rolled over trying to keep her out of the range of his weapons. Not the best at hand-to-hand fighting, Sam thought as Vala punched him squarely in the jaw and then snatched his zat from his suddenly lax hand.

Sam climbed down from the roof more carefully, only dropping down when she was a few feet above the ground. Vala was searching the man, and came up with a second zat, which she tossed to Sam.

Sam crouched to check the man for ID, and wasn't surprised when she found none, only a billfold containing cash, which she didn't let Vala pocket. She did come up with a cell phone, and, most importantly, a set of car keys. She brandished the keys and pointed to the car, and both women moved as one, climbing into the car and pulling the doors shut as silently as if trying not to wake up a sleeping neighbor's baby.

The last question was whether these were the keys to the right car. She slid them into the lock, turned it, and was rewarded by the sound of the engine turning over. She put the pedal to the metal, tires squealing, and Vala let her head flop back on her headrest, relief written in every line of her body.

"That was a bit dicey."

"Piece of cake," Sam said.

"What would you have done if they weren't the keys to either of these cars?"

"Remind me to teach you how to hotwire a car," Sam said. "But only if you promise to use the knowledge for good."

"I'm entirely trustworthy," Vala said. "Can we have that cake now?"

"As soon as we get back to the base, the cake is on me."

Daniel woke up in a heap on wet stone, and peeled himself up with an effort, his head ringing. "Somebody zatted us," he said, and then remembered more clearly what had happened. "I think we zatted ourselves."

"Looks like," Mitchell said. "Where's Carolyn?"

Daniel scrambled up abruptly. "She was just here," he said, realizing even as he said it that they'd probably been lying there for a while.

"Dr. Lam!" Mitchell shouted. "Can you hear us?"

Daniel shone his flashlight toward the entrance to the large cavern, and saw no mysterious darkness, only wet rock and the dim filtered sunlight illuminating the cave floor. "It's moved deeper into the cave," he said. Either the beast wasn't as susceptible to zat fire as they were, or the mysterious field of darkness around it had somehow reflected the zat fire back at them without stunning whatever was within the cloud. Either way, it looked like their zats were currently useless as weapons.

"Taking Carolyn with it?"

"Let's find out," Daniel said, and headed up through the passageway out into the large cavern. The sun had sunk below the level of the crack in the ceiling, and the sky visible through the crack was rapidly darkening from blue to purple as night closed in. He swept his flashlight beam across the cave floor. There were deep prints in the silt of the cavern floor, the claw prints that looked almost like hoof prints, but he couldn't see any new human footprints. "It looks like the tracks go this way."

"Toward the room with the Ancient writing in it?" Mitchell said, following Daniel toward the tight crack in the rock that led to the passageway with the inscription. "And through this place where we're going to get stuck, again?"

"Yep." Daniel shone his flashlight through. "At least this time the creature isn't right on the other side."

"That's comforting, I guess."

"Would you prefer I told you it was right on the other side?"

"Let's just get through here," Mitchell said, shrugging off his pack and wedging himself through. Once they were both on the other side of the tight squeeze, Daniel repeated the passphrase. The door slid open again, to reveal the chamber beyond, still lit by the glow from the platforms. In the collapsed corner of the room, the water was rippling.

"If it took her down there..." Mitchell said, his expression growing tight and unhappy.

"No, it couldn't have. There's not enough room — even if it can swim underwater, a big creature dragging something the size of Carolyn couldn't have gone underwater without disturbing the fallen stone. And there's no sign that something was dragged over here. No prints, no blood."

"There's blood here," Mitchell said, shining his flashlight on the floor. He moved the beam to follow the trail, ending up pointing it at the central pillar, the one that might once have held Excalibur.

"Where does the trail go from there?"

"Nowhere."

"That's not possible," Daniel said. "Unless…" He felt around the pillar. "Unless there's some way to open this thing that we haven't figured out."

"Like maybe having the dagger of King Arthur?"

"I hope that's not it. No, that's probably not it, or it would be the other pillar that opens. And I don't think it's having the ATA gene that does it, or else why would the creature bring Carolyn in here in the first place? It couldn't know she had the gene. If it's carried her off somewhere, it has to have a way to open the door on its own."

"I hate this kind of thing," Mitchell burst out. "I hate riddles. I wish for once Merlin, or whoever made this place, had just written down some clear instructions rather than 'hey, want to open the door and save your friend, that's great, but you have to answer a riddle about when the sphinx goes on one foot first.'"

"I don't think there's a riddle about the sphinx going on one foot."

"You get my point, Jackson."

"Yes, I get your point." He was feeling around the platform as he talked, hoping to find some hidden catch or pressure point, some easy way of opening a door or hidden chamber that something large and reptilian could have stumbled onto. "I think Merlin thought of them not just as security measures but as, I don't know, tests of how worthy people were to find out his secrets."

"You think worthiness is about how well you solve crossword puzzles?"

"No, but I'm not Merlin. I didn't build this thing, okay? I'm just down here trying to figure it out so we can maybe get one tiny step closer to finding the Sangraal. And that's not just one crossword puzzle, it's a hundred crossword puzzles with most of the pieces in dead languages and a big hole in the middle where somebody set the paper on fire."

"How about figuring it out so that we can find Carolyn and Collins?"

"Believe me, I'd like to do that, too." Daniel ran his hands through his hair without caring that he was probably streaking it with mud. "Okay. What do we think is through this door, if it is a door?"

"We don't know."

"Think," Daniel urged. "We're guessing that the Questing Beast is carrying its victims off somewhere. In order to…"

"Eat them, presumably," Mitchell said flatly.

"Except that it was eating something when we ran into it. I mean, when you think about it, if you're the only big predator down here, why would you need to carry off your prey to eat it? What's going to argue with you? No, you'd carry off food that was too big for you to eat in one sitting, so that you could store it."

"Are you sure we aren't indulging in wishful thinking here?"

"No," Daniel said, blinking at the question. "No, of course I'm not sure, but we have to go with the theory that means they may still be alive, because dismissing the possibility means dismissing the possibility of rescuing them. And I'm not willing to do that."

"Okay, that's fair," Mitchell said after a moment. "So you think it's dragged them off to some kind of larder."

"Where you'd store food," Daniel said. "Where a beast that's been stabbed with a dagger might have crawled off to seek shelter… or, wait a minute, maybe it's not fifteen hundred years old. At least, maybe it's only technically fifteen hundred years old."

"You know the connections between the things you're saying? Put in the part where you tell me what they are."

"It was wounded," Daniel said. "And this place is clearly

some kind of armory, or armed camp. What if there's a stasis chamber down there? That would make sense if Merlin wanted to make sure that badly wounded knights could be kept alive until he could treat them. For that matter, it would make sense of some of the legends about King Arthur — that he's not dead, he's just somewhere sleeping."

"So there's a stasis chamber. How did the beast get to it?"

"It can't be a password or a puzzle. Unless this thing is a lot more intelligent than we're thinking, it couldn't work out a puzzle, or say a password even if it had heard one."

"Besides, even if you're Merlin, and you're kind of a son of a bitch, you'd think you wouldn't make people solve a riddle if they're standing there bleeding," Mitchell said, and then looked up sharply, his eyes lighting with an idea. "Hey, you don't think…"

"It's worth a try," Daniel said, following the thought. "You want me to…"

"It was my idea," Mitchell said, and pulled out a knife. He drew it quickly across the heel of his hand, wincing as he did, and pressed his hand to the stone.

With a grinding groan, the platform slid out of the way, and Mitchell stepped smartly back to avoid being knocked off his feet. It revealed a stairway descending into the same soft lighting that illuminated the chamber.

"Bingo," Mitchell said.

"It got down there the first time because it was wounded," Daniel said. "And it can open it when it's carrying a victim, because of the blood, and presumably when it comes back out, it's still covered in blood. But after it swims through the water, it can't open the chamber anymore until it's fed again."

"That would be comforting, except that it's probably down there right now."

"Probably so," Daniel agreed, drawing his pistol. "After you."

"I always wanted to slay a dragon when I was a kid," Mitchell said. "You?"

"Not so much. I was more interested in talking to them. I liked the stories where dragons are these wise, ancient creatures who… but I'm aware that what we're dealing with here isn't a dragon. It's not even the mythical Questing Beast, just a really big, nasty lizard."

"Life is full of disappointments, Jackson."

"Don't I know it," Daniel said, and followed Mitchell down the stairs.

Vala flung herself down into a chair at the mess hall table and contemplated the cup of coffee in front of her. It would certainly serve the function of keeping her awake, but she wasn't sure she wanted to be kept awake. Sam was on the phone in the corner, arguing with some kind of vehicle-related authorities about her car.

"Look, I just want it towed to Colorado Springs. Well, I didn't have much choice about abandoning the vehicle. I can't come pick it up right now, I'm at work." Sam rolled her eyes and waved one hand in frustration, and Vala made what she hoped was a sympathetic expression. "All right, fine, I will as soon as I can. Yes, I'm aware of the storage fees. Yes. Thank you. You've been so helpful." Sam hung up the phone with gritted teeth. "There has got to be some way to get someone to go pick up my car. I'm going to go talk to Landry about it."

"Good luck," Vala said, and waved goodbye. That left her with the coffee and one mess hall worker who was reorganizing cups of Jello. The woman didn't appear interested in chatting, and neither did the cup of coffee. The coffee still smelled suspiciously alien, and at the thought, Vala remembered with vivid intensity the taste of the morning tea that Tomin had made her while she was pregnant with Adria. It had been bitter stuff, but she had choked it down with her best smile because she recognized it for a kindness.

She wanted to believe she had appreciated the tea because it was a sign that she had played her hand well, and made him truly believe in her pretended interest. Not that she had taken it as a sign that he would be a safe haven for her and her daughter. Vala knew better than to believe in safe havens. And yet, surely a baby deserved one if anybody did. Tomin would have been a good father, she thought, if he'd ever had the chance to be. Probably a much better father than she would have been a mother.

Let's not pretend, she told herself. If Adria had been a normal baby, Vala would assuredly have left her with Tomin the first chance she got to run. If not when she was a baby, at least not a very little baby, she would surely have found a way to run before Adria was grown. The idea of settling down as a village wife was absurd. Ludicrous.

That must have been what she was thinking of, when she was drinking the tea. That Tomin would have been a good father for her baby when she left her baby behind. The thought made an ache start deep in her chest, an ache that she firmly dismissed as a strained muscle from being zatted and thrown in a car trunk rather than anything as sentimental as heartbreak.

"May I join you?" Teal'c said. Vala looked up and smiled brightly, relieved to have someone's company other than her own. Her inner self was apparently a hideously depressing conversationalist.

"Of course," she said. Teal'c inclined his head in acknowledgment and put down his tray.

"I recommend consuming food in addition to coffee," he said. "Despite what Colonel Carter believes, coffee is not a substitute for meals."

"I expect you're right," Vala said. She retrieved a dish of Jello and a slice of pie from the serving line and returned to the table with them. Teal'c raised an eyebrow at her tray but didn't comment. Both foods were predictably edible and wouldn't remind her of anything but the last few weeks' worth of experiments in consuming mess hall meals. Tau'ri food had proved by turns bland, bizarre, and interesting, but she wasn't in the mood for interesting at the moment.

"I understand your excursion was more eventful than predicted."

"What's a little kidnapping? On the whole we had a lovely time."

"When I was first on Earth, I found it instructive to observe the lives of ordinary Tau'ri," Teal'c said. "Their world is rich, and few of them understand how fortunate they are in their freedom. But at the same time, they are not all wealthy or fortunate. There is much variety in their lives and in their world."

"It's just a little backwater world compared to some," Vala said. "There are all kinds of technology they don't have. But pretty. It is pretty."

The trip outside the mountain, and the briefer excursion the day before, had brought home to her how long it had been since she'd set foot outside, or been in a crowd of people without having to perform "sincere and serious." It was a role like any other, but it was a tiring one, and there was little chance of getting to be anything else anytime soon. The fact that she might actually be sincere and serious when it came to helping the Tau'ri defeat the Ori made the performance, if anything, much more alarming.

"You need not live on base permanently if you remain here," Teal'c said. "It is possible for off-worlders to be granted permission to live in Colorado Springs."

"Then why don't you? Not that I don't adore the decorating scheme here — it's very martial — but there is an entire world out there where people have windows and colors other than gray and slightly less gray."

"I have made the experiment," Teal'c said. "It required deceiving many people about my true origins."

"I've never had a problem with that."

"And interfering in conflicts between the Tau'ri attracted the attention of the Trust."

"I am wonderful at not interfering."

"Then you might do well. I could not honorably stand aside

and watch violence or crimes be perpetrated without rendering assistance."

"Now you're talking like a policeman."

Teal'c inclined his head, looking more flattered than insulted. "It is an honorable profession."

"In a lot of places I've been, policemen exist to help the rich keep what they've stolen or extorted from the poor."

"As the Jaffa did under the Goa'uld," Teal'c said. Vala winced, wondering if she'd gone too far, but he didn't sound angry. "I recognize the problem, but I do not think that the solution is to allow motorists to crash their vehicles into one another with impunity. And I am not certain that liberating the possessions of those in power in order to sell them to other wealthy individuals serves the purpose of improving the lot of the poor."

Vala shifted uncomfortably, feeling that was a little close to the mark. "It depends on who we're defining as the poor."

"Weapons merchants and antiquities smugglers?"

"It sounds so bad when you put it that way."

"Revolution is an honorable goal. Individual criminal acts do little to advance that goal, especially when they are not aimed at the Goa'uld but at individuals who have desirable possessions but little in the way of political power."

"You say that as though those things don't go together."

"Not always in a simple way."

Vala took a long drink of the coffee, trying to ignore its bitterness. "Besides, you can't have a revolution by yourself."

"Indeed you cannot," Teal'c said. "It is important to acquire friends."

"I know all about making friends," Vala said, but it was possible that really what she meant was accomplices or marks or conquests. Trying to count the number of friends she had who didn't fall into any of those categories was so depressing she stopped at once.

"Then you will do well here. I have worked with Colonel Carter and Daniel Jackson for many years. It would be difficult to wish for better friends. And Colonel Mitchell is an honorable man as well."

"A little too honorable, maybe. I'm not sure he's the type to understand how certain… regrettable decisions might have been made in certain people's pasts."

"I do not believe there are no decisions in the past that Colonel Mitchell regrets," Teal'c said. "There are no warriors whose hands are entirely clean of blood. And he must certainly know that my own are not."

The conversation was skirting close to the edge of other parts of Vala's memory that she usually kept firmly shut in a box as unneeded on the voyage. The subject of the Jaffa and their more morally questionable duties was not likely to improve her mood, only remind her of too many unpleasant scenes she'd witnessed from a vantage point that didn't allow her to do a thing about them.

"I do not believe it is necessary to be innocent of all past wrongdoing in order to behave with honor," Teal'c said. "There is always a choice to be made."

"What choice would that be?"

"What we intend to do today," Teal'c said, looking far more serene than Vala suspected she had ever felt.

CHAPTER TEN

CAM made his way cautiously down the stair, listening for any sign of movement from below. He heard nothing, but halfway down the stairs his flashlight beam once again disappeared into darkness.

"I don't hear anything," Daniel said from over his shoulder. "Before we could hear it breathing."

"It's got to be down here, though."

"Along with Carolyn and Collins."

"All right," Cam said, reaching the bottom of the stairs and bracing himself. "Here we go." He reached out with his left hand and touched rough stone. There was nothing to do but take another step forward into the darkness, hoping his foot would touch stone rather than scales or teeth.

He bumped into something knee-high, and recoiled with such force that he collided with Daniel behind him.

"On your side here," Daniel said.

"Not an animal," Cam said. He bent down to feel the edge of what he'd found, and touched straight lines rather than the curving shape of scales. He felt metal under his fingers, and then the stinging buzz of some kind of force field. "Maybe a stasis chamber."

"Which might have Carolyn in it."

"Or a large, angry reptile."

Daniel brushed against him, clearly crouching down to feel the edge of the chamber. "There's a story like this," he said.

"The lady and the tiger. I know. Only in the story, he gets a hint. We don't get a hint."

"I thought you hated puzzles anyway."

"I do," Cam said. "And I'm still not sure how we know if Merlin wants us to find the lady or the tiger. The Ancients haven't exactly been our best friends every time we've tangled with them so far."

"We know that Merlin wanted to defeat the Ori," Daniel said.

"The enemy of our enemy is our friend?"

"It's what we've got. And I think I've found the control panel for this thing."

"You're waiting for me to tell you whether to push buttons, aren't you?"

"Jack hated it when I pushed buttons without asking him first."

"I can see why." Cam took a deep breath and cocked his pistol. "Push the buttons, Jackson. Let's find out if it's the lady or the tiger."

"Here we go," Daniel said. Cam strained to listen, the small sounds of Daniel pushing buttons seeming to echo through the room. There was a crackle as the force field dissolved under his fingers, and he reached down and felt something warm, and then something hard and distinctly scaly, rising as if a serpentine head was lifting under his hand.

"Please don't move," Carolyn's voice said out of the darkness.

Cam froze. "It's in there with you, isn't it?"

"Oh, yes. It's looking at me right now."

"Do you want me to shoot it?"

"Not yet. I've got my hand on the dagger."

"Think 'off,'" Daniel urged.

"I'm trying, it's just a little hard to concentrate under the circumstances."

"You can do it."

The darkness vanished, not like a cloud dispersing, but like turning on a light switch in a dark room. Carolyn was crouching at one end of a long, deep stasis chamber, big enough to lay three men in side by side. The beast was crouched at the other end, its oddly short legs folded under it, its long snakelike neck reared back, eyes fixed hungrily on Carolyn. Its head swayed to follow her movement as she wrapped her hand tighter around the dagger. Cam couldn't help noting that it had razor-sharp teeth in a powerful jaw.

"Try a warning shot," she said.

"And if that doesn't work?"

"Then definitely shoot it, please shoot it," Carolyn said fervently. "But let's try this first." Her whole body was taut with the effort not to move.

"Daniel, warning shot," Cam said. Daniel let the muzzle of his pistol drift down toward the floor, keeping the motion slow enough that Cam hoped it wouldn't attract attention. He raised his own weapon, and the beast swung its head around to track the motion with amber reptilian eyes.

"Here we go," Daniel said, and fired.

The beast exploded into movement, and Cam jerked around to track it; Daniel was already doing the same as it boiled over the edge of the stasis chamber and charged across the floor toward the stairs. It roared as it went, a booming snarl that reminded Cam a little of an alligator, and as the sound echoed off the stone, he thought for a moment that it did actually sound like the baying of hounds. Then all he could hear was the sound of its pounding feet and slithering scales as it retreated into the room above.

"Of course, now it's between us and our way out," Daniel said.

"I'm hoping it'll keep running all the way to the water," Cam said. "Besides, now we should be able to zat it without knocking ourselves out." He turned to Carolyn. "You okay?"

"I'm okay," Carolyn said, but her mouth was tight. "I think it dragged me down here by the leg. We'll see how walking goes. But I'm all right."

"All right in that special SGC sense," Daniel said. He was roaming the length of the room, and crouched by another large stasis chamber set into the floor. "Here's Collins." He deactivated the second stasis chamber, and bent to check the man lying in it. "He's still alive, but he's unconscious."

"Let me see," Carolyn said, and began levering herself out of the stasis chamber. Cam helped her out, letting her lean on his arm. She handed him the dagger as if unsure why she still had it in her hand, and he handed it to Daniel in turn as she hobbled over to the other stasis chamber. "Oh, not good," she said. "It looks like it shook him by the neck. He's got a pretty nasty head injury, and beyond that, I do not want to move him until we get a stretcher down here."

"That could take a while," Daniel said.

"So turn the stasis field back on," Cam said. "That should keep him in one piece until we can get a medical team up here. But we are not moving him without a stretcher. You got it?"

Daniel nodded, and activated the field again. It sparkled on, and then dissipated again, at the same time that the lights in the room dimmed to darkness.

"Or maybe not," Carolyn said.

Cam looked around. "You think we blew a fuse?"

"We didn't do anything the creature hasn't already been doing," Daniel said. The lights brightened again, and both stasis chambers activated, Collins' still face blurring as if seen through ice over deep water. "I'm guessing there are power fluctuations that turn the field on and off at intervals," Daniel went on. "The creature must have learned it was a safe place to bring its prey. And if occasionally it got caught in the field itself, it would always be able to get out when the field deactivated again."

"Mystery solved," Cam said.

"If only they were all that easy."

"You call this easy?" Carolyn said, looking up at them and shaking her head. "We've still got to get down the cliff."

"Jackson, go back and get us a medical team with some rescue equipment," Cam said. "Take the dagger with you, because I know it's going to make you crazy worrying if you're going to somehow lose it again."

Daniel was still looking around, feeling at the walls as if hoping that one of them would open for him. They stayed stubbornly made of stone. Cam suspected that he was a little disappointed not to find King Arthur sleeping in a stasis chamber, not that Cam thought King Arthur could really solve their problems at the moment. He'd rather have a brilliant physicist with intimate knowledge of the Ori's vulnerabilities, if he got to choose. "I'm just wondering if Excalibur might be down here somewhere too."

"What do we think that does?"

"I don't know," Daniel said. "It could be a tremendously powerful weapon that could help us against the Ori. It could just be a sword."

"We don't really need a sword, Jackson."

"It would make me feel more confident that we were getting somewhere," Daniel said. "We've been going around in circles now for so long."

"We're getting somewhere," Cam said. "Like Vala said, now we know one more place where the Sangraal isn't."

"There are a literally infinite number of places where the Sangraal isn't."

"Even so," Cam said. "Go on, get moving back to the gate. And how about you bring me back a cup of coffee, too?"

Daniel's mouth twitched sideways. "You want me to order a pizza, maybe a few beers?"

"That sounds nice," Carolyn said.

"I'm not sure General Landry would agree," Daniel said.

"No one expected Sherlock Holmes to do his best work on an empty stomach," Cam said.

"I have an MRE in my pack," Daniel said, and offered it to Cam.

"That's cruel, Jackson. Cruel."

"I'll see what I can do," Daniel said, but Cam figured the pizza would probably have to wait.

It took the better part of an hour for Daniel to make it back to the gate, although he took some comfort from the fact that the beast was nowhere in sight when he ascended, and had hopefully retreated through the watery exit to wherever it prowled when it wasn't basking in the warmth of the Ancient devices. The climb down the rocks was harrowing enough with no one to spot for him. If he wound up pinned between boulders or under a rock fall, it would be a long wait before anyone came looking for him.

He couldn't blame Mitchell for listening to Carolyn, though. And he suspected there was more to his caution than just respect for her professional opinion; he'd been pretty badly injured himself, and it couldn't have helped that whoever rescued him had dragged him out of his shattered 302 cockpit with their main goal being keeping him from freezing to death. He'd spent nearly as much time in the hospital as Daniel had spent dead.

He had to respect a guy who could come back from that to going full steam ahead in command of a gate team, and he had to admit that Mitchell was a good leader. It wasn't Mitchell's fault that Daniel had never been entirely comfortable with the idea of being led. And it certainly wasn't Mitchell's fault that he wasn't Jack. Daniel was aware on some level that he ought to make more of an effort to make friends, given that they were going to spend most of their waking hours together for the foreseeable future.

Making friends with Jack had never required an effort; keeping from killing him on occasion had. Mitchell didn't rub him the wrong way like that, at least. It was just harder to make friends when they didn't instantly click the same way, even if it meant being spared the intensity of the arguments that had marked his disagreements with Jack. Hard to let someone else into the circle of friends who had become as close as family.

And outside that circle, he was aware that he had increasingly few friends. It was hard to talk to anyone in his field when all he could say was "I'm working on a military contract… no, I can't tell you anything about it." Even talking about his research interests couldn't go on very long before it got into dangerous territory.

It was possible, when he came right down to it, that most of his friends had always better been described as colleagues. He'd been part of the camaraderie of other grad students, bonding over their dissertations and the hard labor of digs, but there had been few people he'd gotten close to.

Sarah Gardner had been one of them, and he found his mind drifting back to her as he dialed the gate. She'd apparently been willing to talk to Mitchell, even if she hadn't been enthusiastic. Maybe it was worth making an effort to look her up again. If they didn't talk about work… but then, they had always talked about work. He wasn't sure what was left between them if they didn't have the bond of that shared interest to unite them.

"Problems?" Landry asked when he finally stepped through the Stargate and out into the gate room.

I'm not sure I actually have a life outside the SGC anymore, he was tempted to say, but he suspected that Landry didn't believe in having one himself. "We ran into some reptile problems," he said. "We're going to need a medical team with a backboard to evacuate Collins. Dr. Lam hurt her leg, but she's walking around on it, so I don't think it's too bad. And we did find King Arthur's dagger." Daniel brandished the dagger. "At least, that's what I think it is. I want to get Sam to take a thorough look at it, and also compare it to some of the references in Merlin's library."

"I'll tell Colonel Carter you found the prize at the bottom of the cereal box for her."

"Are she and Vala back from Denver?"

"They're back," Landry said. "They showed up in a car belonging to some nice men who tried to kidnap them. Apparently somebody took exception to their talking to Dr. Niles and tailed them on their way out of town. Colonel Carter had to leave her own car behind. She made it extremely clear she's not happy about that."

"Are they all right?"

"I sent them down to the infirmary to get checked out. I assume that if there'd been grievous bodily harm involved, Colonel

Carter wouldn't have stuck to complaining about her car."

"I don't know, Sam might. What did they find out?"

"Dr. Niles claims she wasn't involved with either of them. Says they were both pressing their suit, she said no, Oliver wouldn't hear no for an answer. But she didn't kill them and doesn't know who did. Which gets us exactly nowhere."

"Except that somebody thinks she knows something, or they wouldn't have tailed Sam and Vala after they saw them talking to her," Daniel said. "There must be something we're missing."

"Figure it out," Landry said. "We're running short on time."

It took another two hours to get Mitchell and Carolyn back through the gate along with Collins, who was awake and complaining that he didn't want to be carried, which suggested less of a bleak prognosis than Daniel had been afraid of.

"You're not going anywhere but a nice infirmary bed," Mitchell said. "But Jackson promised to order you a pizza."

"That's not exactly what I said," Daniel said, but he decided the cause was lost. "Sure, if you want it for breakfast. I'll have to bring it down through security."

"He'll be here," Carolyn said.

"Nothing wrong with pizza for breakfast," Collins said.

"Just don't forget to tip," Daniel said. Collins gave him a shaky thumbs-up, and Mitchell gave Daniel a sideways nod of approval. They might come to understand each other yet, he thought, and just hoped they'd all live that long.

"So what have you got?" Sam asked, finding Daniel in his office cleaning mud off an ornamented blade. "I hear you found Arthur's dagger."

"And I hear you got kidnapped."

"Just a regular day at work," Sam said. "We got a license plate number, and Cam is going to run it and see what pops up. And my car is a mess." She leaned over Daniel's shoulder to look at the dagger. "Tell me about this thing. I'd like to think something went right today."

"It requires the ATA gene to activate, and it doesn't work on people who have the ATA gene," Daniel said. "Once it's activated, it works pretty much constantly."

"Then where's the power source? Most of the Ancient devices we've tested that stay on once they're activated create a pretty serious power drain. This thing has been working for, what, over a thousand years?"

"You tell me," Daniel said. He slid it across the table to her, and Sam played with it in fascination. It felt like a perfectly normal dagger, if heavier than she thought a kitchen knife the same size would have been.

"If it really absorbed light, that would explain the power source," Sam said. "And would make it a pretty useful solar-powered generator."

"I'm sensing a 'but' coming."

"But if having the ATA gene protects you against its effects, then it's acting on people's brains, maybe affecting the optic nerve, not actually absorbing light," Sam said. "Which makes the physics less questionable, but also makes it less likely that this is going to revolutionize power generation for us. If I had to make a guess, I'd say that it's been drawing its power from the stasis chamber where the beast was taking its prey."

"It's still an important piece of history," Daniel said, which made Sam hesitate to ask the next question that was on the tip of her tongue. He gave her a wry look that made it clear he saw through her. "You want to take it apart, don't you?"

"I think it would be useful to figure out how it works," she said. "I'm not sure there's a lot of strategic potential here, but it's probably a good idea to try to understand the effect in case someone figures out how to use it against us."

"Like the Ori."

"Yeah. I have to say, I miss the days when we could figure that Ancient technology was mostly intended to help us."

"You mean like the Dakara superweapon?"

"Well, that was originally intended to be helpful. Maybe the

Ancients' definition of 'helpful' is a little questionable, but at least they weren't actively trying to enslave humanity."

"I think Merlin intended the weapons he made for Arthur to be helpful. It's just a question of whether the Ori have figured out the same tricks." Daniel shook his head. "Besides, I'm not sure it's ever been exactly an unmixed blessing to have the Ancients trying to help us. They have their own agenda. They're not as heavy-handed about pursuing it as the Goa'uld or the Ori, but ultimately they're doing what they think is best for the universe, which doesn't always line up very neatly with what we think is best for us."

"We've learned a lot from them. And from the Asgard."

"I know. There's just always a price."

"But given that we've already found this particular piece of Ancient technology, and that it exists whether we like it or not—"

"You should check it out. Sure. I'm just starting to wonder exactly how much of a devil's bargain the Sangraal is going to be when we actually find it."

"Maybe it'll be easy to use and do exactly what it says on the label without any unfortunate side effects," Sam said. "That would be different."

"I'm just not holding my breath," Daniel said.

Back in her lab, Sam examined the dagger. It looked to her like the hilt might come apart, given pressure in the right places. She secured the dagger in a vise and used a pair of small screwdrivers to poke at the suspicious depressions in the dagger's ornamentation. They gave immediately, and the pommel of the dagger slid out, revealing a control crystal encased within a larger translucent casing, inset with metallic contact points for the control crystal.

"Okay," Sam said, removing the casing and teasing out the control crystal. "Let's see what makes you tick."

Half an hour with the control crystal made it clear that, as usual, she only had the most rudimentary idea of what made it tick. She'd identified some of the programming on the crystal, but she guessed that the effect the dagger had on the minds of people without the ATA gene was caused by the interaction between the control crystal and the larger crystalline housing.

The most interesting thing she'd figured out so far was that the control crystal itself required the ATA gene to activate, but that there didn't seem to be any such limitation built into the crystal structure of the dagger. That meant it might be possible to program one of their own control crystals to activate the dagger without requiring the gene.

She set both crystals into one of their jury-rigged crystal programming devices, a combination of Ancient and Asgard technology that she still couldn't believe worked. It began reading out its best interpretation of the programming on the Ancient crystal. Sam scrolled through line after line of code, cutting out the parts that referenced requiring the ATA gene for activation, and then set the machine to duplicating the crystal.

Next up was finding out who had kidnapped her and figuring out what to do about them. She hesitated, wanting to wait for her duplicate crystal to be finished so that she could test it, and then shook her head. Science was going to have to wait.

"These guys are with the Trust," Cam said, shutting the door to Landry's office firmly behind him. "We ran the plates on the car, and they came up as involved in a Trust operation that the NID was tracking several months ago. And that cell phone has encryption on it that sure didn't come standard with someone's one-year contract."

Landry let out a puff of breath. "I'm not entirely surprised to hear that."

Cam stared at him. "With all due respect, can I ask why you're not surprised? Because up until this point, we've all been going on the assumption that Oliver was killed for personal reasons. Nobody's suggested that he was involved in any research that the Trust might be interested in. He was putting together pieces of ceramic pots."

"That's what he's been doing for us lately," Landry said. "Sit down, Colonel Mitchell."

Cam didn't particularly feel like sitting down for a friendly chat at the moment, but it clearly wasn't a request, so he settled into the visitor's chair.

"Vincent Oliver was an agent for the NID for four years," Landry said. "This was back before the SGC ever existed. Oliver was working on digs in the Middle East, and the NID was using him to keep tabs on some situations there. I don't know the details, and I couldn't tell you about them even if I did. Three years ago, Oliver got back in contact with an operative of the NID. Apparently he was looking for more work like the operations they'd used him for before. As you can imagine, poking around dig sites wasn't their priority anymore. They suggested that his skills might be more useful to the SGC."

"And we took him onboard knowing he'd been an NID operative?"

"I understand there was some debate about it. General Hammond felt that since Oliver's ties to the NID predated the Stargate program, and he'd never been involved in more than some routine surveillance work, it was safe enough to bring him onboard. O'Neill was less convinced, but he wasn't the one calling the shots at that point. We've kept an eye on him ever since, and nothing's come up as a red flag."

"I think this is a pretty big red flag."

"You don't have to tell me that, Colonel."

"No, sir," Cam said, knowing he therefore probably shouldn't have said it. It was just hard to control his temper in the face of finding out that Landry was sitting on information that had to be crucial to the case. "I'm still not sure why you didn't tell me about this when you assigned me to investigate Oliver's death. It's not too classified for me to know about, or you wouldn't be telling me now."

"And you don't like being kept in the dark. I didn't expect you would," Landry said. "You're a smart man, Colonel Mitchell. You tell me, why did I wait for you to turn up a connection between Oliver and the Trust on your own, rather than telling you that I knew you'd probably find one?"

Cam thought about it. "You need this clean," he said. "You're afraid if you gave us the idea, we'd seize on the first sketchy evidence we found that supported your suspicions rather than considering all the possibilities."

"More than that," Landry said. "Oliver's contacts at the NID are some pretty well-connected people. If we're going to accuse the man they specifically recommended we hire of being a spy for the Trust, we'd better have an absolutely ironclad case."

"Because in effect we're going to be accusing them of planting a spy on us."

Landry nodded. "Congratulations, Colonel. You might learn to play politics yet."

"This still feels pretty unfair to the team," Cam said. "Not knowing what they were walking into almost got Sam and Vala killed."

"It got them captured for about ten minutes, and we got a license plate and cell phone out of it, which I'm sure the NID will be grateful for, when and if we decide to hand it over to them. But you're right, handling it this way meant one of you was going to walk into something you weren't going to like. And after I finish with you, the next thing I get to do is apologize to Colonel Carter and Vala for blindsiding them, which will be all kinds of fun, I'm sure."

There wasn't much Cam could say in response to that except, "Yes, sir."

"Besides all that, if we're accusing Oliver of being a spy, that needs to come from someone who isn't personally connected to the case. The last thing we want is for it to be brushed off as an attempt to blame anybody but one of our own." It sounded like an offhand remark, but it rang alarm bells in Cam's head. He'd been pretty sure until this moment that the idea that Carolyn had anything to do with the murder had already been put firmly off the table.

"Why would someone think there's a personal connection, sir?" Cam asked quietly.

Landry scowled at him. "Think you're so smart, don't you, Colonel?"

"You told me I was a minute ago, sir."

"Don't remind me." Landry hesitated, the pause drawing out uncomfortably long. "Has Dr. Lam told you about her last phone call with Vincent Oliver?"

"She hasn't mentioned a particular phone call."

"This one was memorable," Landry said. "Two days before Oliver died, I went down to ask Dr. Lam a question and overheard her saying some pretty harsh things about his character and personal habits. She ended up by saying that she was, quote, 'going to kill him,' end quote."

"We all say things we don't mean in the heat of the moment," Cam said after a momentary pause.

"I know that," Landry said sharply. "I don't really believe that she took the first opportunity to poison him with a rare toxin found only on an alien planet. But if anyone else overheard her talking to Oliver like that, it's going to put her back under suspicion in a situation where it's very probable that her boyfriend was an agent for the Trust. Now that's going to look like one of two things. Either she was in it with him, or she found out about it and got so mad that..." Landry tapped his fingers expressively on his coffee cup.

"You can't believe Carolyn did either of those things."

"I don't," Landry said firmly. "What I believe is that you'd better get to the bottom of this, and fast. Understood?"

"Yes, sir," Cam said.

Cam found Carolyn in the infirmary, checking Collins' vital signs. Her own leg was wrapped in bandages, but she looked to be putting weight on it easily enough. "We need to talk," he said.

"Sure. Just let me finish this."

"Now would be good," Cam said.

Carolyn raised her eyebrows. "Okay. Tammy, can you finish this up?" A nurse came in and took over, with only a sideways look at Cam to show that she was curious about why he was dragging Carolyn away.

Carolyn led him into her office and closed the door. "I take it you've found out something about Oliver."

"Yep. I've found out that you argued with him on the phone just a couple of days ago, and you didn't tell me about it. Apparently you told him you were going to kill him. Does this ring any bells?"

Carolyn winced. "I might have said something like that."

"You told me that breaking it off was a mutual decision. Do you want to reconsider that?"

Her eyes slid away from him. "Okay, you know when I said that we weren't clicking?"

He nodded tightly.

"We *really* weren't clicking. Vincent was getting… I hesitate to say paranoid, because certainly it's not that I think there was anything clinically wrong with him, but he was getting more and more suspicious."

"Suspicious how? Like he thought you were cheating on him?"

"No, nothing like that. We weren't even that serious. No, it was over work. We had some overlapping interests — he was making a study of toxins found on various pottery and weapons that we'd collected — but when I expressed any interest in his work, he got suspicious. He'd talk to me for maybe five minutes about his work, and then turn around and demand to know why I was asking so many questions. It was incredibly off-putting."

"But that was weeks ago."

"It was. We hadn't really been interacting since I broke it off—"

"I thought Oliver broke it off."

"It really was mutual. We had a fight, and neither of us would apologize, and that was the end of it. We didn't talk until he sent the weapon down to the infirmary for us to analyze. I didn't even think about it; I'd been working with him on analyzing other toxins he'd found, so I did the analysis on this piece as well. He called me as soon as he got the report back and saw my name was on it. He claimed I was prying into his business, said that he knew what I was up to and he was going to report me to the proper authorities... just ridiculous stuff. I lost my temper and told him that I'd kill him if he ever treated me that unprofessionally again. I swear that's all there was to it. It was just one of those things you say when you get mad."

"Oliver was working for the Trust," Cam said.

"You can't be serious." Cam just let that statement lie there, not feeling that he really needed to point out it wasn't the moment for jokes. "Oh, my God. Was that why he was so suspicious? He thought I was going to find out whatever he was up to? What was he up to?"

"We don't know," Cam said. "We might be a lot closer to figuring it out if you'd told me the truth in the first place." He held her gaze, angrier than he had expected to be. "What happened to being on the same side?"

"I am on your side," Carolyn said. "And I believe you're on my side, but... look, I knew I'd behaved unprofessionally about this. I shouldn't have lost my temper, especially not when I was on the phone at the SGC. For that matter, I shouldn't have dated someone I worked with in the first place."

"There's no rule against you dating a civilian."

"No, but look at the mess it got me into. It doesn't have to be against regulations for it to be a bad idea. I didn't figure I'd get a lot of sympathy from anybody for that."

"I'm having trouble feeling a lot of sympathy for you right now, that's for sure," Cam said.

"I really am sorry. And I swear I have told you everything I know."

"You'd better have," Cam said. "Because Landry's trying real hard to believe you didn't do this, and I don't want him to change his mind."

CHAPTER ELEVEN

DANIEL woke up to sunlight through the window, and struggled with his usual moment's disorientation as he tried to figure out what planet he was on today. Earth, he decided after a moment, and reached for his glasses. They resolved a sunlit blur into his familiar bedroom, the sheets rumpled and the book he had been reading the night before now tumbled to the floor.

He dressed and made coffee on autopilot, still not really awake, and switched on the news to make sure that he hadn't missed any important world events while on another world entirely. The coffee did the job of making it seem possible to face another day, and he concluded that he hadn't missed a war, major natural disaster, or the discovery of alien life. He gathered up books that might prove useful, ransacking his shelves for anything having to do with Welsh versions of Arthurian legend, and balanced the books under one arm as he headed out the door and down to his car.

One of his neighbors, a well-dressed elderly woman who reminded him a little of Catherine, was coming back from walking her dog. He exchanged smiles and nods as he passed her on the stairs. It was a small reminder that he did still live in the real world, although his relationships with his neighbors were necessarily kept on the level of mild small talk; he couldn't even answer "so what do you do for a living?" with much honesty, let alone tell them how his day at work had been.

He headed down to get his car, anticipating that the drive to the base would finish the process of shifting gears from puttering around his apartment to being perpetually ready for mortal danger. After ten years, he still missed living in a city with public transportation — one of the other reasons he was still sorry he'd missed the chance to go to Atlantis was that it had been appealing to live where he worked without that meaning living in an underground bunker — but at least he'd managed to find an apartment this time that had a parking garage so that he didn't have to spend winter mornings scraping snow off his car.

The garage was quiet, most of his neighbors either off earlier to deliver children to school or lingering over their own coffee, although one car was pulling out of its parking space as he entered, a visitor's car rather than one he recognized. Someone in the building had a more eventful social life than he'd managed of late. Daniel made a beeline for his own car, steadying the books under his arm as a volume on Welsh poetry attempted to make its escape.

The sound of squealing tires brought his head up in time to see a black SUV barreling straight toward him. He leaped out of the way, but the car still clipped him. He tumbled over the hood, books flying, and hit the ground hard, rolling and letting his momentum carry him into the lee of a parked car, where he crouched, trying to get his breath back and his feet firmly under him.

The SUV slammed on the brakes, and he could hear its doors opening. Zat fire spat toward him, and he hauled himself up and over the cement wall that separated the ascending and descending ramps in the garage, throwing himself to the ground on the other side and rolling to get between cars. Bruised limbs protested, but all of them obeyed him, so he assumed nothing was broken. He'd stick with that as a working theory for the moment, anyway.

He heard doors slam and the SUV's tires squealing again as it pulled around the end of the parking garage and sped towards him again. He was close enough to the parking garage's stairwell that it seemed worth sprinting for it. He reached the stairwell door, threw himself through it, and slammed the heavy metal door behind him as he heard the SUV screeching to a halt outside.

Down had more promise than up, as he liked the idea of

being out on the street better than the idea of being penned on the top floor of the parking garage. He pelted down the stairs and grabbed for the handle of the street door as zat fire crackled against the cement walls behind him. Out the door, and there was a city street between him and the shelter of the coffee shop across the street.

Daniel dove out into traffic, nearly getting run over once again by a car that honked and swerved to avoid him. He held his breath, expecting at any moment to feel the numbing sting of zat fire, and slammed through the coffee shop door, swinging around half-expecting to see his pursuers at his heels.

"Dr. Jackson!" the girl behind the counter exclaimed. "In a hurry this morning?"

Across the street, he could see the stairwell door closing, as if someone had looked out and then retreated back into the building. To get their car? If they'd seen where he'd gone, he would have expected them to cross the street after him, unless they thought it would be easier to pile his unconscious body into their SUV than to haul him out on foot.

"Need to make a phone call," he said, and put his back to the corner to do it, keeping his eyes on the window. Sam's cell phone rang and sent him directly to voice mail, a sign that she was already on base. So did Mitchell's, and Daniel swore under his breath. That put them both a good half hour away, or maybe more given the time it would take them to get out through security during the morning rush.

A black SUV cruised down the street, and Daniel tensed, although he couldn't have sworn it was the same one. He regarded the parking garage through the window. The idea of crossing the street and trying to reach his car was still unappealing.

Carolyn didn't pick up either, although it was early for her to be getting into work. He wondered if she'd left the base at all; between her injured leg and the cloud of lingering suspicion over her, she might have decided it was easier to sleep in one of the guest rooms for the night. There wasn't any point in trying Teal'c. He needed someone who wasn't on base yet.

Daniel considered other possible late-rising saviors, and dialed Bill Lee. His phone rang long enough before he picked up that Daniel was on the verge of hanging up.

"Dr. Jackson? Don't tell me there was a meeting this morning."

"Somebody just tried to kill me," Daniel said. "I'm in the coffee shop across from my apartment building. I need you to come get me, fast."

"Sure, yeah, I've just got to get dressed," Bill said.

"Do it fast. These guys are friends of ours, and they mean business."

"I get it," Bill said. "You want me to call the base?"

"They can't get here fast enough. You're, what, half a mile away? Stay on the phone, I'll let you know if anything changes."

The girl behind the counter was looking at him wide-eyed. "Dr. Jackson? Do you want me to call the police?"

He muted his phone for a moment. "No, it's fine."

"Seriously?"

He was pretty sure that any danger she was in would only increase if she got any more deeply involved in his morning. The Trust were interested in him, not in the coffee shop where he usually stopped for breakfast. "Seriously."

"Okay. Do you want a danish?"

"Not today, thanks."

"On the house."

"What's going on?" Bill asked in alarm. Daniel heard a thump, possibly the sound of Bill tripping and running into the side of a car because he was trying to run while still pulling on some article of clothing, and then the sound of a car door closing.

"It's fine," he said. "I'm just keeping an eye out."

"Who are we talking about here? Is this the Trust?"

"Seems pretty likely." The black SUV came by again. He was pretty sure now that it was circling the block, trying to figure out where he'd gone. He stayed clear of the windows, his back to the wall, even though he was aware how crazy that made him look.

The girl put the danish down on the table in front of him, wrapped in wax paper, and he nodded his thanks to her. She backed away, still looking as if she felt she ought to call the police, but was at least momentarily distracted by another customer coming in with the words "tall half-caff latte" on her lips the moment she stepped through the door.

"This is a bad thing," Bill said.

"Just tell me you're on your way."

"I'm on my way. I don't have a gun, though."

"I do. But this is a crowded city street." He glanced at the girl, who had started pulling a shot of espresso. "I don't want a firefight."

"You know, I don't think this happens to people who work in other places," Bill said.

"Just tell me—"

"I'm on my way. I mean, even if you're a policeman, people don't usually shoot at you when you're off duty, do they?"

"I don't know," Daniel said. "Maybe they do, I don't know." A black SUV pulled up to the curb outside, and he hit the ground, ducking to one side of the windowsill and reaching for his pistol. "They're right outside. If you hear gunfire, hang up and call the police."

"I'm right outside. The coffee shop across from your apartment building, right?"

Daniel risked a glance around the window frame and saw Bill behind the wheel of the SUV, peering into the shop with a worried expression. He relaxed, letting his head fall back against the wall in momentary relief.

"You didn't tell me you drove a black SUV," he said, straightening up and trying to look like he hadn't been about to reach for his gun. He picked up the danish, which seemed to reassure the girl behind the counter that he wasn't about to engage in violent combat. She gave him a nervous smile, nodded thanks.

"You didn't ask."

Daniel moved to the door and shouldered it open, slipping out and into the passenger side door of Bill's car in one motion. "Go, go, go," he said.

"I'm going, I'm going!" Bill pulled out into traffic, and Daniel winced as he swerved in his lane, nearly side-swiping oncoming traffic.

"Wrecking the car won't help."

"I'm just not in an awful hurry to get captured by guys with guns again. I don't know about you."

"That wasn't my most fun day, either," Daniel said, although he thought he'd come out of their South American adventure a lot less shaken up than Bill. He was used to it, though; being kidnapped, shot at, tortured, and threatened with death had become a humdrum part of his work day. It was surprising to realize how much he resented it intruding into his off-duty hours. It was the same feeling of violation he'd had when he'd realized that Osiris had been not just in his dreams but in his house.

"But then again I guess this happens to detectives all the time, right?"

"I think depends on the detective," Daniel said. He usually preferred cozy mysteries to the kind that involved car chases and shootouts. Generally no one tried to kill Hercule Poirot or Miss Marple; they remained concerned but impartial observers working out an intellectual puzzle, rather than fighting for their lives. Sherlock Holmes faced more threats to life and limb, but at least they didn't usually involve criminals invading Baker Street. Daniel frowned out the window, watching shops and restaurants that he had begun to feel a tentative attachment to roll by. "I'm going to have to move again," he said.

"Yeah, but we'll probably catch these guys, though, right?"

"I still won't feel good about the Trust knowing where I live."

"At least they're not trying to figure out where I live," Bill said, and then glanced at Daniel sideways. "Probably, right?"

"You're not mixed up in investigating Gideon Oliver's death," Daniel said.

"Because I just moved into a new place with a T1 line," Bill went on, wincing. "It's hard to find someplace with really good networking capability—"

"You're probably fine," Daniel said. He watched the used bookstore where he'd found the volume of Chandler's Phoenician grammar that he'd been missing for years recede in the rearview mirror. "But I'm starting to really dislike these guys."

"Well, they're also trying to take over Earth so we can all be slaves to the Goa'uld," Bill said. "For me, that kind of does it right there. I'm against that."

"That too," Daniel said. He started to say that he didn't like it being personal, but that wasn't it; it was always personal for him, and had been personal ever since the day the Goa'uld took Sha're away from him. He just liked to pretend sometimes that there was a part of his life where that didn't matter, and where he was just a researcher with a contract military job who puttered around his apartment reading and drank coffee and didn't worry about aliens taking over the world, the same way that Jack had always used his weekends to watch football and overcook steaks on the grill.

And it was easier to believe those things when people didn't show up at his apartment when he was off work and try to run him over with their cars. He shook his head and took a bite of his danish to fend off further conversation.

"You don't suppose that could be poisoned?" Bill said.

Daniel stopped chewing and examined the pastry. It looked perfectly normal for a cherry danish, with the only inherent danger being the chance that whatever dye made the cherries fire-engine red probably caused cancer in rats. "Why would I think it might be?" He chewed and swallowed, feeling it was a risk he could take.

"Well. Oliver was poisoned, someone's trying to kill you...

no, you're right. They probably wouldn't poison all the danishes in the shop where you get your breakfast just to get to you. That's getting paranoid."

"Very," Daniel said, but it was hard to get much pleasure out of his breakfast even so.

Cam summed up his conversations with Landry and Carolyn over breakfast in the mess hall. Sam and Teal'c listened with interest, and Vala with as much interest as she seemed to be able to manage on her first cup of coffee. He was getting the impression that she wasn't really a morning person. Daniel hadn't shown up for work yet, and Cam was trying hard to believe that he was following a lead rather than either late or down the rabbit hole of some unrelated line of interesting research.

"So that's where we are," he finished. "And we've got about twenty-four hours to wrap this up before we have to come clean to the NID and accuse them of planting a spy on us in the process, which is going to be the world's biggest distraction from everything else we have to do."

"Terrific," Sam said, pouring herself another cup of coffee. "Where's Daniel?"

"Late," Cam said shortly. "And, yeah, this is a mess. I'd say that we need to check out Oliver's involvement with the NID, except that we can't go through Landry, and we can't let the NID know what's going on or we might as well hand this all over to them right now." He hesitated, but decided that if he asked the team for their opinions when he wanted them, it might help his chances of shutting them down when he had heard all the opinions he needed. "Any ideas for where we go from there?"

"I might have one," Sam said. "Malcolm Barrett. We've worked together a number of times, and before this business with Ba'al, I would have said I trusted him without a doubt. He's sensible and helpful, and he's done a lot to uncover the corruption that was going on in the NID."

"I think the fact that he was recently brainwashed by Ba'al and helped him escape with our list of gate addresses does change things," Cam pointed out.

"Well, yes," Sam admitted. "But I've been keeping in touch, and apparently the NID is confident that he's almost ready to go back on duty."

"Almost ready isn't ready."

"They're briefing him on his next mission. They wouldn't be giving him access to classified information if they weren't absolutely confident that he's back to his old self."

"It hasn't been that long," Cam said. "At all."

"Come on, we've all been in that place," Sam said. "Is there anyone sitting around this table who hasn't been brainwashed or possessed or mind-controlled into doing things that you never would have done if you were your normal self?"

Cam raised his hand. When no one else followed suit, Sam added, "All right, maybe not you. But all of the rest of us have been through something like what Barrett went through, and you still trust us." Cam wasn't certain he trusted Vala, but he understood Sam's point. He just wasn't sure how far it went.

"I do trust you," he said. "But that's because I know you."

"And I know Barrett," Sam said. "He's one of the good ones. Believe me, I'm not planning on giving him much information, just trying to get some background information out of him. My biggest question is how much information I can get out of him without having to go on the record about why I need to know. I don't know how much he'll be willing to bend the rules just because I ask him to, although he has bent them before for a good enough reason."

"This would be a good reason," Cam said.

Teal'c nodded. "If there are still agents of the Trust working within the NID, they must be discovered and eliminated."

"Especially with the Ori threat taking so much of everyone's attention," Sam said. "The last thing we need right now is for the Trust to seize the opportunity to make another move.

Ba'al's already proven that he can get his clones into the SGC itself and get them out again with the information he wants. He's likely to try again."

"Why Oliver, though?" Vala asked. "I'm still not sure what the Trust could have actually gained from having him as a spy."

"Good question," Sam said. "Most of his work is classified, of course, but it's not what I'd call top secret. The main reason it's classified is that it reveals the existence of the Goa'uld and the Stargate program, but the Trust certainly knows about all of that already."

"It might not be his work," Cam said. "He's been in a position to observe who's on SG teams, where they were going and when, any unexpected visitors we've had… there's a lot that could have leaked. That may even have been part of what tipped off Ba'al that we'd been looking for the Sangraal."

"Whatever information has been leaking, we need to start figuring out what it was," Sam said. "At the same time that we're figuring out who killed Oliver and whether it was related, or whether we're just dealing with a really unfortunate coincidence."

"I do not trust coincidences," Teal'c said.

"Neither do I, but sometimes that's what you get," Cam said. He turned to Sam. "How sure are you that Barrett's not still a threat?"

"If the NID are putting him back on duty rather than keeping him locked up tight, I'd say they're pretty sure. He's got a lot more of their sensitive information than he does ours. Unless we think the entire NID is bent —"

"In which case we're in a lot of trouble."

"But I don't think so. We have every indication that they've cleaned up their act. And if they're willing to trust Barrett, I am, too."

"I don't know about the NID or Barrett, but I do trust you," Cam said. "See what you can get from Barrett without over sharing. I'm going to call Jackson and see if he feels like coming in to work today."

"He's probably following up some lead," Sam said.

"It would just be nice if he'd tell me what lead that might be."

"Wouldn't it?" Sam asked. "He's always been like this. Don't take it personally."

"I try," Cam said.

Sam went back to her lab to call Malcolm, nestling her coffee cup in between the pieces of a Goa'uld hand device that she had been carefully dismantling back before anyone had been murdered.

"Colonel Carter," he said when he picked up, sounding pleased. "What can I do for you?"

"I need a favor," she said. "Can you meet me for coffee in the next couple of hours?"

"Give me half an hour," he said, after only a short pause.

"Without using my name when you explain where you're going."

"That bad?"

"Not an emergency from your point of view," Sam said. "Just a favor that would need to be off the record."

"And you can't tell me what it is on the phone."

"I'd rather not. Do you know where the Blue Mug is?"

"Yep. I'll meet you there in thirty."

"This is business, not a coffee date," she felt that she had to say. "Just, you know, wanted to make that…"

"I know, you're seeing someone else," he said. "That is, you are still…"

"It's still complicated," she said. "And I'm still unavailable. And this is a really awkward conversation, so I'll see you there in thirty."

"On my way."

In the coffee shop, Sam settled herself at a corner table where she could watch the entrance, and reflected that there had been a time when she didn't pick her tables in restaurants for their strategic value. Sometimes she thought that she was coming to understand Jack all too well these days. Malcolm came in a minute later, and stopped to pick up a cup of coffee at the counter before coming over to join her.

"Sam," he said, a little uncomfortably. She smiled at him, wanting to make it clear that she didn't hold a grudge.

"How are you holding up?"

"Like I said, I'm doing much better," he said. "Which is a relative thing."

"Believe me, I know about that." There was another awkward pause, and Sam decided it was best to move on to business and skip further small talk. "What do you know about an archaeologist named Vincent Oliver?"

Malcolm's eyebrows rose. "Why do you want to know?"

"That's the delicate part," Sam said. "I can't tell you why, except that we think he may have been involved in some criminal activities."

"May have been?"

"I can't give you anything else. Believe me, I would if I could, and for that matter I will if I can. I'm asking if there's anything you can tell me about Oliver off the record. Whatever you've got, I'll owe you a favor."

"I think we're past keeping track of who owes who a favor," Malcolm said. "And I trust that you wouldn't be asking for this off the record if it weren't important."

"It's important."

"Okay. Vincent Oliver worked for us for about four years, from 1986 to 1990. I can't tell you what he was doing for us, but it's a matter of public record that he was working on digs in the Persian Gulf. When things in Iraq heated up, his university cancelled his digs, and he wasn't in a position to be of help to us for several years. We checked back in with him in 1992, but at that point he was uninterested in more work."

"But that changed."

"It did. In 2003, he contacted us again, saying he was interested in reestablishing our relationship. At that point, we were still cleaning house and not in a position to bring anyone else on board until things stabilized for us."

"And the surveillance work that he'd been doing for you wasn't a priority anymore."

"I can't comment on that," Malcolm said, with a little nod that she took for assent. "It seemed like with his academic credentials and the work he'd already done for us, he was a perfect fit for the Stargate program, and we referred him to you."

"Tell me honestly, was that a plant? Was Oliver supposed to be reporting on our people to your people? I'm not going to blame you if that's true. I know it wouldn't have been your call."

"Not to the best of my knowledge. We made sure General Hammond, and then General O'Neill, knew about Oliver's background. He wasn't reporting to any of our people as far as I'm aware. We really just couldn't use him, and we thought you guys could."

"Did Oliver have any contact with the, ah…"

"Unwanted trash we removed when we cleaned house? Again, not as far as I know. One of our people knew him back when he was working for the NID. I talked to him when Oliver contacted us again. He said Oliver was reliable, a perfectionist, an almost painfully honest man. Once we overpaid him by ten dollars by accident, and he sent the check back."

"So you don't think it's likely that he got involved with any of your… trash."

"Is that where this is going?"

"I can't comment on that."

"I didn't know him personally," Malcolm said. "But we got good information from him, and he never showed any signs of being anything other than a pedantic, observant scientist who wanted to make a few extra dollars on the side. Now, a lot of people have ended up tempted when someone offered them a lot of extra dollars on the side. I won't say it couldn't have happened with Oliver. But I'd be surprised."

"Thanks," Sam said. "That was what I wanted to know. If you come up with anything else on Oliver, anything that doesn't require you to go through official channels to find out…"

"I'll let you know," Malcolm said. "If you'll share what you've got when this thing is over with. Whatever this thing is."

"I'll bring you into the loop as soon as I can. There are… complicating factors."

"Aren't there always," Malcolm said. He shook his head. "It's not like we don't have enough problems lately."

"I wish I could tell you that it looks better from where I'm sitting," Sam said.

Malcolm smiled sideways. "No such luck, huh?"

"I'm not sure knowing more about what we're up against from day to day is really comforting," Sam said. "Except that we may be in a position to do more about it. But I can't talk about that either."

"And everything I've got, you either know, or I can't tell you." He leaned back in his chair and took a drink of his coffee. "So. How about this weather?"

"I hear we might get some rain," Sam said, and sipped her own coffee.

"I'm sorry I'm late," Daniel said as he walked into the briefing room. "Somebody tried to kill me this morning." Cam put the brakes on whatever smart remark he'd been about to make. He'd been hoping Daniel had a good excuse for his absence, and he figured that counted as a good excuse.

"Are you all right?" Sam asked. Vala looked alarmed as well, and Teal'c even more somber than usual.

"I was hit by a car and shot at, but I'm fine, thank you for asking. When we're done here, though, I want Landry to send somebody to go find the books I dropped."

"As long as the books were the only casualties," Cam said. He figured that was a win.

Daniel didn't look like he thought it was. "I'm not all right with the books being casualties. This stuff doesn't just come up for sale on Alibris every day."

"I'm sure Landry can send somebody to go get your books," Cam said. He resolved to let Daniel ask him, already hearing Landry asking him if SG-1 needed an airman assigned full time to pick up things they left lying around all over the state. "How about the people who tried to kill you? Anybody we know?"

"Well, I'm thinking it's our friends with the Trust," Daniel said. "They know SG-1 is investigating Oliver's death because they trailed Sam and Vala from Niles's apartment. And the guys who went after me had zats. I'm guessing they assumed I knew something that was worth silencing me for, which is actually ironic, because I have next to no idea what's actually going on."

Neither did Cam, but apparently the bad guys thought they should. Cam wondered what they ought to know and why they were supposed to know it. "You're an archaeologist, and Oliver was an archaeologist, so…"

"So maybe there's something in his work that I'm supposed to have noticed by now, only I haven't. If he was smuggling reports out to the Trust, I doubt he would have been stupid enough to type them on his work computer or write them out in longhand in a notebook while conveniently leaving the imprint of his writing on the page below."

"Although that would be convenient," Vala said. "Have we looked?"

"I was crawling around caves with a weird reptile that tried to eat me, and then I was hit with a car," Daniel said. "No. I haven't searched Oliver's office."

"I took a look around," Cam said. "I found a bunch of stuff that looks like what I'd expect to find in an archaeologist's office. Books, weird little carved things, and enough pottery for a million flea markets. But I haven't looked in every book or under every piece of furniture for secret messages."

"Because it doesn't make sense for there to be any," Daniel

said, looking frustrated. "If he was reporting to the Trust, he'd just call his contact on the phone, or meet them in person. There's no reason for passing messages unless there was a huge amount of information to convey, and even then, he could have carried the files out on a CD or written it all down on a sheet of paper. What he wouldn't do was leave anything in his office."

"Unless he was planning to hand off the information to a contact, but he got killed before he could do it," Sam said.

"Which is possible," Teal'c added.

Cam acknowledged that with a nod. "You're not wrong. But I think we should consider whether we have this the wrong way round. We've been assuming that Oliver was passing information to the Trust, and that somebody found out and killed him for it."

"Or that his death was unfortunate coincidence," Teal'c said, sounding as if he didn't believe in unfortunate coincidence for a minute.

"He's got the connections to the NID, we were jumped by the Trust, and then so were you," Sam said. "It sure looks that way to me."

"Sure, but hear me out," Cam said, turning the idea around in his head and trying to figure out if it made sense. He figured if it didn't, Daniel would tell him instantly where he'd gone wrong. "What if we have it backwards? Oliver wasn't working for the Trust. Oliver found out that somebody else was working for the Trust, and they killed him to keep him quiet."

There was a momentary silence around the table as everyone considered that.

"Why do you think that?" Daniel asked. It was a far less scathing deconstruction of his theory than Cam had expected from him, and he leapt forward into the breach.

"Barrett told Sam he thinks Oliver was on the level."

"That's second-hand information," Sam pointed out.

"It's the information we've got. Everyone who worked for

Oliver says that he was a jerk, but an honest jerk. From everything they've said, does he sound more like the guy who would be sneaking around trying to keep anyone from finding out that he's a spy, or the guy who would look under every rock until he found a spy?"

"Well, when you put it that way," Daniel said. "I see your point. And it does provide a better motive for someone to kill him than we've heard so far. But you know, if that's true…"

"There's still a spy in the base. And it's probably Chen, Jefferson, or Carr."

"For what it's worth, my money's not on Chen," Sam said. "I know it does involve accepting that it's a coincidence that she was also involved in illegal activities, but if she were a spy for the Trust, I don't think she'd have gotten mixed up in this kind of smuggling scheme at the same time. It would put her work for them in too much jeopardy."

"Unless she just really likes money," Vala said.

"I don't think the Trust would use her if they knew she was trying to run that kind of get-rich-quick scheme. It's possible that she was keeping it a secret from them, but that just sounds awfully risky to me."

"I agree with Colonel Carter," Teal'c said. "And if Dr. Chen were an operative for the Trust, I would expect her to have suggested that Da'shak provide information in exchange for the artifacts, rather than simply negotiable goods."

"Unless he's lying," Vala said.

"Yes, unless he is," Daniel said in frustration. "But we have to draw the best conclusions we can from the information that we have. And everyone isn't always lying."

Vala shrugged one shoulder as if she was tempted to argue that point, but kept quiet. Cam forged ahead.

"You don't think he's lying," he said to Teal'c.

"I do not. I believe that if such a request had been made of him, he would have added to his many attempts to justify his actions that at least he had not betrayed our people's secrets to the Trust."

"I mean, you don't think he really sold information to the Trust."

"It is possible that I merely do not wish to believe it," Teal'c said after a moment. "Da'shak has behaved dishonorably, but I did not believe him to be a man who would spy for the Goa'uld. But perhaps it would be wise for me to question him again. He has a prominent position in the councils of the Free Jaffa, and for him to be providing information to the Trust could be disastrous."

"Great," Cam said. "We've thought of a way this situation could be worse."

"We need to check all three of their backgrounds and see if we can find any possible ties to the Trust or the NID," Sam said. "And Niles, too, for that matter."

"See if you can dig up anything," Cam said. "Or if Barrett can dig up anything for you."

"I hate to say this given what I was just arguing a minute ago, but someone should probably search Oliver's office and see if they can find any of his notes," Daniel said.

"A minute ago you said —" Sam began.

"I know, I know. But if there's any possibility that Oliver wasn't the spy, that he'd caught a spy instead, he didn't go to Landry with that information right away. Why would he wait?"

"Because he didn't have enough proof," Sam said immediately.

Daniel nodded. "That's my guess. He was meticulous, methodical. He would have been assembling some kind of proof to show Landry, even if it was just a record of everything he'd noticed that was suspicious. And he might well have kept that in his office."

"Or at home, if he was afraid of the spy finding it," Cam said. "Daniel, I want you to go over Oliver's office with a fine-tooth comb. Sam, check his computer. Teal'c, go see what you can find out from Da'shak. And Vala, let's go check out Oliver's house."

"Are we feeding his cat?" Vala asked.

"Oliver's dead, and he lived alone, and nobody knows he's

dead, so I'm assuming there's no one who's going to mind you breaking in. Just be subtle getting in the front door. After that, you can roll the place." He could see Vala raising a finger to ask a question, and fended off the one he guessed was coming. "Yes, if he has a cat, we can feed it. It's probably getting pretty hungry by now."

"What are we waiting for?" Vala asked, producing a set of lock picks seemingly out of thin air and swinging them around on one perfectly manicured finger.

Cam waited another moment for anyone at the table to argue with him or insist on choosing their own assignment. When no one did, he decided he had to be doing something right. "Not a thing. Let's go, people. We're running out of time."

CHAPTER TWELVE

DANIEL thumbed through books and examined pieces of pottery, hoping for some clue to why Oliver had died. It felt more than usually morbid, although his profession involved spending a tremendous amount of time with the relics of the dead. Usually he was at peace with the fact that the objects he handled had belonged to men and women who died long ago, and merely tried to treat them with the respect that their original owners would have wanted.

Over the last ten years, he'd also gotten alarmingly comfortable working with objects whose owners had died much more recently, occasionally because he or people he knew had killed them. This still felt different, not like examining unearthed artifacts or weapons brought back from the field, but the awkwardness of walking into a house where someone had recently died and not being certain it was all right to flip through a magazine.

He was doing a lot more than flipping through magazines, and finding little to show for it. Reference books he'd already read, a few articles that were new to him and that he resisted the temptation to skim, and objects that remained stubbornly free of bloodstains, blackmail letters, or bullet holes.

He had ransacked Oliver's desk drawers, which contained nothing but organized office supplies — his own were a rats' nest of disorganized office supplies, the emptied contents of his pockets at various random times, and small odd objects he hadn't managed to find a permanent home for on his shelves. He would have to get Sam to search Oliver's computer more closely, but it had been logged on at the time of Oliver's death, and he'd taken a cursory look. The files contained nothing more suspicious than PDFs of articles on archaeology and a few saved email forwards of the "Archaeologists love their mummies" variety.

He was starting to despair of finding anything relevant when he hit a section of museum catalogs, organized by date and location. Most were glossy volumes with extensive descriptions of the pieces within, but the most recent was a visitor's guide to the Denver Museum of Mesoamerican Art, describing an exhibit of Olmec pottery that had only opened a few days before. It was a slim brochure, not the kind of thing that was sold, but the kind someone would have picked up at the museum itself.

Daniel took the brochure back to his own office and called Mitchell's cell phone. "This is a long shot," he said without preliminaries. "Have you found anything that suggests Oliver visited the Denver Museum of Mesoamerican Art last week?"

There was a pause at the other end. "How did you know that? We found a ticket stub in his pants pocket."

"Always go through their laundry," Vala said as if leaning over Mitchell's shoulder. "You can learn astonishing things from someone's laundry."

"I don't want to know," Mitchell said. "Anyway, it's a ticket stub from, yes, the Denver Museum of Mesoamerican Art, dated Tuesday the 18th. And that is just about all we've found, except enough books for a small library and some very organized sock drawers."

"Keep looking," Daniel said. "I'll check out the museum connection."

"You do that."

Daniel frowned at the pamphlet. Oliver had been scheduled to work that day. It was possible that he'd run over to Denver on a weekday, but he would have needed a good reason. There wasn't anything obviously Mesoamerican about the poisoned weapon they'd found; it was possible that Oliver had suspected a relationship between its toxins and some sort of plant found in Mexico or the Southeastern United States, but the museum didn't seem like the obvious place to go to research that.

One picture was circled in the pamphlet, a vase in the shape of a fish with a gaping mouth. It was a pretty piece, typical of fish effigy vessels, but Daniel couldn't see anything particularly special about it. He flipped the page, and saw that Oliver had made notes in his crabbed handwriting, describing the piece's size and noting its location in the museum.

It was the only thing he'd found that nagged at him. He turned the brochure over to reveal the museum's phone number, and picked up the phone again to call.

"I'd like the curatorial department... ah, pre-Columbian. Yes." He waited to be connected, and then said, "This is Dr. Daniel Jackson. I'm working with Dr. Vincent Oliver on some research into Olmec fish effigy vessels, and I was wondering if he'd made an appointment to speak with someone on your staff. He's actually in the hospital — well, yes, I'm afraid it may be serious, and I just wanted to see if he'd made arrangements — you'll check? Thanks, I appreciate it."

He waited, thumbing through the rest of the brochure. Nothing else was circled, and there were no further notes to provide enlightenment.

"Dr. Jackson?" The woman on the other end of the line sounded apologetic. "I don't have any record of an appointment for Dr. Oliver, and Dr. Moreno says she doesn't recall a phone call from him. Did you want to make an appointment?"

"That's all right. Under the circumstances — I think it had better wait until he's feeling better. Thank you, though."

He replaced the receiver thoughtfully, and then called Walter. "Can you tell me if Dr. Oliver took any time off the week before he died?"

The pause was brief. "He had a dentist's appointment scheduled last Tuesday," Walter said.

"I don't suppose you know the name of his dentist."

"I can find out."

"That's all right." He'd certainly visited the museum, whether or not he'd visited the dentist as well. And if their theories were correct, he'd been on the trail of a spy at the time, or had been a spy himself. Not exactly the time to go sightseeing.

He hadn't left his notes in his office. Would he have left them at home, or in a safe deposit box? Maybe, and he'd see what Mitchell and Vala could turn up. But suppose he'd suspected that someone was onto his activities. He'd seemed increasingly paranoid. Maybe that had just been the awareness that someone really was out to get him.

In that case, he might have felt the need for a hiding place for his notes that wasn't linked to him at all. And the open-mouthed shape of the vase was certainly suggestive. It might have struck Oliver as the ideal hiding place. Time for a trip to Denver, he thought.

The phone rang as he was considering what to say when he called the museum, and he picked it up still absently running through possible excuses in his head.

"This is Daniel Jackson."

"Daniel," Sarah Gardner said. She paused for a moment, as if surprised to have gotten him rather than his voice mail. "It's good to hear from you."

"It's good to hear from you, too. I hope things are going well for you."

"You mean, better than the last time you saw me?" she asked dryly. "Yes, you could say that. Although I'm not sure what I said then that made you think I wanted to become a consultant for the Air Force."

"Yeah, I'm sorry about that," Daniel said. "They were in a tight spot, I wasn't here to deal with it, and I just thought you might be able to help them. I figured if anyone had the information they needed, it would probably be you."

"You're trying to flatter me," Sarah said. "You can keep doing that, though, I think you owe me."

"I appreciate your help," Daniel said. "I truly do."

"I'm not sure how much help I've really been," she said. "I've asked around, but I still haven't heard any indication that artifacts like the ones you're looking for have turned up on the antiquities market."

"Thanks for that," Daniel said. "We're pretty sure at this point that they went to… a more distant buyer."

"Oh, well, then," Sarah said dryly. "I don't think the agencies I've been working with probably have jurisdiction there, so we'll leave it at that. I'm relieved."

There was a momentary pause, which Daniel considered filling with *So, how have you been?* He could see where that would lead, down a conversational path that would make it seem natural to suggest getting together for coffee the next time they were in the same town. Except that they weren't likely to be in the same town anytime soon, and even if they were…

He couldn't answer the return question, couldn't tell her how he'd been in any meaningful way. Even though she already knew about the Goa'uld and the Stargate, there would always be too many things he couldn't tell her. He understood that some military relationships worked that way, but he didn't find the secrecy appealing. Half the point of having a relationship was having someone to talk to.

"Thanks for all your help," Daniel said. "I appreciate you being willing to take Colonel Mitchell's call."

"You're welcome," Sarah said. He wasn't sure if he heard or imagined a touch of wistfulness in her voice. "Stay well, Daniel."

"You, too," he said, and put the phone down before he could change his mind.

Sam was finishing up with Oliver's computer when Vala came in and sat down opposite her at her workbench, spinning around on her chair one way and then the other in restless motion that suggested she was as frustrated as Sam by their lack of progress so far. "What are we doing?" Vala asked.

"I've been going through the computers of all the suspects, and also Oliver's computer," Sam said. "And not finding a whole lot. Chen paid her bills online, and I managed to get into her bank account and credit card accounts; she's telling the truth about having financial problems. Jefferson just registered for San Diego Comic-Con. Apparently his dark secret is that he's a geek."

"How dark a secret is that?"

"I'm joking. He has some harmless hobbies that are shared by a lot of the science staff. Also his file structure is a mess, but I don't think it's an attempt to hide anything, I just think he's not very organized."

"And Carr?"

"Carr's more of a cipher. His work computer really doesn't have anything on it that's not work-related. That's... not exactly suspicious, but not informative. And then there's Oliver."

"The jackpot," Vala said, putting her elbows on the table and leaning forward in interest. "The motherlode of secrets. We hope?"

"We hoped," Sam said. "I've searched Oliver's computer. I can't find anything that isn't work-related. If there's a code involved, it's so subtle that I don't think I'm going to be able to figure it out, and certainly not in the next twenty-four hours."

"Well, that's not good," Vala said.

"I'm afraid not."

"Do we have anything else?"

"Not on the case. I think I've managed to get the internal mechanism in the dagger that Daniel brought back to respond to one of our control crystals. If we can reverse-engineer some of the mechanisms in the crystal core, they could be very useful to us. We might be able to reliably disrupt zat fire so that it reflects back at whoever's firing the zat without harming whoever's holding the crystal."

"I sense a catch coming."

"The catch is that I can't figure out how to alter the crystal's programming so that whoever's holding it can actually see what they're doing. Right now, if you pick up the crystal and turn it on, the lights go out for you and everybody else in a five-meter radius unless they have the ATA gene."

"There are situations where that could be useful," Vala said.

"I can think of some, too. But even if we could duplicate the whole mechanism, it's not something we're going to be issuing to combat teams anytime soon."

"Do we have any good news?" Vala asked plaintively. "I was hoping for some good news."

"It's lunchtime?" Sam offered. "Although I really want to take another look at this control crystal programming and see if I can figure out where I'm going wrong. Want me to get us sandwiches, and you can see if you have any ideas?"

"I could do that," Vala said. She looked like it pleased her to have someone ask for her advice. Sam felt she understood that all too well, having been in too many boys' club meetings where she'd had to push to make herself heard and would have waited forever if she'd waited until someone asked her what she thought. "Just not the yellow paste, if you don't mind."

"I think that's supposed to be egg salad," Sam said.

"Which part is egg and which part is salad?"

"If you figure it out, you tell me."

Teal'c stepped out of the Stargate onto the surface of Dakara for the second time in as many days. This time he had to spend some time hunting before he found Bra'tac taking his evening meal with a number of the other Jaffa, soldiers rather than politicians by the look of them. They were clustered around Bra'tac as other warriors had always done, drawn to his insight and to his knack of making friends in unexpected places.

"I need to speak with you," Teal'c said. "But it can wait until you have eaten."

"I doubt that," Bra'tac said. "The Tau'ri are generally in a hurry." He picked up his cup and a piece of bread and followed Teal'c outside to sit on a low stone wall facing out towards open desert. "Not much like home," he said.

"It is not much like Chulak," Teal'c agreed. "But you seem

to be making your home here at present."

"What else can I do? They need me here. There are times when I grow tired of politics," Bra'tac said. "And then I understand better your decision to remain among the Tau'ri rather than returning to us."

"It is not only because I have no taste for politics."

"You cannot deny that is one reason."

"I cannot," Teal'c said. "As you cannot deny that the weapons of the Ancients are our best chance of defeating the Ori."

"That may well be so," Bra'tac said. "You are not the only one who has said such things of late. I would prefer to rely on our own strength, but…" He made a gesture as if casting something aside. "The Ori are powerful, their ships outmatch our own, and they take our worlds as their playthings. It is a persuasive argument that we must have better weapons."

"I will take what weapons we can find," Teal'c said. "As we have used the weapons of the Goa'uld and of the Tau'ri to our advantage. We are not in a position to turn down any tools that may be of use to us."

"Do not say any. Some prices are too high to pay."

"What do you mean?"

Bra'tac shook his head. "Nothing. Nothing. Only that Se'tak's rhetoric disturbs me. I begin to wish that we had destroyed the Superweapon after all."

"It is too dangerous to ever be used," Teal'c said.

Bra'tac shook his head. "You grow naïve among the Tau'ri. Weapons will always be used. But enough complaints from an old man. What did you come here to tell me?"

"I was correct in my suspicions," Teal'c said. "Da'shak was receiving stolen property from the Tau'ri, and selling it to enrich himself. He justified his behavior by claiming that the artifacts did not belong either to the Tau'ri or to our people, and that therefore they were free for anyone to claim and profit from. I believe he feels ashamed of his actions, yet his shame did not restrain him from dishonorable means of gaining wealth."

Bra'tac let out a hissing breath. "This is terrible news," he said. "I had hoped that you were wrong. Da'shak could have been a powerful leader for our people, but I see that he has chosen otherwise."

"That is not all I have come here to tell you," Teal'c said. "We believe the man who was murdered may have been killed because he discovered a spy for the Trust working within the SGC. It is possible that the spy may have been the one who stole the artifacts and sold them to Da'shak. If there is any chance that he was selling secrets as well, we must know."

"I have heard nothing that would make me suspect that were true."

"And yet, could you possibly know?"

"Possibly, yes," Bra'tac said. "Se'tak is not a trusting man, and he has taken one piece of my advice since he came to power. All those who have access to council secrets who are not themselves council members have been deliberately provided with pieces of false information. Nothing that it would harm them to believe, but secrets that it would be tempting for them to share with the Goa'uld. Our own agents, and those of the Tok'ra, report back to us if the Goa'uld appear to believe the rumors we planted."

"But we have no agents on Earth," Teal'c said.

Bra'tac lifted an eyebrow. "Do we not?"

"No agents there in secret," Teal'c said, although he realized he could not be entirely certain that was true. "That would violate our treaties with the Tau'ri."

"That is true enough," Bra'tac said after a moment. "Though that in itself is a council secret, and there are those who would feel safer if we had agents of our own who did not arrive through the Stargate." Teal'c hesitated to ask whether Bra'tac was one of those people, unsure whether he wanted to know the answer, and Bra'tac moved briskly on. "Da'shak was told that we are planning a base on Kelvak," he said. "If the agents of the Tau'ri hear such a rumor from the Trust, we will know that he has been false."

"And if we do not?"

"Are you asking me for a way to prove a man's loyalty beyond doubt?" Bra'tac shrugged. "You are not speaking of brainwashing, but of simple disloyalty. You are too old to believe in a magical means of determining that."

"But never too old to value your advice."

Bra'tac sighed, looking up at the chalky sky. "Find Da'shak and see what he has to say for himself," he said. "You said he showed shame at his actions. That does not sound to me like a man who is an accomplished liar. Speak to him yourself and decide whether you believe that he has betrayed our people as well as his principles."

"I will speak with him."

"You will have to find him first," Bra'tac said. "He has left his home on Imrak and resigned his position here. Whether that is guilt at his actions or the fear of being discovered as a traitor, I leave for you to find out."

"What are you doing?" Vala asked as Daniel reached for the phone again. Mitchell and Vala had both wandered in just as he was preparing to make arrangements for his visit to the museum, which meant answering a lot more questions than he had been planning to have to answer.

He covered the receiver with his hand. "The museum is closed Thursdays," he said.

"Nice work if you can get it," Mitchell said.

"So that their curators can actually get some work done without any visitors there. I'm going to call and see if I can get an appointment to take a look at that vase anyway."

"No, you're not," Vala said, and pressed the button to hang up the telephone. There was no way to call again short of wrestling with her for the phone, which would have been undignified. He settled for narrowing his eyes instead.

"I just explained —"

"What if they say no?"

"Well, they might," he said, envisioning his own response to being asked to meet with a person he'd never heard of on a day when he'd planned to get some uninterrupted work done. "I'll just have to be persuasive."

"It's much easier to persuade someone that you already have an appointment than it is to persuade them to give you an appointment," Vala said. "Believe me, I know."

"I am not going to ask how," Daniel said. "But you may actually be right."

"I may be," Vala said, with a slightly uncertain smile. "So you do think I'm right?"

"I think that I can plausibly claim that Oliver made an appointment, or should have made an appointment. If that doesn't work, my next move is to explain that it's a matter of national security and get in that way."

"Get *us* in." Daniel's skepticism must have shown on his face, because she went on, "Didn't you say that I ought to see some of your planet's cultural institutions?"

He was trapped at that point; he had, certainly, but he'd been thinking about natural parks or monuments, neither of which contained a lot of valuable and portable items that could be sold for cash on another world. He didn't think that even Vala could make off with Mt. Rushmore or a sequoia, although he wasn't planning to present that to her as a challenge. "Mitchell?"

Mitchell looked up as if startled. "I'm sorry, are you actually asking me what you ought to do?"

"You're in charge."

Mitchell's smile was crooked. "Strangely enough, yes, I am," he said. "Take Vala with you and go check out the museum. Figure out whether Oliver left notes in that vase. Try not to steal it, but if you have to steal it, do what you have to do." Vala's eyes lit up, and Daniel shot Mitchell a discouraging look, which Mitchell ignored. "We need to find the Trust's agent and figure out what they're up to. The last thing we want is to find the

Sangraal and have the Trust grab it out from under our noses."

"All right. We'll go check out the museum."

"Meanwhile, I'm going to see if Sam has found anything interesting in Oliver's computer. And I'm going to go check on our guests, who I think we can now officially upgrade to prisoners."

Acquiring a motor pool car took some time, and wasn't assisted by Vala flirting with the airmen in the motor pool. That produced more distraction than efficiency, and Daniel felt they were lucky not to be issued a transport truck or ambulance rather than the car they were finally cleared to borrow.

"Is that just a reflex, or what?" She had turned off the charm the moment they got into the car, and was now staring out the window with furrowed brows.

"Is what a reflex?" she asked, a shadow of the charm returning as she turned to face him and crossed her long legs. It was a defense mechanism, he thought, something like a porcupine's quills. Not that he lacked defense mechanisms of his own. Jack had once accused him of talking to avoid communicating, and while he still felt that wasn't entirely fair, he had to admit there was some truth to it.

"What you were doing back there."

"Just smoothing our way," she said.

"You don't have to."

"There are enough rocks in the road," she said.

"Bumps in the road. I think."

"You know what I mean."

"I suppose I do." He knew there had been a lot of bumps in her road lately, and wished he could think of a way to express sympathy that she might possibly accept. "You know, I'm sure that Adria—"

"Let's not talk about dreary work," Vala said, tossing her head. "I'm supposed to be having a cultural experience. Tell me about Mesoamerican art."

"Well, the Olmecs developed a civilization in parts of modern-day Mexico about 1600 BC," Daniel said, a near-instinctive reaction and a neat deflection of the conversation as well. "They're post-Goa'uld, but I have wondered if there's some lingering influence from the Omeyocan—the giant aliens—or Coatlicue."

"Giant aliens?"

"It's a long story," Daniel said. It was easy to fall into lecture mode as he explained Nicholas Ballard's discoveries in Central America, and the team's later exploration of the worlds where the Omeyocan had sheltered humans while making war on the Goa'uld. Vala listened with interest, and then unerringly picked out the one detail he wanted least to talk about.

"So who's this Nick?"

"My grandfather," Daniel said shortly. They had reconciled to a certain degree, but he'd still never entirely forgiven Nick for failing to take him in after his parents' deaths. Or maybe he had forgiven him, but not in a way that erased their estrangement, any more than Daniel thought apologies had entirely made Nick forgive Daniel's dismissal of his theories about the crystal skulls as crazy.

"So am I going to meet him?"

"No. What about you, do you have any relatives?" He meant the question as his own deflection of a subject he didn't want to talk about, and realized too late how closely it probably cut at the moment. At this rate, this game of conversational judo was going to end with them both lying bruised on the mat.

"Well, everyone has parents, don't they? At least one. Or we wouldn't be here."

"I'm sorry."

"I have absolutely no idea what you're talking about," Vala said.

On that promising note, they pulled into the museum parking lot. It was deserted, although signs warned that cars would be towed if they didn't belong to museum visitors. Daniel parked anyway, and hoped they didn't mean it.

He found the staff entrance and rang the bell. After a few minutes, a woman with her dark hair pulled back in a ponytail answered the door. She was wearing jeans and a worn denim shirt, but there was something in her age and bearing that said "curator," not "intern."

"I'm sorry, we're closed today," the woman said.

"I have an appointment with Dr. Moreno," he said.

She frowned. "I'm Dr. Moreno, but I don't recall any appointments scheduled today."

"You said your colleague had arranged everything," Vala said, looking at Daniel with a wide-eyed expression of distress.

Daniel shot her a "don't help" look. "I'm Dr. Daniel Jackson, with the United States Air Force. I'm working with Dr. Vincent Oliver — he's the one who made the appointment."

"Yes, Melissa asked me about that, but I told her I didn't recall speaking to Dr. Oliver."

"Oh, gosh. I must have misunderstood — all those layers of phone tag. Vincent swore he was going to make the appointment, but I'm sure he's been distracted by all his medical issues — he's in the hospital right now."

"I'm sorry to hear that," Dr. Moreno said, although her expression hadn't noticeably thawed.

"I don't suppose there's any way… he was going to try to arrange for us to take a look at your fish effigy vessels. It's for a paper on Olmec ceramic techniques." He considered invoking his University of Chicago mentor's name, but a background in Egyptology wasn't going to make this any more convincing. He decided to gamble on Nick instead. "My grandfather, Dr. Ballard, did some preliminary work on this back in the 1970s, and I'm trying to follow up on some of his theories."

"Ballard," Dr. Moreno said. "I've read his work." Daniel held his breath for a moment. "Some of his monographs on his Mayan excavations had some useful field notes in them, although his theories about the pyramids and crystal power got a little wacky."

"Maybe a little," Daniel said uncomfortably.

"He's better than some. I don't know what it is about grubbing around in pyramids that makes Anglo archaeologists decide they're in touch with the spirit of an ancient jaguar god, or whatever their favorite brand of woo is this week."

"Wacky," Vala agreed. Moreno turned to her expectantly.

"This is my assistant Vala," Daniel said. "She's helping out since Vincent wasn't able to come out to the museum — he's actually going into surgery today."

"Well, this is awkward," Moreno said. "I really don't have the time blocked off for this, but… at least come in and have some coffee, we'll talk." She opened the inner door and gestured them through. "My office is the last one down the hall. I'll meet you there with the coffee."

Vala leaned in conspiratorially as soon as Moreno had disappeared down the hallway. "We're in."

"Stealing the vase is a last resort," Daniel said. "We're clear on that, right?"

"Trust me," Vala said, with a radiant smile.

"Da'shak?" the gray-haired woman said, handing Teal'c a plate. Having had no luck asking after Da'shak in the council halls, he had turned to the dining hall, where council members and travelers there on business took their mid-day meal. "I know him. He comes in here often, but I have not seen him for three days."

"Is that unusual?" Teal'c said, taking the nearest seat. It was early for the mid-day meal, and the long trestle tables were largely empty, only a few small groups clustered together in conversation over their food.

"He usually only goes home to Imrak for a single day," the woman said. "I hope nothing has happened to him. He has kept to himself since Chulak fell to the Ori."

"I hope their stay there will be short," Teal'c said.

"We all hope," the woman said, giving him a look that was as effective as Bra'tac's scoldings at making him feel once again like a child before his prim'ta. "We hope that someone is doing something about it."

"The Tau'ri are seeking a weapon that will be effective against the Ori. I will return to helping them as soon as I find Da'shak."

"I would look on Imrak. He went back there three days ago, and as far as I know, he has not been back."

Teal'c shook his head and addressed himself to his food. No one he had spoken to so far had seen Da'shak after he told Bra'tac he was resigning his position. He ate quickly, unwilling to spare much time from his search, and used the time to observe the other people eating. He could not hear the conversations going on at tables around the room, but they did not look, on the whole, like happy ones.

There was no way of finding out more about how people were taking the change in leadership, and to what extent they agreed with Se'tak's call for an attack on the Ori, without spending time that Teal'c could not steal from his appointed mission. It made him wonder whether Bra'tac was right; it was clear that he was needed on Dakara, and he could not keep his finger on the pulse of politics there while he was busy on SG-1.

At the same time, all their political wrangling of the council would be for nothing if the Ori continued seizing world after world, and he had seen nothing to make him believe that the weapons and ships of the Free Jaffa were sufficient to stop the Ori in their crusade. If they could not find the Sangraal, or invent some weapon of equal usefulness against the Ori, it was a near certainty that his people would once again be enslaved. He did not believe that was a final defeat — if anything, their escape from the Goa'uld's hold on their minds and bodies had convinced him that any slavery could be overthrown in time — but it would be a staggering setback, and one he was determined to prevent.

And the sooner he helped solve this problem for the Tau'ri, the sooner they could return to their search for the Sangraal. He carried his dishes to stack them with other dirty ones, and set off for the Stargate.

CHAPTER THIRTEEN

DESPITE what Da'shak had told Bra'tac, Teal'c felt it was possible that Da'shak had returned to his home, if for no other reason than to collect another load of belongings. Certainly his furnishings had been far more than he could have carried with him on his way to Dakara to resign his position in a fit of remorse.

Teal'c dialed Imrak, and once again stepped out into a chillier morning. He used the walk to town to plan a search, considering who he might question and where he might look for signs of Da'shak's intentions.

In the end, he needed none of his plans. Da'shak was sitting outside his house on a low wall, a pack at his feet, as if waiting for some transport to come and take him away.

"Teal'c," he said, flinching as if some internal vision had come to life. "What are you doing here?"

"I might ask you the same question," he said. "You told Bra'tac you had abandoned your home here."

"I have. I mean to," Da'shak said. "I tried to go to Chulak."

Teal'c shook his head. "You cannot reach Chulak through the chappa'ai. The Ori are sensible enough to block the gate and use their ships for transport."

"Perhaps I can charter a ship," Da'shak said.

"With the proceeds of the stolen goods you have received?"

"At least then I will be fighting for our people," Da'shak said hotly, his chin coming up. "You are right, Teal'c; I have behaved with dishonor. At least I can use the profits I made to the benefit of our people."

"How do you intend to defeat the Ori, should you reach Chulak?"

"I will certainly not defeat them by staying here."

"No," Teal'c said. "But you might have done more for our

people as an aide to the council, even if that work is more tedious and less likely to result in personal glory."

"They would hardly accept me now."

"Your own actions are the cause of that." Teal'c considered him. "But I do not think that you are a spy as well."

"A spy?" Da'shak scowled at him. "Who says that?"

"The circumstances suggested it might be the case," Teal'c said. "The Tau'ri archaeologist who was killed appears to have made an enemy of the Trust. If his killer were selling information to the Trust, you would have been a tempting source."

"Green never asked for anything of the sort," Da'shak said. "I would have reported it if he had attempted to buy information."

"Even if he had sold you stolen artifacts for gold first, so that reporting him would mean exposing your collaboration with him?"

"At least I would have turned him away," Da'shak said, looking down at the paving stones beneath his feet as if they were suddenly interesting. "I am no traitor. And I swear he asked for nothing but precious metals that he could sell on Earth."

"I am inclined to believe you," Teal'c said. "Not because I trust you, but because if you were a spy, you would not be running away from the position that has provided you with information to sell. You would be pleading for forgiveness and another chance to be taken back into the counsels of our people's leaders."

"Instead I will go and fight," Da'shak said. "If I can find a way."

"There are battles enough," Teal'c said. "If you cannot reach Chulak, I am certain that you can find a battlefield to suit you." He was tempted to leave it there, and then decided he could not. "And they will need people to rebuild, on Chulak, when the Ori have gone, as we rebuilt after the Goa'uld had gone. Do not throw your life away for nothing. It is too valuable for that." He shook his head at the hopeful light in Da'shak's eyes. "That is not forgiveness," he said. "Only the truth."

"I will think on what you have said," Da'shak said.

Teal'c was not at all certain that he would; next to the uncertainty of chartering a ship into a war zone or setting off to find some unspecified battlefield, he thought it would prove all too attractive to simply slink back into his house and settle down again among his comforts. But that remained to be seen, and his work was elsewhere.

"I hope that you will," he said, and set his steps toward the Stargate again.

"So tell me," Moreno said when she returned with the coffee. "What's the Air Force's interest in Olmec pottery?"

Vala had no idea what might be remotely plausible, so she turned to Daniel with her best "you answer that one because you're so terribly dominant and in charge of this situation" expression. Daniel looked like he was choosing his words carefully.

"They're funding our dig in a location where there are some joint training activities going on with the Mexican Air Force," Daniel said. "And that's really all I know about that. I think it's really mostly a public relations thing — providing a reason that they can talk about for cutting down trees and digging up hillsides."

"As opposed to reasons that nobody wants to talk about?" Moreno raised an eyebrow. "I know, I know, you don't know. But that's a good way to get into very bad situations. If you don't mind giving you one piece of advice, I'd get out before you get burned."

Daniel shook his head stubbornly. "Not in the middle of dig season."

"Well, it's your neck. You just want to see our pieces?"

"I'd like to take some measurements."

"That's all in our catalog. I can get you the catalog descriptions —"

Daniel was already shaking his head. "I need to see the actual pieces. I'm interested in the angle and depth of the scale marks."

"I don't suppose you've got some identification on you?"

Daniel handed over a little plastic card with his picture on it, and nudged Vala. After a moment she remembered that she had one as well. She fished it out of her pocket and handed it over with her most innocent expression.

"Just a military ID?" Moreno asked her.

"She's Canadian," Daniel said.

"Well, I don't guess this is a nefarious Canadian plot. If it's specifically fish effigy vessels you're interested in, we've got pieces in storage and several on display. Where do you want to start?"

"Let us start with the ones on display," Daniel said. "You don't have to take them off display for us, unless they're in a locked case."

"They're not," Moreno said. "We keep the jade figurines in the same room in locked cases, and there's apparently a shortage of locked cases around here. Either that or someone's decided that the public can't appreciate anything they can't put sticky fingerprints on and ruin. The ones in actual easy reach are on alarmed bases, but I can turn the alarms off for you."

"That would be very considerate of you," Vala said.

Moreno led them through a series of service hallways out into an open gallery that looked like museums on any planet; pedestals and cases that were designed to be nearly invisible next to the works of art they showcased. These were mostly pottery, although Vala did see the jade figurines and masks in their locked case, pretty and portable enough to make her fingers itch, and several large vessels made of gold, all in locked cases of their own.

Moreno approached a pedestal on which rested a vase that did, indeed, look like a large-mouthed fish frozen in perpetual surprise. Or perhaps perpetual hunger; she was reminded uncomfortably of Goa'uld symbiotes, and let her gaze wander back to the jade.

"I've disabled the alarm," Moreno said. "You can take your measurements."

Daniel extracted a tape measure, miniature flashlight, and notebook from his pockets, apparently tools he found as necessary to feeling dressed for the day as she did her lockpicks, and approached the vase.

From the way his face fell the moment he glanced inside, she could tell that it was empty. Still, he recovered quickly, and puttered about making measurements while Moreno looked increasingly bored. Vala turned a slow circle, wondering where the notes could possibly be if they weren't in the fish.

The problem with them being in the fish, when she thought about it, was that the pedestal that held the fish had been alarmed. Surely shoving a sheaf of notes into it would have set the alarm off. On the other hand, the other fish vessels that she could see in the room were in a locked case, and surely Oliver couldn't have stood there and picked the lock in front of a room full of visitors.

She pursued the thought, drifting around the room as if bored herself with Daniel's perfectionist measurements. He would have had to put the notes somewhere within easy reach, because even if he waited until the gallery was empty, he couldn't have counted on more than a moment of privacy before more visitors walked in.

A large vase, easily the size of her torso, sat on a high display platform in the corner of the room. On its surface, fish chased other fish in bright ceramic color. She stretched on her toes, and decided that a tall man could easily drop a sheaf of notes into the vase. On the other hand, getting them back out again was a much taller order.

She looked up, and decided that it was doable; the ceiling featured exposed beams that it would be easy to dangle from even without the assistance of rope or a harness. What they needed was a distraction. She briefly considered just shouldering the vase off its perch, and decided that would be too much of a distraction. Instead, she shot Daniel a meaningful glance.

He ignored the meaningful glance. She cleared her throat,

and he ignored that too, although Moreno looked at her sideways in disapproval. Finally she said, "Didn't you want to look at that using the…" She added a vague gesture that she hoped suggested some sort of appropriate piece of Tau'ri equipment.

"Microscope?" Daniel finished after a moment's pause.

"One of those."

Moreno gave her an odd look, but said, "Why not, I'm not getting any work done right now anyway." She put on a pair of gloves that had been jammed in her pocket and picked up the fish vase carefully. "The lab is through here."

"Have you been having trouble with the funding for your lab equipment?" Daniel said, engaging her in conversation as they went. "It's hell trying to get the Air Force to understand why we need half of the things we do."

"You should try foundation funding," Moreno said. Vala tuned out the rest of their conversation, only lending it enough attention to make sure that they were still talking, not returning to pay attention to what she was doing. That wouldn't last long, though, unless Moreno was more careless than she seemed.

It was tempting to climb the nearest pedestal, but she suspected it was alarmed. Up to the ceiling it was, then; a handy bench provided the opportunity, and it was a moment's work to scramble up to dangle from the ceiling. Reaching a position where she could reach the inside of the vase was trickier, and involved suspending herself in an undignified position.

She tried not to be grateful to her father for his instruction in various forms of larceny and confidence schemes, but there were moments when she couldn't help appreciating how skills she'd learned at his knee had proved useful later in life. So many people lacked basic tools for overcoming life's little obstacles, like the ability to climb like an acrobat to retrieve valuables, escape out windows, and hide from situations that had gone unexpectedly sour.

She peered down, and saw something light-colored that might have been paper. Encouraged, she stretched to grab for it, dangling by her knees, her fingers barely touching paper. She had just managed to grasp it between her fingers when she heard Daniel's voice, and her head snapped up in alarm.

"— and the new thermodynamic imaging processes —" Daniel saw her, and for one frozen moment she was afraid he was going to blow their chance by standing and staring. Instead he swung around without hesitation. "I'm sorry, I just realized I left my pen — I can get it, just, which way was it again, left — no, right at the first door and then all the way to the…"

"I'll show you," Moreno said, turning around herself. Vala relaxed, letting her head roll back in relief, and then stretched her arm again. She closed her hand around the pages in triumph and extracted them from the vase, pulling herself back up to the ceiling beams and swinging to jump for the bench. She had just scrambled down from it and was repairing the damage to her hairstyle from dangling upside down when Daniel and Moreno re-emerged.

"You'll have to excuse me, my hair is just unmanageable in this weather," Vala said.

Moreno nodded cautiously, thankfully not commenting on the fact that there wasn't a cloud in the sky, and replaced the fish vase on its display pedestal. "I'll need to unlock the case for the next set," she said.

Daniel raised an eyebrow questioningly at Vala, and she nodded as imperceptibly as she could. He frowned and glanced at his watch. "We should still have time to make that meeting with the dean, don't you think? We've got… oh, wait a minute…"

"Was that today?" Vala asked in theatrical horror. "I thought it was tomorrow. We're going to be late if we don't leave right this minute."

"You're completely right," Daniel said. "Thank you, Dr. Moreno, I appreciate the help, but we'll have to schedule an appointment to see the rest of the pieces — at this point it may need to wait until Vincent is out of the hospital, so…"

"So we'll call you," Vala said, following Daniel as he retreated from the room.

"I'm glad to be of help," Moreno said, shaking her head at the two of them.

"What did you get?" Daniel said once they were out in the parking lot.

Vala brandished the sheets of paper. "I don't know yet."

"You didn't look?"

"There's an old Earth saying that Teal'c taught me," Vala said. "Never count your money while you're sitting at the table." She looked longingly at the car's controls. "I could drive and you could read."

"No."

"It isn't even your car. How hard could it be to learn?"

"You don't have a driver's license."

"That doesn't matter unless you get caught."

"You read, I'll drive," Daniel said, and slid behind the wheel.

"Colonel Mitchell," Carolyn said as Cam came into the mess hall. He had intended to grab a sandwich and go, and ended up standing awkwardly by the cafeteria line, too close to Carolyn's table to pretend he couldn't see her. It wasn't very fair of him to run away, either, given that she probably couldn't chase him with her wounded leg. "Can we talk?"

"Briefly," he said, picking up the sandwich and joining her at her table. "I need to see how our suspects are getting along. Our other suspects."

"Of course," she said, and then looked up at him. "Just please tell me you don't actually think I did this."

"I don't think that," Cam said. "I think you lied to me, and I'm still not happy about that."

Carolyn pushed cubes of Jello around a dish with her spoon. "I know. I shouldn't have lied — well, I didn't exactly lie, I just didn't tell you everything."

"You let me think that you weren't mad at Oliver, and that

there wasn't any good reason to suspect you of having killed him."

"There wasn't. There isn't."

"There's enough of a reason, and it puts us all in a bad position. Look, I know it's weird for you working with Landry. If I had to work with my dad, it would be weird for me. But right now you're in exactly the position you said you never wanted to be in. If you were anybody else, you'd be cooling your heels in guest quarters right now with the rest of the suspects."

"Do you think that would help? I wouldn't mind catching up on some reading."

"I'm more interested in catching our spy. If you've got anything else, anything that might possibly be useful to us, I want to hear it."

"I've been trying to come up with anything that might possibly be relevant, but I really can't think of anything. It's still hard for me to believe that Oliver was working for the Trust."

Cam realized with a guilty twinge that she was still a step behind. "I'm starting to think maybe he wasn't working for the Trust."

"But you said —"

"It's looking more like he caught someone else working for the Trust, and they took him out. Which makes this whole thing even messier, because it suggests we've still got an agent inside the base."

"Oh, my God," Carolyn said. She put down her spoon and pushed her tray away. "You should put me in custody right now."

"That's not a confession, is it?"

"No, I didn't kill him and I'm not a spy. But you have no way of knowing that except that you don't want to believe it. You're right, I shouldn't get special treatment because I'm Landry's daughter. That's the opposite of what I've ever wanted. I want him to believe in me, not to be stupid on my account. If I were anybody else, the idea that I was a spy would be at the top of his list of theories about what happened to Oliver."

"I can't just arrest you."

"I'm not saying throw the book at me, just… you should know where I am and what I'm doing. For both our sakes. If there's still an agent in the base, and somebody's still leaking information, I don't want there to be any question of whether it's me."

"You can finish your lunch first," Cam said.

"I'm pretty much done with this."

"All right. I can go lock you up, if you're really serious about this."

"Dead serious."

"Jackson had better find Oliver's notes," Cam said. "We need some answers here."

He escorted Carolyn to one of the unoccupied guest rooms. All the guest rooms were depressing in their motel-room sameness, like base housing but without anything to suggest that people really lived there rather than just passing through. He hated to leave her stuck there, and hated even more that he was planning to lock the door when he left. "Last chance to get me off the hook of having to explain this to Landry."

"Sorry," Carolyn said. "If someone could bring me the pile of medical journals on my desk, I'd appreciate it."

"This isn't all because you're guilty about lying to me, is it?"

"Let's just say I don't want to create any more problems for anyone," Carolyn said. "I've got more of a motive than you thought. You should take that seriously."

"For what it's worth, I really don't think you did it."

"For what it's worth, I'm glad," Carolyn said as he closed the door.

He went down to check on Chen next, and found her much as he'd left her before, pacing the guest room nervously and insisting the moment he came into the room that she hadn't killed anybody. "All I did was give the artifacts to Green to sell for me, and all he asked Da'shak to give him for them was gold, not any kind of information about the Jaffa. I don't want to know anybody's classified secrets. I'm not a spy."

"You know that would be more convincing coming from someone who wasn't a thief."

"Just because I stole the artifacts doesn't mean I don't care about what we're doing here," Chen said hotly. "Do you think I want the Ori to take over Earth? Or the Goa'uld? I have nightmares about that. I don't want everybody I know to be enslaved by aliens. I can't imagine how anybody could want that. I just wanted some money."

"Sometimes people don't think very much about the consequences of what they're doing," Cam said.

"I think about the consequences," Chen said. "I've had friends who went on off-world missions and didn't come back. The last thing I want is for any more of my friends to die."

"Those friends," Cam said. "Do you think they'd be proud of you if they knew what you'd been doing while they were out putting their lives on the line?"

"No," Chen said, almost a moan. "I screwed up. I know that. But I *didn't kill anyone.* I'm not a spy, and no matter what you do to me, you can't make me admit to something that isn't true."

"I think I left the thumbscrews in my other uniform jacket," Cam said. "All right, sit tight, I'm going to see if Green has anything to say today except that he wants to see a lawyer."

"He'll tell you the same thing," Chen said. "He wanted the money too, but he would never sell secrets to the Goa'uld. They're the people who've been shooting at him and his friends for years. How can you even imagine that he'd cooperate with them?"

Cam refrained from pointing out that getting shot up by the Goa'uld might be exactly what inspired someone to decide cooperating with them was better than the alternative. If Chen hadn't come up with that bad idea on her own, Cam didn't want to suggest it to her. He preferred it when people couldn't even imagine why a person would cooperate with the Goa'uld; it discouraged them from even trying.

In fact, Green had nothing to say except that he still wanted to see his lawyer. "You can't keep me here without a trial forever," he said, crossing his arms over his chest.

"Cool your jets," Cam said. "You'll get a lawyer in a day or two. In the meantime, sit back, enjoy the fine hospitality of the SGC, and think about what you're planning to say at your court-martial."

Next up was Jefferson, who was also pacing when Cam let himself into his guest room, the television playing in the background but with the sound off. He didn't look like it had been very successful in distracting him. "Tell me you found the guy who did this."

"Not yet," Cam said. "I was wondering if there was anything else you wanted to tell me about that."

"I told you everything I knew. Listen, is there any way I can get back into the lab? I'd feel better if I at least had something to do."

"I can bring you a deck of cards," Cam said.

"I found one," Jefferson said, pointing out the solitaire spread on the table behind him. "Solitaire's just not that much fun. You always know how it's going to come out. The interesting thing about archaeology is that you never do know."

"Dead people usually stay dead."

"Sure, and their stuff stays the same until you dig it up, but you never know what you're going to find. No matter how much you think you know about the past, there are always mysteries. There's always some reason people had for doing what they did that you don't know, or some weird kind of object you never thought you'd find that turns up and changes everything you thought you knew. And that's just regular archaeology. That's before you take a job and you find out that basically everything you learned in school is wrong because most of Earth's history involves getting jerked around by a bunch of different aliens."

"Sorry about that," Cam said.

"It's great," Jefferson said. "Well, not most of what actually happened, but it's great to feel like we've figured out one big piece of the truth. It's like wearing a blindfold all your life and finally getting to take it off. We've solved one of the big mysteries. If we can do that, we should be able to figure out anything."

"Now you sound like Jackson."

"Dr. Jackson is terrific," Jefferson said. "I wish I had more opportunities to work with him, but I understand he's busy out there in the field." There was a light in his eyes that Cam recognized, the expression of someone who wasn't really satisfied with a desk job.

"Have you applied to be on an SG team?"

"A few months ago. They said there weren't any openings for civilians right now, but they'd consider me if they put together another science team. I figure that's better than a flat no, right?"

"A lot better," Cam said. "And I guess if you were trying to get out there in the field so that you could report to Goa'uld contacts, you wouldn't tell me, so there's no point in asking, right?"

"What do you think, that I'm some kind of spy?" Jefferson frowned. "Is that why Oliver was killed? Was he mixed up in some kind of spy thing?"

"Why, was there something that made you thinks so?"

"I guess not, just… there was that argument he had with Carr. I thought it was over something personal, but Oliver was always looking over people's shoulders, you know? He had his nose in everybody else's work, he went behind them and checked over what they were doing, and I think sometimes he looked into other people's notebooks when we left them lying around. If somebody had information they shouldn't have had…"

"You think that was what he was arguing with Carr about."

"I don't know. It's just that if there's some kind of spy connection… I think that would make sense with what I heard, as much as that it was a fight over Patricia."

"Dr. Niles says she wasn't dating either Oliver or Carr, but that both of them were being pretty insistent about pursuing her."

"I didn't really notice anything like that," Jefferson said. "She spent time talking to both of them, and maybe they were hitting on her when I wasn't around. When I was around, it was all work talk. She used to stay late in the evenings so that she and Carr could compare notes — I guess maybe he was the one who suggested it, although she never made any excuses not to stay or seemed like she was trying to get out of it. It was always, sure, I'll meet you in the mess hall for coffee and we can go over those notes."

"I'm talking to Carr next," Cam said.

"Ask him what he was arguing with Oliver about."

"I already did. He said it was about Patricia Niles."

"I'm just not sure I believe that," Jefferson said, and Cam wasn't sure he believed it, either.

He made his way down the hall to Carr's guest room, and used his security code to unlock the door. He stared in, and then reached for the intercom to call Landry.

"We've got a problem," he said to Landry.

"What's the problem? And what's this I hear about you arresting Dr. Lam?"

"She arrested herself, ask her about it later. But Carr's gone."

"What do you mean gone?"

Cam turned a circle, looking around the empty room. "Gone. Not in here anymore. He was locked in, and now he's not."

"Pull the security tapes," Landry said. "I want to know how he got out."

"At least maybe we've found our murderer," Cam said.

CHAPTER FOURTEEN

CAM tore through the halls to Sam's lab at a run, and found her taking some kind of crystal object out of a large piece of machinery. Probably she'd explain what she was doing with both if he asked her, so he deliberately didn't do that; there wasn't time. "Pull the security footage from both guest rooms, and from Chen and Green's cells," he said. "For the last couple of hours."

"I can do that," Sam said, slipping the crystal object into her pocket as she sat down at the computer. "I take it there's a problem."

"Carr's gone missing."

"Ouch," Sam said. "Okay, here we go." She ran the footage forward, and they watched as Carr read a book, Chen and Green paced, and Jefferson napped. "I'm not seeing anything out of the ordinary," she said. Then Jefferson's door opened, and Cam sat up straight. "That's just lunchtime," Sam said. A mess attendant put down a tray, and went out again.

She delivered a tray to Carr's guest room next, but while Cam was expecting to see Carr jump her and force his way out, instead she left calmly, and Carr began eating his lunch. The woman left the trays for Chen and Green with the security officers guarding them, and they passed them inside after she had gone.

"So where is he?" Cam said.

"Wait and see." The footage continued speeding forward. Jefferson had woken to eat his lunch, and was now pacing. Chen was sitting in a corner, Green still eating the last of his lunch. Carr had pushed his tray aside and reopened his book.

Then the room door opened. "Freeze frame," Cam said.

Try as he might, he couldn't see who had opened the door. "Do we have a camera in the hallway?"

Sam's fingers flew across the keys. "I'm afraid not." She ran the footage forward, and they watched Carr put down his book and leave the room, the door shutting behind him. "Someone must have opened the door for him."

"Unless he somehow managed to program it to open for him at a certain time."

"We don't have any indication that he has the computer skills to do that," Sam said. "I'll see if I can find any indication that the security systems for the base were tampered with that way. But until I do, it's simpler to assume that someone let him out."

"We need to do a sweep of the base," Cam said. "I can't believe he got out through base security. He's got to be down here somewhere."

"We've got Oliver's notes," Daniel said as soon as he got Landry on the phone. He was manfully resisting the urge to try to read and drive at the same time. In the passenger seat, Vala was frowning at the notes they'd retrieved from the museum.

"Good for you," Landry said. "What do they say?"

"Ah… that would be the catch. It looks like they're in some kind of code. I think it may just be a simple substitution cipher, but I'm not sure the language he wrote it in originally was English, and unless it's English or Ancient, Vala can't read it even if she works out the code."

"I just love trying to work out ciphers in alien languages I don't speak," Vala said. "How many vowels in a row are plausible in Earth languages? Is four too many?"

"It's going to have to wait until we get back," Daniel said into the phone.

"Get back as soon as you can. Carr's missing."

"What?" Vala was twisting herself into a pretzel shape trying to lean over close enough to hear, and Daniel reluctantly put the phone on speaker. "Did you say Carr is missing?"

"Missing," Landry said. "As in we can't find him. Either he let himself out of a locked room, or somebody let him out. I'd very much like to know what's in those notes of yours, in case it turns out that they shed some light on the problem."

"I'm driving as fast as I can," Daniel said.

"Well, I don't see how that can possibly be true," Vala said. "Sam's vehicle goes much faster than this. Or are the ones that the military uses generally defective?"

Daniel decided that he was going to take away from that the hopeful note that Vala was calling Sam by her first name, which suggested that getting shot at together had been a bonding experience for them, and not speculate about just how fast Sam had been driving. He hoped Vala would bond with the rest of the team. He needed Vala to bond with the rest of the team, because being the focus of her undivided attention while they'd been trapped together by the alien bracelets had made him more than a little crazy.

"We have laws about that kind of thing," Landry said. "Don't get arrested, Jackson. Just get back here as fast as you reasonably can. I want some answers."

"So do we all," Daniel said.

They arrived back at the base to find that they had to talk their way through an extensive security cordon before they were able to leave the elevator. Vala turned on the charm again, which he suspected only made the security guards more suspicious. Finally he managed to persuade them that neither he nor Vala had Gideon Carr hidden under their clothes — Vala came perilously close to demonstrating that — and headed for Landry's office.

"We've locked the base back down," Landry said when Daniel and Vala got there. Daniel refrained from saying that he never would have guessed. "I did give orders that the guards were supposed to let you two through."

"They did eventually, they just didn't look happy about it."

"We're doing a complete sweep of the base. If Carr's still here anywhere, we're going to find him."

"Do you think there's any chance that he's not?"

"We have security cameras on all the entrances and exits. Even the one that involves crawling through access tunnels. There's no way he could have gotten out of here without sounding a dozen alarms."

"Unless he was very, very good at disabling them," Vala said.

"Which we don't have any reason to believe, so I'm choosing to believe that he's here somewhere. We've just got to find him."

"We found Carr," Mitchell's voice said abruptly over the intercom. "He's in one of the storage rooms on level 26. Sir, he's dead."

"I'm on my way," Landry said, and Daniel and Vala followed him at a run.

The storage room was one of the ones used for long-term storage of food supplies, and Carr sat on one of the large boxes, propped up next to an oversized bag of potatoes. He was clearly dead, his eyes open as if in surprise. A zat was lying on the floor by his feet, and Daniel reached to pick it up.

Mitchell held out an arm to stop him. "I'm hoping for fingerprints," he said.

"You think he was murdered?" Vala said. There was a note lying on a nearby crate, torn from one of the ubiquitous SGC notepads, and she leaned over it to read it without touching it. "This looks like a suicide note to me."

I can't do this anymore, the note read. *I want out. This is the end*

"There's no period at the end of the sentence," Daniel said.

Mitchell gave him a sideways look. "So?"

"I'm not sure this is where the sentence originally ended. The paper's torn. The note breaks off abruptly. There's no signature, no 'sorry about the mess' or 'you'll be sorry when I'm gone' or anything else you typically see with a suicide."

"You think the note was torn from something Carr had already written," Mitchell said.

"I think it's a good possibility," Daniel said. He looked around. "There's no pen in here, no notepad. Check the room where he was staying. See if there's a torn piece of paper that matches this, and whether the piece of paper under it is indented. If he wrote on a notepad, there should be marks, grooves, in the paper underneath—"

"I think I get the picture," Mitchell said. "Anyway, if he had a zat, and he wanted to off himself, why break out before he did it? Why not do it in his guest room and spare us all hunting for him all over the base?"

"And if he managed to break out, then why would he kill himself?" Vala said. "On the other hand, if someone else was planning to kill him, why would they break him out?"

"Because the isolation rooms have cameras," Daniel said. "And whoever broke him out didn't want to be seen, because we'd recognize them. Which implies that we've still got an enemy agent in the base."

Landry's radio sounded. "Unscheduled off-world activation," Walter said. "It's Teal'c's IDC."

"Open the iris," Landry said. "And get a medical team down here to check for fingerprints and verify the cause of death. We're going to keep searching the base, and he can help. Not you, Dr. Jackson," Landry said when Daniel moved to follow him and Vala. "You crack that code."

"I thought I'd see if you could use some help," Sam said. Daniel was frowning over the sheets of paper he'd brought back from Denver, a stack of books by his side and a number of false starts at decodings on the paper in front of him.

"Thanks. I could use some." He slid the paper over to her, and she leaned down to examine his guesses.

"That can't be right," she said.

"I don't think it is. I think the original's in Latin, not English."

Sam felt she would have been on a firmer footing if the message consisted of more technical vocabulary, rather than probably revolving around spies and descriptions of archaeological activity. "My Latin is… mostly Ancient."

"Even so, I'm not getting anywhere."

Sam looked at Daniel more closely, and sat down at the table next to him. "You're worried."

"It's Carolyn," he said. "I was really sure that she didn't have anything to do with this."

"We still don't think she does, do we?"

"She went out of the way to give herself an alibi right before Carr disappeared. She told Mitchell to put her in an isolation room, and he did."

"That's good, right?" Sam offered. "Because if she was in an isolation room, she can't have been the one who let Carr out."

"Unless she programmed the door to open, and then put herself in isolation so that it would look like she had an alibi," Daniel said. "Or unless there's another person in this, and Carolyn knew what they were planning and wanted to make sure she couldn't be blamed."

"You don't think that."

"I don't know," Daniel said, pushing the papers away in frustration. "We don't know her the way we knew Janet."

"Nobody's ever going to replace Janet," Sam said. It still made her chest ache to remember that Janet was gone, but she was trying these days to talk about her more, to remember everything they'd shared together, if only for Cassie's sake. It wasn't fair to Cassie to let her memories of Janet slip away, or to let Janet become one of the parts of SG-1's shared past that they all agreed not to talk about because it hurt too much. "Carolyn's not Janet. But she's never given us any reason to think that she's a spy."

"That's pretty much the definition of being a good spy."

"Okay, but why would she need Carr, if our theory is that she might be his accomplice? Carolyn has top-level clearance. If she were trying to spy on the SGC, all she'd need is a contact with the Trust. She wouldn't need to work with Carr. There's nothing he could find out that she couldn't find out herself. Even the archaeology stuff, if that's of any possible interest to the Trust—Carolyn was working with Oliver, she must have had access to the archaeology lab."

"Which is just what bothers me," Daniel said, leaning back in his chair and looking up at the ceiling as if he could find the answers to their problems there. "Maybe the Trust was just making sure they had all their bases covered. Two agents in case one of them got caught."

"And in that case, one of them was supposed to take out the other one?" Sam shook her head. "Can you really imagine Carolyn doing that? Not even imagine her stealing secrets. Maybe everybody has some button you could push that would persuade them to do that, I don't know. But can you imagine her killing Carr in cold blood and then faking a suicide note, really?"

"No, I can't," Daniel said. "But I can't be sure that's not wishful thinking. Not about anybody we've known for less than a year. I can't be absolutely sure about Carolyn, or Vala, or even Mitchell and Landry, and it drives me crazy, because, I don't know, what if I gamble on them when it really matters and it turns out…"

"They're not trustworthy?"

"I guess so."

She put her shoulder against his for a moment. "We can't know, right? So we're back in the same place we were when we first joined the SGC. Just hoping we're trusting the right people. That worked out pretty well for us."

"I already knew I could trust Jack," Daniel said. "I stopped doubting him after Abydos. Well, mostly stopped doubting him. I knew he'd do the right thing when it counted."

"But you didn't know me, or Teal'c."

Daniel turned up his hands, granting that, but still didn't look entirely satisfied. "It was different back then."

"We were younger," Sam said. "And we didn't know how scary the world out there was. But by the time we'd been working together for a year, you would have put everything on the line for any of us. You know that's true."

"I'd do that for Mitchell and Vala now," Daniel said. "Maybe not because I trust them that much, but… because I have to trust them that much. Which I guess is my answer." He shook his head. "You know, I don't think it's true that there's a way to persuade anybody to steal secrets. You wouldn't, Jack wouldn't, Teal'c wouldn't. I'm certain of that."

"I hope not," Sam said. "I'd like to think that no matter what somebody offered me…"

"And that's an interesting question, when you think about it," Daniel said, his expression sharpening. "What do we think the Trust offered Carr and whoever else he was working with?"

Sam shrugged. "Money?"

"Maybe, but there have got to be safer ways to make money."

"Like stealing artifacts and selling them to the Jaffa?"

"At least that doesn't involve working with people who kill you if you double-cross them, or use you as a host for…"

Their eyes met. "We should find out whether anybody has medical problems that would make becoming a host sound attractive, shouldn't we?" Sam said.

"Or being healed with a sarcophagus. That's the big enticement the Trust can offer that nobody else can. It might not even be the spy, it might be a relative, someone they know…"

"It's going to take some time to hunt down that information about everybody on the base," Sam said. "And time is just what we don't have."

"So let's ask Carolyn if she can tell you off the top of her head who might have been tempted," Daniel said. He shrugged at Sam's expression. "You want us in, let's be all in. She didn't do it, that's that, so we can trust her information."

"Okay," Sam said. "I'll ask Mitchell to do that, and we'll figure out this code." She pulled her chair around to get a better view of the sheets of paper in front of him, which made it at least possible to decipher Daniel's handwriting.

"I've found a bunch of things that aren't the key to the cipher, unless the message contains a lot of Xs in a row."

"That's a start," Sam said. "Let's go from there."

"I want you to know this was Jackson's idea," Cam said as he sat down across the table from Carolyn in the isolation room. Good to her word, she'd been working her way through stacks of medical journals, although the television was on as well, CNN playing silently without an audience. "He thinks we ought to trust you."

Carolyn put her head to one side. "Should I say that I'm pleased that he trusts me, or that I'm sorry that you obviously don't?"

"He's choosing to trust you," Cam said. "And so am I, so here's my question. It's possible that the Trust offered their agent — or agents — more than just money. The one thing we know they have that money wouldn't buy is either the opportunity to become a host, or if somebody was too smart to make that particular devil's bargain, the chance to use a sarcophagus."

"Which is also a devil's bargain," Carolyn said.

"But one that might seem awfully tempting to someone who didn't care whether it made their soul less shiny, or whatever it is those things do."

"They're addictive and destructive to people's personalities," Carolyn said. "And we're pretty sure they're the reason that the Goa'uld are universally unpleasant people, and mostly extremely mentally unbalanced. I don't know if they really erode people's souls. We didn't cover souls in medical school. I can tell you as a medical professional that I wouldn't recommend using one except as a last resort."

"And there are a lot of people who might appreciate having that last resort."

"Which I've always understood to be the reason why we don't keep one around," Carolyn said. "We could go out and get a sarcophagus. But then the next time that someone had fatal injuries, we'd use it. And then the next time that someone had injuries that were going to end their career. And then one of us would start getting old. You know General Hammond has heart problems."

"I know. I know. Believe me, I thought about it myself." He'd wished, during his slow recovery from the crash, that he didn't know about the sarcophagi, so that he couldn't resent the fact that other people's injuries had been healed in a flash of light while he kept waking up to his day after day. He was doing a better job with not resenting, these days, but he still didn't have any trouble understanding the temptation to use the technology if they'd had it readily to hand.

"I'm sure you did. And imagine the temptation for a doctor. Do you think it would be easy for me to let people die, or suffer permanent disabilities, knowing that I could prevent that if I used the sarcophagus? I'm glad that decision isn't in my hands."

"Well, the Trust aren't big on ethics. I need to know if there was a reason why anybody in this picture might have been tempted."

"There's such a thing as medical privacy."

"And I'm trying to catch a spy."

"I know." Carolyn paused for a second, choosing her words carefully. "Without getting into specifics, no, I don't know of any reason why any of the archaeologists working with Dr. Oliver would try to get access to Goa'uld healing techniques. That doesn't mean they didn't have any relatives or friends who might have benefitted from them. But they were all generally healthy."

"Including Dr. Niles?"

Her pause was longer that time. "She was also generally healthy. However, she has a close relative with a degenerative disease. That's as much as I feel like I can say about that, honestly."

"That's probably all I need. Would a sarcophagus work on that kind of thing?"

"Probably not," Carolyn said. "It might alleviate symptoms, but it wouldn't cause a permanent cure. Of course, from the Trust's point of view, that might be all to the good, right? But the only thing that I know of that would allow permanent healing of a degenerative illness rather than an acute injury is to be joined with a Goa'uld symbiote."

"Which is definitely a cure that's worse than the disease."

"We know that," Carolyn said. "But there's no telling what the Trust promised. It's possible that they offered to find a symbiote that would join with Niles's relative long enough to heal them and then move to a new host."

"But they'd be lying."

"Oh, yeah. Bigtime."

Cam shook his head. "I don't really want to sympathize with a spy and a murderer. But if Niles is mixed up in this, it sounds like she may have gotten played."

"Which still doesn't excuse the spying and murdering."

"No, but it makes a little more sense," Cam said. "All right. Let's see if Jackson has broken that code yet. I'd really like to know if Oliver said anything about Niles."

"Cam?" Carolyn said as he started to leave. "Thanks. For trusting me."

"I'm doing the right thing to trust you, right?"

"You are. Of course, that's probably what I'd say if I were an agent for the Trust."

"I'm trying not think about that."

"I suppose you're wondering why I've called you all here," Mitchell said when SG-1 and Landry were assembled around the conference table. Daniel frowned into his coffee cup, trying not to laugh. Vala put her head to one side curiously, Teal'c looked amused, and Landry looked unamused. Mitchell hurried on. "Jackson, what have you got?"

"Well, Sam helped me break the cipher Oliver was using for his notes," Daniel began. "She realized that it was based on a—"

"Good work, let's cut to the chase," Landry interrupted.

"The Trust's original spy was Patricia Niles," Daniel said, after a momentary pause to distill the information down to its purest form. "Oliver got suspicious when he noticed her accessing computer files she had no reason to be interested in. He decided to play detective and plant some files with intriguing names to see if she would open them, and she did. Oliver should have gone to you at that point, of course."

"You're right about that," Landry said.

"Instead he apparently decided to do a little cloak and dagger work of his own. He doctored up a file to look top secret — he says there wasn't anything actually top secret in it, just a lot of really boring material on planets we surveyed years ago. He left it on his desk and left Niles alone in there, with a hidden camera to snap pictures. Apparently he got some very nice shots of Niles flipping through the folder."

"So where are they?"

"What?"

"The pictures. The proof."

"Ah… they were apparently on Oliver's computer, but we didn't find anything like that when we searched Oliver's computer, which suggests that someone deleted them after Oliver's death."

"But not Niles, because she was in Denver at the time," Landry said.

"No. Niles realized that Oliver was onto her, which explains her sudden departure from the SGC. Oliver had already gotten suspicious about the amount of time she'd been spending with Gideon Carr."

"Suspicious in a romantic sense?" Vala asked. "Or in a cloak and dagger sense?"

"I think more the latter," Daniel said. "I don't know whether Carr ever actually had any romantic interest in Niles, or whether the whole thing was a cover for their spying, and it ultimately doesn't matter. Either way, it looks like Niles talked

Carr into feeding her information after she left. The last thing that Oliver says in his notes is that he was planning to confront Carr about it."

"That doesn't seem to have worked out very well for him," Vala said.

"I guess not."

"We need to pick up Niles," Mitchell said. "But there's still a problem here. Niles couldn't have killed Carr. There's got to be another agent still here on base."

"Yeah, and unfortunately there's nothing in Oliver's notes to suggest who that might be."

"At least it's a starting point," Sam said. "And once we have Niles in custody, she may be willing to tell us who else they were working with."

"The trick may be finding her," Mitchell said. "Let's hope she's either at work or at home. If we have to stake out her apartment and wait for her to come back, it may be a long night."

"We're not going to have to do that," Sam said. In answer to his raised eyebrows, she shrugged and said, "I put a tracker in her car. We can use that to trace her movements."

"I thought you said you were sympathetic to her," Vala protested.

"Not that sympathetic."

"All right," Mitchell said. "I'll take Sam and Teal'c and go have a little chat with Niles. Jackson, make sure there's nothing you missed in those notes."

"There's not," Daniel protested immediately, but then subsided. "I'll check again."

"What about me?" Vala said.

"You're going to be searching the base with me," Landry said. "If there's anything out of the ordinary, I want to know about it."

"Just don't hurt my car," Cam said as Sam changed lanes. The tracker had put Niles at the edge of the University of Denver campus, heading north toward the green expanse of

Washington Park. It was probably the easiest place to stop Niles without bystanders getting in the way, and Sam had no intention of letting her outdistance them. "Sam…"

Sam shook her head at him. "I'm not going to hurt your car." Cam's Mustang was a pretty sweet car, and she really didn't want to mess it up, but she also had less sympathy after the wreck the Trust had already made of her own car.

"Maybe I should be driving."

"You and Teal'c are faster on foot. Whoever's behind the wheel is going to be the last one who can jump out of the car. And, no offense, but if we're going to have a car chase, I'd rather be driving."

"We're not going to have a car chase," Cam said. "Are we going to have a car chase?"

"It is to be hoped that we will not," Teal'c said.

"I still think we should have swung by my place to pick up my motorcycle," Sam said. "Just in case."

"We aren't going to need your bike," Cam said. "Because we're not going to have a car chase. Just for once, something's going to go smoothly and without a hitch, right?"

"You said it," Sam said.

"Okay, the signal's showing up a block ahead of us. We're just going to pull in behind her, nice and easy, and follow her."

"Pulling in behind her," Sam said, as she spotted Niles's cream-colored sedan in the lane in front of her. Even in the gathering dusk, the car's color made it easy to tail. "I'm going to give her a couple of blocks and then let her know we're here."

"She's going to catch on sooner than that if you stay on her bumper. Try and drive casual."

"Maybe I should have let you drive," Sam said. "You're as much of a backseat driver as Colonel O'Neill."

"I would not advise trying to drive this vehicle from the rear seat," Teal'c said.

"She means I'm telling her what to do," Cam said. Sam caught Teal'c's eye in the rearview mirror; from his amused expression, he knew that perfectly well. She wasn't sure that Cam had entirely figured out Teal'c's sense of humor yet.

In front of her, Niles' car changed lanes, and then accelerated. "Uh-oh."

"I said drive casual," Cam protested.

"Next time, you do the tailing," Sam said. "She knows we're behind her. Let's see if she'll pull over." She sped up to crowd Niles' rear bumper, but Niles pulled ahead of her again, weaving back and forth in her lane and winning honks from oncoming drivers.

"I told you we were going to have a car chase," Cam said.

"We're not going to have a car chase," Sam said. "That would be dangerous." She glanced over her shoulder to check for space, wrenched the wheel around to dodge to Niles's left, still mostly in her own lane, and swerved to nudge Niles' fender, trying to encourage her to pull over.

Instead Niles slammed on the brakes, falling behind as Sam swerved back into her lane to avoid oncoming traffic, and then made a hard right turn.

"The paint job, the paint job," Cam said.

"I'll get it detailed," Sam said, trying to turn in time to follow Niles. Her rear tires squealed, and the street corner loomed in front of her. She had to swerve back into her lane, admitting defeat. "Which way is she going? I can take the next right and try to get in front of her."

"Do that," Cam said. "She's still moving."

"If she figures out that we've got a tracker in her car, that's it," Sam said. "She'll ditch the car and we'll have to go after her on foot." The next right turn was coming up, and she hit the brakes hard, wrestling the car into the turn. "Is she still heading east?"

"She's turning north," Cam said. "I think she's heading up the side of the park.

"Perfect," Sam said. She turned north herself, and could see Niles's taillights in the distance. Too far in the distance; she sped up, the streetlights at the edge of the park flying by as she gained on the cream sedan.

"You know if we get pulled over for speeding we're not going to catch her," Cam said.

"I know what I'm doing." She was gaining on the car, and flashed her headlights. The car only sped up, the dark expanse of the park flying by to her right.

"This would be an advantageous place to stop her," Teal'c said.

"Way ahead of you," Sam said. She honked and floored the gas pedal, tapping Niles's rear bumper.

"My car," Cam said through gritted teeth.

"Unless we want to zat her while she's driving…"

"She deserves it," Cam said, but put his hands over his eyes. "I know, I know, just do it."

Sam pulled into the opposite lane the moment there was a lull in the oncoming traffic. She jockeyed the car forward until she was even with Niles, and then slammed into her, forcing her car off the road. They barreled along over grass and sidewalks, until finally Niles's car plowed into a raised flowerbed and came to a stop. Sam threw on the brakes herself, and glanced sideways to make sure Cam had taken his hands away from his eyes.

He was already moving, his hand on the car door, and Teal'c had his door open already. Sam stepped out on the driver's side and drew her sidearm in one motion. "Dr. Niles! There's nowhere for you to go!"

Niles opened her own car door and scrambled out. For a moment, Sam thought she was going to bolt away between the flowerbeds toward the lake beyond, but then she shook her head and raised her hands, showing Sam her open palms.

"Search her," Sam said.

"Way ahead of you," Cam said, already patting Niles down for weapons. "She's clean," he said, but pulled her hands down so that Teal'c could cuff them behind her back anyway.

"I'm afraid we're going to need you to come back to the SGC

with us and answer a few questions," Sam said.

"Like why you've been spying for the Trust, and who your little friend in the SGC is," Cam said.

"You don't really care why," Niles said. "And it doesn't matter what you do to me right now. Do you think I'm the only one who's working for the Trust? They'll succeed without me. I don't think I'm going to be sitting in a military prison for long."

"Succeed at what, letting the Goa'uld take over Earth?" Cam said. "That doesn't sound like too hot an idea to me."

"There are compensations," Niles said. "Their technology, to start with. Don't you understand that they can do things we've only ever dreamed of? All those science fiction fantasies you ever had as a kid are going to come true."

"More like nightmares," Cam said.

"For the ones who oppose them. But the humans who give them Earth…"

"Will be really privileged slaves when we get our new overlords, I get it," Cam said. "We've heard this one before."

"These are not new promises," Teal'c said. "My own people have learned better than to believe them."

Niles let out a humorless breath of laughter. "Your people? Your people already have all the advantages that the Goa'uld can give their servants," she said. "Do you think I don't know that the Jaffa live for centuries?"

"Only as hosts for the Goa'uld young. A privilege that the Goa'uld could withdraw at any time if one of us failed to please them."

Niles was shaking her head at Teal'c. "You don't think that's still a pretty good deal? So you had people telling you what to do. Everybody has that, one way or another. You don't get old for hundreds of years, you can heal yourself if you get hurt, you don't get sick—"

"Who's sick?" Sam asked, trying to make her voice gentle. "A relative?"

"My sister," Niles said. Her face was bloodless, her mouth

set in a grim line. "She has ALS, Lou Gehrig's disease. She's going to die."

"I'm sorry about that," Cam said.

"Being sorry won't fix it. The Trust contacted me right after I took the job at the SGC. They said they could cure her, and all they wanted in exchange was information."

"And you believed them?" Teal'c asked, his voice dark with skepticism.

"Not at first. They said they'd prove it, though. They told me to bring her to them and they'd show me. I had to lie to her. I couldn't tell her about aliens, she'd think I was crazy. I said I had a friend who worked at a clinic, that they could get her into a trial of a new treatment… they had a setup in a warehouse, with everything set up like a clinic. They told her the sarcophagus was a kind of radiation treatment. It scared the hell out of her, but she was willing to try anything. She wants to live."

"They put her in a sarcophagus," Sam said.

"It helped," Niles said. "But it didn't last. She's been in the sarcophagus three times, and each time it works a little less."

"And each time it takes a bit more of the person you knew as your sister away," Teal'c said. "In the end, she will be a stranger to you."

"You think she cares about that? I told you, she wants to live. Whether she's the same or not. If that's what she wants, that's what I want her to get. But the sarcophagus isn't working anymore anyway. She needs a Goa'uld symbiote."

"Do you understand what that means?" Sam said. "The host personality is entirely taken over by the Goa'uld. She'd be trapped within her body, unable to do anything but watch while a Goa'uld used her body to do awful things."

For the first time, a hint of doubt showed on Niles's face. "That's not what they told me."

"News flash, they lie," Cam said.

CHAPTER FIFTEEN

DANIEL checked over his decoding of the notes one last time and then tossed the whole sheaf of notes aside, certain there was nothing it could tell him that he didn't already know. He also had no idea where to begin looking for Carr's killer; he'd already told Landry and Vala they should search the circuitous system of tunnels they used as a back door to the base during their tests for prospective new SG team members, but they'd come up with nothing but a new appreciation for the amount of climbing required during those practice exercises.

He spread out his photos of the dagger and the chamber with the pedestals instead, comparing them to the illustrations in the book where he'd originally found the gate symbols, and then to every other source he could find. One of the books showed copies of an illuminated manuscript that depicted Arthur and his knights next to what might have been an even smaller fragment of the fragmentary gate symbols, and he examined that one more closely. There was a shape in the drawing that might have been a dagger, although if he hadn't known that, he would have assumed from its shape that it was a key.

A sword, a dagger, a key; there was something in that that nagged at him, and he flipped pages in one of the books of Welsh poetry in English translation, rifling past the Triads and stopping at a translation of the Battle of the Trees. It was a different translation than he was used to, or possibly interpolating lines of another poem, as several of the surviving versions did:

I have been a narrow sword,
I have been a darkness in the air,
I have been a key to tales.

A narrow sword—that might be something like a dagger. And "a key to tales"… figurative, maybe, but there was something about the shape of the pedestals that was nagging at him, some reason he had been immediately certain that they were meant for weapons to rest on. He picked out the printed photo of the pedestal that had seemed dagger-sized, and held it up to the light. He thought he could just make out a fine outline on its surface, as if it were suggesting where the dagger might be placed.

It made him itch to go back at once and try placing the dagger within the outline. They'd been so distracted by Collins' injury and the possibility of the beast returning that he hadn't even considered the possibility that the dagger might open one of the other pedestals. But there was no time for that, now. They had to find the Trust agent, and fast.

He put the book aside, hoping that there would eventually be time to return to the caves and investigate. It can't all be an unending series of crises, he told himself, and tried to believe it.

"You can tell us all about the pretty promises they made you once we get you into a cell," Cam told Niles. They couldn't keep having this conversation in a flowerbed next to a wrecked car unless they wanted the police in attendance. "Your friend Carr is dead, by the way." He thought he saw surprise on her face at that, a stiffening of her whole body, but she only nodded. "And as soon as you tell us who the other agent in the Mountain is, they're going down with you. If you tell us now and spare us a whole unpleasant interrogation, it might go easier for you."

Cam wasn't sure that making threats was really his strong suit, and found himself perversely wishing that Vala were around to play the bad cop. Certainly Niles only raised her chin defiantly, looking like she'd never watched the kind of TV shows that would have told her that the bad guys were supposed to confess and throw themselves on his mercy at that point.

"I don't believe that for a minute," Niles said. "And I don't care anymore whether it goes easy for me or not. You've probably killed my sister, and you can all go to hell for that." She smiled, an expression that sent shivers down Cam's back.

He glanced at Sam, wondering if he should cut this off as unproductive ranting. She shrugged, leaving the decision up to him, which he appreciated, even though that meant he had to make it. He decided to let it ride; those TV detectives certainly got good results from letting murderers brag about their evil plans, even if he suspected that the murderers' lawyers would have advised them not to make statements that began "Yes, I did it, and he deserved it, too."

"I'm just sorry that you're here and not at Cheyenne Mountain," Niles said. "You'll have to go to hell a little behind schedule."

Cam frowned. "What are you talking about?"

"I called my friends at the Trust when I saw you following me, to tell them that you were onto me. Their agents in the mountain aren't going to be any use to them anymore — apparently they've already decided that Carr was more of a liability than an asset."

"We'll find whoever killed Carr," Cam said.

"It's too late. They've already finished the job they've been sent to do. Did you think they were just smuggling information out? They've also been smuggling equipment in. Right about now, their remaining agent will be setting the timer on a bomb powerful enough to destroy the entire mountain and bury the Stargate under half a mile of solid rock."

It was tempting to believe that Niles was bluffing, but if there was any chance that she wasn't —

"Call the mountain, now," Cam said to Teal'c, and Teal'c stepped a little away from Niles and withdrew his cell phone from his pocket.

"Why would Ba'al want to do that?" Sam asked. "We know Ba'al is the one who's been pulling the strings at the Trust. He wants to use the SGC to get what he wants, not to take us out entirely."

"Oh, this isn't Ba'al's plan," Niles said. "There are a lot of people in the Trust who are on board with inviting the Goa'uld in, but not with that Goa'uld being Ba'al. His clones have been acting… erratic, and he has a reputation for being hard to predict."

"You mean hard to manipulate," Sam said. "You know, playing that kind of game with any of the Goa'uld is suicidal. Plenty of people have tried."

"My contacts are people who were in the old NID," Niles said, ignoring Sam's point. "They're not running Ba'al's agenda; they figure they're better off if they make their own plans. Of course, in order to do that, they need to get you and the Stargate program out of the way. I wasn't really sure about that, but you know what? At this point, I'd cheer them on."

Cam looked a question at Sam, and she nodded reluctantly. "It's plausible. A lousy idea, but an old NID kind of lousy idea."

Cam drew his pistol and leveled it at Niles. "Where's the bomb? And who planted it?"

She shook her head. "You're not really going to shoot me."

"You're right, I'm not going to kill you. We don't do that kind of thing." Cam lowered the pistol to point it at Niles's kneecap. "But take it from me, when you're sweating through rehab in prison, you may wish that I had."

Niles licked her lips nervously. "I don't know where the bomb is, and even if I tell you who the agent is who planted it, that won't help you disarm it."

Cam thumbed back the hammer on the pistol, the noise sounding very loud despite the hum of passing traffic. "Let me worry about that. I want a name."

Niles took a deep breath, and at the same time it registered to Cam that one of the passing cars was slowing. He turned his back to make it less obvious that he was threatening someone with a gun, and then there was a single sharp crack, and the car's tires squealed as it accelerated away. Niles's head went back as if in surprise, and she crumpled to her knees.

Cam reached to help her, and caught her weight as she fell. She had been shot neatly through the temple, and her eyes were wide and unseeing. Cam lowered her to the ground, his hands coming away bloody as he let go. He wasn't sure it was ever going to stop shocking him to watch someone die like that, there one moment and gone the next. He wasn't sure he wanted it to.

He heard the squeal of tires. "Get under cover," he said. "They're coming back around."

"I believe we can take them," Teal'c said, drawing his zat.

"Still, I'd like a little more of an advantage."

Sam scrambled behind the cover of the car, and made room for Cam to join her. "This seems familiar."

"So what did you and Vala do?"

"Get zatted."

"Let's think of another plan," Cam said.

"Sounds good to me."

Vala was investigating a featureless storage area that seemed identical to every other featureless storage area on the base; it contained metal shelves, boxes of what in this case proved to be paper and other supplies for printing out the endless reports that the Tau'ri adored, and a bare light bulb hanging from the ceiling that barely illuminated the room. It did not contain a lurking spy, not that she had expected it to.

If she were a spy, she had concluded some time ago, and she were planning to commit murder, she would either have a foolproof plan for escaping, or be trusted enough that she wouldn't have to escape; she'd just go back to her job and be doing something completely innocuous while the search boiled past her. There didn't seem to be much point in saying that, though, as Landry seemed in no mood to give the search up as a lost cause.

Alarm sirens sounded, and she looked around, still failing to notice any major threat from the boxes of office supplies. The door flew open, and Daniel stood in the doorway, looking harried. "Slight change of plans," he said. "We're not looking for a spy anymore. We're looking for a bomb."

"A bomb."

"You know, an explosive device—"

"I know what a bomb is," she said testily. "Just fill me in a little bit, please."

"The Trust has an agent. They've planted an explosive. Don't ask 'where,' that's what we've got to figure out. Landry's evacuating non-essential personnel, but we've got to keep enough people down here to find this thing."

"Where would it do the most damage?" Vala said.

Daniel shook his head. "I don't know. No, the gate room. Everything else can be replaced, but the Stargate can't."

"I doubt they have explosives that can actually blow up a Stargate."

"No, but if they bury it in rubble, it's going to take us a long time to dig it out."

"Or if they block the main exit from the mountain and leave us all buried in here." It was not a pleasant prospect to wind up trapped under so much rock.

"Or that," Daniel granted. "Although then we could always use the Stargate to leave."

"Maybe that's just what they want us to do."

"You're overcomplicating this."

"I'm trying to stay a step ahead," Vala said. "You have to get into the minds of your enemies."

"That would be a lot easier if we knew who our enemy was."

"Well, if it's not Chen—"

"It doesn't make sense for it to be Chen. If she'd blown up the base, she'd have lost her source of artifacts to counterfeit. And it's not Carr, because he's dead. And it's not Niles, because she's in Denver."

"Then that leaves Dr. Jefferson," Vala said.

"Who's in custody."

"He could have planted the bomb before Oliver died, for all we know. And we didn't strip-search the archaeologists when we put them in custody—"

"Obviously a mistake."

"—so it's possible he's been sitting in there with a remote control that would let him set off the bomb at any time."

"So let's find him and have a little chat."

Jefferson was still in his guest room, and thankfully not either missing or dead. He was pacing again, and spun to face them as they entered. "What's going on? The base sirens are going crazy."

"You tell us," Vala said. She was getting tired of being the good cop. "You planted the bomb, didn't you? It's all part of your nefarious plan. Well, we're onto you." She advanced on him, and had the satisfaction of watching him take a step back. She lowered her voice to Qetesh's most dangerous purr. "Tell us where the bomb is, or I personally guarantee that you'll regret it."

"What bomb?" Jefferson asked, sounding baffled.

"You know very well what bomb." She leaned in, going on tiptoe so that she could glare down at him. "And you don't want to know what happens to people who lie to me."

"Ah, Vala, that's probably enough. It doesn't look like he knows about the bomb," Daniel said. Vala gave him a look that hopefully communicated approval for his efforts at playing the good cop. Jefferson took another step back, and she pursued, driving him back against the wall.

"What bomb?" he protested.

"You know perfectly well—" Vala began.

"There's a bomb in the base," Daniel said. "Planted by an agent of the Trust."

"That's terrible," Jefferson said. He looked around nervously. "So should we be evacuating right now, or…"

"So that's your plan," Vala said. "Plant the bomb, and then escape during the evacuation. Fiendishly clever, but it won't work." She glanced sideways at Daniel, uncertain whether this was one of the areas in which Tau'ri treatment of prisoners differed significantly from Goa'uld practice. "Will it?"

"We should probably let him evacuate," Daniel said. "Under guard, of course."

"Being under guard wouldn't stop me from escaping," Vala said.

"I don't think Jefferson's going to flirt with his guards until they're distracted and then kick one of them in the face," Daniel said.

"No. No, I won't be doing that," Jefferson assured them.

"He's the one who planted the bomb. He ought to stay here and suffer the consequences."

"I did not plant a bomb!" Jefferson burst out. "How could I have done that? I've been locked up in here ever since we found out Oliver was dead. And before that, it's not like I have access to explosives."

"Your confederate in the Trust would have taken care of that," Vala said.

"I don't know anybody in the Trust," Jefferson said. "And if I had a confederate in the Trust who could smuggle things onto the base, why would they need me?"

"To put the bomb in the gate room where it would do the maximum damage to the base."

"I don't have access to the gate room," Jefferson said. He crossed his arms. "I'm a civilian contractor. I'm not cleared to go off-world, and no one handed out explosives to me when I was hired. I don't know anything about this. Really," he added when neither of them answered.

"Okay," Daniel said after a pause. "You wait here, and I'm sure a security guard will come to help you evacuate."

"How sure are you?"

"Practically positive," Vala said. She followed Daniel outside, and stepped up into a conspiratorial huddle, from which Daniel extracted himself by stepping six inches back. "Do we believe him?"

Abruptly the siren stopped sounding and the warning lights went out.

"Okay," Daniel said after a momentary pause. "This could be good or bad."

"SG-1, report to the archaeology lab," the intercom announced.

Daniel and Vala sprinted for the archaeology lab, and Vala swung around the doorway to see Landry and Sgt. Siler confronting a tangle of wires and lights under one of the countertops in the lab.

"I take it we found our bomb," Daniel said.

"Looks like it," Siler said. He crouched and peered at the wiring, and then reached in with a pair of clippers. Daniel tensed, and Vala edged back to flatten herself against the wall of the lab. She preferred to keep a certain healthy distance from people who were poking things that might explode.

Siler snipped three wires, and the lights on the device went out. He pulled it out cautiously and set it on the counter. "Here's your bomb."

"That was easy," Vala said.

"Yes, it was," Siler said. He was frowning. He didn't seem to be a habitually cheerful person, but Vala thought he might have showed a little more relief under the circumstances.

"But?" Daniel prompted Siler.

Siler prodded at the device cautiously, prying away wires. "Nothing. Easy is good. Looks like someone took a couple of sticks of plastic explosives and wired up a timer for it. It's safe enough now."

"Presumably one of our archaeologist friends," Landry said.

"Presumably," Daniel said.

"You don't look happy either."

"We still need to find the spy," Daniel said.

"So get on that," Landry said, and followed Siler out of the room, Siler carrying the defused explosive at careful arm's length.

"You know, he's right, you don't look happy," Vala said.

Daniel shook his head. "That wasn't much of a bomb. It might have taken out the archaeology lab, but how much of a loss is that? I mean, to science, and to me, obviously, yes. But this wasn't a naquadah generator or anything that might have had a chance of leveling the mountain. It might have done some damage to particular computer systems if it were right on top of them, but even taking out the gate room computers wouldn't be a permanent setback, just an annoyance."

"It would certainly set us back in looking for the Sangraal."

"Sure, but as far as I know, the Trust doesn't have any particular reason to stop us from looking for the Sangraal. If anything, it would be in their best interests for us to find it so that they can snatch it out from under our noses. Delaying us doesn't help them. Taking us out completely might, if they're gambling that the Ori will leave this planet alone if it isn't connected to the Stargate system, and the Trust can make it their new base of operations."

"That doesn't sound like a very good gamble," Vala said grimly. "I don't think the Ori intend to leave any planets just lying around for the Goa'uld to play with."

"Probably not," Daniel said. "But these guys don't always make winning bets. If there's anything we know about the Goa'uld, it's that they're overconfident. And as for the ex-NID men in the Trust, they've been jerked around so many times that I doubt they're sure what they're trying to do, except take us down."

"So you think this was… what, a decoy?"

"I think this was a decoy," Daniel said. "An underpowered bomb in a place we'd be certain to search? I can't prove it, but if I had to bet right now, I'd be betting that there's another bomb."

"Which might be anywhere," Vala said, her stomach sinking. "We may never even be certain that it exists until it explodes."

"Except that we're going to stop that from happening," Daniel said, as if he were perfectly confident in that. Maybe he was. Maybe he was just that good, and SG-1 was just that good, except that most of SG-1 wasn't there. There was only Vala, and while usually she had every confidence in her ability to pull one trick after another out of her sleeve — even while not wearing anything with sleeves — she was beginning to feel that her stock of tricks had run dry.

"If we find the bomb before it goes off," she said. In that moment, she didn't believe they would. It was all one with the events of the last few months; every time she had thought she had the situation mastered, and had a plan for what might happen next, the ground had fallen out from under her feet again. Now she was finding it hard to even grasp for a vision of a future that didn't end in either imminent fiery death or fleeing the SGC.

And yet she hadn't run. Every instinct developed in the last decades of her life should have been screaming at her to escape with her own skin intact and leave those who couldn't be saved to the slim hope of rescue by someone else. And yet she hadn't run.

"Hey," Daniel said, low and urgent. Surely he hadn't seen anything that looked like fear or doubt on her face. She would never be so transparent. Could never afford to be so transparent. "Vala. I need you to help me figure this out. I need someone to bounce ideas off of. To help me think. I always have. Now work with me. We need to figure this out."

She took an unexpectedly shaky breath, and then another. "All right. If that wasn't what the Trust was planning to use to destroy the base, what are they planning to use?"

"Something smuggled in from outside, like Niles said. Something that the agent brought onto the base."

"So how did they get it onto the base? Everyone has to go through the security checkpoint. This isn't like taking artifacts back and forth to study. Even Sam couldn't just walk onto base with a bomb in her backpack and get it by security."

"So it didn't come in through security."

"Then it didn't come in on a person."

"Supplies," Vala said. "All these supplies. Storerooms and storerooms of them. Paper and cups and parachutes and blue Jello. How do they get down here?"

"They're brought in by truck," Daniel said. "They're unloaded into the main part of the base, and then they come down the elevator. But any kind of unusual shipment of supplies would be sorted through, opened, recorded."

"What about the usual shipments of supplies? We must get cases of blue Jello down here every day. Surely no one opens every case to make sure it's really blue Jello and not little cups full of high-powered explosives."

"Except the kitchen workers," Daniel said, and then stopped, staring off into the middle distance. "The kitchen workers. Who are in a position to listen to anything that's been said in the mess hall."

"Where we talk about our missions."

"Where we've talked about this case."

"So come on. What are we waiting for?" Vala said, and strode off toward the elevators, confidence at least temporarily regained.

Cam ducked further down behind the car as Sam began rummaging in her pockets. "What are you doing?"

"I think I may have another plan. You may or may not like it."

Zat fire spit above his head. In the distance, he could hear the sound of sirens, but too far off to suggest that the cavalry was about to arrive. "I think I like it."

"I have the darkness generator I extracted from Arthur's dagger in my pocket."

"Okay, I do like it," Cam said after a moment. It would get them across the park unseen, and if the Trust agents tried to shoot them, they should be zapped by the same feedback effect that had knocked him and Daniel out.

"Just keep in mind that we won't be able to see where we're going any more than they'll be able to see us. And that it may stop zat fire, but it won't stop bullets."

"Believe me, I'll be keeping that in mind," Cam said.

"Also, we won't be able to use our zats either once I turn it on. If I can turn it on. It was behaving a little erratically when Vala and I were testing it."

"I think I liked this plan better before I knew this much

about it," Cam said. "On my mark, we take our best shots, then you turn it on."

Teal'c nodded assent, and Cam took a deep breath.

"Ready," Sam said.

"One, two… go!"

Cam stood to fire his zat, and ducked down behind the car before he could see whether his shot had landed. Beside him, Teal'c was doing the same. Sam fired, and then raised her left hand holding something crystalline and about the size of a lighter. She squeezed, and the world went dark.

Cam felt her take his hand, and he reached out to grab Teal'c by the sleeve of his jacket. He let Sam pull him along, cutting sharply to the right across the gardens, and managed not to swear when he tripped over a flowerbed and ended up having to scramble up into the flowers. He managed to get down the other side without falling on his face, and then he heard the sound of zat fire, and the air around him went wild with electric flashes.

It looked and felt like electricity striking out in all directions, but it didn't touch him, and Sam and Teal'c were still on their feet beside him. There was a thump from behind him that he hoped was the sound of a stunned Trust agent falling into a flowerbed. Cam didn't turn around to find out, but kept jogging blindly across the lawn as fast as he could, hoping he wasn't about to slam into a tree, late-night dog-walker, or lamppost.

Teal'c shrugged out of his grip, and Cam started to protest before he realized that the only way for Teal'c to scout out the situation was to get far enough away from Sam that the darkness generator wasn't still working on him. Tree branches lashed Cam's face, and he put out a hand to fend off a tree trunk. He circled it and put his back to it, tugging Sam close enough that she could hear him without his raising his voice above a whisper.

"Now what?"

There was a gunshot, a single soft pop that Cam hoped any late-night parkgoers didn't shrug off as the sound of a car backfiring or a champagne cork leaving the bottle. The best thing for any bystanders at this point was to get out of their way. The sound of sirens was getting closer, though, and Cam didn't think the police were going to put the gunfire down to anything innocent. He was torn between being glad for the reinforcements and afraid that the cops would just go down in a storm of zat fire, especially since he didn't think the Trust agents were going to be very restrained about shooting to stun and not to kill.

"Where's Teal'c?" Sam asked, and he could feel her waving her arm and feeling the air.

"Here," Teal'c said, returning and gripping Cam's arm. "We are nearly to the lake."

"Let's not fall in the lake," Cam said.

Sam turned a half-circle without letting go of Cam's hand, as if trying to visualize the space she couldn't see. "We could head for the boathouse. At least that would be some cover." Another gunshot cracked, this one closer. "I think they've figured out that the patch of total darkness is us."

Cam nodded, despite knowing it was a useless gesture. "So let's use whatever cover we can find."

Teal'c set out in what Cam hoped was the direction of the boathouse and not the direction of the lake. The last thing they needed was the noise of falling in and splashing around in the water. He put his trust in Teal'c's sense of direction, and let himself be towed along in Teal'c's wake.

Another zat fired, and the cloud of darkness exploded with lightning flashes again. Cam made a mental note that these particular Trust agents were slow learners. The thump that followed was uncomfortably close, though. It was gratifyingly followed by a splash, and the sound of someone conscious swearing. Hopefully they'd bother to pull their companion out of the water. He couldn't worry about it at the moment.

Teal'c stopped abruptly, and Cam ran into him, and then into the boathouse wall. He felt his way around as they circled the building and reached the stairs. They climbed the stairs, and then he felt something metal and barred in front of him, a gate preventing him from going further.

Sam's hand in his pulled downwards, and when he reached out he could feel her crouching to place the darkness generator on the stairs of the boathouse. Teal'c was already moving out of the way, and Cam ducked down and then rolled across the stairs and down, painfully, on the other side.

He could see his hands in front of his face as he came up to crouch in the shelter of the steps, as if he were seeing them through a dense fog. Sam came thudding down beside him, and he motioned the other two around the corner of the boathouse.

He got around the corner himself and turned to watch as two black-clad forms approached, covering the stairs with pistols. Apparently they'd finally learned the lesson about zats. He couldn't see anyone else closing in, and hoped they finally had the advantage.

He drew his own zat, waiting for a clear shot. If he could take down one of them before they reached the pool of darkness, he hoped the other one would realize how badly he was now outnumbered. Sam had her zat out as well, and after a sideways glance at her, he lowered his own. She had years more experience with the weapon, and was probably better able to make an educated guess about how long she could wait to shoot before risking a stunning backlash.

Sam fired, and Teal'c leaned out from cover as one of the two Trust agents dropped convulsing to the ground.

"Put your hands up!" Cam called. "We've got you covered." The remaining man gave them a weighing glance, and then dived for the pool of shadow. Cam gritted his teeth. "Really?"

"They're not dumb," Sam said.

"Except that now we've got them trapped."

"Unless they can get the boathouse gate open."

There was the sound of a gunshot and a bullet ringing off metal, and Cam ducked back behind the corner before realizing that the shot hadn't been aimed in his direction. The sound of the Trust agent shooting the lock on the boathouse gate, he figured. The darkness began to move, then, receding through the gate into the open expanse between the columns of the boathouse. Apparently he'd stumbled over the darkness projector and made a really good guess about what it did. Cam was really starting to dislike this guy.

"Freeze and put your hands up!" he shouted. "I will shoot!" He leveled his pistol, preparing to take the shot even though he suspected the guy wasn't standing in front of the gate anymore. At least they had him penned down, and they could go in after him at their leisure, maybe even with some police backup—

"Freeze and put your hands up yourself," a voice said from behind him. He turned, lifting his hands slowly without dropping the gun, and found himself staring three police officers in the face. None of them looked in the least bit friendly.

"Sir, drop your weapons!" the one female officer yelled. "All of you, drop them!"

Cam let the pistol drop. "Hey, we're on your side," he said.

"We're with the United States Air Force," Sam said. "This is a matter of national security."

"Uh-huh," the first policeman said. "And I guess the lady you shot back there was some kind of spy?"

Cam was suddenly very aware that his hands were covered in blood. "We didn't shoot her," he said. "The men who were chasing us did."

"Yeah, tell us another one," the man said, but the other two officers exchanged more thoughtful looks.

"This area may not be secure," the woman said. "Assume there may be a second shooter."

"I'm not a first shooter," Cam said in frustration. "We haven't actually shot anybody."

"The man you are seeking entered that structure moments ago," Teal'c said.

"Check it out," the woman said, and then jerked Cam's hands behind his back to cuff him.

CHAPTER SIXTEEN

THE MESS hall was emptying again as the evacuation sirens resumed sounding. People were moving quickly enough, but Daniel heard fewer expressions of concern as they shouldered their way against the stream than complaints that there was always some false alarm to prevent people from doing a full day's work in peace.

There were moments where Daniel thought that Sarah might be onto something. It was possible that he was crazy to work for the military rather than in a job with fewer bomb threats in an average working day and fewer armed attackers cornering him in his parking garage. On the other hand, when he'd joined the SGC, he hadn't been able to get one of those jobs, and now he knew he could never be satisfied turning his back on all the secrets he'd uncovered.

A day off, he told himself. If they found the bomb — when they found the bomb — and they'd wrapped up this mess with the Trust, he'd take a day off. He ignored the realistic voice in the back of his head that said that he wasn't going to be able to stand to take a day off until he found the Sangraal, and that Landry probably wouldn't authorize one until the Ori were defeated, whenever that might happen.

"It's just as well that I don't have cats," he said, and then realized from Vala's expression that he'd said it aloud.

"What would the cats do?"

"I'd never get home to feed them."

"Ah," she said sagely, as though that were meaningful to her, although he was aware that it was probably so far outside her own experience that he might as well have been speaking in gibberish. She was still listening, though, waiting for him to go on, and it occurred to him that in her own way she was trying to understand them, even if sometimes it was hard to believe she was even making an effort. There was so much about their culture that had to be completely incomprehensible to her, without even Teal'c's advantage of having come from another organized military, and yet she was still managing to keep up and even beginning to blend in.

"This isn't how normal people live," he clarified.

She shrugged one shoulder, looking tired. "I really wouldn't know."

The mess hall sergeant came out at that moment, a big man with close-shaved hair, and Daniel cleared his throat. "Ah, Sergeant Cross? I need to talk to you for a moment."

"I thought we were evacuating," Cross said, with a glance at the steaming pans on the cafeteria line where meatloaf was rapidly drying out. "Again."

"That's what we need to talk to you about."

"We're looking for someone suspicious," Vala said.

Cross raised an eyebrow.

"It's possible that someone on the mess hall staff has been smuggling unauthorized material onto the base," Daniel clarified. "I wanted to know if you'd noticed any suspicious behavior, anyone who was being secretive or opening boxes you didn't expect to be opened."

"If I'd noticed anything suspicious, I would have reported it to General Landry," Cross said, sounding a little annoyed. "I'm not in the habit of watching people do suspicious things in my department and just figuring it's none of my business."

"Of course you're not," Vala said, turning on the sudden brilliant charm that seemed to disconcert so many men. Cross didn't seem to mind it when she leaned sympathetically into his personal space. "But I'm sure you keep a close eye on your people, and you might have picked up on something that bothered you on an almost subconscious level, not enough to report, but just a sort of a gut feeling."

Daniel wasn't sure that Cross's gut feelings were what they were looking for here, but he held his tongue, reserving judgment. He wanted to see where Vala was going with this, and it wasn't going to help if they both started pursuing different lines of questioning.

"I don't know about any gut feelings," Cross said. "I try not to rely on gut feelings, unless it's about the food we get sent down here, which sometimes in my opinion is not what it should be. It's one thing when you're in another country, but when we're sitting here in Colorado Springs, the lettuce shouldn't look like rabbits wouldn't even eat it."

"This is an emergency," Daniel couldn't help saying from between gritted teeth. "We're looking for someone who may have planted a bomb in the base."

"So it would be terribly helpful if you could tell us any little suspicions you may have about anyone on your staff," Vala said.

"I don't have any suspicions I haven't reported already. Of course there was that business with Miss Vickers, but she said she was just lost, and that's easy enough down here."

"Assume we don't know anything about Miss Vickers," Vala said, which was considerably more patient than the words on the tip of Daniel's tongue.

"Cora Vickers, she's one of the civilian mess hall workers. One of the security guards found her wandering around in a secure area a couple of weeks ago. She said she just got turned around and couldn't find a door to go through that didn't say 'Keep Out.' I reported it to General Landry, but that was the only problem we ever had with her, and I wasn't going to fire someone for getting lost once."

"Of course not," Vala said. "I've wandered into all kinds of secure areas entirely by accident. It could happen to anyone."

Daniel heard himself make a strangled noise and turned it into a cough. "Where can we find Vickers right now? Has she already evacuated?"

"She and Airman Weiss were turning off the grills and the fryer," Cross said. "It's a fire hazard to leave them hot when no one's around. She should be out any second. Or I can go get her for you."

"We'll find her," Daniel said. "I'd rather not give her a chance to get away."

"There's nowhere you can go from the kitchen but the storage rooms. And those don't go anywhere but the elevator up to the warehouse where we store the deliveries from outside."

"Does Vickers have access to that warehouse?"

"There's no reason for her to go up there, but we don't keep the elevator locked. It's not like we're trying to keep the potatoes secure from the kitchen staff."

"I don't think potatoes are the problem," Daniel said, and headed for the kitchen door.

"If you'll just call General Landry at the Cheyenne Mountain Air Force Base…" Sam began, and then was cut off as her own hands were cuffed behind her. "Oh, you really don't have to do that."

"I think we do," the woman said. The other officer was patting Cam down, and found his zat.

"It's a cell phone," Cam said. "Experimental Air Force cell phone."

"You have the right to remain silent," the woman said. "If you give up that right, anything you say may be used against you in a court of law."

"We do not desire to remain silent," Teal'c said.

"We don't have time for this," Cam said. He looked at Teal'c, whose hands were still free, and nodded. He hoped that the nod communicated his intention well enough. If not, he figured that Teal'c had his own ideas, and that he could trust they would be good ones.

Teal'c stumbled abruptly, going down to one knee. "I believe I have been hit," he said, and bent over.

"Teal'c, buddy, where did they get you?" Cam said, crowding in closer in hopes of creating as much confusion as possible. Teal'c stayed down, and for a moment the icy suspicion crept in that he really had been hit, and that his tretonin-fueled healing wasn't handling it the way that a Goa'uld symbiote would have.

Then Teal'c came up with a zat in his hand, firing at the female police officer before he could raise it above her knees. Cam put out his foot and tripped the other man, going down himself as he'd known he would, and rolling to get distance between them.

"Go, go, go," he urged, and saw Sam taking off around the corner. Teal'c fired the zat again, and the second police officer went still. He turned, expecting to see Sam hightailing it back toward their car, and saw her heading up the boathouse stairs instead.

"Hey, Carter! Our ride is that way."

"We need to get the darkness generator back from the Trust agent who took it into the boathouse," Sam said, despite the fact that her hands were still cuffed behind her back. So were his, which suggested to him that any unnecessary excursions were a bad idea.

"We need to pull out. I'm not taking a vote," he said when she opened her mouth to protest. "There's a situation going on back at the base, we need to be there and not here, and if we need somebody to interrogate, there's this guy here," he said, nudging one of the fallen Trust agents with his foot. "We're not going in there and playing blind man's bluff with an armed fanatic with our hands cuffed behind our backs just so that you can get your toy back."

Sam took a deep breath, and then let it out. "You're right."

"Glad to hear it," Cam said, as Teal'c picked up the fallen Trust agent and slung him over his shoulder. "Now move, people."

He ached already from the fight at the boathouse. He suspected Carolyn would tell him that throwing himself down stairs and kicking police officers weren't a recommended workout. They were almost to safety, though, sprinting toward the garden and Niles's wrecked car where it stood next to a police cruiser, Teal'c making good time considering that he was weighted down by one unconscious spy.

Cam heard more sirens at the same time that he saw a black SUV swerving off the road and heading toward them.

"Everybody just had to call for backup," he said. "All right, lose the baggage." Teal'c dropped the Trust agent, and the three of them reversed course and ran. Behind him, the sirens were coming closer, but he was more worried about the SUV, which was steering directly toward them and seemed determined to run them down.

Trying to outdistance the SUV across flat grass was a lousy idea. Teal'c fired his zat, but the driver managed to swerve so that the zat's energy crawled harmlessly across the SUV's hood, crackling and spitting but not bringing the vehicle to a halt. Their only choices for finding cover were trees that wouldn't shelter them from anyone firing at them from the car, the lake — a bad idea with their hands cuffed — or the boathouse.

"Boathouse," he said. Shots spit at the ground beside him, kicking up dirt, and he put his head down and ran faster. He took the boathouse stairs recklessly fast, and Teal'c had to catch him at the top to keep him from pitching forward onto his face.

"Our guy isn't up here," Sam said, looking around. The open, columned boathouse was dimly lit, but there was a notable absence of an area of impenetrable darkness.

"Also, there's not a hell of a lot of cover," Cam said, ducking behind a pillar. "You think he went into the lake?"

Teal'c looked. "I see nothing, but in the darkness, he might well have escaped into the lake."

"I didn't hear a splash," Sam said. "I think we would have noticed the splash." She looked around. "There's a bottom floor to this place, with a kitchen and bathrooms. I think the door is around the side of the building."

"Are you sure?" Cam said. The SUV had screeched to a halt, and its doors were opening, letting out more men in black who did not look like they had good intentions.

"Pretty sure," she said.

"Good enough for me."

"Only it'll mean going over the railing with our hands still cuffed."

"I love this kind of thing," Cam said, already moving toward the railing. "I say to myself when I get up in the morning—" Teal'c grasped his arms and half-lifted him over the railing, lowering him by his jacket. He kicked his legs, hoping to touch ground, and didn't. "—that what would really get the old blood going is to get handcuffed and dropped off a—oof!"

He didn't expect to stay on his feet when he landed, and he didn't, but at least he managed to fall well, rather than keeling over on his face. All those hours of parachute training might still come in handy in his present life, he reflected, even if he wasn't likely to be ejecting out of any more planes. So, that was good to know. Teal'c dropped Sam down beside him—to Cam's annoyance, she landed on her feet—and then climbed down himself.

"The door's probably locked," Sam said.

Teal'c zatted it, but the door didn't pop obligingly open. It was probably a simple key lock, not something modern and high-tech that could be zapped into failing. Teal'c slammed it with his shoulder instead, and the door groaned and slammed open, its lock splintering.

"We are going to owe the parks department some money," Sam said, heading in.

"Tell me about it," Cam said. "Maybe we should sign up to do one of those things where you pick up litter."

"I believe we have other priorities," Teal'c said.

"I mean, later. After we win the war with the Ori."

Teal'c covered the hallway in front of him with his zat, pulling out a penlight with the other hand to penetrate the darkness, while Sam shouldered the door closed again. "See if you can find something to break these handcuffs," Sam said.

Teal'c turned around, shining the flashlight beam on the walls and the battered door. "Is it likely there will be an axe in this facility?"

"There might be a fire axe. Look for a box with a fire extinguisher."

Cam explored down the corridor cautiously, very conscious of how vulnerable he was with his hands pinned behind him. "There's a light switch."

"Let's not take out an advertisement that we're here," Sam said.

"Fair enough." He couldn't see much revealed in the beam of Teal'c's flashlight but bare hallway. "What do they actually do down here?"

"It's used for events," Sam said. "Receptions, that kind of thing." She sounded oddly uncomfortable.

"I have found the fire extinguisher box," Teal'c said. "It does contain an axe."

"Great."

"I believe if I break the glass, it will trigger an alarm."

"I think we're past the point of caring about that," Cam said. He could still hear sirens outside, and the alarming sound of gunfire. "It sounds like they're mixing it up out there."

"And one of the Trust agents may still be down here," Sam said. "All right, maybe it is time to take out an advertisement that we're here. Just get us out of these handcuffs."

Teal'c smashed the glass, and the alarm sounded, a brassy, brittle clanging. Added to the sound of sirens and gunfire, Cam couldn't help thinking of it as the sound of things failing, fairly spectacularly, to come off without a hitch.

The kitchen was a long, narrow space full of metal trays on racks, equipment that Vala assumed produced heat and cold as desired, and sinks full of dishes. No matter how cooking was accomplished on the various worlds she had visited, there was always someone who had to do the dishes.

An airman wearing an apron was turning off equipment, and looked up frowning as they entered. "You can't be back here," the man said. "It's a restricted area."

"Cora Vickers?" Daniel said.

"She was right here," the man said, and glanced around as if expecting her to be behind him. Vala caught a glimpse of movement behind the door at the other end of the room, and she dashed toward it, slamming through the door. On the other side, she could just see Vickers retreating down a long corridor. A plain woman with colorless hair caught back in a severe knot, she was someone people probably never looked at twice. In other words, the perfect spy.

Vala ran after her, Daniel at her heels. She rounded the corner at the end of the corridor just as Vickers was punching the button to summon the freight elevator.

"Oh, no, you don't," Vala said, slamming her against the wall. "You're not getting away that easily."

"Let me go!" Vickers said, struggling to get free. "You don't know what you're doing. The whole base is going to explode. We have to get out of here right now, or we're all going to die."

"We already found the bomb in the archaeology lab," Daniel said.

"That ridiculous thing?" Vickers said. "I told Carr that wouldn't fool anyone, but he insisted that it would distract Oliver if he started snooping around looking for explosives before Carr could get the poison into his coffee."

"Well, it didn't distract us," Vala said.

Daniel patted the woman down for weapons, and found none. "Tell us how to defuse the real bomb."

"We know the Trust smuggled it in to you in the supply shipments," Vala said. "Probably disguised as those very strange mashed potatoes." She overcame the urge to ask how it was possible to give a vegetable the consistency of a building material. "Tell us where you planted the real bomb, and we'll defuse it. If not…" She mimed an explosion with her fingers, and Vickers squirmed, looking longingly at the freight elevator as its doors closed.

"I can't," she said.

"Try," Daniel said. He didn't raise his voice, but his expression suggested that it would be a bad idea to assume he was currently playing the good cop.

"I mean, I really can't. What do you think they sent me, a big ticking bomb with an alarm clock wired to sticks of dynamite?"

"Why don't you tell us," Daniel said.

"You know it's hopeless anyway," Vickers said. The elevator doors were closing, and Vickers closed her eyes for a moment in despair, and then opened them with a harder expression. "The Goa'uld are going to take your planet, and you'll be the first ones they use as hosts."

"Funny thing, I thought it was the Ori who were going to take over Earth," Vala said.

"It's getting hard to tell one set of overconfident megalomaniacs from another," Daniel said. "Maybe we need a scorecard."

"Helping the Goa'uld is the only way to save ourselves. They can save us from the Ori. The Ori won't stand a chance against their powers."

"That's news to me," Daniel said. "And news to Ba'al, as far as I know."

"They can deal with anything," Vickers said. "They're gods. I was skeptical at first, but they've shown me their powers, and now I believe."

Vala let her head roll in frustration. "The Goa'uld are certainly not gods," she said. "They—"

"Blasphemer," Vickers spat.

The word hit her like a punch to the gut, far too reminiscent of far too many unpleasant scenes from the past.

"Do you know what I think is blasphemous?" she found herself saying. "The idea that any real god would treat any human being the way the Goa'uld and the Ori treat us, like disposable toys they can amuse themselves with and throw away when they're done." Vala wasn't sure where the words came from, only that she couldn't restrain them. "If there's any justice in the universe, gods should be good."

"Don't be a child. You ought to know that there's no such

thing as good and evil," Vickers said. "There's only power."

"The bomb," Daniel said. "You want to talk about power? Right now, you have the power to save yourself by telling us where the bomb is. And if you don't, we're all going to die, and you're going to die with us."

"It's not a bomb," Vickers said scornfully. "We're in a base with a self-destruct system that uses nuclear explosives. There's no way any bomb you could sneak in here would do a more thorough job of destroying the base and burying the Stargate than those explosives will."

"And there's no way you have the codes to trigger the self-destruct."

"The Trust built a device designed to hack into the base's computer systems and rewrite the programming of the self-destruct system so that it doesn't require the usual codes to activate. As soon as it's finished disabling all the security measures you could use to get control back, the base's automated self-destruct system will activate, and you won't be able to stop it."

"But you must have be a way to stop it," Daniel said. "Some code, some password... what is it?"

"I don't know it," Vickers said. "I activated the device using a remote control. Then I destroyed the remote control, as ordered. I don't know where Carr placed the device, and I don't know what password he set. Without the password, you can't turn it off." She shook her head. "The base is going to explode. I'm not going to tell you where the device is so that you can waste time trying to deactivate it. You can't. But if you let me go right now, I'll show you the quickest way out of the base. You can survive along with me to serve our new..."

Vala zatted her, watching her collapse to the ground with a certain degree of satisfaction. "I was getting tired of this conversation, weren't you?"

"Admittedly I was," Daniel said. "We've got to find the device Carr planted before it activates."

The warning lights abruptly began flashing again, and a new

set of sirens blared. "Self-destruct system has been activated," a recorded voice warned. "Self-destruct in fifteen minutes."

"Too late," Vala said.

"New plan," Daniel said. "We find the device and figure out a way to deactivate the self-destruct before it goes off."

"How do we do that?"

"Carr only had access to limited areas of the base," Daniel said quickly. "His office, Oliver's office, the archaeology lab…"

"We've searched all those places," Vala said. "I think we would have noticed an unexplained device attached to any of those computers."

"Where else has Carr been? He's eaten in the mess hall, he's gone to the bathroom —"

"No computers in the bathroom."

"He cut his hand," Daniel said. "He cut his hand and had it treated in the infirmary. Where there are plenty of computers, and where it's easy to wind up waiting by yourself while the doctors treat someone else."

"Surely Dr. Lam would have noticed a doomsday device attached to her computer," Vala said. "Or are we back to considering her an accessory?"

"I still don't buy that," Daniel said. "Even if I believed she would murder someone, I don't believe she's ready to blow herself up to help the Goa'uld conquer Earth. She's not a fanatic. And there's a lot of equipment in the infirmary."

"Let's go find a bomb," Vala said.

Watching Teal'c break Cam's handcuffs with an axe made Sam wince, even though she trusted that this wasn't going to end in accidental amputation. Cam jerked his wrists apart with a sigh of relief, and Teal'c looked pointedly at Sam. She held her arms out behind her back and tried not to flinch as he took aim.

"Lucky you knew about this place," Cam said.

"Mm-hmm," Sam said. She planned never to admit that

she had seen the boathouse floor plans as part of her abortive wedding planning; the idea that she had seriously considered putting on a white dress and holding a bouquet of flowers in a Denver boathouse while Pete waited for her at the end of the aisle seemed like a bout of temporary insanity, as hard for her to explain now as some of the things she'd done under alien influence. If she ever planned another one, she was determined to stick with Air Force uniforms and a venue that didn't scream "bridezilla" —

Her wrists jerked as Teal'c smashed the handcuffs apart with the axe, and she was able to tug them free of each other, although she was left wearing jagged metal bracelets she would have to deal with later. Cam was already moving down the hall, and Sam started to remind him that he was unarmed, and then decided that he probably didn't like back-seat driving any more than she did.

"Teal'c, cover the door," Cam said.

"I am the only one with a weapon."

"A weapon you can't use against the jerk with the darkness generator. Just make sure we don't get any more company, and me and Sam will take care of our friend down here."

"I think we can handle it," Sam said. She fell into step behind Cam. "So how do we play this?"

"I'm open to ideas."

"I think we need a distraction."

Cam peered cautiously into a half-open door, and then pushed it open the rest of the way. Inside was a dressing room, with empty clothes racks and a mirror in front of a table littered with abandoned hairspray and bobby pins. Sam felt more spiritual kinship with whatever bride had left a roll of duct tape.

She considered the strategic possibilities of duct tape and hairspray, but it was in an environmentally safe plastic pump rather than a satisfactorily explosive metal can. Her gaze drifted upwards to the steam pipes that ran along the ceiling.

"That might be distracting," she said, pointing up.

"I bet it would be. Go get the axe."

They explored further down the corridor, Cam now with an axe in one hand and a penlight in the other, and stopped in front of a door that Sam suspected led into the small boathouse kitchen. Cam shone the penlight at the bottom of the door, and the beam disappeared into darkness.

Sam grabbed the door and jerked it open at the same time that Cam swung the axe hard at a joint in the pipe. It spewed steam, and Cam grabbed it and pulled it down, spraying steam into the room.

There was a yelp and a gunshot, and Sam crouched low, trying to put her back into the corner. Cam barreled into the room, his arm up to shield his face from the steam, and she heard the solid thud of him colliding with someone as he disappeared into darkness.

Sam threw herself after him, and wound up in an extremely confusing tangle of arms and legs. Her hand closed on something cold and crystalline, and she threw it as hard as she could. The darkness lifted into a dim fog, with just enough light to see that the Trust agent was wrestling with Cam for a gun, its muzzle lifting by inches toward Cam's face.

"Don't even try it," she said, and punched the man. He went limp, his hand opening, and Cam grabbed the gun from him.

"Out cold," Cam said. "You've got a mean right hook."

"I try," she said. She glanced over at the pool of darkness in the corner. "Think we can use this thing to get out of here?"

"It might be worth a try," Cam said.

She felt around in the corner until she retrieved the device. "All right. Let's try this."

They retraced their steps until Teal'c's voice sounded out of the darkness. "Come no farther," he said.

"It's us," Sam said. "We're going to try to use this thing to get out of here."

"A wise decision," Teal'c said. "The noise of gunfire outside has stopped."

"Goody," Cam said. "Let's find out who won."

Sam cautiously felt for the door, and pulled it open. There was the sudden, distinctive sound of a gun being cocked. "Police!" a woman's voice called. "Come out with your hands up!"

Sam froze, hoping that the woman would believe the door had opened on its own.

"Get them up! Right now!"

Sam slammed the door shut. "One of them can see us."

"That's not supposed to be possible," Cam said.

"She must have the ATA gene. Of all the rotten luck…" At that moment her phone began ringing. She fished it out and answered it by feel. "I'm going to have to call you back, I'm a little busy right now," she said.

"So are we," Daniel said over the phone. "We need your help defusing a bomb."

CHAPTER SEVENTEEN

THERE was a pause on the other end of the line, and Daniel thought for a moment that Sam hadn't heard him. "Okay," she said finally. "We're pinned down here. We've got police outside who think we're probably serial killers, one zat between the three of us, and an unknown number of Trust agents on the loose, but, sure I'll talk you through defusing a bomb."

"It's not exactly a bomb," he said. They'd found the device wired to one of the computers in the infirmary, completely unnoticed in the tangle of wires that ran to and from diagnostic equipment. It looked very bomb-like, with a countdown timer that was mirroring the self-destruct system's occasional unhelpful reminders that they now had eight minutes left before a nuclear explosion leveled the mountain. "It's apparently hooked into the base's computer system. We've tried disabling the self-destruct countdown, but it's not taking anyone's passwords."

Landry was pacing the room, glaring at the device as if he could disable it by the sheer force of his anger. Carolyn was sitting very still watching it, as if it might not have its destructive effect if she kept it under observation at all times. She hadn't evacuated with her patients, which Daniel felt proved her innocence fairly conclusively. It was clear from her very stillness that she didn't want to die.

"Okay," Sam said. "There's a back door that should get you access even if the computer's not taking the usual passwords." There was the sound of gunfire and then pounding in the background.

"Sam—"

"I know, we're handling it," Sam said. "Get someone to a keyboard. I want them to enter the following code."

Daniel put the phone on speaker and set it down in front of

Vala. Sam began reeling off a long string of numbers and letters. Vala typed them in as Sam spoke. "That should do it," Sam said.

"Password accepted," Vala said.

"Colonel Carter, you wouldn't have an unauthorized backdoor access into the SGC's computers, would you?" Landry said.

"No, sir," Sam said. "That would be against regulations."

"Good for you," Landry said.

"Try disabling the self-destruct," Sam said. The mechanical voice of the self-destruct system intoned *six minutes to self-destruct.*

"I'm trying," Vala said. "I'm entering the commands, but it's not working."

"Okay. Enter this diagnostic code." She provided another string of letters and numbers, which Vala obediently typed, her mouth pressed tight together in concentration.

"Enter command access password," Vala said. "Tell me the password again."

Sam repeated the code.

"Password incorrect," Vala said. "Why is password incorrect?"

"Vickers said that Carr set a password on the device," Daniel said. "She said we wouldn't be able to disable the countdown without entering the password."

"That's probably what it's waiting for," Sam said. "I could try a brute force crack on it, but I don't think you have time for that. Do you have any idea what password Carr might have used?"

"Five minutes to self-destruct."

"Put your hands up!" someone shouted over the phone. There was a clatter that might have been a cell phone falling to the floor.

"Sam…"

"You have the right to remain silent. If you give up that right —"

"I'm telling you we can explain —"

"Hey, I can't see anything! They're using some kind of gas —"

"What are you talking about? I can see just fine."

"We're with the United States Air Force, and there's been an accident with a top secret test of a prototype weapon that affects the vision centers of the brain — if you'll just listen to me for a minute, I'll explain everything —"

Daniel muted the phone. "So it sounds like Sam's a little busy right now," he said. "We're going to have to figure this out on our own."

"I have no idea what password Carr used," Carolyn said. "I barely knew him. If it were Oliver, I'd guess he used something really complicated and memorized it. He was careful like that. But for all I know, Carr might have used ABC123."

"Four minutes to self-destruct."

"He'd do better than that," Daniel said. "He'd assume that if we found the device, we were going to try to crack the password by brute force. So it wouldn't be something easy to break that way. But he'd have been nervous, under pressure, trying to plant the device quickly while none of the medical staff were paying attention. That suggests he'd use something easy for him to remember, right?"

"What if it doesn't?" Vala asked. "What if we have no idea? You don't always have all the answers. Not every mystery is there for you to solve."

"We have to believe there's an answer," Daniel said. "Because if there's not, we'll never solve it, and we're all about to be blown up in a nuclear explosion, which at least is likely to be a more painless death than some I've had."

Carolyn's mouth quirked in something that might have been a smile. "I suppose you could try to Ascend," she said. "At least that would get you out of here."

"I think that revolving door is closed," Daniel said. "Besides, I haven't given up on solving the problem."

"You never give up on solving the problem," Vala snapped.

"Neither do you, or you'd be dead, so *help me*," Daniel said urgently.

"Three minutes to self-destruct."

"I gave the order for medical personnel to evacuate," Landry said to Carolyn. "Why are you still here?"

"If I ran, it would look like I was guilty," Carolyn said.

"That's better than being dead."

"Not if you believed it."

"We are not going to die," Daniel said. "What do people use for passwords? Their kids' birthdays, their pets' names, the name of their cabin or their boat or their favorite sports team or cartoon character…" He realized he was making his best guesses at Jack's passwords. "What would Carr use as a password?"

"We're assuming it's something we can know," Vala said. "Because if it's the name of a dog he had as a child, we can't know, and we're going to die." She sounded calmer now, interested in the philosophical problem. "So it has to be something we can work out, like… a dog he's already told us about, or the name of his favorite Ancient artifact, or a book that he left bookmarked with a note that says 'this is the password I'm using to set a bomb'…"

There was something there, something that snagged in the back of his brain.

"Two minutes to self-destruct."

"A book," Daniel said. "Carr published a book before he came to work at the SGC. He bragged about it, which drove Jefferson crazy because he wasn't ever going to be able to publish any of his research since he started at the SGC. What was the name of the book?"

He'd meant it as a rhetorical question, but Vala closed her eyes and furrowed her brow. "*Ceramics Techniques of the Predynastic Period: An Overview*," she said. In answer to his look, she shrugged a little. "You have to notice things in our profession," she said.

He wasn't sure if she meant treasure-hunting or being on an SG team, but he'd take it as a gift either way. "Try that," he said.

Vala typed in the words. "Password incorrect."

"Try the first letter of each word."

"Password incorrect."

"He probably used a number. What number? The publication date of the book. He'd remember that. And he published the book in…" He tried to remember Carr's CV. He could see it on his desk, next to a cup of cold coffee, some morning when he'd only half been paying attention to the stack of applications for the archaeologist position, but he'd picked it up and he'd read it and he'd noticed the one major publication, a book that came out a few years earlier in…

"*One minute to self-destruct.*"

"1991, try 1991."

"Password incorrect."

"No, the first letters of each word in the title, and then 1991. CTOTPPAO1991. Try that."

"I wouldn't have believed you were guilty," Landry said.

Carolyn held his gaze. "I wasn't willing to take that chance."

Vala typed, and Daniel held his breath as she hit the enter key.

"Password accepted," the screen blinked.

"*Thirty seconds to self-destruct.*"

"Cancel the self-destruct!"

"I'm entering the command," Vala said. "I can't tell if it's working or if it's still counting down…"

In front of Daniel, the numbers on the device were still scrolling. 00:00:19 … 00:00:18 … 00:00:17… 00:00:17… 00:00:17. They stopped, and he closed his eyes in relief.

A shrill alarm went off, and he flinched, and then realized it was his cell phone. He picked it up and answered it.

"Daniel? Are you there? Talk to me."

"We're all right, Sam," Daniel said. "The bomb didn't go off. Obviously."

"Obviously," Sam said, sounding as relieved as he felt. "Things got a little interesting here, but Barrett just got here with the NID, and they're helping sort things out with the local authorities. I really owe him some answers at this point."

"Tell him we've solved the mystery," Vala said.

Daniel nodded to her. "Yes, we have. We'll fill you in when you get back, and then you can fill Barrett in."

"Will someone get this timer thing out of my infirmary?" Carolyn said, turning around as if suddenly busy so that no one could see her face. "Some of us have work to do."

Landry ignored her, which seemed to be what she was hoping for. "I expect a full debriefing, including an explanation of exactly what's been going on around here," he said.

"Can we take five first?" Vala asked hopefully. She still looked rattled, if very pleased not to currently be dead.

"Under the circumstances, you can even make it ten," Landry said.

"So I suppose you're wondering why I've called you all here together," Cam said.

Landry gave him a look. "Once again, Colonel Mitchell, the answer to that is no."

"I'm sorry," he said. "I've just always wanted to say that."

"And now you have. Twice. So how about that report?" Landry prompted.

"I'd be interested in hearing that, too," Colonel O'Neill's voice said over the phone. "I assume that's why you've called *me* here. Or at least called me."

Cam cleared his throat. "The report, yes, sir. Here's what we figure happened. Oliver was paranoid, all right, only it was that special kind of paranoia where they really are out to get you. He discovered that Niles was spying for the Trust, and when he let on that he knew about her activities, she quit her job before he felt like he had enough evidence to turn her in."

"The problem was, she'd already recruited Carr," Sam said. "When Oliver realized that Carr had been spending a lot of time with Niles, he started putting the pieces together. He began compiling evidence to build a case against the two of them. In the course of doing that, he realized Chen was also behaving suspiciously."

"Only it turned out she wasn't a spy, just a thief," Daniel added.

"The thing I still don't get is why it didn't occur to him to bring any of these suspicions to me," Landry said. "Or for that matter, to you, Dr. Jackson. You'd think it would be the kind of thing any reasonable person would report."

"We like it when people tell us they've noticed spies in the SGC," O'Neill said.

"Oliver was a perfectionist," Daniel said. "And he was always reluctant to go out on a limb with his theories. It bothered him too much to think that people might not believe him." There was a dry note in his voice that suggested that he was all too used to the idea of not being believed himself.

"Besides, there was his past association with the NID," Sam said. "It certainly made us suspicious when we first found out about it."

Daniel nodded. "So I think he was trying to build the perfect case against Carr, and even then, he would have preferred it if Carr had been willing to confess. That's the one thing we couldn't have ignored."

"Oliver was worried about Carr finding his evidence, so he stashed a copy in the museum," Cam said, picking up the thread of the story again.

"Thankfully in a place where it was easy for us to retrieve them," Vala said, although Daniel gave her a sideways look at the word "easy."

"He also kept files on his computer, but Carr managed to access those remotely and delete them after Oliver's death. Oliver collected evidence and collected more evidence while Carr and Niles funneled information to the Trust, but finally he decided he had to stop making notes and actually do something about it."

"Unfortunately, his choice of what to do was unwise," Teal'c said.

"Do you think?" O'Neill said.

"Unwise about sums it up," Cam said. "He decided he had to

get Carr to confess. He put the pressure on, but Carr wouldn't promise to turn himself in. And when he confronted Chen about her thefts, she decided to try a little blackmail along with stealing, and told Oliver that if he didn't give her time to make a confession on her own terms, she'd tell everyone he was having an affair with Niles."

"Which he wasn't," Sam said. "But given his association with the Trust and the phone calls he'd been making to Niles, he was afraid it would look like he was conspiring with her. I think at that point he must have realized he was in over his head, but he gave them both more time, hoping that they would both decide to turn themselves in and make full confessions."

"I'm guessing they weren't planning to do that," O'Neill said.

"No one with any sense would have," Vala said.

"Regardless of whether that is true, Carr and Chen did not choose to confess," Teal'c said. "Carr seized upon his first opportunity to kill Oliver in a way he hoped would be accepted as either accident or suicide."

"A little risky if there was a bomb scheduled to go off in a few days, don't we think?" O'Neill said.

"All he'd done was placed the device, and the decoy designed to distract us if we started looking for a bomb," Sam said. "He didn't know that the Trust was getting ready to use it. And he probably assumed that Vickers would rescue him in plenty of time for him to get clear if we even decided to put him in custody. Instead she — or her superiors at the Trust — wrote him off as a liability. She killed Carr and activated the bomb."

"Tell me that Niles recruited her, too," Landry said. "I do not want to believe that four separate people we hired all turned out to be crooked."

"We think that Vickers and Niles were both plants by the Trust," Cam said. "Vickers is a true believer, the kind of whacked-out person who really thinks the Goa'uld are gods, and Niles went along with the Trust because they promised to cure her sister's illness." He shook his head. "I don't guess there's anything we can do about that."

"Other than put the sister under surveillance and make sure she's not being used by the Trust, probably not," Sam said. "The Tok'ra might have been willing to take her as a potential host, but there's no guarantee there would be a symbiote available for her, and given that she was willing to be a host for a Goa'uld… that would probably be a deal-breaker for them."

"Come on," Cam said hotly. "This woman didn't know anything about the difference between the Goa'uld and the Tok'ra. She just didn't want to wind up lying in a hospital bed not able to get out of it. I think we can all imagine what that would be like."

"I know," Sam said, and there was a wealth of sympathy in her eyes. "But there are a lot of people we can't help. Except by doing what we do, going out there and finding things and people that can help us advance medical technology here on Earth."

"True enough," Cam said, but it took some of the satisfaction out of solving the case to think about Niles's sister, and about Niles lying bleeding in his arms and Vickers facing trial for the crime of having bought a bill of goods the Goa'uld were experts at selling the galaxy over. There was a reason he'd never wanted to be a detective. He'd rather fight any number of mythical beasts if he didn't have to feel bad about slaying them.

"Besides, it's still better than what would have happened to her if she'd become a host for the Goa'uld," Sam said.

"That's probably true, too," Cam said.

"The fun of leading SG-1," O'Neill said. "Still glad this is the job you asked for, Mitchell?"

"Yes, sir," Cam said, knowing that O'Neill had seen his share of victories colored by regrets. And any day when they saved the mountain from being blown up couldn't be such a bad day after all. "One hundred percent."

"That's what I thought you'd say."

"I did promise Barrett a full explanation in exchange for his help," Sam said.

"You can give him one along with our thanks," O'Neill said. "Don't forget to tell him that our investigation is complete and no further assistance from the NID is required."

"Will do, sir," Sam said.

"All right. Good work. I assume one of you will call me the next time there's a crisis, so, maybe not until tomorrow."

"We'll try to give you a whole day off," Landry said, and cut the connection. "Good work, SG-1. Go get some rest. Colonel Mitchell, I hope you won't take it the wrong way when I say that I sincerely hope you never have to do this again."

"Amen to that," Cam said.

"So I'd like to go back to P2H-144 with Merlin's dagger," Daniel said as they began the next day's briefing. "The more Sam and I have looked at it, the more we think that the darkness-generating effect isn't its original purpose, it's more like a useful side effect. I've been looking at these pictures of the pedestal that the dagger was probably originally resting on, and there are some markings here that look very similar to the outline of the dagger."

Vala craned her neck to see as Daniel spread out more photos. "I think it's a key," he went on. "I think the whole point of the dagger is — yes, it's a useful weapon, but it also opens a second chamber out of the main chamber, one that contains information that you can only reach if you have the dagger."

"And we think this why?" Landry asked. He looked as tired as Vala felt.

"If you go back to some unorthodox translations of the early Welsh poets —"

"On second thought, I think I'll take your word for it, Dr. Jackson," Landry said. "Colonel Mitchell, assemble your team and go check out Dr. Jackson's latest theory. If you find the Sangraal, call me. If you get attacked by the Questing Beast again, call for backup. Otherwise, I'm going to enjoy a few hours of peace and quiet."

"Yes, sir," Mitchell said. "Gate room, fifteen minutes."

Vala lagged behind, letting the others leave and the sound of their voices retreat down the hall. "At least it's not five," she said.

"You'll get used to the Air Force," Landry said. "Or come to hate it. One or the other."

She knew that was probably her cue to leave, but hung back nevertheless. "I'm just wondering," she said.

"What are you wondering, Vala?" Landry asked, sounding resigned enough that she thought he might answer her question if she asked it.

"How certain you were that Dr. Lam wasn't the murderer."

"I was absolutely, completely… ninety-nine percent sure," Landry said. There was a pause while he gazed out the window toward the Stargate. "It's that one percent that kills me."

"You can't trust anybody one hundred percent," Vala said.

"Yes, you can," Landry said. "That's something you ought to find out, if you don't already know it. You ought to be able to trust your own daughter completely and utterly. Even when she's got motive, means, and opportunity. Even when she's in a situation that looks bad, and lying about it so that it looks worse. I ought to know my own daughter well enough that I wouldn't feel a single little particle of doubt."

"And instead you believed she might have done it."

"I believed it was remotely possible that she could have done it."

"Well," Vala said, turning to regard the Stargate herself. "I think there are always reasons why people might do terrible things. Whoever they are. However much you care about them. We all have those temptations. What matters is that we choose not to do those things. I think. Do you think?"

"I think," Landry said. The silence drew out again, but it felt like a friendlier silence. "Tell me something," Landry said. "What Colonel Carter said about Niles's sister. That whatever happens to her, it's better than becoming a host for the Goa'uld."

"Do I think she's right?" Vala suggested when he didn't go on.

Landry shrugged. "I figure you'd know if anyone would."

"I think that where there's life there's hope," Vala said. "And I think that if I don't go get my pack, I'm going to run out of my fifteen."

"You still have seven," Landry said, looking at his watch. "Plenty of time if you run."

"I'm on my way," Vala said, and ran to keep up with her team.

Daniel placed the dagger gingerly between the almost imperceptible markings on the stone pillar, while Cam kept a close eye on the door, not wanting to be surprised by any unexpected reptilian visitors. He hoped the Questing Beast had been as scared of them as they had been of it, and would be steering clear. He didn't really want to kill the thing. It had survived this long by sheer dumb luck, but some days, so did they.

For a long moment, nothing happened, and Cam was beginning to think that for once, Daniel's hunch wasn't going to pan out. Then the dagger began to sink, a section of the stone sliding cleanly down into the pillar.

Brilliant light rose in its place, filling the room with a golden glow. The light shifted and resolved itself into a human figure, and then into the increasingly familiar holographic form of Merlin. He began speaking in Ancient, with a beatific smile that Cam found more than a little annoying.

Daniel looked transfixed, though, and Sam, Vala, and Teal'c were all listening as if they followed at least some of what he was saying. Cam wondered if there was an Ancient for Dummies crash course, and if so when he would have free time to take it. Maybe those tapes that you were supposed to listen to in the shower. He'd have to ask Daniel to make him some if they didn't have any already.

Daniel's face fell abruptly, and Cam didn't need an instant translation to figure that out.

"This place doesn't have anything to do with the Sangraal, does it?"

"No," Daniel said. "Merlin talks about this as a resting place for Arthur and his knights in their quest for the Sangraal. They didn't find it here, and we're not going to find it here, either. This was just a way station, a place for them to arm themselves and recover if they were injured."

The hologram dissolved, although the pillar of light remained. The part of the stone that had sunk into the pillar slid back up, cutting off the beam of light, but it was empty now, and the dagger was nowhere to be seen. "How do we get the dagger back?" Sam asked.

"I don't think we do," Daniel said. "I think if we were the ones who were supposed to have the dagger, we wouldn't need the information. If we need the information, we obviously didn't need the dagger."

"That's how the Ancients think?" Cam asked.

"That's how the Ancients always think," Daniel said. "They measure out the information they give us in tiny pieces, and there's always a price. All these games, all these tests… it's all part of wanting to control everything we do, while still being able to tell themselves they're not interfering. They won't help us, but they'll make us work for every scrap of information that we get."

"Well, we're not playing their game," Cam said. "We're looking for the Sangraal, all right, but for our own reasons, not for theirs. And we're going to find it, whether or not Merlin or Morgan le Fay or anybody else thinks we're worthy to have it. We're going to defeat the Ori, and we're going to defend Earth, and I don't doubt that for a moment, because we've got the best team working on it. The best there is. All right?"

Sam smiled crookedly. "You do a good pep talk."

"It's the truth and you know it. So we didn't find the Sangraal today. We solved a murder, kept the mountain from being blown up, and didn't get chased by a giant reptile again."

"It is true that we have not been pursued by a giant reptile today," Teal'c said.

"So let's keep it that way and get a move on back to the Stargate. How do we feel about movie night?"

"With popcorn?" Vala asked hopefully.

"You always have popcorn. Daniel, haven't you taught her that you always have popcorn with movie night?"

"Pizza is also a traditional movie-watching food of the Tau'ri," Teal'c said.

"I think in honor of the occasion, we definitely need a Sherlock Holmes movie," Daniel said.

"You mean Conan Doyle," Vala said. "Or was he the sidekick?"

"I was thinking more Hitchcock," Sam said. "Teal'c, wouldn't you rather have Hitchcock?"

"It is true that I prefer his films to the adventures of Sherlock Holmes."

"There are some Agatha Christie TV series…" Daniel suggested. "Stately manors, locked rooms, the butler did it…"

"Perhaps something with more action," Teal'c said.

"The Maltese Falcon?" Daniel offered less enthusiastically.

"Did the bird do it?" Vala asked.

"I am making an executive decision," Cam said. "No, people, we are not voting on this. We have had enough of mysteries. We are watching a movie, it's going to be a comedy, and nobody is going to die in it. That's an order. Now, you've got until we get back to the Stargate to decide what movie we're watching, or no pizza for you."

As the sound of heated debate broke out behind him, Cam smiled, and thought he might get the hang of leading SG-1 yet.

STARGÅTE SG·1.

STARGATE ATLÅNTIS

Original novels based on the hit TV shows **STARGATE SG-1** and **STARGATE ATLANTIS**

Available as e-books from leading online retailers

Paperback editions available from Amazon and IngramSpark

If you liked this book, please tell your friends and leave a review on a bookstore website. Thanks!